WEST OF THE SUNSET

A STORY OF DANGER, ADVENTURE AND LOVE

PAUL F. MURRAY

Inquiries and Book Orders should be addressed to:

Great Writers Media
Email: info@greatwritersmedia.com
Phone: 877-600-5469

ISBN: 978-1-960939-54-8 (sc)
ISBN: 978-1-960939-55-5 (ebk)

Also by Paul F. Murray

The Freedom Series:
Freedom's Long March
The Gifts and the Fruits

ACKNOWLEDGMENTS

The author wishes to acknowledge his editor, Bill Greenleaf, who was instrumental in helping to shape the book into its final form and who gave strong support to the plot and the characters as written. The help of staff at Fort Bridger, Wyoming State Historical Site also was most useful.

DEDICATION

This book is dedicated to the pioneer emigrants who braved the dangers of the Oregon and California Trails in the 19th century, creating an American history saga in the Western states that is every bit equal to the stories of Plymouth, Massachusetts and Jamestown, Virginia. Despite multiple hardships, they kept on going.

CHAPTER ONE

"What the damn hell you staring at, kid?"

Tyler Linders backed away from the batwing doors of the Independence Saloon. He resented being called a kid at his age but he quickly raised his arms and hands to show he meant no harm. "I—I wasn't staring, sir," he replied, breathing heavily.

"Yes, you were. You was staring right at me, kid," the thin-faced, toothy man muttered from underneath his plainsman's hat. "I don't like being stared at. I just lost fifty dollars in a poker game to some bigger-than-his-britches young saloon card sharp that looked only a couple years older than you."

"I'm s-sorry, sir," Tyler said. He wanted no fight with this man who had a pepperbox revolver stuck in his pants "You came out of the saloon door just as I was about to walk past it. I didn't want to bump into you."

The angry man in the plainsman's hat looked Tyler over for a thick moment. His eyes stony and unblinking, he appeared to Tyler to be assessing him, weighing him mentally, trying to decide if he wanted to continue this sudden confrontation.

Finally, he took a step to start moving on down the boardwalk. "Well, see that you don't," he snapped. He turned his head to walk away slowly.

Tyler turned to walk fast in the opposite direction among the mercantile shops of Independence, Missouri. *Testy*, Tyler thought to himself.

Behind him, Tyler heard someone else walk out of the batwing saloon doors and say, "Easy there, Crabbage, or you'll be picking fights with everybody in the whole wagon train before we even get halfway to Oregon. Buckman ain't going to allow . . ."

Tyler heard no more as he let go of his suspenders and broke into a half-run across the dusty street back in the direction of the gathering wagons. Past the livery a sea of white-canopied covered wagons stood scattered in no particular order. Families and heads of households were talking, joining together, planning the journey on the Oregon Trail. Some of the wagons had brightly painted wooden boxes in shades of blue, green, even an occasional red. "Oregon or bust" signs had been mounted on the backs or sides of some of the wagons. Others of the wagons, appearing to be mostly those of single men, had "California '52" or "California or bust" signs. Tyler knew that Pa intended to hit the trail for Oregon, and was not going to be tempted otherwise by the smell of gold in California.

In the far distance along the Missouri River, steamboats brought still more prospective emigrants and their belongings. Freight wagons met them at the docks.

Nearing Pa's wagon, Tyler forgot about the incident outside the saloon a moment earlier. The sunshiny, unusually warm mid-April day certainly portended a safe trip, or so Tyler wanted to convince himself. Independence, Missouri to the Willamette Valley of Oregon was a 2,000 mile journey through rattlesnake-infested dry plains, across flowing rivers rife with quicksand, across snow-dense mountains cutting up the sky, past stampeding buffalo herds numbering in the thousands, and through the lands of Indians who would just as soon they stayed clear away from their hunting grounds.

The sea of wagons owned the large grassy prairie right outside Independence and its array of false-fronted mercantile supply stores. Tyler sat back down at his canvas-covered wagon as his father had asked him to do, keeping an eye on their supplies while his father talked with other families heading west, to see who was heading out on the trail to Oregon the earliest. The earliest wagons on the trail had the best grass for their animals, less dust to eat from other wagons farther ahead, and the best chance of getting over the mountains before snow started falling come autumn.

Of course, as Tyler reminded himself, the first folks out on the trail also ran the greatest risk of being caught in a surprise late-spring blizzard, and of their having their animals, and possibly themselves, freeze to death. No way around it—heading out on the Oregon Trail was a gamble. Making it all the way to the Willamette Valley depended, naturally, on luck, but also upon finding the right group of people to travel with and then being able to hire the right man to be the wagon train captain, or have the best wagon captain agree to take you on with his train. At least all of that was what Pa's trail guidebooks said and what the scuttlebutt among the prospective pioneers the past few days had been. The captain would preferably be a former mountain man with long years of experience dealing with Indians, dust storms, prairie fires, tornadoes, and other dangers of the Trail, and knowledge of the quickest and safest mountain passes.

Brushing back his dark hair bangs and then gripping his suspenders, Tyler couldn't help chuckling when he saw some of the items people actually thought they were going to take all the way to Oregon. Two families loaded grandfather clocks into the backs of their wagons. At least a dozen families loaded bookcases into their wagons. Other families loaded up crates of books, extra pots and pans, large kettles, extra clothing, family heirlooms such as jewelry or quilts, even a piano in one case, and other assorted bric-a-brac which would likely be dumped all along the first half of the Trail, as families came to grips with the reality of how much weight their animals could pull uphill and over dale.

The people themselves sometimes also arrested Tyler's attention. Most of the travelers were young, people in their twenties or early thirties, with small children, it appeared. Tyler noticed occasionally families with older teenagers, like himself, at age nineteen. Young women about to make the journey certainly caught his eye, but then his hopes would quickly fade. No sooner would Tyler espy a lovely young brunette, blonde or redhead, than some little toddler would run up to the young lady and call her "mommy," with a smiling young husband following quickly behind to kiss her.

Tyler hoped his Pa could hook up with a sizeable wagon train, and not simply because larger wagon trains tended to discourage Indian attacks. Larger wagon trains had larger numbers of young, single women to choose from than did smaller trains. Naturally, as was always the case, there was a fair amount of courtship among the single men and single women in any wagon train. Beyond Cupid, though, there were economic reasons for finding a wife on the journey to Oregon. By virtue of the 1850 Donation Land Act passed by Congress, married men were entitled to 640 acres of land in Oregon, while single men had to content themselves with half that amount, 320 acres.

Pa, even though he was a widower, would still qualify for 640 acres. Tyler planned to get his own 640 acres of prime Oregon farmland, however, not 320 acres. That would require getting hitched before he went to the land office in Oregon City at Trail's end.

His dark eyes squinting in the sun, Tyler surveyed his prospects. One gal who was definitely not married was a fair young blonde-haired girl, who, from a distance of about one hundred feet, looked quite intriguing. She sat on the back of her family's wagon in her pastel blue bonnet enjoying the company of five young men Tyler's age or slightly younger semi-circling her.

Way too much competition. Tyler looked away, resting his left elbow on his left knee.

Another wagon caught his attention, about seventy feet ahead and to the right. A tall, middle-aged man in a blue military uniform with white trim, epaulets, and a funny, Napoleon-like hat, got down out of the back of one of the wagons and talked to four red-coated military men. Tyler remembered his father telling him yesterday evening that the funny-dressed Napoleon look-alike was a duke or baron or something from Austria-Hungary, and the fancy pants soldiers in bright red uniforms with metal bangles from the Austro-Hungarian Empire were there to serve him. Hapsburg, the duke's name was, or something like that. He was a tourist, plain and simple, out to see the sights along the way.

There were always a few such types in every decent-sized wagon train, Tyler recalled Pa saying, rich Europeans who wanted to make the Trail trip and see the American West, then stay or go back to where they came from, as the mood suited them.

A cute, long brown-haired girl in petticoats got out of the wagon next and was given a big hug by the duke. Obviously his daughter, she was equally as attractive as the other girl, just in a different way, with blue eyes, and a nose slightly thickened at the end but nevertheless well-sculpted.

And she was by herself, not surrounded by a bevy of admiring wanna-be suitors.

Just great, Tyler thought to himself. The one teenage girl he'd seen in the whole kit and kaboodle of a hundred assembled wagons who was alone was Miss Untouchable European royalty. Probably no coincidence that she was alone. Tyler resolved not to waste any of his time pursuing *that* one. She was probably stuck up as all get out, and would no more deign to talk to the likes of him than she would talk to a goat or a hog.

"Hey, Tyler, keep a sharp eye on the oxen," Magnus Linders shouted. "We'll be heading out at sunrise tomorrow."

Magnus Linders strode back toward his wagon, accompanied by a tall, thin-bearded thin-faced, thin-nosed man in classic mountain man-style buckskins.

"I'm keeping my eyes on 'em, Pa," Tyler responded. "They're not going anywhere."

"Yeah, I saw you keeping your eyes on 'em," Pa remonstrated, "the oxen, among other things. But I reckon that's okay. I was young once too, believe it or not."

"I'm not sure I do," Tyler said underneath his breath. He grinned at his father, Magnus Linders, a caring man whose bark was always worse than his bite. Magnus had a medium-muscled body and a kindly, stubbled face. He only shaved when the mood suited him, usually once every four or five days.

"Where's Penny?" Magnus asked, his arms akimbo.

Tyler jerked a thumb in the direction of the wide Missouri River a couple of hundred yards to the north, lined with aspens and cottonwoods. "Penny went to the river to wash some clothes. Figure it'll be our last chance to wash clothes for awhile."

Magnus looked to the silk-clad man. "The Missouri's kind of muddy, ain't it?"

"Depends on the time of year. It should be okay this time of the spring. The snow melt from the mountains hasn't really kicked in yet."

"Tyler, this is Mr. Henry Buckman," Magnus introduced the deerskin-clad man. "Mr. Buckman is going to be our wagon train captain. I've agreed to join the wagon train party he's forming and I've paid him money for the privilege. I'm confident he'll get us to Oregon safely."

"I've been all around the mountains we'll be passing through," Buckman declared, rubbing his stubbly dark whiskers. "I've also got a couple of guides to help me, just for extra measure. Press Doolittle and Silas Maple are a couple of mountain men that together have seen every nook and cranny of the Rockies and beyond. There'll be over eighty wagons and four hundred and fifty people in our wagon train, for safety purposes."

Buckman cast a quick glance at the left back axle and iron wheel hub of the Linders wagon, briefly feeling the outward-flaring spokes of the wheel with his fingers.

"I've asked around," Magnus emphasized. "All the supply and mercantile folks say that Mr. Buckman here is the best there is. We're lucky there was still room for us in his wagon train."

Tyler tried to sound nonchalant. "You said, Mr. Buckman, there'd be over four hundred and fifty people in our wagon train. Who all is in it, 'sides us?"

Buckman's arm swept the wide plaza outside the false-fronted mercantile stores. "Just about all of these wagons you see around us—the Burneys, the MacNaughtons, the Allertons, the Zuriches, the Jonas Smith family, the Colledges, the Hancliceks, the Bennetts, the Palmerstons—" Buckman kept naming families, but Tyler gleefully noted inwardly that when the wagon captain had said "the Palmerstons," he had pointed a hand directly at the wagon occupied by the attractive blonde girl in the blue bonnet.

"—the Hapsburgs, the Clevengers, the McGuigans, the Cullenders—"

"The Hapsburgs?" Magnus asked. "They're part of our train?"

"Well, yeah."

"They're planning on traveling all the way to Oregon dressed like that?"

"Not really." Buckman gestured toward all the mercantile supply stores a couple of hundred yards away in the town of Independence. "I told Franz Hapsburg and his soldiers with him that they'd better pick up some trail clothes before we head out—regular cotton or silk shirts or buckskins, suspenders, and trousers. I was kind of surprised when I didn't get any argument from him. Hapsburg wants the whole Western American experience, I guess."

Tyler looked back in the direction of Independence, Missouri, the most westerly town in the most westerly state, the jumping off point for the Promised Lands of the West Coast. Everywhere he could see hundreds and hundreds of wagons on the grassy plain facing the town. Thousands of people were heading out on the Oregon and California Trails. Tens of thousands. Men loaded agricultural tools, sacks of flour, dried bacon, and salt pork into their wagons. The all-important water barrels were attached to the sides of the wagons. Those would become of life-saving importance once the wagon train got beyond the North Platte River.

Some pioneers still were loading treasured possessions onto their wagons—a favorite rocking chair, large decorative clocks, enameled chests full of clothing and other goods, stacks of books, even a sofa on one wagon. Again, Tyler reminded himself, much of this stuff would be left by the trailside once the wagons got deep into their journey with wheels and axles breaking down and oxen or horses giving out. A lot of these folks must never have picked up and read a guidebook for advice.

Pa had made the decision that they would travel light. Beyond the bare necessities—food, water, clothing, blankets, tools and seed—only their departed mother's Bible, Tyler saw, was among the items to be taken. All of these folks with their fancy possessions would even out soon enough, or else risk having their oxen and wagons break down nowhere near Oregon.

Still, Tyler looked in the direction of Mr. Buckman, who watched cross-armed, as people loaded all of this stuff into their wagons. Maybe it was okay to carry extra weight if Buckman allowed it?

Tyler nervously ran his fingers through his thick dark hair and then across his clear, slope-nosed face as he sauntered up to Buckman. "I see all these people taking most of their possessions," Tyler said. "My Pa and I had to leave a lot of stuff behind. Maybe we didn't need to?"

Buckman eyed Tyler casually. "Son, these greenhorn folks with their brains inside their asses won't even make it to the Platte loaded down as so many of 'em are. And if I'm to be the wagon master of this train, then, so help me dammit, these folks are gonna do what I told 'em."

Tyler followed Buckman's glance toward a canvas-covered wagon about a hundred feet away where a man and two teenage sons had hauled a wood-burning stove, no less, and stood trying to figure out how to load it onto their wagon.

Buckman started toward the family with the wood-burning stove. "Lawton, I told you to leave the heavy stuff behind," he declared. "You'll never make it anywhere near Oregon carrying something that heavy. You won't even make it to Fort Laramie, unless you're figuring to buy a dozen oxen to haul your wagon, and even then, something as heavy as that stove is gonna wear hard on your axles."

Lawton, a husky, thick-boned man with a cropped beard and no mustache, put his arms on his hips and glared back at Buckman. "Ain't no way I'm leaving it behind. I paid fifty dollars for this stove just now."

"Well, then, somebody took you for fifty dollars," Buckman snorted. "But if you're in my train, you're starting out without that stove. I'm not holding up the train for any stragglers with overworked oxen. We'll never beat the first snows on the mountains come fall that way."

"Well, then, head on out without us," Lawton barked. "We don't need you or anyone else. We'll get to Oregon just fine on our own."

"No, we won't," snapped a bellied, pug-nosed middle-aged woman in a light green bonnet, approaching. "The Indians'll murder all of us within 200 miles of here if we travel by ourselves."

Buckman turned to the woman. "Mrs. Lawton, I can assure you that the Indian dangers on the Trail are greatly exaggerated, although you are correct that the danger increases for people traveling in small groups. Full-blown Indian attacks on larger wagon trains are more the stuff of eastern dime novelists. But the real trouble comes when wagon oxen can't go on or an axle breaks because the wagon is overloaded. That's what my real concern is. If you lose your oxen, do you have the money to buy new oxen at one of the forts along the way? Does your husband know enough carpentry to fix a broken axle or make a new one?"

Lawton grabbed Buckman by the shoulders and wheeled him around to slam a right fist to his jaw. "I paid you your money, Buckman, so we'll just take whatever we decide we want to take. You got it?"

Buckman was barely fazed. He clutched Lawton's shirt collar launched a fist into Lawton's stomach that knocked the wind right out of him. Buckman drilled a left fist to Lawton's jaw that pummeled him rolling to the ground. A spurt of blood from Lawton's lower lip reddened a spot in the dusty dirt.

Lawton's wife jumped in front of her husband to stop him from continuing the fight. "It's okay, Elrud, it's okay," she said, putting her hands on his chest as he rose. "We'll go back to the general store and see if we can get our money back. We don't need the stove."

Lawton looked at Buckman with narrowed red eyes beneath his clipped bangs and he felt his lip, wiping more blood off. He looked at his wife, then at Buckman again. "All right, you win for now, Buckman. But this ain't over," Lawton promised. "You and me are gonna meet again sometime . . ."

Tyler turned to walk away. People in the wagon train were already fighting one another and were at each other's throats, and they hadn't even left Independence yet. Why couldn't they all at least get a few hundred miles under their belts before tempers started growing short?

Tyler found himself heading back toward the Palmerstons, and their beautiful blonde daughter. Tyler saw the Palmerston girl still sitting on the lowered back of her family's wagon, with her bonnet off. Two boys near his age still stood by her, glaring at one another and shouting at each other. This Palmerston girl was going to be a source of trouble on this trip as the single boys vied, and even fought each other, for her attention. Well, she *was* strikingly beautiful, with long blonde hair down to her waist, her flawless skin, piquant, slightly upturned nose, and bright blue eyes. Then she saw Tyler noticing her. She smiled at him.

Tyler bashfully turned his head away but he glanced at her smile. Maybe there was a chance here after all. She'd noticed him, despite the heavy competition. The two boys in front of her pushed and shoved each other as they yelled at each other, and the Palmerston girl seemed to enjoy the male head-butting for her attention.

Over by the hitch rail in front of the nearest Mercantile, Tyler saw his twelve-year-old sister, Penny, apparently finished with laundry-washing and looking cute in her yellow pinafore, white blouse, and blue bonnet, talking to a much older boy with sandy blonde hair. Tyler knew the boy's name, Alain Laurent, but not much else about him. The name sounded French Canadian. Presumably, Alain Laurent planned to be in the Buckman wagon train. Penny seemed quite bright-eyed and smiley, talking with Alain. Well, Tyler reflected, his Pa had met his Ma when he was eighteen and she was fourteen, and they had married a couple of years later. Still, a boy who looked to be age seventeen developing an interest in his twelve-year-old sister represented a situation which bore close watching, especially when he saw Alain Laurent try to hold hands with Penny, and she, not shy about letting him. Indeed, Penny's face glowed as she looked at her new male friend. It was the first time he'd seen Penny truly happy since Ma had died a year earlier.

"Tyler! Tyler! Get over here and help me load up the seed bags and tools."

Pa was calling. Time to stop relaxing and get back to work. "Coming, Pa."

While he walked back toward Pa's wagon, Tyler couldn't help but take in the whole exciting scene. Pioneers, including many who fancied themselves such, loaded their wagons, chatted with their neighbors, lounged about the wooden boardwalks in front of several general stores, a couple of millinery shops, multiple saloons, the red-brick courthouse, two blacksmith shops, or even a nearby white-steepled church.

Yes, pray. Many of these folks would never make it all the way to Oregon or California. Some would "see the elephant" and head right back east-ward at the first sight of Indians, the first sight of desert, the first sight of high mountains, whatever. Others would succumb to disease along the Trail.

The first few hundred miles of the journey, up to the Platte River—some folks even said up to Fort Laramie—would be an exciting, glorious lark, with plenty of grass for the animals, plenty of water from nearby rivers, few if any Indians, and a powerful sense of anticipation as the pioneers saw the promise of the Far West ahead of them in the setting sun each evening.

The region beyond Fort Laramie where the grass gave out, the water became alkaline, if there was water anywhere at all, and the Sioux, Crows, Shoshones, Arapahoes and Cheyenne Indians lurked menacingly, now that was the region that separated the genuine pioneers from the pretenders, the wanna-bes, the pikers, the mere dreamers.

The folks who would actually make it to Oregon traveled light and small. Their wagons were no more than ten feet long, not the huge Conestogas made famous farther east. The "To Oregon" or "Oregon or bust" signs on the back of many of the wagons were vaguely amusing to Tyler. Pa had said that many of these wagons, and the people who owned them, would go "bust" well short of their goal.

Magnus loaded a heavy bag of grain seeds into the back of the wagon. Tyler grabbed the next bag. It was heavy, maybe fifty pounds. He could barely lift it into the wagon.

"That's why Buckman doesn't want folks taking a lot of bric-a-brac with 'em," Magnus said. "Think what it'll be like for the oxen just to haul the stuff we need, let alone something like a heavy stove." Pa, weary wrinkles framing his dark eyes, looked toward the Lawton wagon and sighed, shaking his head, "What were those people thinking?"

Pa took a moment to walk around the wagon as Tyler watched. The long, pointy-ended wagons were not what most people traveled to Oregon in. Tyler recalled how his father had been advised to buy the ten-footer wagon that wouldn't exhaust the oxen before they even got to Fort

Laramie. Away thirty feet from the wagon, Drake and Dru, the two broad-shouldered main oxen of the six-animal team that would haul the wagon, grazed placidly and seemingly oblivious to the challenging ordeal in front of them.

"How far is it to Oregon, Tyler?" Penny asked, approaching.

Tyler turned. Penny stood in her yellow pinafore and white blouse, with her blue polka-dot bonnet pulled to the back of her neck. She half-smiled, her clear-faced, thin-nosed expression hopeful yet seemingly masking the worry beneath. Her long brown hair fluttered in the western breeze. Her dark brown eyes shone.

"Two thousand miles, Penny."

"Do you think we'll make it?"

"Yeah, well, I guess."

Penny lowered her expression for a solemn moment, her straight little tan nose downcast, then she raised her head again. "You don't sound like you really think we'll make it."

"We'll make it, Penny," Tyler said impatiently. *Riding, walking or crawling, we'll make it.*

"We'll get there, Penny," Pa declared, "even if I have to carry you the last thousand miles, we'll make it."

CHAPTER TWO

"Gee haw! Gee haw!" Magnus Linders snapped the whip over the heads of Drake and Dru, yoked directly in front of the wagon. The other two teams of oxen strained in front of Drake and Dru. Pa did not want to whip their skins, but still get the message across. It was time to move against the flower-strewn and breeze-swept grassy prairie after ferrying across the Missouri River.

The oxen pulled against their yokes. The wagon lurched forward as Tyler sat in the front box with the reins. He knew that he would have to spend most of the journey walking, and he wanted to enjoy sitting for as long as he could. Pa walked alongside, guiding the oxen. Penny rode on the outward-extending box seat next to Tyler. The wagon bounced along annoyingly.

The white-canvas-covered wagons formed themselves in no particular order behind Buckman, the mounted wagon master, and his scouts, the sub-captains Silas Maple and Press Doolittle, plus the small herd of horses and cattle that Buckman and his sub-captains kept. No doubt their experiences in the mountains during fur-trapping days would be priceless before this journey was over.

The wagon train forming itself was an exciting time for Tyler. Pa had said that Buckman's wagon train would have eighty-five or more wagons, with over 450 pioneer emigrants in it bound for Oregon. Some families had more than one wagon. That Hapsburg feller and his fancy-pants daughter had two wagons, one for themselves and the other for the Austro-Hungarian soldiers accompanying them. The pioneers and their wagons worked to line themselves up four or five abreast. Already the dust had kicked up, a foretaste of the journey ahead. Also looming large up ahead was the paucity of trees. A few scattered cottonwoods broke up the wide-extending prairie, with the sky coming right down to the ground on the horizon. Soon they would be dependent upon buffalo chips for their fires.

Tyler wondered again how many of these four hundred and fifty-plus pioneers would actually make it all the way to Oregon. Some would find the lure and temptation of gold in California too much to resist and would turn off to the southwest. Others would see that mischievous, mythical elephant and turn around to head back East. Still others would find only death, and a grave, before reaching their goal of the Willamette Valley in Oregon. Indeed, Tyler wondered, would he, Pa, and Penny make it?

Yet now was not the time to think of such things. Now, it was time to enjoy the excitement. The oxen bawled and complained, the drovers shouted and cracked their whips. The wagons started toward the Golden West.

Tyler looked around him. The MacNaughton wagon lurched forward to the left about thirty feet, while the Colledge wagon was to the right. The Ellises, Hancliceks, Palmerstons, and Clevengers were in the immediate front, while a half-dozen more wagons lay further still in front of them. Tyler heard the creaking movements of dozens of other wagons behind them.

Buckman rode in front of the wagons. The wagon master had said he was giving everyone a break on the first day—the sun was up as they started. He had warned every family in the train that there would be many a day when the wagons would be rolling while the moon was still up.

"Be up by 4:30 a.m., 5 a.m. if you feel you just have to sleep in," Buckman had told Tyler and four or five other nearby families yesterday. "We're on the trail by 6 a.m., earlier than that if we can. We can't and won't wait for families with kids that don't want to get out of bed. If we do, we'll never make it to Oregon before the snows hit the mountains in early fall. Those that aren't ready to move in the morning when I am, can be at the back of the train and eat the dust coming from the wagons that got started on time. Or, they can be left behind."

Tyler kept these words in mind as the wagon moved forward with eight others. In the distance he saw Buckman the wagon master raise his hands for the five columns of wagons to halt. It took about twenty feet for Tyler to hold up on the reins and get Drake and Dru to stop completely. Other wagons ground to a halt at more or less the same distance.

Buckman lowered his arm and Tyler thought he was going to turn around and speak. However, Buckman continued to look ahead toward the West, toward a line of low, lightly-forested hills in the far distance, and a narrow river. Beyond those hills lay the Oregon Trail.

A sense of mysticism overcame Tyler, a feeling of awe, a sense of an adventure great and stunningly profound. As the Pilgrims had set out from Plymouth, England in 1620, as Daniel Boone and his followers had left North Carolina for Kentucky in 1767, as Lewis and Clark had set out to cross the North American Continent in 1804, so was this wagon train of men, women, and children about to embark upon a heroic journey that would place them among those earlier hallowed ranks.

"To Oregon!" Buckman shouted across the prairie.

"To Oregon!" one of the pioneers behind him yelled.

"To Oregon!" several more men shouted. The chant was taken up by dozens, then by hundreds of others, by those who would never make it, by those who would turn around, by those who would stop along the way, by those who would end their journey in lonely trailside graves, and by still others whose journey would end in the Willamette Valley near the Pacific, people whose sheer guts and overachieving determination would carry them past hostile Indians, flooded rivers, dry deserts, snow-capped mountain barriers, and ultimately to the golden, green, fertile West Coast. Oregon was a land of dreams fulfilled and hopes met, or so the many would believe.

Buckman took his reins and started forward again. Tyler snapped his oxen reins and the wagon lurched forward once more in sync with the other wagons.

"This is exciting," Penny declared. "We're finally starting."

"Let's hope we're still excited about this when we're crossing the desert," Tyler said.

Van Buren Colledge rode on the front of his parents' wagon, as their black slave walked alongside. What the status of the Colledges' slave would be once the train left Missouri was unclear. Kansas was either "free" or "slave" territory depending upon who was asked.

Dennis and Helena Palmerston walked alongside their wagon as blonde Rachelle and her two younger brothers rode on the wagon board. With the constant lurching—not to mention the drain on the oxen's energy—Tyler wondered how long any of them would care to ride.

Renford MacNaughton whipped his two oxen teams mercilessly. Tyler felt for the poor beasts, who were really too small, and cheap, to try to haul a 3,000-pound wagon that was probably overloaded.

Kitty-corner to Tyler's right ahead of them Tomas Hanclicek calmly called out "gee" and "haw" to his wagon team as though he had done it a thousand times before, although Tyler was sure he hadn't. Alongside Tomas, his thick-bonneted wife worked the beads of a rosary. Their older son handled the reins. A young, brown-haired Hanclicek beauty, whose name Tyler had heard was Marta, walked with her Slavic parents.

Tyler made note to try to keep his wagon close to the Palmerston and Hanclicek wagons. The Ellis twins weren't bad-looking, either. Billie Kay and Kelly Jay, Tyler had heard their names were. Tyler unconsciously kept running his fingers through his dark hair, trying to keep his long bangs out of his eyes and his appearance neat.

Excitement gave way to mundane travel. Tyler felt his eyes grow heavy with the relentless plodding of the oxen and back and forth rocking of the wagon which acted as a somnolent. The morning sun was warm, with no breeze now, which exacerbated the effect.

Crossing the Blue River seemed simple enough. Narrow and shallow with a firm, rocky bottom, the Blue hardly seemed portentous of what Tyler knew lay ahead. Pa walked alongside the wagon through the water, with the waves never rising above his knees.

The wagons moved through an area of short buffalo grass, mixed with blue pasque flowers. "This is like a spring trip!" Penny said excitedly, surveying the landscape and the other wagons confidently heading west. The prairie spread out like a yellow, waving sheet. The blue sky above seemed a deeper shade than further east. A few small puffy clouds sailed overhead

"They say the first hundred fifty miles or so through Kansas are like a picnic," Magnus said. "Enjoy it while it lasts."

Tyler watched the Colledge wagon close by, listening to the banter between Jonathan Colledge and his slave.

"…can't let them walk too fast, Tuck. They've got a long way to go ahead of them. Make sure the oxen pace themselves," Colledge said.

"Yessuh," the slave Tuck said. "I is understandin'."

Tyler turned to the MacNaughton wagon to his left. Renford MacNaughton kept whipping his bawling, complaining oxen on their backs. MacNaughton was trying to get to Oregon on the cheap side, using only two teams of oxen. Probably the MacNaughton oxen would give out by about Fort Laramie or so. MacNaughton had likely bought his oxen on the cheap side as well, as they were smaller in size, and likely thought that if he was mean enough to them they would perform like regular-sized oxen.

Next Tyler observed the Ellis wagon ahead. The wagon moved along at a steady pace over the prairie grass at the same speed as Tyler kept his oxen going. Through the back flaps of the wagon Tyler could see the Ellis twins inside. Pa Ellis walked to the wagon's left. Presumably, Ma Ellis rode up front.

The first day's journey rolled through perfectly flat terrain amidst grass that was high enough to offer good livestock forage but not so high as to create resistance to wagon travel. The wagon train easily moved among and around low hills which offered no barrier to passage.

After twelve noon Buckman called a halt to the wagon train travel to give people a chance to enjoy their first "nooning." It was a break from the grind and a chance to relax. Tyler jumped down to enjoy a ham sandwich while sitting on the ground in the shade of the wagon with Penny and Pa.

"How long will it take us to get to Oregon?" Penny asked.

"Maybe five months," Magnus said while munching on his sandwich. "Hopefully no longer than that." He swallowed and added, "We got to get past the Rockies before there's snow. I'm sure we will. Buckman's a good leader and he'll get us there."

Tyler smirked with his thin lips. "Just so we don't end up like the Donner Party."

Magnus halted just as he was about to take another bite. He glared at Tyler. "Don't bring that up while I'm eating."

After an hour of resting the journey resumed. A pleasant, warm, benign afternoon appeared to be an omen of good fortune. All of the wagons kept pace. None fell behind. The fresh oxen steadily pulled their heavy loads. Friendly greetings were exchanged among neighboring wagons and families.

When Buckman called a halt to the day's travel at about 5 p.m., the wagons formed themselves into a rough circle. Buckman spread the word that the purpose of forming the eighty-seven wagons into a gigantic circle hundreds of feet in diameter was to keep the livestock enclosed at night.

Once the wagons had completed this traditional ritual, campfires were lit; evening meals of coffee, beans, bacon or salt pork were prepared and consumed.

Truly it seemed like a community picnic to Tyler. He sat back against a wagon wheel enjoying the company of thin-faced Timothy MacNaughton as together they ate their chili beans. Tyler guessed that Tim was about his same age and would be a good companion on the journey.

Tim appeared feisty. His pimply face contorted. "Buckman said this wagon circle is to keep the livestock in, but I know better," he said. "Really, it's to set up a defense barrier if the Indians attack."

"What kind of crap are you talking about?" Tyler demanded. "There ain't no Indians around here."

"But there will be," Tim retorted. "Buckman wants to get us used to forming a defense position for the night. There'll be Indians attacking us soon enough, probably as soon as we get to the Platte. Actually, I'm looking forward to it, fighting the Indians, I mean. I read all about it in this novel I read before we—my family, I mean—left Indiana. This one guy who was the hero of the novel, he killed ten Indians that were trying to kidnap his girlfriend. Killed 'em all, he did, then married the girl."

Tyler thought for a moment, observing a fiddler nearby and four couples who danced a quadrille to the music. "Actually, Tim, I'd just as soon not think about Indians," Tyler said.

MacNaughton rose and dusted off the seat of his pants. "Suit yourself," Tim snapped. "Me? I can't wait till the Indians attack. I'm gonna fight 'em all off and afterwards have every girl in this wagon train swooning over me, maybe even Rachelle Palmerston."

As young MacNaughton walked away to finish his chili, Tyler glanced a hundred feet to his left. At the Palmerston wagon, Rachelle had set up court. Eight or nine boys surrounded her as she sat on the wooden back flap of her family's wagon, each boy trying to get her attention. Her blonde hair fluttered in a gentle breeze. Her blue pinafore dress over a blue blouse covered cleavage that was larger than most Tyler had seen.

Tyler barely knew Rachelle, he admitted to himself, but he knew her type—in that one percent of girls whose beauty stood out exceptionally above the other ninety-nine percent, and they darn well knew it and acted like it.

He turned away. Over to his right, standing in front of a large group campfire, a preacher man had gathered a couple of dozen listeners in a semi-circle around him. He'd heard the preacher's name was Reverend Michael Thomison, a Methodist circuit-rider. Probably some folks drew a bit of comfort from knowing there was a man of God traveling with them on this long journey.

Reverend Thomison gripped his Bible in his right hand. ". . . Abraham didn't know what the Almighty had in mind, when the Almighty ordered him to leave the land of his father Terah in Ur, the land of his ancestors, and travel all the way to the land of Canaan," the good Reverend thundered. "But Abraham went anyway. He trusted the Almighty . . ."

When an older man sitting on the ground listening to Reverend Thomison leaned back, Tyler saw that one of those listening rapturously to the tale of Abraham and the Almighty was Penny. She was with that seventeen-year-old Alain Laurent, who also listened to Thomison.

Tyler doubted that the muscular, broad-shouldered Laurent boy was the religious type. Probably he was just trying to impress Penny—or Pa—that he was a God-fearing, upstanding young man. Well, so be it.

"You're Tyler Linders, aren't you?"

Tyler looked up and there was Kelly Jay Ellis, with her brown-eyed, clear, gently dimpled face, upturned but slightly thick nose and three feet of brown hair. Or was it her identical twin, Billie Kay Ellis, smiling at him?

"I sure am."

"Hi. I'm Kelly Jay Ellis. Kelly Jay for short. Some of us are getting together to have a young folks' dance. You want to join us? We need more men."

"You don't have to ask me twice." Tyler leaped to his feet. To his sheer delight, Kelly Jay Ellis took him by the hand and led him over to the west side of the wagon train circle which the young people had claimed as their own. A thin-bearded man of perhaps thirty-five years handled the fiddling.

Tyler did a couple of two-step dances with Kelly Jay Ellis. He had an opportunity to ask her why she and her twin sister, unlike many identical twins, seemed to delight in looking exactly alike.

"You even wear the same clothes," Tyler remarked, observing Kelly Jay's broad-shouldered blue dress. "Do you enjoy confusing people?"

"We have some harmless fun with it," Kelly Jay replied in the midst of a whirl. She stopped suddenly, though, and turned serious. "That's how I found out about how bad my erstwhile fiancée's drinking problems were," she declared. "I knew Jess liked to drink too much every now and then, but I'd naively hoped he'd change if I just gave him some encouragement, so I never told my Pa. One day, though, Billie Kay went to visit Jess' family's farm to buy some seed. Jess thought it was me. He had whiskey bottles in both hands, and he was darn near passed out drunk. He could barely apologize in a real slurred way. Billie Kay told my Pa, and that's one reason—among others—why we left Pennsylvania for Oregon. Pa wanted to get me as far away from Jess as he could, so he'd never find me. Pa had always wanted to go West, and Ma finally agreed after hearing about Jess' drinking and how he still wanted to marry me even after that incident."

Billie Kay Ellis asked Tyler to dance next. Tyler happily danced with Billie Kay, and then with several other girls whose names he didn't know and couldn't remember afterward. Not that it mattered. Tyler figured that he would see them again and again and again as the journey progressed. Truly, Tyler reflected, this was a picnic, a celebration, a special moment in time on this first night of the odyssey. Ten miles down, only 1,990 miles to go.

Always, though, Tyler reverted to reflecting upon the Ellis twins, Kelly Jay and Billie Kay, who seemed to relish their identical looks. They wore their hair the same length and style and they wore the same type of blue plaid schoolgirl type dresses and dark socks. They had the exact same facial features—well-formed, round-ended noses, slightly round faces, light brown skin, and light brown, exuberant eyes.

When Tyler stopped for a moment to rest, he noted the Hapsburg girl, Angelique, watching the party from beside her father's wagon, with her father's four soldierly escorts nearby. The soldiers were dressed in silk shirts and jeans now—they probably felt weird in that Western attire. Tyler could not read Angelique's thoughts from her expression. She had one hand on a wagon wheel, another hand on her hip, as if interested but not sure what to do about it. Her clothes, interestingly, were buckskin breeches and shirt, hardly European in style. She was still European royalty, however, and Tyler knew she was flat-out unapproachable. No sense getting to know her when she was no doubt spoken for by some handsome prince in Europe. Tyler knew he could never match that kind of competition, not even in his most exotic dreams.

Rachelle Palmerston came late, with a retinue of sorts, of no less than nine or ten boys accompanying her. Rachelle kept her haughty sharp chin up. Dance she did, with the more debonair-looking, handsome boys. When one short, heavy-set, pudgy-faced older teenage boy dared to ask her to dance, Rachelle burst out laughing, as did the other boys surrounding her. That, apparently, was her answer when a boy who was not debonair or handsome had the effrontery to ask her to dance.

"You're not in Rachelle's league, Quimby, and you know it," one laughing young man called out as the unfortunate pudgy-faced young man tried to slink away and hide his embarrassment and his heartfelt deep hurt.

Tyler watched as the poor fellow retreated without a word, shame-faced, in front of a couple of dozen other young partiers. With all of the dangers and trials that lay ahead on this journey to Oregon, Tyler hoped that at some point

Rachelle would need help from that boy she'd embarrassed so rudely, and would not get it.

"Get those kids out of the way! Get 'em out of the way!"

Startled, Tyler forgot the dance and ran toward the direction where he'd heard the man's screams coming from. He leaped over a wagon tongue to see what was happening. Buckman's herd of twenty cattle that had lagged behind the rest of the train were not stampeding, but they were hurrying toward a small water pond a few hundred feet away amidst the grass. Directly in their path a small group of toddler-age children played together, oblivious to the cattle heading straight at them. If they didn't move, the cattle would crush them under their hooves.

Three mothers frantically ran for their children but they would be mowed down as well if they got in the way of the cattle. A thick-bearded man raced on horseback toward one side of the moving cattle. He twice fired shots from a new-style revolver over the heads of the cattle. He could not fire at their hooves without danger of a ricochet hitting one of the toddlers.

The bearded man on horseback shrieked at Tyler. "Grab some stones and throw them at the cattle coming at you!"

Tyler grabbed two large pebbles off the ground and hurled them at the nose of the front steer. Two other men fired rifle shots just over the heads of the cattle. The report of the rifle shots and the stones hitting the front steer's nose veered the cattle hard rightward just before they would have crushed the toddlers, who now saw the danger and ran screaming with their mothers out of the way of the rest of the cattle.

Another thick-bearded man, this one in a red and black plaid mackinaw coat, came riding up on horseback to confront the first man Tyler had seen.

"Maybe you could keep a little better watch on the livestock, Silas?"

"Maybe I could get more help from you with that, Press," Silas retorted.

Tyler remembered the two men's names now. Press Doolittle and Silas Maple, Buckman's two scouts and right-hand men.

Press looked like he would say more in anger, but he checked himself. Slowly, he nodded. "Well, yeah, maybe. We nearly had our first deaths on this trip just now, and we're hardly started out."

Tyler looked with bitter eyes at Silas Maple. "Why didn't you just shoot the cattle?" Tyler demanded.

Silas Maple returned Tyler's stern look. "Because one shot wouldn't a-stopped any of them critters, son, so there. 'Sides, we may need them cattle further on down the Trail."

Now, Tyler recalled that the cattle were supposed to serve as an emergency food supply, in case provisions grew short in the desert. But only twenty cattle for 450 people? Huh!

Oh yeah, Tyler told himself. Not all 450 people in this train would survive to Oregon. By taking only twenty cattle, Buckman was thinking not of how many people in his wagon train had started out, but of how many would be left by the time they might need emergency food supplies.

CHAPTER THREE

"Y"ou did fine this morning," Pa said. "Just keep cracking the whip over the heads of Drake and Dru at a steady rate every few minutes and it keeps them in a steady rhythm. That's important for the long haul, no pun intended."

Tyler leaned back against the wagon wheel to enjoy eating some dried apple slices. This nooning business was a warm, relaxing time. "So far, it looks like Drake and Dru are doing as well as any of the other oxen. They don't have any neck bruises yet."

"Let's hope it stays that way," Pa said. "Where did Penny go?"

"She's relieving herself."

Interesting how the women and girls handled those situations. Tyler recalled twice now the past couple of days, on the nearly treeless Kansas prairie, having seen pairs of women blocking the view from the wagons as another woman relieved herself. He'd tried not to stare at the odd sight. There wasn't a single outhouse on the whole Oregon Trail, outside of at a few forts along the way.

Tyler looked around. It was largely the same people as yesterday, and the day before that, in the wagons nearby. The

MacNaughtons to the left, Ellises ahead, Hancliceks to the right, and behind them, the Clevengers and the Hapsburgs. The wagons looked to be in good shape so far, with axles thoroughly greased and white canvas tops still sturdy.

"Pa, when do we get to the Blue again?" Tyler asked.

"The guidebook I got, and Buckman, say we should be there by the fourth or fifth day," Magnus replied. "Don't worry. We're not gonna run out of water. If we have to, we can catch rainwater when it rains."

Tyler checked Pa's guidebook again and saw that the next thing named "Blue" wasn't the river again, but rather a low, tree-lined summit called Blue Mound. The wagon trains could easily move past Blue Mound, low but elongated in the distance.

Tim MacNaughton leaned against his father's blue-painted wagon box. He looked at Tyler. "Hey, our first mountain," Tim declared. "We're in the mountains now."

"Hardly," Tyler said underneath his breath. Blue Mound might have been considered a mountain in Indiana. Pile about twenty Blue Mounds on top of each other, and you might have a mountain like in the Rockies 500 miles further on, Tyler reflected.

It turned out to be the Red Vermilion River ahead, Buckman said as he rode past informing everyone, not the Blue River, that would need crossing once the journey resumed. But this next crossing would be the very first signpost, as it were, on the Trail. It would be the signal that they had actually started out to Oregon. Buckman announced that for anyone who needed it, the Red Vermilion was clear, pristine water, despite its name.

Tyler reminded himself that rain, although an inconvenience, also was a reliable, pure source of water, at least for now on the first several hundred miles. Later on, rain would become highly unreliable and the rivers muddier.

"I may jump in the water. It's kind of warm out today," Tyler said, looking at the placid stream in the distance.

"The water'll still be kinda cold at this time of year," Magnus responded, "even if the air is warm."

"Well, yeah, maybe," Tyler said. "I suppose it's—"

"Get ready to move!" Buckman shouted to everyone around as he rode past again. "Nooning's over."

"I've only had half an hour, maybe less," a harsh voice muttered.

Buckman dismounted. He walked over to a wagon about thirty feet away and just behind the Linders wagon. A shaggy-haired, thinly dark-bearded man wearing a greasy blue shirt and dirty suspenders glared at Buckman.

"What's your name—Stoneman or something like that?" Buckman demanded.

"Stonehouse. Brinton Stonehouse," the shaggy-haired man replied.

"Well, Mr. Stonehouse, you got a late start this morning after sleeping in later than everybody else, till 5:30 a.m. or so." Buckman made a sweeping motion at the flower-strewn prairie. "Everybody else was up and moving by the time you got up. So you had to play catch-up. If you want to have a full nooning from now on, Mr. Stonehouse, then you get moving in the a.m. the same time as everybody else. I ain't giving special privileges to you or anyone."

Buckman turned to walk away, looking around. "Spread the word—we're moving again."

Stonehouse's expression burned during a tense, quiet several seconds when no one knew if he would argue further. Tyler took another bite of a dried apple slice, watching the scene carefully.

"Yeah, and you have a nice day too," Stonehouse sarcastically muttered at Buckman.

Buckman kept moving away, apparently not wanting to continue the confrontation with Stonehouse any further.

"Was there a fight?" Penny asked, walking up in her brown calico dress and bonnet.

"Not yet," Tyler said, gripping his suspenders. "Those two haven't seen the last of each other, though, I'm thinking."

Tyler rose to take his place next to Drake and Dru. He pulled the whip loose from its hold at the left side of the wagon. He took a cursory look at the dish-shaped wheels and iron axle joints. All was well, so far.

Twenty feet away, Tim MacNaughton looked at him with an annoyed expression. "That Buckman thinks he's big shit," Tim snorted. "We ought to get together and stand up to him. What does he think he is—a dictator?"

Pa glared at Tim as he mounted the wagon board to take the reins. "Actually, yeah, for the duration of this journey, Buckman *is* a dictator and he's got a right to be. We signed on to his wagon train voluntarily. He's got a tough task, trying to get as many of us through as safely as possible and being our leader across a couple of thousand miles of unorganized land with no real law or civilization. He has to be hard and tough. A wagon master who's nothing but a shrinking violet would never get us through to Oregon. Wagon trains that don't have strong leadership end up breaking apart and with people scattering, ending up alone by themselves in the middle of nowhere."

Renford MacNaughton walked around his oxen team. "Just the same, I'm keeping an eye on what Buckman does." The thin-bodied, bespectacled elder MacNaughton put a hand on his son Tim's shoulder. "There's no law that says Buckman has to be our wagon master all the way to Oregon."

Tyler looked at Pa, who glanced downward and shook his head.

"We've barely gone fifty miles and already there's dissension," Magnus said. "It's sunny weather, warm, no buffalo stampeding around us yet, no Indians yet, and already people are starting to feel edgy."

Tyler drew close to his Pa. "You think it'll get worse when we get farther along?"

Magnus pursed his lips, sighed heavily through his nose, and snorted. "What do you think?"

* * *

The wagon train continued on for another five hours. By the time the wagons circled for the night, nearly twenty miles had been covered, or so Buckman announced. With Buckman's hard-nosed leadership, the wagon train was making better-than-average time for an oxen-drawn group of wagons.

Tyler had no reason to doubt what the wagon master said. He felt footsore from walking for long stretches, and butt-sore from sitting for long stretches on the bouncing wagon. Still, Tyler was glad to participate in the nightly party. It was quickly becoming a tradition. Each evening the younger set gathered for dancing and socialization, with some guy named Bruce Mallory supplying the fiddle music. Tyler had his eyes on the Ellis twins, Kelly Jay and Billie Kay. He did three dances with Kelly Jay and one with Billie Kay. No need to choose one of them, not with 1,945 miles to go, or thereabouts. Tyler also told himself that it would not be smart to come on to either of the Ellis girls too quickly and risk scaring them away.

"Keep that bull away from the wagons while people are eating!"

Tyler turned around from the music. It was Buckman, dismounted and yelling at that Lawton fellow again as the latter herded a dark-haired bull away from the circle of wagons and out into the prairie for grass.

Suddenly the bull lurched around and with a sharp bellow and horns lowered headed straight for a small boy who had thrown a stone at it.

"Help! Mom!" The terrified boy tried to run away but the bull charged after him. Lawton did nothing to stop his bull from attacking the boy.

Buckman raced around one wagon to get as close to the 1,500 pound behemoth as he dared. Lawton stood and watched. Buckman fired a pistol right over the bull's head which distracted the creature away from the boy. For a tense few seconds, the bull looked like it might turn its full narrow-eyed wrath on Buckman, who doubtless knew that a single pistol shot from one of his new-fangled revolvers wouldn't even slow the bull down, but at length, the bull decided eating was better than fighting, and sauntered off.

"Thanks for your help, Lawton," the wagon master muttered sarcastically. Buckman took off his plainsman's hat and slapped it against his knee. "Keep a better eye on that thing."

"Don't go shooting at my bull," Lawton demanded. "I'll need it in Oregon for breeding purposes. He's been a good money-maker for me. And tell the kids to leave my bull alone. He's ornery just like any bull is. Just try throwing a stone at him and see what happens!"

"Keep it under better control from now on," Buckman said. The wagon master turned to walk away, choosing to avoid a full-blown confrontation with Lawton just yet. Buckman and Lawton had a clear dislike for each other, which presaged trouble further along the way.

Returning his attention to Mallory's fiddle playing, Tyler thought that still, even though he didn't want to be too forward, it might be smart to hint to Kelly Jay, who had been the first to invite him to dance on that first evening, that he could be a-wanting to get to know her better as time marched on. He sought her out, standing near her parents' wagon with its big "To Oregon!" sign on the back.

"Hi, Kelly Jay," Tyler declared. He desperately looked around for something, anything, to comment on. "Looks like the oxen and cattle have got plenty of good grass hereabouts. Buckman's keeping the spare herd fat and meaty, if we ever need 'em."

"Well, yeah, I suppose," she responded, smiling, but with her arms crossed over her light green calico dress.

"Tell me, Kelly Jay, where did you learn to dance so well?" Tyler asked. "You could probably teach me quite a few new steps."

"Well, yeah, I suppose," she said, smiling and half-chuckling. The end of her long perfect, upturned nose flared ever so slightly as she grinned.

"You're not going to be too tired tomorrow night to dance some more, I hope." Tyler spread his arms and hands. "In all sincerity, Kelly Jay, you're one of the best Reel dancers I've ever seen. I just feel a lot less self-conscious when I'm dancing with someone who knows what they're doing better than I do and can teach me proper."

She stretched out an arm and put a hand against the wagon box while putting her other hand on her hip. "Why, thank you, Tyler, that's very sweet of you to say that," she declared, beaming as broadly as a sunflower.

Tyler felt he was on a roll here, and he reacted instinctively. *Go with it.* "You know, Kelly Jay, I really appreciate how you invited me to the dance that other night. I mean, I mean . . ." Tyler didn't know for sure what he meant. "That was very, real kind of you, and, well, Kelly Jay, since your family and mine travel so close together, maybe . . . maybe we could share a nooning together sometime? You and I alone, I mean. I . . . I'll b-be real honest, Kelly Jay, I think you're really a special young woman." Tyler involuntarily let out a sigh of relief—there, he'd said it and made his intentions clear.

"Hmm," she said uncertainly. She moved her head from side to side as if pondering the idea. Finally, she said, "Well, yeah, I suppose."

Tyler brightened instantly, but then his face fell. He asked, "Are you saying that because you really want to or because 'Well, yeah, I suppose' is all you hardly ever say?"

"Well, yeah, I sup—" She burst out laughing and slapped her hip as she looked away momentarily.

"Did I say something funny when I asked you to share a noon lunch with me?" Tyler demanded.

She looked at him with her brown eyes sparkling and her laughter merry. "Tyler, I'm not Kelly Jay. I'm Billie Kay," she said. "I'm Billie Kay. Sometimes it's fun for me and Kelly Jay to fool people a little."

Tyler's fists balled and his even teeth clenched. "So you can make fools out of people like me? Is that it? What I just said was meant only for Kelly Jay's ears, not yours. What I just said was absolutely none of your business, Billie Kay." He turned to stalk angrily away, feeling embarrassed and idiotic.

Billie Kay hurried after him and put a hand on his shoulder to stop him. "Tyler, Tyler—I'm sorry," she declared. "Please, let me apologize to you. I'm truly sorry if I did anything to hurt you."

She forced him to turn around and look at her. There was sincere contrition evident in her brown eyes and hang-dog expression.

"I'm sorry, Tyler, and I apologize from my heart. I mean it. Let me tell you right from my heart I wasn't trying to offend you. I would never do that to you or anyone. Forgive me?"

Tyler couldn't resist the urge. "Well, yeah, I suppose," he muttered.

A wan little smile returned to Billie Kay's tanned face. "Thanks, I appreciate your accepting my apology. I would never hurt anyone, nor will I stand by and see someone be hurt. Believe that about me. You're a wonderful guy to say those things."

"All right, fine." Tyler swept his brown bangs out of his eyes and turned to walk away again.

"And Tyler," he heard her as he moved away from her. "I know what you were getting at. I'll tell Kelly Jay that you'd like to share a nooning with her sometime. But she's just gotten over a bad relationship with a man back East. She may not be ready just yet for another serious relationship."

Tyler put his hands up and half-looked back at Billie Kay. "Okay, fine. I understand if she doesn't want to."

He walked on. Besides, earlier, Rachelle Palmerston had smiled at him again, even as she had walked past him with a half-dozen young men in her retinue. Oh, how Rachelle's long blonde hair cascaded down her blue pinafore dress back!

Tyler thought he might actually suck up the courage to ask Rachelle to dance, and damn the other guys surrounding her. He sat on the ground watching her dance, debating his next move. Those same two boys glared at each other, each jealous of the other for being attracted to Rachelle. Van Buren Colledge was one of the two boys.

"Hey!"

Tyler felt a kick in the butt. He looked up. Pa needed him.

"Penny's with that seventeen-year-old Laurent kid again," Pa said, rubbing his dark whiskers.

Tyler looked in Penny's direction. There she stood, fifty feet away, holding hands with Alain Laurent as together they watched the Reel dancing.

"Anything wrong?" Tyler asked.

Magnus spit out a chew of tobacco off to the side. His dark eyes stretched wide. "Nope, nothing's wrong, I hope. If that Laurent kid can keep Penny occupied and happy and content on this long trip, then fine and dandy. But I aim to make sure that that Laurent kid minds his manners around our twelve-year-old Penny. Why don't you go over and just kinda, sorta get acquainted with him? Just as subtly as you can, just so he knows we're watching him. Understand?"

Tyler got up and dusted off the bottom of his trousers. He gripped his suspenders and headed toward Alain and Penny. He circled around several dancing couples and had to pass by Reverend Thomison again. The preacher was gathering a growing flock. Tonight, Thomison thundered away about the Hebrews on their forty year journey from Egypt to the Promised Land and how the Lord took care of them en route.

Hopefully the Lord would do a better job of taking care of this wagon train on its much longer journey from Independence, Missouri to Oregon Territory's Willamette Valley. Tyler felt no desire to spend four decades on this trip.

Tyler approached Alain and Penny, holding hands, and waved a hello at them. "Hi, Allen."

Laurent smiled politely, nodding. "Tyler."

Penny frowned. She pushed her hexagonal reading glasses up her sharp-featured nose on her tan-brown face. "His name isn't Allen," she declared. "His name is Alain. A-lain. And his last name's not pronounced 'Law-rent;' it's Lau-ron. He's French Canadian by way of Vermont."

"I'm sorry, Alain. I promise I'll remember."

Penny's expression softened and she looked at Tyler with mild condescension. "Would you tell Pa not to worry so much," she said. "Alain is my good friend that I met when his parents' wagon train was parked next to ours for awhile in Independence. Alain and I are fine together."

"So Tyler, how's it going?" Alain asked.

Tyler smiled and greeted him like nothing was amiss. "I'm just enjoying the music." He shook hands with Alain. "If it's like this all the way to Oregon, this trip is going to be one long party." He knew better, but he could think of nothing else to say.

"Once people've walked a couple of hundred miles I doubt they'll be as interested in sashaying around in the evening," Alain said. "Like as not, they'll be too tired and they'll probably be smart enough to realize they have to save their strength."

"I'm not too tired to dance yet," Penny declared.

"Then let's go!" Alain said. He held out his arm and Penny took it. Off they went into the exuberant dance.

Alain did have rugged good looks with his clear, half-circular, thin-nosed face and sea-blue eyes, Tyler had to admit to himself, and he could see why Penny was attracted to him with her first girlish crush. Alain always had his square jaw clean-shaven. His clear eyes and sandy blonde hair bespoke of earnestness and forthright character.

Penny's long brown hair whirled and twirled as she laughed and danced with her seventeen-year-old nascent boyfriend. Tyler let out an involuntary sigh. He saw how some of the girls older than Penny with more mature beauty looked at Alain Laurent. He saw how Rachelle Palmerston looked at Alain—with longing. Rachelle watched Alain as he danced arm-in-arm with Penny.

"Tyler!"

He had to turn away. Buckman of all people had called out to him.

"What do you need?" Tyler asked as the wagon master approached on foot.

Buckman's frayed whiskers and dirty buckskin shirt were already showing promise of the uncivilized pioneer leader that he was starting to look like. "I need you to help with the first watch tonight," Buckman said, walking up. "That Austro-Hungarian guy and his four guards will be helping you."

"That Hapsburg guy?"

"Yeah, him." Buckman switched his long Kentucky-style rifle from his right arm to his left. "Make sure the live-stock all stay within the wagon circle overnight. Don't let any of the cattle or oxen get outside the circle."

"You expecting any trouble tonight?" Tyler asked.

Buckman apparently knew what Tyler was driving at and he spat out a chew of tobacco disgustedly. "No, there ain't gonna be no 'trouble' tonight. When we get another hundred miles closer to the Platte is when we got to start watching for Indians wanting to steal livestock. You think I'd let that high-falutin' tinhorn dandy Hapsburg stand guard tonight if I was expecting any real trouble? No, for now, it's just that we can't afford time in the morning looking for missing livestock."

Without waiting for an answer to his rhetorical question about Hapsburg, Buckman turned and walked away.

Yep, Tim MacNaughton was right. Buckman was a dictator. "I need you to help with the first watch tonight," he'd said. End of discussion. That was okay, though, Tyler told himself. Maybe being asked to do guard duty this early on the journey meant that Buckman wanted to train him for a leadership position further down the road in the mountain country. Maybe Buckman intended to make him a wagon train captain at some point, or would make him one if he showed enough willingness to take on extra responsibilities.

Maybe, being a wagon captain would give him a leg up on the stiff competition for Rachelle's attention and admiration. "Oh, but why the hell do I have to think of her all the time?" Tyler asked himself out loud.

"Think of who all the time?" a sandy-haired kid named Brent McGuigan asked, walking by leading a cow. He was one of those two boys most interested in Rachelle.

"Never mind," Tyler snapped.

Tyler ventured back over to his own wagon to speak with his father, smoking a corncob pipe as he sat on a three-legged stool. "I'm helping out with the first watch tonight, along with that Hapsburg character."

"Yeah, I heard," Magnus said, removing the pipe from his mouth. "Buckman wants me to stand second watch tonight. I'm going to be tired tomorrow, so you'll have to do most of the driving."

"That's fine, Pa. I can handle it." Tyler knew that by "driving," his father meant walking next to the oxen and keeping them moving.

Tyler felt a certain manliness about doing guard duty. The dancers continued in their Reels, quadrilles, and twirling, Penny and Alain among them. He caught Penny's attention. "Don't worry, Penny, if I'm out late tonight," he called out. "I've got guard duty for the first three hours of the night."

Tyler knew he didn't really need to tell Penny that—Pa would no doubt have told her. His real audience that he hoped had overheard him was the crowd of puffed-up pretender-boys hanging around Rachelle, and Rachelle especially. He furtively glanced in the direction of the femme fatale and her wanna-be suitors. A couple of the boys looked at him. They could talk all they wanted about whatever they'd done in the past, or what they had made up about themselves. Let them build themselves up verbally. He could demonstrate to Rachelle by clear deeds that he was a bigger man than all of those other guys. He was one of the first ones to be tapped for nighttime guard duty.

CHAPTER FOUR

yler watched the fiddle-playing and dancing, but ever so coolly did not join in. Soon, Tyler fetched his Sharps rifle. Whenever anyone asked him why he was carrying his rifle, he answered as nonchalantly as possible, "Got guard duty tonight." None of those who asked him, though, were of the high-and-mighty Rachelle crowd, as that group was completely self-absorbed.

As darkness started to fall and the pioneers headed off to their tents and sleeping rolls for the night, Tyler sauntered over toward the Hapsburg wagon. Duke Franz Hapsburg, in faux buckskins, or perhaps they were real, sat at a campfire with his daughter, Angelique, also in buckskins.

"I guess they both want to look the part," Tyler whispered to himself, sighing.

There was no such masquerade from the four Austro-Hungarian guards. In full red dress uniforms once again, ridiculously out of place on the Kansas prairie, they stood with their rifle butts on the ground.

As Tyler approached the Hapsburg wagon, one of the guards half-raised his rifle. "*Halten-zie!*"

Tyler obeyed but looked at Duke Franz Hapsburg. "You speak English?" he asked.

"I think so," Hapsburg replied with barely a trace of an accent, and a half-smile to boot.

"Hmm. Very funny." Tyler couldn't help returning the half-smile. "Buckman told me that I have the first watch with you and your—your friends here."

Hapsburg rose from his fire. "And so it is. Buckman said something about that. Perhaps we should get started." He nodded to one of his personal guards, who dutifully climbed into their second wagon.

Tyler didn't feel this Hapsburg fellow looked like the typical European royalty that he'd seen in picture books. Hapsburg was slightly paunchy, not thin, but with a short, thin nose, a wisp of a mustache, and keen, alert hazel eyes.

Tyler took note when the guard emerged from the wagon with not one but two Hawken rifles, one of which he gave to Duke Hapsburg and the other to Angelique.

"Angelique, come here." Duke Hapsburg had pronounced her name "Ahh-jhel-ique."

"*Ja, fater?*" Angelique drew close to him and brushed her three feet of brown hair behind her back.

"We're in America," Hapsburg said. "We should talk English as much as we can."

"Yes, father, it is as you say."

Hapsburg looked at Tyler and then at his daughter. "Our job tonight is to keep the livestock inside the circle of wagons," he said to them both.

Angelique nodded. She apparently understood English perfectly.

"The cattle, the oxen, the sheep and chickens, any or all of them may try to wander off at night," Hapsburg went on. "If they get outside the circle of wagons they'll take off anywhere and everywhere and we'd never find them. You've seen how dark it gets out here on the prairie with no city street lamps to light up the night."

Again, a nod from Angelique.

What if wolves come around?" Tyler asked.

Hapsburg shrugged unconcernedly. "Shoot them." He turned and explained to the four guards in German what needed to be done. All four men nodded their understanding.

"Let's get to it then. Let's spread out," Hapsburg suggested.

Tyler started moving on the outside of the wagon train, cradling his Sharps rifle. With eighty-seven wagons, the circle of wagons stretched nearly a quarter of a mile because the wagons were too far apart. Even Tyler could see that. He wondered if Buckman's reputation was perhaps based upon knowledge of the land and the trail, but not wagon handling. Cattle and sheep could easily move outside the circle.

Men and women hurried to grab or herd runaway cattle, sheep, chickens, horses, and oxen back toward the interior circle. Tyler watched carefully. He moved in the opposite direction from some of the Hapsburg guards. When he passed them Tyler repeatedly wondered how long they would wear those ghastly red European uniforms with the bronze buttons, bangles and epaulets when they had earlier worn Western wear. Did they realize they weren't in Europe?

Oh well. If people laugh at them enough times, they'll learn soon enough.

One who looked right at home in this frontier was Angelique Hapsburg. Doing guard duty apparently at the invitation of her father, she was dressed in buckskins over a blue silk trader-style shirt, and she wore a narrow-brimmed plainsman's hat. Angelique looked the part of a pioneer girl *non-pareil.* Women did not normally perform guard duty, but Angelique apparently wanted to. Perhaps she intended to have the complete frontier experience, as her father apparently did.

Angelique smiled politely as she passed Tyler. She looked all business. This newly-arrived European girl who resembled a classic west-of-the-Mississippi American, was a curious enigma. She could dress like a European princess if she wanted to, but did not.

Tyler passed her and she passed out of his mind. It had started getting dark not only because the sun had just gone down but also because thick dark clouds had gathered in the west, moving toward the train. A lightning flash gave warning of what was coming.

As luck would have it, Tyler saw the Palmerston wagon up ahead. Rachelle had momentarily torn herself away from the dancing to fetch herself a drink of water from her family wagon's large keg beside one of the five-foot back wheels. Her entourage of male admirers had stayed behind at the dance. Here was a chance to talk with Rachelle, draw her attention to himself, and show off a bit that he was on guard duty.

A red-and-white cow grazed placidly near an opening between the Palmerston wagon and the one behind it. Tyler saw his chance. He shifted his rifle from his right to his left hand and approached Rachelle. "That your cow?" he asked her, pointing.

Rachelle took a drink from the dipper roped to the water keg as though she hadn't even heard him.

"Oh, Rachelle, is that your family's cow?" Tyler asked again.

She put the dipper down. "Yeah, it's ours," she said without looking at him.

"You might want to keep it a little farther away from edge of the circle," Tyler said. "If it wanders off at night we'd never be able to find it."

Rachelle's face showed disgust. "Don't worry about our cow," she muttered, walking away. "Betsy's not going to wander off."

As Rachelle stalked back to the dance, Tyler cursed himself. What, if anything, had he just accomplished? Getting a reaction like that from Rachelle Palmerston was worse than if he'd just kept his mouth shut and ignored her. Negative attention from her moved him backwards from his starting point with her, not forward.

A loud thunderclap from the northwest brought Tyler's attention back to more immediate concerns. Inside the circle of wagons the cattle and sheep reacted with frightened bawls and bleating plus terrified neighs from the horses. Tyler wished now that the wagons were bunched a little closer together. If there was a storm, a lot of these animals were going to panic and run. He knew there was no way that he, the two Hapsburgs and their four soldiers would be able to hold back a stampede of hundreds of animals. They were barely past the Red Vermilion River and already many of the wagons would have to drop out if they lost their animals.

"Put the barrels out between the wagons! Fill in the gaps with crates, boxes, oxen chains or whatever you've got. Oxen chains work best."

Tyler turned around to see who was talking and he saw Angelique Hapsburg, with quick presence of mind and knowing exactly what to do, yelling at people about how to cut off escape routes for the animals.

Tim MacNaughton nearby took up the chant. "If you've got anything big that can fill a gap and prevent an animal from escaping, do it!"

Tyler waved an arm at the people near him. "Move your barrels into the gaps," he shouted. "Move 'em into the gaps before the storm gets here and stampedes the animals."

"Don't let the animals escape! Fill in the gaps," rang out across the camp.

Everywhere emigrants took up the cry. Anything that was okay to get rained on, and a few things that weren't, were thrown into the gaps between the wagons to keep the animals penned inside the circle if the storm broke.

"Somebody help me with this, please," a voice begged.

Tyler saw a gray-haired man trying to unload a water barrel as his equally gray-haired wife stood helplessly by.

"Let me give you a hand with that," Tyler declared. Putting his rifle down, he hurried over to help the elderly man unstrap the oversized twenty gallon water barrel from the side of his wagon. It was bulky as he lifted it. The elderly man helped him carry the nearly full water barrel about ten feet to set it down in front of the wagon behind.

"Whew," the elderly man said, holding his back.

Tyler wondered why the couple had such a large water barrel. Most wagons had one, ten gallon barrel and they only used that on long dry stretches of trail. They carried enough water for each day's use in canteens and canvas water bags.

A rush of cool wind foreshadowed the approaching storm. Horses, oxen, cattle, and sheep, mooed, neighed, bawled, moved and shuffled uneasily about.

"Ephraim Allerton."

Tyler turned and saw the gray-haired, gray-bearded man extending his hand. He smiled and shook the man's hand. "Tyler Linders. Glad to know you."

"This is my wife, Abigail."

"Pleased to meet you, Tyler." She nodded politely.

"The same." One of Abigail's eyes looked to be of glass reflecting campfire light; she probably had only one good eye to see with.

"We're traveling from Kentucky," Ephraim said. "There's going to be a war someday soon back East between the northern states and the southern states. That's what everybody's saying. And when there is, Kentucky'll be caught smack in the middle of it. I figure, get out of there while we can. Our son and his wife and our four grandkids left for Oregon a year ago. We decided we'd follow 'em. What's your reason for heading west, Tyler?"

Tyler grinned sheepishly. "No special reason. Our Pa decided after our Ma died that he'd like a little more elbow room for farming than we had in Missouri, that's all."

Ephraim gave Tyler a couple of hearty claps on the shoulder. "That's as good a reason as any for heading West."

Looking around, Tyler saw nervous emigrants trying to herd their animals close to their wagons. The Colledges' slave, Tuck, took a switch to a cow.

"Git. Git near the wagon," he ordered the cow. "You'll be out of the wind and the worst of it, that a-ways."

Whether or not the cow understood Tuck, the cow nevertheless obeyed.

Jonas Smith herded a pig underneath his wagon, cursing it all the while. Zach Bennett tied his horses to his wagon as they neighed their concern about the approaching storm.

"Easy, boy, easy," Will Burney said as he settled one of his oxen down.

A thunderclap sent a half-dozen horses running from the center of the circle toward the wagons. Several heavy crates set between two of the wagons stopped and turned them.

Another thunderclap sent more horses and oxen running. Again crates, barrels, oxen chains, and a dresser stopped and scattered them.

Tyler glanced up at the clouds. The storm was actually moving away from the wagon train. The wind had become gentler, less threatening.

Ephraim and Abigail also looked up at the sky. Abigail drew closer. "Maybe we'll miss this one," she said

"Maybe," Ephraim agreed tentatively.

A tense few minutes followed. The clouds pushed themselves southward and a half-moon came out. More lightning ensued. More thunderclaps, but from further and further away.

Buckman walked the edge of the circle. "Next time, park your wagons closer to each other, with wagon tongues and oxen chains forming an enclosed circle," he ordered through his growing whiskers. "I hope everyone's learned a lesson tonight. I told you people to do that, but nobody listens to me."

Perhaps the wagon train had escaped this first mild encounter with trouble. *The picnic's over, though,* Tyler thought to himself. From this point on, for anyone who hadn't believed it before, it was clear now that getting to Oregon was going to take hard work and sweat, and some luck.

* * *

The drizzly rain came down steadily. The gray clouds overhead from horizon to horizon depressed the spirit. Granted, the rain had enabled some of the travelers to replenish their water supplies. Rainwater had a tangy cleanliness to it that river water often lacked. Still, Tyler felt miserable as he walked and drove the oxen. His wet clothes felt clammy and cold.

Pa slept in the bed of the wagon. Penny read a book quietly just inside the front wagon fold. One thing that was fortunate, Drake and Dru had gotten the hang of this wagon-pulling business, and so needed less whip-cracking over their heads as they pushed the other two yoke of oxen forward.

Gradually, Tyler felt mesmerized and sleepy from the rhythmic undulating of the Ellis wagon just ahead, and the Burney wagon in front of the Ellises. Behind, the MacNaughton wagon and then the Colledges followed immediately. Another thirty-seven wagons trailed the Colledges, some behind and some to the sides. The once-pristine white canvas tops of the wagons had started to get dirtier.

In the middle of the pack, Tyler was at least grateful that the rain had tamped down the dust. Ahead, he saw the Ellis twins talking just inside their wagon, but they paid no mind to him. Tyler regarded them as a lost cause. If they had had any real interest in him, as he thought particularly of Kelly Jay, they'd have done something other than ignore him. He had seen Billie Kay, for one, spending a lot of time walking beside a tall kid whose name Tyler thought was Justin Something-or-other. Or at least he thought it was Billie Kay. The identical twins kept up their game of wearing the exact same clothes and hair styles.

Tyler asked himself again why he cared so much about the young women on this journey. They were a distraction. But always the thought returned to him: *640 acres, not 320.*

Again, the Ellis twins had dressed annoyingly alike with identical blue pinafore dresses. Kelly Jay looked at him briefly, or was that Billie Kay?

Increasingly, Tyler hated to admit to himself, he was smitten, smitten, smitten with Rachelle Palmerston and no one else really mattered. Not good. He was not Rachelle's type. He was a Rachelle dreamer, like so many other young men on this journey were, or were becoming. Tyler knew that he would ignore every other young woman on this journey, and that he would have eyes only for Rachelle Palmerston. She was indeed a femme fatale, the kind of beauty who could blind men's eyes to other young women who would be easier pickings, and Tyler knew it. But he also knew that he was drawn to her as iron to a magnet, and he knew that he would be indifferent to all others. Again, not good. He wished that there had never been a Rachelle Palmerston on this wagon train. Had such been the case, he would gladly have focused upon the Ellis twins more and earlier. But the reality was, there was a Rachelle Palmerston on this wagon train, and Tyler knew that he could never escape that reality.

The rain came down and showed no signs of letting up. Tyler looked around him. Mr. Hanclicek gamely drove his wagon walking beside his oxen as the rest of his family huddled inside the wagon's canvas covering. The Colledge slave, Tuck, drove his oxen while the Colledge family stayed dryer, if not dry, inside their wagon. Young Van Buren Colledge, another of Rachelle's suitors, poked his head outside every now and then. Ahead, George Ellis walked beside his oxen. To the left now, Tim MacNaughton held the reins of his team from the jostling wagon board. Renford MacNaughton held the whip and drove his oxen hard, as he always did.

Looking southeast, the endless land seemed to gently slope downward toward a gray patch. At first, the patch seemed indistinguishable from the gray sky. As Tyler peered harder, the patch became clearer—the Big Blue River. Its colors reflected the gray of the sky. But it signaled the halt to the journey for today. There was a ferry, but it was too late in the day to haul all eighty-seven wagons in the Buckman company, as it was starting to be called, across the river before dark. Buckman would want to keep the wagons together, not separated by the river. Likely, rain or shine, the wagons would all be ferried across tomorrow.

Ahead, the first wagons had begun to form a circle with Buckman directing. The two buckskin-clad scouts, Press Doolittle and Silas Maple, doubled back.

"Start forming up," Doolittle ordered. "Keep the wagons close together."

Tyler gently urged Drake and Dru to the right. He snapped on the right rein and the oxen, all six of them, moved in the correct direction. The four columns of wagons gradually merged into one. Tyler worked the Linders wagon in behind the MacNaughton wagon and just in front of the Colledge wagon. He pulled up as close behind the MacNaughton wagon as possible, with Drake and Dru and the other oxen almost touching the back of the MacNaughton wagon. Water kegs, oxen chains, and a table would have to fill in the gap once the yokes were removed. Tyler observed that some of the wagons were angled behind the ones in front, making less room for livestock to escape the center circle at night.

Tyler unhitched the oxen and turned them loose to graze upon the thick yellow-green grass inside the circle near their wagon. The cold rain continued into the evening and for the first time, there was no dance, no sermon by Reverend Thomison, no campfires, no glad talk among friends or among wagon neighbors getting to know one another. With the rain coming down relentlessly, families crowded inside their wagons or inside their tents, which had varying degrees of being waterproof.

Glad that his Pa's wagon was among the more water-tight,, with plenty of linseed oil overlay, Tyler still wished that he could change out of his moist clothes. However, with Penny inside the wagon and not much room anyway with the two plows and other farming tools and seed bags, he couldn't. Tyler had to set up a small pup tent that Pa had brought, in order to change his clothes, with a dry bluish cotton shirt and jeans.

Tyler crowded back inside the wagon underneath the canvas. Penny sat reading one of her books, a McGuffey's reader, Level Four, while Pa with pipe in mouth whittled at a duck decoy, or what looked somewhat like it. Tyler couldn't really be sure. Pa himself probably wasn't even sure. Often he'd start whittling one thing, and end up having carved something quite different from what he'd started. It was just Pa's way of collecting his thoughts without having to share them with anyone.

"How long before we get there?" Penny asked.

Tyler leaned back against two of the seed bags inside the wagon. "You're asking that question already?" he responded disgustedly.

"It's okay, Tyler," Pa snapped. "Your sister simply asked a question. You don't have to be snide about it."

"I was merely saying that—"

"How many more miles?" Penny demanded, brushing her brown bangs back beneath her blue sunbonnet. "How far have we come so far?"

Tyler sighed. "We ain't Mormons so we don't count the miles, exactly." He couldn't repress a grin as he glanced at Penny. "Every day we cover between fifteen and twenty miles, though. That means we were 2,000 miles from Oregon when we started. We've covered maybe a hundred miles since we left Independence, so now we're 2,100 miles from Oregon. After tomorrow, we'll be 2,115 miles from Oregon."

Penny looked at him quizzically with her big brown eyes out of a clear, quiet bespectacled face. Her expression turned harsh. "You're just funnin' me," she muttered. She slapped his arm. "Quit it!"

Tyler shoved her back angrily.

"All right, knock it off, both of you!" Pa shouted, taking pipe in hand.

Tyler felt embarrassed. Their family quarrels were none of the MacNaughtons' or Colledges' business if they could hear nearby.

"We're not that far, actually, from Oregon," Pa said. "Maybe a thousand miles. Oregon Territory on the map starts at South Pass."

"That isn't Oregon," Tyler muttered. "She means, how far is it to where we're headed in the Willamette Valley? That's about 1,900 miles from here, or about five months' journeying ahead of us still."

Pa let out a grunt, then muttered, "Why didn't you just say that to begin with?"

Tyler was about to let out a smart-alecky response but he thought better of it. Cabin fever—it was starting already. Before this journey was over, Tyler worried that he and Pa and Penny were certain to get on each other's nerves altogether too often.

CHAPTER FIVE

Tyler manipulated Drake and Dru behind the Allerton wagon waiting for the ferry to take them across the Big Blue River. Beyond the river, the trail wound through a valley replete with cottonwood and alder trees. Prairie grasses waved and undulated. The sun was out and it was a beautiful day. The tree-studded river valley beckoned. The large ferry could accommodate two wagons at a time. The only holdup was Ephraim Allerton.

Ephraim stood arguing with the ferryman, a burly dark-bearded man who stood with arms folded, giving nothing.

"You're charging four dollars to take my wagon across?" Ephraim stormed, beard and fists shaking. "Do we look like a bunch of almighty New York millionaires to you?"

"No, you don't," the muscular ferryman snapped back. "You look like a bunch of dirt-faced hardscrabble farmers with money. If you can afford a wagon, you can afford to pay for a ferry."

"Ephraim's right." Another man, dark-bearded and surly and whose name Tyler didn't know, joined the argument. "We'll have to pay for a lot of ferries on this trip. We need to save our money for further up the line. What if we have to pay for more supplies at Fort Kearny or Fort Laramie? You think they'll cut their prices just because we had to overpay you?"

The ferryman glared at Ephraim Allerton and his fellow upset traveler. "Hmm," he grunted. "You can always try fording the river with your covered wagon if you don't want to pay me. The river's over twenty feet deep in the center. Or, better still," the ferryman pointed toward the east, "turn your wagons around and head back to Independence or wherever you came from. I ain't forcing you to take this ferry."

"We'll pay you fifty cents!" Ephraim bellowed.

"If I only charge you fifty cents I'll have to give money back to the people who've already crossed," the ferryman retorted.

"Seventy-five cents!" the other emigrant snapped.

"Oh, Dillon, why don't we just do what the ferryman suggested and forget about this whole idea of going to Oregon?" A sour-faced young woman, quite pretty inside a yellow bonnet, approached Dillon, the surly, bearded man whose name Tyler hadn't known. "Me and the kids never wanted to leave Jefferson City. You know me and the kids didn't want to. It was all your idea, and you can't even afford it. You know, Dillon, if you want to go all the way to Oregon, then go. Me and the kids are going to walk back to Missouri alone if we have to." With that, Dillon's pretty wife turned and walked away, the discussion over as far as she was concerned.

"Agatha, wait." Dillon ran after his wife. "Let's talk about this. C'mon, we don't need . . ." His voice trailed off.

Abigail Allerton now came forward. "Ephraim, four dollars is the going rate for river ferries, I've heard. Just pay the man and let's get across the river. We're holding up everyone else."

Ephraim glared with a wrinkled pout at the ferryman. "Oh, all right then," he snapped. "You've got us over a barrel."

"Four dollars in advance," the ferryman said. Tyler thought he detected a trace of a smirk on the ferryman's face.

Ephraim disgustedly slapped four greenbacks into the ferryman's palm.

Pa walked around his wagon to take in the scene. "Is it just me or do I get the impression that Ephraim Allerton's going to make more and more of an issue of these ferry tolls the further along we get?" Pa asked.

Tyler glanced backward. "Why? You think Ephraim's going to end up shooting somebody?"

"It could come to that at some point," Pa said, turning to walk away. "Or else he'll do what that ferryman also suggested, try to ford a deep river on his own."

Ephraim got back on the wagon board and urged his team forward again. His six oxen nosed their way onto the flat-surfaced ferry. A pair of thin rails and a gate kept wagons from going over the side.

Once the Allerton wagon was loaded aboard, the ferryman waved a hand at Tyler. "Next!"

Tyler cracked a whip over the heads of Drake and Dru. The two oxen moved forward toward the ferry. On either side Tyler saw other emigrants watching him.

"You're a little too far over to the right," Brent McGuigan declared.

Tyler clapped his hands near Dru's head, and in reaction, Dru and the other oxen headed straight for the right center of the large ferry, next to the Allerton wagon.

"That's it, boys," Tyler said. "Nice and easy."

The wagon's wheels clicked on the edge of the ferry and Tyler halted Pa's wagon right beside the Allerton wagon.

"Stay on the wagon boards," the ferryman ordered. "Don't get down." He walked around the wagons and shut the gate behind the two wagons. A young boy, maybe thirteen-years-old, came on board and held out his hand. Tyler gave him four dollars.

The ferryman and the young boy, no doubt the ferryman's son, pulled on ropes at the sides of the ferry to get it moving toward the other side. Tyler held onto the oxen reins tightly. Drake and Dru bawled only mildly as the ferry swayed slightly. A stiff breeze whipped up foot-high waves on the 200-foot wide river. Below the spume, Tyler could see a catfish swim lazily along. By the time the ferry reached the middle of the river Tyler had a sweeping view of the vista. The trees blocked the view straight ahead but to the northwest—in the direction of Oregon—the horizon stretched far, far into the distance. Sunlight came between a crack of sky separating two clouds. The clouds assumed a gold, orange, and red color which produced an ethereal, mystic, heavenly effect. The message in the clouds seemed to be: "Ahead is the promised land, look at it!"

"Whoops!" A sudden lurch to the right by the ferry caused Drake and Dru to bawl loudly. Tyler cracked his whip over their heads.

"Stay on your wagon," the ferryman demanded. "We're fine. This happens all the time. The water's just a little choppy today."

Tyler looked over the side again and saw seaweed sticking up to within a couple of inches of the surface. He thought he saw a big bass moving through the seaweed, but with the roughed-up water, he couldn't be sure. Tyler promised himself that once they got to Oregon, he was going to do some fishing again.

The ferry approached the opposite riverbank. A small dock jutted fifteen feet out into the river. The ferry nosed into the shallow water at the opposite end and eased up against the leather abutment of the dock.

The ferryman jumped onto the dock to secure the fastening ropes. "See, a nice, safe trip," the ferryman said to Ephraim. "Safety is worth a few bucks."

Tyler saw Ephraim mutter something unintelligible under his breath.

When the ropes were secure, Ephraim moved his wagon forward off the ferry. Tyler followed as Pa took Drake's bridle and guided him off the dock.

Once on the dock, Tyler snapped the reins and Drake and Dru pulled the wagon onto firm ground again. Ten other wagons had made the ferry crossing ahead of the Allerton and Linders wagons. Tyler saw that the MacNaughton wagon had been one of the early crossers.

Tyler brought his wagon to a halt and jumped down.

Tim MacNaughton was there to greet him. "We're on the other side of the Big Blue now," Tim said. "The Platte is next, another couple of hundred miles or so. We're at a point now that we got to start watching out for Indians. We're gonna start seeing Pawnees, and maybe some south-roving Sioux."

"Aw, are you still worried about Indians?" Tyler demanded.

"Yeah, I am." Tim's brow knitted and he put his hands on his hips. "You should be too. Everyone should be. Trust me, they're gonna attack at some point. They pretend to be friendly and wanting to trade, but all they're really doing is sizing us up, trying to find out our weaknesses. That's what happened in that novel I read."

"You know, Tim, if you really believe that, then you're probably going to do something really stupid when we finally do see Indians," Tyler declared. "You'll be so jumpy that—"

"All right, let's get the wagons moving again!" Buckman ordered, riding by on his chestnut horse. "If we wait till everyone's across, that could take all day. Let's get the wagons moving that we can, and the others can catch up."

"Okay, Tyler, let's get 'em moving," Pa said.

Tyler got back on the wagon board and snapped the reins. Drake and Dru protested but nonetheless slowly got moving again, pushing the other two pairs of oxen forward behind the Allerton and Ellis wagons.

The area the wagon train moved through now was wooded and pleasant. The oak and maple trees had leafed out by this time of spring. The flat, tree-filled, bush-filled landscape by the side of the road reminded Tyler of more easterly terrain.

The Oregon Trail at this point was clear and narrow, two-tracked through the woods. Several miles of the same mundane but comfortingly familiar scenery ensued. Drake and Dru pulled the wagon steadily. Tyler looked behind him at one point just to see who was there. The Colledge wagon followed immediately behind with Tuck the slave, on free territory, ostensibly, still walking beside the Colledges' oxen with whip in hand.

"Hey look!" Penny stuck her head out of the wagon, her eyes popping as she pointed straight toward the northeast.

"There they are," Pa declared, walking beside the wagon.

Tyler looked, then looked some more. Toward the northeast was a long narrow flower-strewn meadow. Large black dots loomed in the far end of the meadow. A couple of the black dots moved. No doubt about it—buffalo. It was not a large herd, maybe twenty animals. But this herd of bison was the first of many to be encountered. The bison herd was another signal that they really were on the Great Plains en route to Oregon.

The wagon train moved slowly past the small herd of bison, which scarcely noticed their passing. Still, the wagon master Buckman kept a wary deep-set eye on the bison as the wagons passed. Tyler observed Buckman, literally tall in the saddle, not slouched.

A sudden inspiration gripped Tyler. "Mr. Buckman, sir!" he shouted.

Buckman snapped his reins, pushed his wide-brimmed hat back, and wheeled his horse. "Something wrong, young Linders?" he asked.

"Uh—no, not really. I was just thinking, I'd like to do night watch again, if it's okay, sir."

"Developing a taste for night watch, are you?"

"Uh, yeah, something like that."

Buckman rubbed his dark-whiskered chin. "Well, all right then. Can you do first watch again?"

"Sure. Be happy to."

"Okay, you're on for tonight then."

Tyler smiled. "Thank you, Mr. Buckman, sir."

Buckman looked puzzled, but Tyler knew what he was doing. Night watch made Tyler feel important, because when he was on night watch, he *was* somebody important. If he became a night watch regular, maybe even a leader among the night watchmen over the wagon train, that gave him status. Tyler half-grinned. Maybe Rachelle Palmerston would start noticing him more.

* * *

This night watch business was becoming routine. For the third night in a row, Tyler took first watch. Buckman told him that he hoped people weren't taking advantage of him, and that everyone had to take their turn at night watch.

Tyler felt a growing sense of importance and prestige. While the young folks had their evening dance and did their twirling, kissing, and eating, Tyler stood stoically watching, leaning on his Sharps rifle and occasionally resting a hand on his .31 Colt cap-lock pocket revolver.

He hoped Rachelle saw him and thought even subconsciously that he cut a figure slightly above the run-of-the-mill. He hadn't talked at all with Rachelle, but Tyler figured he didn't need to. Better, for now, to act somewhat distant and above it all. Let Rachelle get the impression of him, that he was somewhat distant and less approachable than the others, and thus, hopefully, more desirable.

Bruce Mallory again handled most of the fiddle duties at the dance. Looking to be in his upper thirties, Mallory was older than most of the dancers but he seemed to enjoy being around the younger women.

Rachelle Palmerston took turns dancing with a multitude of partners. Regardless of who the young men came to the dance with, sooner or later all of them seemed to get around to asking Rachelle to dance.

That was good, Tyler figured. That meant that Rachelle was not, yet, connected with any one young man in particular. That meant she was still available, with all three feet of her blonde hair and sky-blue eyes.

Tyler watched the dancing as he leaned forward, gripping the barrel end of his Sharps. That was the image that he wanted to project—cool, distant, above it all, a man with responsibilities to protect and serve the wagon train while others partied. He kept his expression steady and slightly glum. Tyler made eye contact twice with Rachelle to be sure she noticed him.

A man with responsibilities had better fulfill them. Tyler figured that he ought to start his rounds. He picked up his rifle and began moving The duties were simple, but critical. Make sure wagons were as close as possible in their nighttime circle. Make sure the animals had finished grazing and were inside the circle of wagons for the night. And of course, watch for any intruders. Although the danger of actual Indian attack was greatly exaggerated, Indians still were known occasionally to try to drive off wandering live-stock, thus the need to keep the livestock inside the wagon circle. There was also a policing function.

"Trust me, tempers are going to grow thin the further along we go," Buckman had said the previous night. "I don't expect you to break up any fights by yourself. But if there is a fight breaking out, come get me or one of the scouts. We'll handle it."

Tyler watched the activities around the wagons as he walked past small emigrant groups and their mostly Dutch oven cook fires. Reverend Thomison had a growing congregation of sorts. Three dozen people, mostly women and children but some men, hung on his every word as he gripped his Bible in grandiose gestures. The Hebrews were still en route to Zion, but Tyler felt certain that Reverend Thomison would have them safely in the Promised Land by the time the wagon train reached Oregon.

One fatso lady whose name Tyler didn't know spent time mending a small tear in the side of a white canvas wagon top. Tomas Hanclicek ran his hands over the iron rims of his wagon wheels. It wasn't a problem yet, but further along in the drier regions, wooden wheels could separate from their iron rims. Aggravation awaited. Another family, the Clevengers, sat on the ground near the water barrel at the back of their wagon, eating a supper of bacon and beans. A coffee pot stood on a pair of poles over the fire. The four Clevenger children, two boys and two girls, drank milk courtesy of the Clevengers' cow. Thirteen-year-old Brit Clevenger, ten-year-old Agnes Clevenger, seven-year-old Luke Clevenger and five-year-old Jenny Clevenger, looked to be playing marbles as they ate.

Tyler was making a point of getting to know who was who on this wagon train, often simply by chatting with folks on his rounds.

"Tyler, how's it going?" Blake Clevenger asked, adjusting his spectacles.

"Mighty fine, how are you tonight?"

"Okay so far," Blake declared.

Telia Clevenger rose to her feet, her red hair tumbling down. "Pretty soon we'll be at the Platte, people are saying," she said hopefully.

"Pretty soon," Tyler confirmed, "another fifty miles or so, two and half more days if we make good time."

"Hey, I won that marble fair and square!" Luke yelled at Agnes.

"No you didn't!"

Tyler left the Clevenger kids to their arguing. He saw that underneath the back axle of the Clevenger wagon there was a small covered milk bucket. The undulating movement of the wagon would churn the milk to butter over the course of a day. Many wagon train emigrants thought themselves real clever for doing that. The problem, Tyler told himself, was that the lid had to be kept on tight. If it ever came loose, the trail dust and dirt could get mixed in with the milk.

Further on down, Jonathan Colledge and his slave, Tuck, lay underneath their back wagon axle, greasing it. Axles were another wagon part that could create problems closer to Fort Laramie.

"I vasn't asking you to not graze your livestock. I vas just asking you to keep a better eye on zem."

Tyler looked ahead. The voice belonged to Angelique Hapsburg, also on watch again and forgetting about watching her accent for the moment. She looked to be in the midst of an argument with a thin but hard-faced man whose last name was Crabbage, who gesticulated wildly at his herd of five cows.

"There ain't enough grass inside the circle for my stock overnight!" Crabbage exclaimed. "Nor is there water except along the river."

"I know zat," Angelique said. "But keep your livestock within a hundred yards of the wagon train. Don't let them go wandering off. We can't take time in the early morning to go hunting for zem if you lose track of zem. We'd never find your cattle anyway in the dark."

"I'll graze my own cattle anywhere I want," Crabbage declared, "wherever I think is best."

Now Tyler remembered where he had seen Crabbage before, just outside the saloon in Independence, Missouri. He was the bellicose man who had taken it personally when Tyler had almost bumped into him accidentally. Crabbage's self-centeredness amazed Tyler. He switched his rifle from his left to his right hand as he neared Crabbage arguing with Angelique. He felt safer dealing with Crabbage now that he carried a rifle.

"You know, Mr. Crabbage," Tyler said as he approached, "you certainly can graze your cattle as far from the wagon train as you want as long as you understand that you'll probably be left behind, if not tomorrow, then eventually. People aren't going to wait for you to find your cattle in the morning."

"We're nearing Indian country," Angelique said, her dark eyes beseeching. "We need to keep tight watch on the cattle and other livestock. The Indians try to steal livestock that's not carefully guarded. The Indians vill leave us alone and let us pass through their country unmolested if we look well-organized and keep close together. But if we spread out and our livestock gets scattered and the Indians steal some of it and we have to retrieve livestock from the Indians, that vill provoke a confrontation that could have been avoided, understand?"

"Yeah, yeah, yeah," Crabbage muttered.

Tyler made eye contact with Angelique as he moved on. She nodded and half-smiled a sparkle-eyed thanks for his help and support. She looked weird dressed almost like some kind of female mountain man, with a red silk shirt underneath a buckskin coat. Tyler also wondered about Angelique's occasional Austro-Hungarian accent. He liked it not.

He moved further around the large circle. Other families grazed cattle, sheep, oxen, and goats outside the circle. One change which occurred now, however, from the first 150 miles, was that most of those grazing livestock outside the circle of wagons stood armed.

George Ellis carried a late-model Hawken, while his wife Melissa Ellis sported an 1850 model Kentucky rifle. Kelly Jay Ellis—or was it Billie Kay?—helped her parents watch over a clutch of a half-dozen chickens amidst their grazing oxen. Billie Kay—or was it Kelly Jay?—appeared too preoccupied with dancing to worry much about chickens or oxen. That was bound to change with time. For now, though, there seemed to be a clique developing amongst the emigrants that wanted the fun to last as long as possible.

Tyler shielded his eyes from the setting sun. To the left lay the Little Blue River. Animals and people could get a clear drink from the Little Blue. Ahead lay the muddier Platte. He saw Pa filling a keg with water from the Little Blue. Penny and that Alain Laurent guy stood near Pa, holding hands.

The sun was setting between two low hills, encircled by yellow, orange, red, and purple clouds—once more, a majestic scene pointing squarely in the direction of mystical Oregon. Small wonder that Oregon seemed like a land just on the border of heaven itself with scenes like this toward the West stirring men's imaginations.

". . . because it's too dangerous and risky having that wagon in our train, that's why!"

Tyler's jerked his attention to the right. Buckman sat his horse just outside the wagon circle, with one of his dirt-bearded scouts, Silas Maple, standing and looking up at him sternly.

"I didn't say they could join the main part of the train," Buckman retorted. "They can follow behind at a safe distance."

Tyler glanced ahead. He saw them now. A lone wagon, drawn by six mules, Two gaunt-looking parents, two children, a small boy and a smaller girl. All four of them walked beside their slow-moving wagon. The woman kept dabbing at the tears in her eyes with a white handkerchief.

People stopped what they were doing to watch in solemn silence. Tim MacNaughton put down his water drinking cup at his wagon keg to watch. The fiddle music stopped momentarily. Blake Clevenger leaned against his Hawken rifle. Telia Clevenger stood against the back gate of their wagon with arms folded, her expression tight-lipped and puckered. Jonathan Colledge watched as he drank from his wagon water barrel. Crabbage tried to shoo his five cows away from the oncoming wagon. Ephraim and Abigail Allerton watched in quiet dread. Abigail stood with a hand to her mouth. All sensed something ominous about the approaching wagon.

Crabbage shook a bony fist at the family. "You keep your distance from the rest of us, you hear?" he demanded. "You hear?"

As the family neared him, Tyler observed them carefully. The middle-aged heavy-set woman who dabbed with a handkerchief at her tears looked to be quietly sobbing. Her bearded husband in a plainsman's hat kept an arm around her shoulders, seemingly trying to avoid any eye contact with the malignant glances around him. The girl also cried. She looked about seven. The boy, about twelve or thirteen, walked gamely on with his head bowed.

"We heard what happened to that wagon group ahead of us," Crabbage bellowed. He shook his fist again. "You keep your distance. We mean it!"

Who is this 'we'? Tyler wondered. What was it about this grieving family that had so many people worried?

Crabbage took up small rock as he glared at the family. "You stay way back, you hear? You hear?" he demanded.

Thirty feet away, Nathan Zurich approached Buckman sitting his horse. "What's going on?" Zurich asked.

Jonathan Colledge snapped, "You haven't heard yet?"

Buckman turned to Nathan Zurich and then looked at the solemn family again. "That family, Renwiler is their name, just buried two of their children earlier this morning. Cholera. The father's name is Ben, Ben Renwiler. I don't remember what he said his wife's name was. The children, the surviving children, are Elizabeth and Preston. They were part of a wagon train up ahead of us. They were returning back East after being kicked out of their wagon train up ahead, when we came along. They asked if they could join us. I didn't know how I could possibly say no to them."

Tyler saw Ephraim Allerton turn to his wife Abigail. "I'm sure I'd have done the same as Buckman. But, still, the cholera now comes among us," Ephraim murmured.

CHAPTER SIX

rabbage shook his rock at the Renwilers. "You stay away," Crabbage bellowed. "You'll poison all of us, you will!"

Ben Renwiler hugged his wife a little tighter. He looked at no one in particular. "We . . . we won't be any trouble," he said. "We'll stay back. You won't even know we're here."

"You stay back, way, way back," Crabbage bellowed again. He thrust his arm backward as if readying to throw his rock at the Renwilers. "You stay clear away from the rest of us. You hear? You hear?"

Buckman lurched his chestnut horse forward. "I'm sure they heard you, Milon," the wagon master muttered.

Tyler glanced up toward Buckman, framed by the orange clouds in the distance. "They buried two children earlier today?" Tyler asked.

"Yup." Buckman nodded, leaning forward. "Elizabeth's twin sister and their younger brother, this morning. Cholera took 'em both."

Tyler glanced back toward the Renwiler family, or what was left of them. Crabbage followed them at a distance, still pointing a long, bony finger at them.

"You're poison to this wagon train!" Crabbage bellowed. "You stay way back; we don't need you spreading your disease among all the rest of us. You hear? You hear?"

Tyler couldn't stand to watch the bitter scene any longer. Crabbage just seemed like the type of person who was happiest when he had someone to be angry with and whom he could scold. Tyler recalled the word "misanthropic" from his spelling bee days.

Approaching his own wagon, Tyler saw Pa with Penny and Alain Laurent.

Pa rubbed his growing beard briskly. "I heard they had a couple kids die of cholera just within the past day."

"Well, yeah, that's what happened, I guess," Tyler said.

"So now we got to worry about cholera," Pa said. "I'd hoped this train would be one of the lucky ones."

"Yeah, so did I," Tyler said. He leaned against one of the forward wagon wheels and folded his arms. "We don't need cholera around here. Still, that wasn't any reason for that Crabbage guy to be mean to those folks after two of their kids died."

Pa took off his broad-brimmed plainsman's hat and rubbed his forehead. "I suppose not," he agreed. "Still, let's keep our distance from 'em just the same, leastways until we can be sure no one else in that family is coming down sick. That's not neighborly, I know, but we got to think of ourselves and our own lives."

Tyler continued on, after another few minutes approaching the Palmerston wagon. Rachelle still lingered with the dancing crowd. But maybe here was a chance to casually get to know Dennis Palmerston, Rachelle's sandy-haired, clean-shaven father. He sat on a high three-legged stool, writing in a notebook.

Tyler smiled and approached. "Keeping a diary, Mr. Palmerston?"

"Matter of fact, I am. Lots of folks keep diaries on these journeys. It'll give people something to read a hundred years from now about this trip."

"Anything interesting happen to you today?"

"Matter of fact, it did, actually. I don't know if you know that guy Stonehouse, I think his name is."

"Brinton Stonehouse?"

"I guess that's what his name is," Palmerston said. "Anyway, he's been just ahead of my wagon for two days in a row now and his wagon is so heavily loaded that his oxen have to go slower. He's been holding my wagon up and everyone behind me, including you. Maybe if it wasn't just me alone talking to him, maybe he'd listen to some sense and lighten his load. When the trail is narrow through wooded areas, it's difficult to simply get around him. Jonas Smith said he'd go with me to talk to Stonehouse if I could get one other person besides him to go with me."

"All right, I'll go," Tyler said eagerly and instinctively.

"Let me get Jonas."

While Tyler waited for Palmerston to return, he asked himself if he'd done the right thing by so hastily agreeing to help Palmerston. Yet he knew he could hardly say no. It was a golden opportunity to get to know Rachelle's father and put him partially in his debt. It was an opportunity not to be refused or squandered.

Jonas Smith had behaved like an even-keeled person, and so Tyler hoped that this upcoming discussion with Brinton Stonehouse would be quick, painless, and reasoned.

Palmerston quickly returned with a bitter-faced Jonas Smith whose gray-streaked beard could not hide his anger. Palmerston also looked furious.

"All right, let's go talk to the bastard," Palmerston muttered.

So much for painless and reasoned discussion. Tyler followed Palmerston and Smith closely as they stalked toward the shaggy-haired Stonehouse.

Stonehouse sat on a stool with a mirror propped up on a wagon wheel axle. He wiped shaving cream off his face as he saw Palmerston, Smith, and Tyler approaching.

"Stonehouse, we need to talk," Palmerston declared.

Brinton Stonehouse rose to his feet, gripping his razor. "I already told you I'm not leaving anything behind. So quit bothering me about it."

"You're not only holding me up, but your heavy-loaded wagon's holding these folks up as well," Palmerston gestured toward Jonas Smith and Tyler. "Plus three dozen people behind them."

"I've got a hundred pounds of books that I ain't leaving behind!" Stonehouse gripped his razor tighter in his fist and held it forward. "Some of my books are worth a lot of money."

"Damn your books, Stonehouse," Smith bellowed, shaking a fist. "You knew you were overloaded when you started out. And you're holding not only yourself up, but others as well. You're going to be responsible for cutting several wagons off from the main group."

"One of my heaviest books is almost two hundred years old," Stonehouse snapped. "It's a first edition by John Locke that belonged to my great-grandfather."

"Who the hell was John Locke?" Tyler demanded.

Palmerston said, "We're not going to inconvenience half the wagons in the whole train. You should have left your books behind with family or friends and had them ship your books to you after you'd reached Oregon."

"I'd probably never see my books again if I left them behind." Stonehouse shook his razor at Palmerston. "And nobody's taking them from me. I dare you to try!"

People gathered around to witness the commotion. Tyler felt suddenly light-kneed. He was neither tall nor muscular, but thin-armed and chested. Stonehouse could beat him silly if a tussle started and that razor could rip his guts wide open.

"Let's see a good fight," one husky man said hopefully. "We could all use some entertainment."

"Stonehouse held me up, too," Renford MacNaughton muttered. "Let's all teach him a good lesson."

"Fight, fight, fight!" other men shouted as they gathered around, anxious for a good show.

Stonehouse jerked his razor one way and then another, threatening Palmerston, then Smith, then Tyler. "First man that attacks me is gonna get sliced up like a mincemeat pie," Stonehouse declared.

Tyler worried what he'd gotten himself into. He did not want to fight Stonehouse but he might not have a choice now. He couldn't appear cowardly in front of all these gathering people, especially Rachelle's father.

"Fight, fight, fight!"

Hair flailing behind her, Angelique Hapsburg came running up to the scene in her buckskin shirt and leggings. "Mr. Stonehouse, why don't you simply ask some of these other people who may have lighter wagons than you if they'll haul some of your books?" she asked.

A stunned silence ensued. Tyler half-smiled. Angelique had stated the obvious solution that others had been too angry to see, or else too desirous of seeing a good, bloody fight to think of or mention if they did.

Men exchanged glances with one another. Some of them looked clearly disappointed that an exciting fight had apparently been avoided.

Ephraim Allerton puckered his lips, then faced Stonehouse. "I could carry some of your books in my wagon," Ephraim said quietly. "It's light enough."

Rubbing his cleft chin, Nathan Zurich took a couple of steps forward. "I suppose, I guess, there's room in my wagon for some of your books," he sheepishly said.

Tyler saw men beginning to disperse. The excitement was dissipating. It was time to move on. He saw Rachelle approaching from the dance, though, to see what was happening with her father. For Tyler, it was time to move on but not before making sure that Rachelle knew that he had helped her father.

"You gonna be okay now, Mr. Palmerston?" Tyler asked.

Dennis Palmerston shook Tyler's hand and gave him a friendly clap on the upper arm. "I'll be fine," Palmerston said. "Thanks for your help, Tyler. I appreciate it."

"Anytime, Mr. Palmerston." Tyler shook his hand heartily. "Glad to help out."

As Tyler left the scene he felt gratified when out of the corner of an eye he saw Rachelle watching him, her face partly hidden by a blue polka-dot bonnet. This was not the time to make a move on Rachelle. He was building his case for her. Tyler told himself that if he was lucky, Rachelle would feel more comfortable around him when he finally did try to make her serious acquaintance. If he was very lucky, his position as a night guard would make Rachelle feel he was more debonair than all of the other young men trying to get her attention. And if he was very, *very* lucky, Rachelle would think so highly of him that she herself would initiate a relationship with him and he wouldn't even have to plot and scheme at all about how to win her.

Hmm. Tyler wondered if Dennis Palmerston might even suggest to Rachelle that she might do well to make his acquaintance?

"Do you think Mr. Stonehouse vould actually have stabbed you or Mr. Palmerston or one of those other men?"

"Huh?" Tyler turned around, knocking the bangs out of his eyes again. Angelique Hapsburg stood looking at him, with rifle in hand across her chest. She gazed at him with gentle brown eyes.

"Do you think he vould have?" Angelique slightly twisted a corner of her lips upward.

"Yeah, I do," Tyler said. "Stonehouse is the type. Glad you thought what to do. Thanks."

Tyler continued on his rounds. Behind him, Tyler felt Angelique watching him. He heard Angelique slowly turn around and head back on her own rounds.

People were already starting to fight with each other. Tyler wondered how strained would tempers get when water began to give out, wagon wheels started coming loose in the drier air farther on, and oxen began failing.

* * *

Tyler kept a close eye on Penny and Alain as they frequently walked together hand-in-hand over the next several days. The way that Penny and Alain looked at one another, it seemed that they were truly smitten with each other. It was a developing situation which bore watching. Pa also watched Penny and Alain, although he tried not to be too obvious about it.

Tyler spent the next few days driving the wagon while Pa walked alongside most of the time. Penny rode in the wagon with her school books, except when she walked with Alain Laurent. Tyler knew he would have to soon forego any thought of riding in the wagon. He must think of the weight he added to the wagon and the extra strain on the oxen. Plus there was the jerky motion of the wagon train as it rolled over the uneven ground surface.

Trees gave way to a flowery prairie. Beautiful blue, yellow, and white flowers decorated the landscape. With few trees in the way now, the wagon train spread out into four separate lines. Tyler again found himself trailing just behind the Ellis wagon.

"Wow! Look at that!" Penny cried.

Tyler looked to his right. A widely scattered herd of buffalo grazed in the warm mid-May sun and gentle breeze. A few high clouds drifted overhead. The scene was idyllic, like an Impressionist painting. Yet Oregon was more beautiful still, with its own flowers, and moisture that produced 200-foot-tall trees and lush undergrowth, plus bumper crops of wheat.

Tyler looked to his left. A row of cottonwoods loomed in the distance across the prairie. It was unmistakable. Tyler pointed excitedly. "There it is! The Platte River. I see it."

"That means we've really started for Oregon," Pa said. "The Platte River is the first really major signpost on the Trail. Next up is Fort Kearny, Chimney Rock and Scotts Bluff. Then on to Fort Laramie. Yeah, we're on our way."

Pa lifted his fist in the air. Other pioneer emigrants joined the chorus of shouts, hurrahs and applause.

"We're gonna get there," Ephraim declared nearby, lifting his hat high above him. "We're gonna be one of the groups that really make it to Oregon."

Silas Maple the scout rode by. "Mr. Buckman says we're stopping here for the night," Silas called out. "It's a good stopping place. It's a good hunting area, and maybe we can bag a few pronghorns or mule deer, even a buffalo or two. Good grazing near the river for the livestock too."

"Sure is," Pa agreed. He turned to Tyler. There'll be a party here tonight for sure."

Tyler drove his wagon toward the river and into position right behind the Ellis wagon. Buckman had stopped the train early for the day, but they had earned it. Three hundred miles closer to Oregon. The train was making excellent time, so far.

That evening Bruce Mallory had his fiddle out early, even before most people had finished their supper. Tyler joined in the fun, dancing with Kelly Jay Ellis, dressed smartly in a light blue calico blouse and a dark blue skirt.

"Thanks, Kelly Jay," Tyler said.

"Oh, you're welcome, and I'm Billie Kay, actually."

Tyler was getting tired and fed up with the Ellis twins doing that to him and others and he thrust up his arms in frustration. "Must you and Kelly Jay keep on trying to make fools of us?" he demanded. "It makes me feel really stupid when I can't tell the two of you apart because the two of you dress alike, and wear your hair the exact same length with the same dark waviness and blue ribbons on top. Why do you feel you have to do that anyway?"

Billie Kay smiled, not the least bit perturbed. "Kelly Jay and I just like to have some fun with it," she said mildly. "Be assured, Tyler, we mean no harm to anyone. We would never want to do that. Thanks again for the dance. I enjoyed it."

She headed over to hold hands with a young man whose name Tyler still only knew as Justin Something-or-other.

Billie Kay looked back at him. "You're a wonderful, wonderful guy, Tyler," Billie Kay said. "You're a truly special guy and I do care deeply about what happens to you. I'll be watching out for you. If you ever need a friend or need to talk to someone, I'll be there for you. Remember that."

Tyler smiled politely, not sure what she meant. If pert, seventeen-year-old Billie Kay Ellis now considered herself his guardian angel, that did him absolutely no good if she was already smitten with Justin Something-or-other. Platonic relationships with young women did not interest Tyler.

Now was still not the time to make a move on Rachelle Palmerston, though. It was another 1,700 miles to the Willamette Valley. There was plenty of time. All the attention that Rachelle was getting from a variety of young men would continue to ensure that she wouldn't settle on any one of them too quickly.

On the other side of the dance circle opposite a half-dozen grazing cows Tyler saw Penny holding hands with her seventeen-year-old French-Canadian-Vermont boyfriend, Alain Laurent. Pa still expressed concern about Penny spending so much time with a boy five years her senior, but as long as Alain minded his manners, Pa accepted it.

Nevertheless, Tyler thought he'd casually saunter over to Alain and Penny just to say hi to Alain, and subtly let him know that he was being watched. Pa was busy grazing Drake, Dru and the other oxen over by the tree-lined river a few hundred feet to the north.

He tried to think what to say to Alain that wouldn't seem too obvious. Tyler looked around the dance circle and at all of the activity within the wagon enclosure. Cows, oxen, sheep, and horses grazed at one end of the circle of wagons. A few goats chomped on corn husks. Other livestock grazed beyond the enclosure, under the watchful eyes of emigrants. People talked in small groups near their campfires, laughing, smiling, happy with the joy of the moment. The Platte had been reached.

Still, something was missing.

"Hey Tyler, what's up?" Alain said with bright-eyed genuineness as Penny grimaced at her brother's appearance.

"Whatever happened to Reverend Thomison?" Tyler asked. "I don't see him anywhere. Usually he has quite a group around him."

"I heard he was feeling poorly," Alain replied. "It's great that we've reached the Platte, but that also means we're getting to where the water isn't so good. You have to boil the water first before drinking it. If you don't boil it enough, or at all, well . . ."

Tyler waited for Alain to add the next bit of news. Alain said nothing further but he didn't need to. His implication was clear. Tyler went back to the dance just to listen to the music. He had no real further desire to dance with anyone but Rachelle if she became available.

Dennis Palmerston caught Tyler's attention as he watched the dancing and clapped his hands. Here was a chance to solidify his friendship with Rachelle's father. Tyler walked over to Dennis, who extended his blonde-hairy hand in greeting.

"Tyler, good to see you again."

"Mr. Palmerston, how are you tonight?" Tyler asked.

"Tired of walking all day today," Dennis replied.

"I heard tell there's going to be a transcontinental railroad through here someday," Tyler said. "People will be able to just sit in a rail passenger car all the way to the West Coast. It'll be too late to help us, though."

"I heard the same," Dennis said. "I don't expect to see a transcontinental railroad, though, probably for oh, another fifty or sixty years. I don't know how they'd ever be able to lay track across the mountains. But maybe in another half-century them engineering science fellas will know enough by then to figure out how to push a rail line through solid rock or over 10,000-foot mountains. But I don't expect that'll happen in our lifetime."

"Probably not," Tyler agreed.

"What the heck is Buckman waving his arms for?"

"I'm not sure, but he sure seems powerful agitated about something," Tyler said, watching the wagon master ride his chestnut horse straight into the center of the dance.

"Everybody, stop the music, stop it now," Buckman shouted. "It's inappropriate."

Bruce Mallory and then Blake Clevenger halted their fiddle-playing in mid-song. Many of the two-step dancers shouted their dismay at this interruption of their regular evening fun.

"What do you think you're about, Buckman?" Brent McGuigan demanded, with fists balling after his dance with Rachelle was halted.

"We ain't hurting nothing," Mallory barked. "We been holding these parties ever since we started out. It keeps everyone's spirits up."

"Can I have everyone's attention, please?" Buckman raised his arms for quiet. "I need everyone to listen to me."

Buckman's seriousness could not be mistaken. Something had happened. People quieted down, and as Buckman took them all in with his worried stare atop his nickering mount, an ominous pall enveloped the dozens of people within the wagon circle.

Tyler gripped his suspenders tightly.

Buckman lowered his arms. "Everybody, I have some bad news to report. A few minutes ago, Reverend Thomison died. It was the cholera. We need to bury him quickly."

Stunned gasps and cries reamed across the multitude amidst the circle.

"No! Not the Reverend," Patience Burney cried out. "The Reverend can't have died."

"He can't," Telia Clevenger exclaimed, echoing fifteen others as she put a hand to her cheek.

"Anybody that wants to look at his dead body, it's in the wagon at the far end of the circle," Buckman said. "I need five or six men to form a burial party. I'm not going to do it myself."

CHAPTER SEVEN

yler stared at the mound of earth and the small wooden cross stuck atop it. With his shovel he scooped another spade of dirt on the mound. Buckman had said a few words sheepishly asking the Lord to welcome one of his own before muttering, "I'm not much of a praying man."

Several people, mostly women who had enjoyed listening to Thomison's Bible-thumping sermons every night, stood around and quietly wept. Every now and then a louder wail was heard.

Reverend Thomison was dead. Why him? Why not someone else? Beneath the grief for Reverend Thomison, a deeper, yet-unspoken worry tore into people's consciousness. Cholera had arrived amongst them. Thomison would hardly be the only victim. If cholera could take away a man of God, then really no one was safe from the disease.

"What did I tell ya? What did I tell ya?" Crabbage muttered, clutching his thin hat. "Them Renwilers get here, and we got cholera killing us now. But does anybody want to listen to me? No, I'm the bad guy for telling them we didn't want 'em"

Overnight and the next morning, people went about their routines of fixing breakfast, tending their livestock, mending wagon canvas covers, or greasing their axles, but a somber quietness had overtaken the wagon train. People didn't talk, or if they did, they spoke in low, hushed voices. An ominous quiet had fallen over the entire wagon train with the first death on the Trail. Who would be the next to die? It seemed disrespectful and frivolous to act as they had before, light-hearted and happy-spirited.

As much as any landmark, Tyler reflected as he ate his breakfast of dried bacon, Thomison's death signaled the end of the "fun" part of the trip. The Renwilers stayed well back of the main body of wagons. Tyler was glad to hear, though, that apparently no one but Crabbage was against them staying.

Surreal normalcy pervaded the next day's journey. The sense of ominous, respectful quiet continued as the wagon train followed the Platte River's length of scattered woods and open prairie. There was no joviality, and talk was kept to a minimum. When two people did converse, it was in low tones.

The sense of quiet, heavy air continued through the nooning. Tyler, Pa, and Penny snacked on their jerked buffalo meat as they sat in the shade of the wagon. Press Doolittle had done some hunting and had provided the meat.

Out of the quiet nowhere Penny asked, "Pa, are we going to die on this trip?"

Pa didn't seem startled by the question. He forced a smile. "'Course not, Penny-dear. We're all fine."

Penny looked unconvinced. She bowed her white-bonneted head. Softly she murmured, "Reverend Thomison was fine till just before he died."

"The Reverend was sick before he died," Pa declared, trying to sound firm. "None of us is sick."

Penny softly sighed. "I reckon not, Pa."

Tyler kept silent, his head bowed. He recalled from Missouri how cholera could strike quickly, mercilessly, without warning. A person could feel fine, then be dead four or five hours later.

"How many wagons are there altogether in this wagon train?"

Tyler turned. It was Ben Renwiler, approaching Ephraim Allerton sitting down by the wagon next.

"This looks like a good big safe train," Renwiler said.

"I hope so," Ephraim declared. "There's eighty-seven, some say, one less without the Reverend. But there's enough rifles and men to keep the Indians from getting any ideas and trying to . . ."

Tyler's attention was arrested by Milon Crabbage, fifty feet away disgustedly throwing a rag down at sight of Renwiler talking with someone.

Shaking a threatening fist, Crabbage stalked toward Renwiler. "You stay away from our wagons," Crabbage bellowed. "You and your cholera, you killed that preacher man. You as good as murdered him, I say! You get away from our wagons or—"

Tyler saw that Crabbage held a table knife.

"No!" pert Patience Burney cried. "We don't need that. We don't need us killing each other." She picked up her calico skirt to hurry through the stem grass over to Crabbage as several men also ran to prevent violence.

Franz Hapsburg came running to the scene. "I heard Thomison was starting to feel sick before the Renwilers arrived," he said.

Stonehouse kicked someone's small cat out of his way and into a tuft of prairie grass as he approached. "That's a crock of you-know-what," Stonehouse bellowed. "Milon is right, Thomison was fine until the Renwilers showed up."

Tyler told himself that he just knew Crabbage and Stonehouse would find each other at some point.

Renwiler seemed loathe to deal with Crabbage. As Crabbage raised his knife from fifteen feet away, Renwiler found his legs and hurried away back to his own wagon and his wife and two remaining children, far off to the side of the main train.

Ephraim rose to his feet as Tyler continued to watch. Pa stood up as well, putting his hands on his hips but saying nothing.

"United States is a democracy," Hapsburg muttered. "You don't make zeh decisions for all zeh rest of us, Crabbage."

"Oh, don't thank me that the rest of you aren't all dead like the Reverend," Crabbage huffed. "If them cholera-ridden Renwilers traveled right in the middle of us, spreading their disease all around, maybe all of you self-righteous good people would be in your graves by now."

No one said anything further, or seemed inclined to continue the argument. Slowly, the scene broke up. Scowling, Hapsburg sauntered slowly away, half looking back at Crabbage. Stonehouse gave the yellow cat another kick as he stalked off.

The journey continued in the afternoon. Renford MacNaughton attempted to lighten the mood by talking of Oregon and his plans once he got there. "I'm going to live in a tree," Renford said as he walked beside his oxen to the left of the Linders wagon.

Pa rubbed his stubbled chin, thinking on that for a moment. "You mean you're going to live in a treehouse?" he asked.

"Nope. What I mean is, them Douglas Firs I heard about are so big around, I hear, that you can take an axe and carve out a place to live in a tree bole. Small but cozy and comfy."

Tyler paid the conversation no mind as Mrs. Ellis let loose with another series of low moans. She rested in the bottom of the Ellis wagon, which was in front of the Linders wagon again as it had been for most of the journey so far.

Cholera was a disease that acted quickly, Tyler reflected again. People stricken with cholera either recovered or else died, seldom after more than twenty-four to thirty-six hours. Mrs. Ellis did not sound like a person who was recovering.

Kelly Jay and Billie Kay took turns wiping their mother's brow and just being with her in her misery. When one of them was with their mother, the other walked beside the wagon, driven by their father as gently as he could. George Ellis tried to avoid chuck holes or gravelly ground.

The worried expressions on the faces of, alternately, Kelly Jay and Billie Kay, told Tyler that they feared the worst for their mother. They knew that their mother had but hours to live.

Pa sensed it too. He did not talk jovially as he walked beside the wagon. Penny also remained somber, not talking excitedly anymore at the sight of grazing buffalo or pronghorns.

The wagon train formed up in its nightly circle again once Buckman had estimated that another seventeen miles had been covered. Tyler observed thirteen-year-old Brit Clevenger driving his family's wagon into position a hundred feet ahead amidst the grass, assisted by his seven-year-old brother Luke guiding the oxen with the whip. Where were their parents, Blake and Telia Clevenger? Were Blake and Telia sick now too?

"We have to stop for a few days and let mother rest," Tyler heard either Billie Kay or Kelly Jay declare while standing nearby. "She's too sick to travel."

"If we don't go on, we'll be stuck by ourselves, alone, right in the heart of Injun country," George Ellis retorted, fingering his Hawken rifle barrel beside his wagon. "All of us will be as good as dead."

With a stick Tyler stirred the small buffalo chip fire heating his beans and dried bacon for supper, oblivious to other activities around him. People talked in small groups in low tones. There was no dance. A few people who had been part of Reverend Thomison's makeshift congregation gathered in the center of the circle to read their Bibles and talk.

Sudden loud wails from the Ellis wagon told Tyler that Mrs. Ellis had just died. Billie Kay and Kelly Jay sounded inconsolable. George Ellis leaped down from the front of his wagon to approach a small group of men, including Ephraim Allerton and Tomas Hanclicek to tell them the news.

The weeping of the Ellis girls kept Tyler awake much of the night in his tent. It was muffled, but occasionally a louder wail erupted from one of the twins in their tent. Tyler tried to ignore the wailing although it kept him from sleeping. The Ellis girls were entitled to their grief.

"Hey, keep it down in there! Other people are trying to sleep," Tyler heard an angry voice shout at the Ellis wagon and tent. "Don't you know other people need their rest? Show some courtesy, damn you!"

Tyler couldn't be sure of whose angry voice it was, but it sounded like Milon Crabbage. He wouldn't have been surprised if it was.

Because the wagon train needed to keep moving, there was little time for grieving. Burials were quick. Tyler again helped with burial duty early the next morning before the sun was up. The thick, well-knitted, foot-tall yellow prairie grass didn't make digging easy. Pa, Ephraim, Franz Hapsburg, Dennis Palmerston, and Renford MacNaughton were among the dozen or so men who did the digging.

"We have to take care of these things as rapidly as we can," Silas Maple declared as he shoveled dirt on Melissa

Ellis's blanket-draped dead body. "If we hold up for a day or two every time someone dies, we'll never make it through the mountains before the heavy snows come. Then we'll all be dead, or worse, just like the Donner Party in '46."

As with Thomison, Buckman said a few words over the prairie grave of Mrs. Ellis as the family and others watched. Tyler got the impression that Buckman was not acquainted with religion at all, for he held no Bible and seemed embarrassed to talk of God, the afterlife and "Melissa Ellis is in a better place" which he could not bring himself to name. He said no prayer.

Although Billie Kay and Kellie Jay wept uncontrollably, Tyler noted that George Ellis did not appear particularly broken up by his wife's death. He stood by impassively as the impromptu funeral took place, expressionless, showing no emotion. He said nothing.

Buckman put his hat back on when the service ended. "All right, let's get the wagons rolling," the wagon master said as if the burial were just another "to do" task.

George Ellis, dark-faced with black whiskers, seemed almost equally more concerned about getting back on the trail than he was about mourning his deceased wife. He put a hand on the shoulder of both Billie Kay and Kelly Jay but firmly said, "Let's go."

He turned to head back to his wagon. The twin girls did not move. They stayed looking at their mother's grave with a small cottonwood cross above it, perhaps unable to deal with the finality of death and leaving their mother's body behind and alone in this broad, sweeping land.

Many walked by, putting a hand on each twin's shoulder or murmuring a few soft words of comfort. Tyler walked past them, unsure what to say. "Sorry for your loss," he told them.

Billie Kay and Kelly Jay nodded their appreciation. "She was a good mother for us, the best," Kelly Jay said tremulously.

"I . . . she . . ." Billie Kay started to murmur, but the words would not come. She simply broke down and wept anew.

"C'mon, let's go!" their father shouted harshly from near his wagon with stern gestures. "There's nothing more we can do for her. Holding up the wagon train ain't going to bring your ma back to life. Like Mr. Maple said, it'll just make us late getting to Ca—Oregon. Now c'mon!"

Kellie Jay looked at her sister. "Pa wants to get going. We'd better do what he says." She gently took Billie Kay's arm to lead her away. Both sisters slowly walked back to their wagon, turning to look back at their mother's grave every step of the way.

Silas Maple rode by on his horse. "We need to roll out within fifteen minutes," he shouted. "It's almost sunup. We're over an hour behind schedule."

Tyler helped Pa hitch up Drake and Dru and the other oxen, who reluctantly let themselves be torn away from a patch of succulent dewy buffalo grass. Tyler marveled how Buckman and Maple could put tragedy behind them so quickly. Grudgingly he had to admit they had a point about beating the snow. It was only late May but already the wagon train leaders were concerned about beating the heavy mid-autumn mountain snow to Oregon.

The wagon train got moving again. The muddy, fast-flowing waters of the Platte River loomed to the right of the four lines of wagons. Mountain snow melt had deepened the Platte. The cottonwoods along the banks looked to be in three or four feet of water.

As the trees thickened, the trail moved away from the immediate riverbank. At one point the trail was a half-mile south of the river. Then the Trail edged back toward the water as the trees thinned and the prairie reasserted itself.

"Look, there they are!" Tim MacNaughton shouted, pointing in the direction of the river as he walked along.

"There who are?" Tyler demanded, circling around the oxen to look.

"The Indians. Don't you see them?"

"Indians. Where are they?"

Tim pointed toward an opening in the line of leafy shrubs along the river. "There's three of them on horses."

Tyler looked past the shrubs and bulrushes to the other side of the Platte. Now he saw them. Three Indian men, likely Pawnees, sat on painted horses a few hundred feet away. Other wagon train emigrants saw the Indians now as well, and a strange, awed silence overcame one and all. Conversations ceased. People watched in silence as the train moved past the Indians. For many of these travelers, Tyler knew, it was the first time they had ever seen Indians.

The three Indians did nothing, except watch the wagon train moving into their territory. They sat their horses like statues. Only an occasional swish of one of the Indian horses' tails proved that they were not sculptures.

The Indians continued watching the wagon train. Tyler wondered what their thoughts must be. Were they seeing another link in a long chain of events that inexorably was leading to the downfall of their way of life? Were they seeing, with heavy hearts, the future of their people? Was that why they sat so motionless and still?

"You can bet that where there's three, there's a thousand more at a camp nearby," Tim declared.

"Let's leave them be," Tyler said, "and maybe they'll leave us be."

People anxiously watched the Indians, who they knew were watching them intently in turn. The Indians' stone-like demeanor was as unnerving as if they had been openly shouting angrily. Certainly, there was no indication on the Indians' part that they welcomed the emigrant wagon train.

As the bulk of the wagon train moved past them, though, the Indians unobtrusively turned around to leave, heading away toward the north.

A palpable sense of relief overcame the emigrants as the three Indians rode off. Conversations started up again, although the focus was upon the Indians as the wagons rolled along.

Tyler looked ahead to Tomas Hanclicek walking beside his wagon.

Tomas wiped his brow. "A narrow escape, hey?" he said.

A narrow escape from what? Tyler wondered. "I guess."

In the wagon to Tyler's right, Bruce Mallory grinned as he walked next to the front of his wagon and cracked a whip over the heads of his team. "How much money you want to bet that we'll be seeing Indians from now on?" Bruce asked.

"A lot." Tyler turned to talk to Pa. "I'm thinking they were Pawnees. We're not quite to Sioux territory yet. What tribe do you think they were?"

"I think they were a tribe that wishes we'd move through their land as rapidly as possible and that just wants to not do anything to slow us down," Pa said, walking beside Drake and Dru. "We'd better keep a closer eye on the livestock from now on, though."

The Trail moved back through another grove of cottonwoods. In the far distance stood the buildings of Fort Kearny. On the other side of the Platte, Tyler saw a large herd of buffalo moving slowly northwestward. An occasional pronghorn grazed among them. There were no more Indians to be seen, for now.

Another two hours of journeying brought the wagon train to a flowered meadow with tall grass. Buckman ordered a stop for the day. The wagons began to form their customary circle.

Press Doolittle rode past on his chestnut gelding. "We need another burial party," he announced. "Blake and Telia Clevenger are both dead."

* * *

Tyler had felt so sorry for people before, but not like this. It was with difficulty that he kept his own emotions in check as he watched the four Clevenger kids at their parents' funeral service after their burial. Buckman had done the right thing this time. Press Doolittle appeared to be a little more conversant with the Bible and Buckman had him say the words. Doolittle read the story of Jesus raising Lazarus from the dead.

But there would be no rising from the dead on this day. Blake and Telia Clevenger had died in each other's arms, Doolittle said. Thirteen-year-old Brit Clevenger bravely and gamely tried to keep his emotions under control. Even he had to brush away tears, though. Ten-year-old Agnes, seven-year-old Luke and five-year-old Jenny made no pretense of even attempting to be unemotional about their parents' deaths. The three younger Clevengers cried buckets. Nor did anyone try to give them false comfort. They had a right to their tears and grieving. They were orphans now. Abigail Allerton placed her hands on little Jenny's shoulders to let her know that she was not alone in her mourning or completely alone in her life.

Tyler turned away from the scene, afraid that if he watched any longer he would burst out crying himself. That was the last thing he would ever want to do. He started walking away toward the wagon and Pa and Penny. Tyler had to circle around a pair of men arguing. One was shaggy-haired

Brinton Stonehouse, another fellow who never seemed happy unless he had someone he could bellow at. The other man had his back to Tyler. When Tyler passed him, he saw that it was Silas Maple.

". . . be a burden on us all now, they will!" Stonehouse snapped. "I'm telling you, we gotta get rid of 'em somewhere."

Silas clenched his teeth and made a sweeping gesture at the wide-open, one-tree prairie. "Does ya see any orphanage around here we could drop 'em off at?"

"Leave 'em at Fort Kearny," Stonehouse muttered.

"Fort Kearny ain't no orphanage; it's a military post," Silas retorted. "There ain't no families at Fort Kearny that'd adopt all four kids together."

Stonehouse clenched his fists. "Leave 'em with the Indians, then" he grunted. "The Indians'll take care of 'em."

Silas straightened up, pausing a moment to meet Stonehouse eye-to-eye. "Was that an idea you meant me to take seriously, or just you trying to make a sick joke?" Silas demanded. "The Clevenger kids will be all right. Brit can handle a team. He's been doing it now for . . ."

Tyler continued on. Silas Maple was capable of handling Stonehouse by himself.

Returning to the wagon, Tyler saw Pa there fixing the usual bacon and beans, with strong black coffee. Pa sat back against one of the three-foot front wheels.

"Where's Penny?" Tyler asked.

Pa ladled out a serving of beans and placed it on a wooden plate. "She's with that Alain Laurent kid again," Magnus said. He handed Tyler the plateful of beans.

"Do you think Alain's maybe, uh, fixing to ask Penny to marry him?" Tyler asked.

Pa gagged and coughed as he tried to swallow some beans without choking. "Don't—don't even mention that idea," Pa gasped. He coughed and pounded his chest. "She's twelve years old. My grandma, my mother's mother, married when she was fifteen. That's the youngest I ever heard tell of anyone in our family getting hitched. I'm not letting Penny marry anyone till at least she's graduated eighth grade."

"I was just funnin', Pa."

"Well, it wasn't funny."

Loud shouting coming from the flowery, live-stock-strewn meadow back of the wagon circle drew Tyler's attention.

". . . better leave this wagon train if you know what's good for you." The voice was Milon Crabbage's. "Four people have died since you and your family showed up. You spread the cholera, you and your family coming here did! I'm warning you, Renwiler, if you don't leave on your own, I'll see to it that you do it at the point of a gun if I have to."

"I've already left two of my family behind buried in the earth, where they can hurt no one," Renwiler retorted. He let his teeth show. "And I'm warning *you*, Crabbage, I've had enough of your bellyaching. If you come after me and what's left of my family with a gun, I promise you I'll be ready."

"Damn you, Renwiler, you and your family are poison," Crabbage went on, undeterred and unfeeling. "More people are going to die if you don't leave."

Pa looked at Tyler. "We'd better see what's going on," he said.

Tyler got up, followed by Pa. They headed around the wagon and saw Crabbage following Ben Renwiler trailing three sheep toward the flower meadow.

Pig-tailed Elizabeth Renwiler approached along with Angelique Hapsburg.

"Mr. Crabbage," Angelique said, "anyone can get cholera if they drink water straight from the river. That's what's causing it. The germs are there if you don't boil your water first. Cholera doesn't just spread because of someone who had it. Cholera can spread without anyone's help. Boil your water thoroughly and you won't have anything to worry about."

Crabbage turned his half-boiling thin face at Angelique. "Well, who asked you for your opinion?"

"I did," Elizabeth Renwiler said. "Angelique is my new friend. She knows a lot about these things after reading a lot of books to prepare for coming out here."

Crabbage seemed about to blow up, but the words caught in his throat. His fists clenched, then relaxed. Young Elizabeth looked at him with puppy-dog dark eyes. Perhaps Crabbage felt unwilling to be seen getting in an argument with a young woman and a young girl.

"I heard about them germ things, but they ain't proved yet," Crabbage muttered.

Nevertheless, Crabbage turned, grunting, still shaking his fist at Renwiler. Grudgingly he walked away. Once again, though, Angelique Hapsburg had helped thwart a potentially dangerous confrontation. As semi-royalty, probably she was used to ordering people around in Europe.

Tyler was distracted by the sound of several gunshots ringing out from the far west end of the circle of wagons.

CHAPTER EIGHT

"What the blazes is going on?" Pa demanded. Tyler was off running toward the direction of the sounds of the gunfire. He leaped over someone's Dutch oven. Another pistol shot rang out. Tyler slowed up as he neared where the sound of the gunfire had come from. Good sense prevented him from rushing headlong into a dangerous situation.

He saw the scene clearly, though. Tim MacNaughton had a new-fangled revolver pistol pointed at a group of about ten Indians riding pell-mell away from him.

"Let that be a warning to you!" Tim shouted at the fleeing Indians. "Tell all your other warrior friends that that's what to expect if they attack this wagon train. Bullets and more bullets if you ever attack this wagon train again."

Other men came rushing up. "Knock it off, MacNaughton," Jonathan Colledge bellowed. "They can't understand a word you're saying."

Buckman stormed up on horseback and leaped down at Tim's feet. He reared the back of his hand and walloped Tim so hard across the mouth that Tim reeled backwards.

"You wet nose greenhorn kid!" Buckman reamed Tim. "Those Pawnees weren't here to attack. They're mostly a peaceful tribe. They came here to trade. They probably wanted to trade some buffalo robes for some grub or some metal pots and pans, which we could certainly have spared. And we could have used the buffalo robes. But now, thanks to you, MacNaughton, we may very well get attacked."

"Hey, I read—"

"You *read?*" Buckman exploded. "You *read* in some dime novel about Indians attacking a wagon train? Indians aren't stupid! They're not going to attack a wagon train with a hundred well-armed men—unless they're provoked. And you provoked them! Now they're likely as provoked as any bunch of Indians I ever seen in my whole damn life. All thanks to you, MacNaughton."

The stupidity of what he had done suddenly seemed to grip Tim. He started breathing heavily through his half-open mouth. His eyes widened.

"They were just here to trade?" Tim asked incredulously.

"Yeah, to trade, nothing more," Buckman bellowed.

"Maybe they were here to trade but they were really here to spy on us," Tim said.

Buckman drew his Colt Navy revolver, forcing Tim backwards. "Wet nose kid, you still don't get it." Buckman pistol-whipped Tim hard enough to force blood from his nose.

"I'm going to need to ask several good men to risk their lives with me to track those Indians to their camp and win back their good will through trade."

"You're going to track them down and *find* them?" Tim asked.

"Yes, I'm going to have to find their camp and try—try—to show them we meant no harm," Buckman said. He turned to face the rapidly gathering crowd. "I'm going to have to ask ten good, brave men to go with me with trade goods to assuage those Indians and keep them from attacking us. Hopefully we can get them to realize it was just a dumb-ass misunderstanding."

Brent McGuigan turned to Tyler and asked in a low voice that Buckman could still hear, "What's he mean by that word 'assuage'? That's kind of a big word, you know."

Buckman stepped away from Tim and faced about three dozen people forming a semi-circle around him. "'Assuage' means, I need ten men to join me in finding that Indian camp, with probably several hundred Indians, go there, bring presents, and apologize to those Indians before they *do* form a war party to seek revenge."

"Say what?" one bearded fellow demanded.

Buckman put his hands on his hips and seemed to eye every man individually. The quiet, pregnant silence burned and thickened. Tyler wanted to hear if Buckman really meant what he had just said. He could see some men, out of the corner of an eye, listening to Buckman from well back of their wagons, and not daring to get any closer.

"I said, I need ten men, ten brave and good men, to go with me, to find those Indians that MacNaughton just shot at. We'll take trade goods to give as presents. Indians like and expect presents. That will show them that one of us shooting at them was all just a big, big mistake. We mean them no harm. We need to make that clear to them. If we don't, then yes, they could attack the wagon train. Or, they could attack Press, Silas or some of our other hunters when they're out alone."

Buckman paused to let the import of what of his words meant sink in. He finally added, "Don't everybody volunteer all at once."

Tyler saw one man with a broad plainsman's hat and a pockmarked face step forward. "I'll go," the man said quietly.

"There's one," Buckman declared. "I need nine more."

"Oh no you don't, Elston Tanner." A bun-haired woman in a polka-dot dress, presumably his wife, pulled the pockmarked faced man backwards. "You've got two kids and a third on the way who need a father. Don't even think about chasing after no scalping Indians."

Buckman looked at the man being pulled away from the scene. "Thanks anyway, Elston," he said. Turning back to the crowd of men, Buckman declared, "All right, we're back to needing ten men, then. I need ten of you. With ten men going with me, the Indians'll know we're not a large enough group to be threatening to attack, but if we are attacked, we are enough to do some real damage before we're all killed. That will hopefully, I say, discourage the savages from doing anything too quickly."

Hopefully?

Tyler saw in his peripheral vision that Rachelle had joined the crowd and was listening. She stood with arms folded over her white blouse and she looked worried. Maybe here was a chance to impress Rachelle with his bravery and importance in a way that might be something a tad more than mere show.

"I'm waiting. Ten men are what I need."

Tyler hesitated. Was impressing Rachelle really worth risking his life? His need to impress Rachelle had its limits. But before he thought it completely through, Tyler found himself slowly raising his hand. "I'll go," he said.

Pa grabbed him by the arm. "Are you nuts?" he whispered harshly. "Are you trying to be some kind of hero?"

"I don't have a wife and family," Tyler said loudly enough for Buckman to hear him. "I'm alone."

"You have a family—Penny and me," Pa bellowed.

Tyler noted that Brent McGuigan, one of Rachelle's more determined suitors, had moved to stand next to her but was in no way looking to volunteer as he had his arms folded and his clear-faced expression tense. Probably he knew he should volunteer but was too scared.

Here was his chance, Tyler knew, to really show up Brent McGuigan and all of her other would-be suitors in front of Rachelle.

"Pa, if I don't volunteer, then some man with a wife and kids will have to go in my place." Tyler could not fool himself. His intentions were in no way noble, but his statement had sounded good. Pa's lowered head and quiet lack of response as he rubbed his whiskers appeared to indicate that he had to see the grim logic behind Tyler's statement.

"I'll go," another man said. This young man, short and pudgy, Tyler saw, had no woman next to him to stop him.

Buckman raised a hand in salute to the man who'd volunteered. "Thanks, Quimby, thanks plenty." Buckman looked directly at Tyler. "You in, Tyler?"

"Count me in," Tyler said before Pa could object further. "I'll volunteer to go."

"Thanks, Tyler. That's two. I need eight more. Who's next?"

Silas stepped forward. "You know that Press and I will go."

"Appreciate it, but I can't allow you and Press to go," Buckman declared. He matter-of-factly added, "If I don't return, then you and Press will have to get the wagon train through to Oregon."

"I'll—I'll go," Tim sheepishly said. "I should go. I created the problem. I should help—try to help solve it."

"Can't allow that either," Buckman said. "Yeah, I agree, you should go, MacNaughton, after the danger you put all of us in by your wet nose, greenhorn stupidity. Stupidity hardly even describes it. Stupidity is something simple and dumb. What you did was butt-huge and incredibly selfish beyond belief. Yes, you *should* go, MacNaughton. Unfortunately, if you go with us and the Indians recognize you as the one who shot at them, they'll open fire at us first and ask questions later."

Buckman turned to face the crowd again. "I've got two men," he declared. "I need ten. I need eight other men to volunteer. Who'll be next to step forward?"

The wagon train captain scanned the crowd with grimly-pursed lips. He fisted the hands on his hips.

Tyler was surprised when another man actually did step forward from the crowd. "I'll go," the narrow-spectacled, thin-whiskered man said.

"Excellent, Lucas. That's three men we have now," Buckman declared. "I need seven more. Who else will volunteer?"

Buckman looked over the crowd of men, some with their wives and children. Tyler observed the men, many of them seeming to watch each other sheepishly out of the corners of their eyes. No doubt, each man hoped another, or others, would volunteer. Each man no doubt hoped that other men would take him off the hook, enabling him to say to a relieved wife or girlfriend, "I would gladly have volunteered to go on the mission to the Indians but I wasn't needed."

"I said, I need seven more men to go with me," Buckman declared more loudly. "Don't tell me that on this whole wagon train there's less than ten men with a backbone."

Tyler glanced at Pa again. He wore a half-smile now, as if strangely proud of him. Tyler looked at other men listening to Buckman. Several of them hung their heads, ashamed of themselves but not ashamed enough to volunteer. A few men turned to walk away. Tyler saw a couple of men being pulled away from the scene by their wives.

"Again, I need ten men, not three, in order to do this safely," Buckman shouted.

"I thought you just said you might not come back regardless," one short, stocky man muttered while gripping his suspenders.

Buckman eyed the round-bellied man angrily. "Or, Mr. Oggerdt, I guess we can all of us stay here, and risk the chance that the Indians really do attack the entire wagon train. Then you're all involved whether you want to be or not. I need seven more men."

Tyler looked around. No one gave any indication of having interest in risking life and limb to placate the Indians.

"Who else will volunteer?" Buckman looked around this way and that, seemingly taking in every man individually with his searching, toothy glance.

Silence. Total, utter, deafening silence.

"There's your answer," Silas declared.

"Seven more men." Buckman looked around.

Apparently Buckman got the picture. "All right then, all you yellow-bellies. I'll do this with three men, three real men, I mean, three real men who are probably the equal or the betters of all the rest of you put together."

Out of the corner of an eye, Tyler saw Rachelle looking at him, then at the other men who had volunteered. Stupendous! This was working out fantastically. What must Rachelle be thinking of him now? Hopefully that Brent McGuigan and the rest of that ilk surrounding her at dances weren't even half the man put together that he was. Being able to dance a reel or a jig when no danger lurked was one level of manhood; being able to protect a wife and family in an unsettled frontier area was manhood on quite another level. Tyler trusted that Rachelle would realize that, and think on it as she danced this evening with the young men who had chosen not to volunteer for the hazardous mission to the Pawnee Indians.

If he returned, Tyler told himself, gulping.

Buckman took one last parting shot at the men walking away. "If you're afraid of the Pawnees, then may God help us all when we get closer to Fort Laramie and Sioux land." He glanced at Tyler and the two other men who'd volunteered. "Be ready to leave in a few minutes." He turned to Silas. "We probably won't be back before tomorrow morning. You and Press will need to get the wagon train moving."

Silas nodded. "I understand. We'll see that everybody gets under motion, with or without you."

* * *

"Godspeed, Tyler." Pa gave him a hug. Pa was not the type to show emotion and he wasn't now. Still, this hugging business was atypical for him. Pa gave him a couple of hearty claps on the back.

When Pa was done, there stood Penny, scarcely breathing. She looked at him with big soulful brown eyes that reflected her sincere little heart. She moved her arms slightly. What should he do? Tyler held out his arms to Penny and she fell into them and embraced him.

"Come back to us, Tyler," Penny said earnestly.

"I intend to." Tyler gave Penny a quick hug and he got away from both her and Pa. Being touchy-feely made him uncomfortable.

He walked over to Buckman, astride his chestnut horse. The two other men had also mounted up. One of them held a mount for him. The other man held the reins of a packhorse.

"You've got weapons, right?" Buckman asked.

Tyler nodded. "I'm taking my Sharps rifle and my .31 Colt cap-lock pocket revolver, though I hope I don't have to use them."

"You're not hoping any stronger than I am," Buckman declared.

Pa handed Tyler his Sharps rifle to go with his waist pistol that he already had stuck between his pants and his shirt. The Sharps went into the rifle scabbard.

Tyler mounted the grayish gelding and took the reins. He glanced at the packhorse. "What are we taking to the Indians?" he asked.

"Some pots and pans, some tobacco, some bright beads," Buckman replied. "Nothing of big value to us. The Pawnees, though, they fancy that sort of stuff. It'll hopefully pacify 'em for what that shit-head MacNaughton did."

Buckman reined his horse around and headed in the direction the fleeing Indians had taken.

Tyler snapped his horse's reins and headed out without hesitation across the prairie, as did the two other men who had agreed to embark on this dangerous mission.

"What are your names?" Tyler asked.

"Quimby—Quimby Freding," the short, portly young man said, extending a friendly hand in greeting.

Tyler shook hands with Quimby Freding. "Might as well get to know each other," Tyler said. "We're going to be depending on each other up ahead."

"Lucas Pfister," the other short man with the narrow spectacles said.

Tyler shook hands with him. "Tyler Linders is my name. Glad to know you guys."

"Looks like we might have a fourth volunteer." Quimby pointed behind him. "Someone's actually coming to join us."

Turning to look behind him, Tyler saw none other than Alain Laurent riding toward them. "What the . . ."

Alain rode up on his palomino gelding, with a Sharps in his rifle scabbard. He smiled as he neared Tyler and tipped his hat.

"Penny asked me to go with you and look after you," Alain said. "How could I say no to your wonderful, beautiful sister?"

All Tyler could think was that, truly, Alain must really, *really* like Penny very, *very* much. Tyler remarked, "I see

Penny is beginning to have a major influence on you if she can ask you and get you to do something like this."

"Aye, she is," Alain declared. "I wasn't present when wagon master Buckman made his impassioned request for volunteers. Penny told me and asked me to go with you. I couldn't say no to her."

"How romantic," Tyler said, half-sarcastically and half-seriously. Both he and Alain were on this perilous mission solely because they wanted to impress a pair of females.

Buckman halted for a moment. "Welcome, Laurent. There's five of us now. We have to convince the Indians of our good intentions. The ten Indians that Tim MacNaughton stupidly shot at are heading toward the southwest. Silas told me there's a camp of about two hundred Pawnees ten miles southwest of here. I'll bet my last pair of britches that's where they're headed."

Buckman snapped his reins and moved on, grabbing the pack horse reins behind him.

As they rode along together, Tyler and Alain followed by Quimby Freding and Lucas Pfister spoke little. It was not a time for light-hearted conversation. Tyler tried to keep his emotions in check by paying attention to the surrounding blue prairie pasque flower, yellow goldenrod, white Queen Anne's lace and other flower types that Tyler did not know the names of. All of the flowers graced the prairie. Low hills along the horizon loomed purple-blue. Choppy, bare outcroppings of rock further along toward the west gave promise of the badlands to be encountered in volume after another 200 miles. Above, a golden eagle soared, and, farther off, several kestrels, all of them probably looking for mice or snakes below them to eat or feed to their young.

"I think I see it," Buckman said, pointing toward the southwest. "Indian encampment up ahead."

Tyler couldn't make out anything except some smudges along the horizon. Doubtless, Buckman's more practiced eyes recognized the pointy smudges as large tepees. After another half-mile of riding, Tyler saw more clearly what looked like about thirty tepees.

"Guess we'll find out pretty soon if we'll live to see another day," Quimby said.

Tyler exchanged somber glances with Alain. "I'd rather be more positive than that," Tyler declared.

"Here, here," Alain agreed. "I don't want to think about what *might* happen, but hopefully won't."

"I just wonder if the Pawnees like to torture their prisoners like the Sioux do," Quimby said.

"Will you stop it?" Lucas demanded. "We've got guns. We can fight if we have to."

"All right, everybody just settle down," Buckman demanded. He looked back at them with a narrowed glance underneath his bushy eyebrows. "The object of this expedition is to help keep the peace. Remember that."

Tyler felt his muscles and senses going numb. He wished now that he would have at least gone on this dangerous expedition for a better reason than merely to impress Rachelle Palmerston. What price glory? Was Rachelle even thinking about him? Or was she too busy dancing with Brent McGuigan and her other admirers to even think of anything else? If she did think of him now, would she consider him a hero, or nothing but a reckless fool?

As they approached the tepees, Tyler saw there were not thirty of them, but probably twice that number. He grew so numb that he hoped that he would not make a sudden instinctive move to jerk his horse around and skedaddle away like a coward. He felt his heart hammer-beating his chest beneath his cotton shirt. Sweat on his brow and armpits gave him a cold, clammy feeling.

The Pawnee Indians, men, women, and children watched the approaching men. Their stony faces showed no emotion, making it hard for Tyler to determine if Buckman's strategy was working or not. A group of about twenty men, warriors no doubt, made their way to the front of the crowd as the women and children slowly moved toward the rear.

One of the Pawnee men turned to yell back to the others. He extended all five fingers of his right hand. "*Sikuhts piita!*" he declared.

Tyler had no idea what the man had said to his fellows, only that he had sounded concerned and annoyed.

Buckman pulled up on his horse and made the peace sign of a hand extended with the palm down. "Does anyone here speak English?" he shouted. "Do any among the Pawnee speak English?"

Tyler waited for an answer to Buckman's question. All of the Pawnees stared blankly. A tense several seconds followed. Tyler gripped the reins of his horse. He could feel the wetness of his sweaty palms. He did not want to run. His breaths came in short, quick gasps.

One older Pawnee wearing leggings and a purple vest that must have been received in trade, or stolen, stepped forward. "No Englis, no Englis," he said.

Buckman looked back at Tyler and the others. "Nobody speaks English. Of course they don't," Buckman muttered. "If they did, it would make our task here way, way, way too simple and easy, now wouldn't it?"

Well, did any of us grow up speaking Pawnee? Tyler asked himself.

Buckman again made the peace sign and pulled the pack horse closer. "Trade, trade," Buckman shouted. "Surely you must understand that word." He pulled an iron pan out of one of the sacks the pack horse carried. "I can't believe nobody here speaks any English at all."

"Buckman."

Tyler followed with his eyes to where Alain pointed. A white man with a thin, sandy-blonde beard and a thick head of sandy hair had emerged from a tepee. The man looked well-dressed, with a silver-blue vest that was slightly smudged with dirt.

"I think I speak English fair enough," the man said. "Of course, in grammar school, English was most assuredly not my favorite or best subject. Arithmetic and geography had more appeal."

"Don't be a wise ass. We need help. Who are you?" Buckman demanded.

"The Reverend Bartholomew Cornleiter at your service. A simple Methodist missionary minister, am I."

"Okay, so you speak English. How well do you speak Pawnee?"

Cornleiter twisted his lips briefly in thought, putting his hands on his hips. "A fair piece. I've been here about a year now."

"I'm a wagon master leading a train of over four hundred and fifty people bound for Oregon. An idiot traveling with us foolishly and thoughtlessly took some pistol shots at a group of Indians from this camp when they approached to engage us in trade. Will you tell them that it was all a grievous mistake for which we apologize. It won't happen ever again."

Cornleiter spoke several words to the Pawnee in a matter-of-fact tone, then several more.

The first response was an angry one from one of the younger Pawnee warriors who yelled loudly and shook his fist at Buckman as if he were speaking not to Cornleiter but rather directly to Buckman.

Another Indian with long braided hair also chimed in with several angry words.

Cornleiter turned to Buckman. The minister sheepishly scratched the back of his head, sighing. "They're telling me they don't believe a word you're saying about this being simply a misunderstanding. If I were you, I'd come up with a more convincing story, and be right quick about it."

CHAPTER NINE

The initial relief which Tyler had felt when Cornleiter had presented himself disintegrated. Tyler exchanged glances with Alain, and the latter with Quimby and Lucas. The minister's presence held no guarantee that the Indians couldn't suddenly decide to do anything they wanted if their bloodlust exploded.

Buckman leaned forward in his saddle. "Tell them we came here to trade. Iron tools for blankets. Maybe they'll believe *that*." He gestured at the packhorse. "Would we have brought all this stuff if we were here looking for a fight? Also, tell them again that what happened earlier was a foolish mistake by whatever their words are for 'stupid greenhorn.'"

Cornleiter turned and spoke again to the Indians behind him. Once more two of the Pawnees responded, but this time more casually, more slowly, and with seeming matter-of-factness. Tyler thought their words sounded tinged with sadness, and a bit melancholy. At least they didn't sound angry this time. Tyler exhaled heavily.

"Well . . ." Cornleiter sighed again, putting his arms akimbo once more. "They say they may be willing to believe you if you have items for trade. But even if what happened was a misunderstanding, they are sure *you* won't let it happen again, but with the very next wagon train that comes through, the same thing will happen again, and then again." Cornleiter rubbed his chin. "I know it's happened before. Some of the Pawnees will approach a wagon train to trade, and they'll be shot at well before they have a chance to make their intentions clear."

Buckman pushed his broad-brimmed hat up, then scratched his whiskers. "Well, whatever. There's nothing I can do about whoever's behind us."

Another tense moment ensued. White man and red looked one another over, each unsure what would come next—fighting or trading, maybe both.

Lucas glanced at the round, gold-plated watch in his waistcoat.

"In a hurry to get somewhere, Lucas?" Buckman asked nervously.

"Nope. Just checking my watch. I've noticed the sunsets getting later and later. I've heard Indians don't like to fight at night."

Buckman shuffled uneasily. "Not only is it getting closer to the solstice, but we're getting farther west. Your watch is set for the time in Independence, Missouri. We're maybe a few hundred miles west of there now. Right now we've got other things to worry about."

"I reckon."

A middle-aged Indian who had been standing off to the side approached Lucas on his horse. "What—this?" he demanded, pointing to Lucas's timepiece.

"It's my watch," Lucas replied, smiling apprehensively. "It tells me what time it is."

Suddenly the Indian grabbed Lucas's watch and ripped it out of his waistcoat.

"Hey! You give that back!" Lucas leaped down to his feet to angrily confront the Indian but Quimby grabbed him by the suspenders and pulled him backwards.

Buckman leaped down also. "Relax. Stay put, Lucas," he ordered. "You can always buy another watch for yourself at Fort Kearny or Fort Laramie, but you can't buy another life for yourself if you lose the one you've got. We need to get off to a good start here with the Pawnee. Let it go."

Tension thickened the air ever more tightly. A couple of dozen Pawnee warriors watched carefully. Tyler saw one of them in back grip the sheath of a large knife around his neck. Would the Pawnee attack them after all, kill them, and take all of their goods anyway? White man and red looked one another over once more, not sure what would happen next.

Teeth clenched, Lucas grudgingly took a couple of steps back and looked away. Smart man, Tyler thought, very smart to swallow his pride. Lucas eyed the tear in his waistcoat where his watch had been ripped free while the Indian proudly showed off his new piece of jewelry to his fellows nearby.

Finally the purple-vested older Indian who had spoken first gestured toward the ground in front of him. "Sit," he said to Buckman, Tyler and the others.

Buckman dismounted and waved toward Tyler and the other men with him to come forward. "Looks like we got some business to transact," Buckman declared. "Grab those two sacks for me from the pack horse."

Tyler grabbed one leather sack while Quimby grabbed the other. Buckman took a seat on the ground and a half-dozen other Indians did the same. Still other Indians stood back and watched pensively. The older Indian who had first invited them to sit took a red colored pipe from a long pouch. He took a plug of tobacco from a pouch about his neck and put it in his pipe. Matches were a trade item. The

Indian took a small box of matches from his pouch. Taking one match, he lit his pipe.

The old Indian took a couple of puffs and exhaled smoke through his mouth and nose. He handed the pipe to Buckman.

Tyler took a seat on the ground, his fears starting to dissipate. Maybe, maybe, his gamble was paying off, and he would get to brag later, within Rachelle's hearing, of taking part in a dangerous mission that most of the other young men had been too frightened to go on.

Alain took a seat on Tyler's left, with Quimby and Lucas seating themselves on the other side.

Buckman took several puffs from the pipe. He then passed the pipe to Alain, who took a deep puff and inhaled too deeply. Alain covered his mouth and coughed several times. The Indians roared with laughter, further alleviating the tension.

Thus forewarned, Tyler politely pretended to take a puff from the pipe but he did not inhale deeply. He exhaled the smoke before the bitter-tasting tobacco could assault his taste buds. He quickly passed the pipe to Quimby Freding.

Quimby and Lucas puffed readily and easily, no doubt having had much experience in the past with pipes. After he had puffed from the pipe, Lucas passed it to the Indian sitting next to him.

The Indians resumed their pipe-smoking until the pipe returned to the old Indian who had first lighted it.

This ceremony concluded, Buckman pulled the two leather sacks toward him and opened them, taking out an iron kettle and iron skillet to demonstrate the items that he had come to trade.

The old Indian examined the iron kettle and nodded his approval. He took the iron skillet and nodded his approval of this item as well. Buckman pulled more items out of one of the leather bags to show the old Indian, tin plates, tin cups, eating utensils, woolen scarves, three silk vests and a pair of trousers.

The old Indian nodded approval of all of these items. He turned around and gestured toward three blanket-covered women behind him. The women disappeared momentarily into a large tepee. Quickly, though, they appeared outside again, each one bearing a couple of buffalo robes which they brought forward. The old Indian gave one of the blankets to Buckman, who ran his fingers through the fur.

"Good, good," Buckman said. "We'll take all of these you care to give us."

As Cornleiter translated, Tyler reflected that the importance of the buffalo robes was not in their quality, but rather in the sense this trade conveyed that all was being restored to a normal state of affairs between white man and red, that is to say, an uneasy truce.

There was no choice but to spend the night at the Pawnee camp. It was too late in the day to start back to the wagon train. Buckman said there was too much danger they'd get lost in the dark, or a horse might accidentally step on a rattlesnake.

Tyler, Buckman, Lucas, Quimby, and Alain all slept crowded together in the same large tepee. Three Indians joined them. All night long, Tyler slept fitfully with his wagon train companions, battling lice and mosquitoes, and lingering fear. He wanted to get out of there safely and ensure that he lived to brag about his exploits among the Pawnee. The Indians slept peacefully, oblivious to all distractions.

The following morning Buckman took his leave of the Pawnees, with the six buffalo robes draped over the pack horse. Tyler breathed a hefty sigh of relief as they rode away from the Pawnee camp without each of them getting a personal collection of arrows in the back.

They rode all that day, not back to where they had last seen the wagon train, but to where Buckman expected it to be after thirty-six hours. When they caught up with the wagon train again it was evening and the wagons had already formed up into a circle. Interestingly, three Pawnees from another camp had approached the wagon train to engage in trade.

Tyler asked himself why he was not surprised that it was Angelique Hapsburg who was communicating with the three Pawnees in sign language. However, he was not so curious that he had any interest in joining this latest discussion about Indian robes and utensils. Tyler felt he had done his share. Rachelle would know of his adventure. He would talk about it casually and make sure that Rachelle knew he had gone to meet with the Pawnees, rather than vice versa.

When he dismounted with Alain, Penny was there to hug them both while Pa gave him a handshake and a hearty clap on the back.

"Alain, you took care of Tyler for me just like I asked you to," Penny said, clapping her hands gleefully. "Hurray, Tyler! Hurray, Alain!" She embraced Tyler and Alain again.

"All of us took care of one another," Tyler said.

Buckman dismounted nearby. "Well said, Tyler," he remarked. "There were just enough of us to confront the Indians safely. If any one of us had gone there alone, he'd have had his scalp lifted after being shot full of arrows."

Tyler heard the fiddle music. The dancing was in progress. He headed toward the music. Bruce Mallory had his fiddle going full strength as the dancers went into a Reel. Brent McGuigan stood next to Rachelle, both of them clapping their hands to the music. Tyler casually looked past them toward several older folks also enjoying the music.

"Hey, Tyler, I see you made it back okay," Ephraim declared. "Good for you!"

"Sure did." Tyler waved a friendly hello. "Got the Pawnees to give us some buffalo robes on top of making peace."

Stepping around several chickens, he hurried on in the direction of Brent McGuigan. Tyler pretended to be watching the dancers as he walked along. Nonchalantly, he looked at Brent and made eye contact with him.

"Hey Brent, how's it going?" Tyler asked unconcernedly.

"Tyler, good to see you again," Brent declared, "And I really mean that. You made out okay with the Injuns?"

The perfect question, with Rachelle listening. Brent had unknowingly done him a tremendous favor. "I guess so, or I wouldn't be here," Tyler replied. He sauntered close to Brent with Rachelle right next to him. "Buckman did just about all of the talking. The rest of us were just there for backup support. I did get to see a Pawnee village, though, and we slept overnight in a tepee."

"Wow!" Rachelle reacted, clasping her hands together. "That must have been quite an experience. Were you scared at all?"

"Well, of course," Tyler replied with the right tone of modesty. "We didn't know what was going to happen, right up to when we left. We got lucky because there was a Methodist missionary guy living with the Pawnees and he knew their language."

"Still, though, wow," Rachelle said. "No doubt about it, that was a brave thing to do, Tyler."

"Well, Buckman was putting the pressure on the men to help him," Tyler said. "Let's hope Tim MacNaughton doesn't do anything stupid to ever make a trip like that necessary again."

"I don't know," Brent murmured. "We passed Fort Kearny early today and picked up a few supplies, then hurried on because it wasn't time yet for stopping for the night. There were some Injuns standing around the Sutler's store, and Tim circled wide around them with one hand on his knife. The Injuns actually laughed and thought it was pretty funny that Tim was so scared of them. We'll be at Chimney

Rock soon enough, then Scotts Bluff and pretty soon Fort Laramie. We'll be in the middle of Sioux country. They may not be so friendly."

"Dance with me." Rachelle grabbed Tyler's arm and half-dragged him out to the dance.

This made the whole episode worth all the risk. Tyler twirled Rachelle around and into the dance they went. She smiled broadly at him, her shiny blue eyes sparkling and her long blonde hair whirling away with the dance moves and the music. The prettiest, most beautiful, most desirable girl in the whole gosh darn wagon train, and Tyler rejoiced that he had her for the moment. He held hands with Rachelle as they whirled and twirled to the fiddle music. He saw other young men watching him, jealous and envious as sin, no doubt. Yet there was Rachelle Palmerston, gripping both his hands as she smiled delightedly at being with him. She genuinely seemed thrilled with his company. Yes, Tyler told himself, this was his goal achieved.

The music ended, but Rachelle continued gripping his hand. "Do another dance with me, Tyler," she beseeched. "That last one was too short."

"Glad to, Rachelle," Tyler said, ecstatic.

Tyler danced three more dances with Rachelle, as she taught him the moves that she'd been learning every single evening on this journey. More young men watched him with Rachelle. Not all of them looked with jealous eyes, though. Tim and even Brent clapped their hands to the music and applauded him, seemingly genuinely happy for him with Rachelle.

After their last dance together, Tyler bowed to Rachelle and she politely curtsied to him. She was out of breath and panting. "Thank you, Tyler. That was fantastic," Rachelle said earnestly. "I think I need to go back to my Pa's wagon and get a drink of water."

"Thank you, Rachelle, I had fun too." Tyler waved at her and she smiled prettily and waved back at him as she took her leave.

With a full and joyous heart Tyler put his hands on his hips and watched other couples dance. Well, no matter. Let other men have their fun with other young women. His early interest, Billie Kay Ellis, seemed to be having the time of her life dancing with Justin What's-his-name. Billie Kay wore her hair a little longer than Kelly Jay now and looked downright attractive in her brown pinafore.

No matter, Tyler told himself again. He had Rachelle. He needed no other.

Tyler's attention was momentarily distracted by young Penny proudly dancing with Alain Laurent again. Strangely, though, Penny had chosen to wear her reading glasses while dancing. Come to think of it, she wore her glasses all the time now. Maybe she figured they made her look older. Well, Penny, bless you. Pa may have his discomfort about a seventeen-year-old boy having twelve-year-old Penny for a girlfriend, but Tyler felt happy for Penny. If Rachelle was the best-looking young woman, then Alain Laurent was arguably the best-looking young man in this whole wagon train, with his thick sandy blonde hair, sea-blue eyes, clear, unwhiskered face and tall length.

Plus, Tyler reflected, at Penny's request, Alain had risked his life to go on the trading expedition with him to the Pawnees. Alain seemed for all the world truly devoted to Penny with every ounce of his heart, and she to him. Penny had made herself quite a catch in Alain.

Tyler decided to have some fun with Penny. "Hey Penny," he called out, "why do you wear your glasses all the time now?"

Penny looked at him for only a split second, then she returned her attention to Alain. "Because I feel like it," she said, somewhat perturbed. Then her warm, excited smile returned. "Plus, the better to see Alain with."

Alain grinned appreciatively at that.

Tyler turned to head back to his wagon. His attention was arrested, however, at the sight of Rachelle walking and holding hands with Van Buren Colledge. Tyler was in her line of sight but she acted as though she didn't even see him. She smiled at Van Buren Colledge as she had smiled at him just minutes earlier. Then they danced delightedly as Rachelle had danced with him moments earlier, with Rachelle apparently not so winded as Tyler had thought.

Carefully Tyler watched everything Rachelle and Van Buren did together, his jealousy and envy surging with every twirling motion they did together. Worse, Mrs. Edith Colledge was watching her son with Rachelle and clapping her hands to the fiddle music and applauding. Clearly she approved of Van Buren and Rachelle being together, and she would likely encourage Van Buren if he had any serious interest in Rachelle.

Tyler bowed his head, sighing. There were three things which Van Buren and the Colledge family had which he did not—money, more money, and still lots more money.

*   *   *

Pa and Tyler walked next to the wagon over the next few days, sometimes joined by Penny wearing her hexagonal spectacle glasses. The Palmerston wagon went well in front of the Linders wagon for several days, so Tyler did not have much contact with Rachelle, and it was hard to watch her at dances, talking and laughing and having fun with young men whom Tyler remembered had slunk away in shame and cowardice when Buckman had asked for volunteers to meet with the Pawnees.

There were distractions in any case. Crossing the South Platte, then heading up the two-mile incline of California Hill were difficult obstacles to overcome. Some of the emigrants forded the South Platte by removing their wagon wheels and floating their wagon boxes across the river. Ephraim Allerton was one of the forders, refusing to pay a $5 charge for a ferry.

California Hill saw a tragic scene when one of the wagons going up the long incline started to go backwards. A small boy whose name Tyler couldn't remember did not get out of the way quickly enough and the wagon ran him over. Another funeral. More tears. Another grave to dig.

Windlass Hill represented still another challenge. Emigrants learned to help one another by holding onto ropes as each wagon was lowered down the steep incline. Or at least some did, Tyler observed. The Colledges lost one of their two wagons when their slave Tuck, getting help from Van Buren but not from Jonathan, couldn't hold onto his rope tightly enough and the wagon went careening downhill and smashed to pieces against a large boulder. Several pieces of Colledge furniture inside the wagon were also smashed.

Standing to the side and watching, Jonathan Colledge erupted in two-fisted anger. "Damn you, Tuck!" he bellowed. "It's going to cost me over two hundred dollars to replace that furniture when we get to Oregon. That bureau belonged to my grandfather and was a family treasure. Thanks to you, Tuck, it's not good for anything now except kindling wood. Don't you dare let the next wagon fall downhill."

"Yessuh, I is understandin'," Tuck said in a beseeching tone. The pained expression on Tuck's face bespoke his fear, and apparently the slave knew he dare not respond in any manner indicating that Jonathan could have helped him. Jonathan casually held his ox whip in one hand.

Nathan Zurich, Tomas Hanclicek, Bruce Mallory, and Tyler helped Tuck and Van Buren with the ropes keeping the main Colledge wagon from taking off downhill.

As Tyler plodded along later, he was lost in thought. The flowered prairie landscape gave way increasingly to patches of badlands—sod tables, pinnacles, hard white clay earth, and the occasional promontory. Tyler barely noticed the scenery and could not enjoy it. His thoughts centered on Rachelle. For twenty glorious minutes he'd had her, or so he had thought.

It was as though she had satiated herself with him in those first moments after he had returned from his trip to the Pawnee Indian encampment. He had risked his life for that?

Dully, Tyler walked along, recalling his effort to ask Rachelle to dance two nights earlier.

"I'm sorry, Tyler, I'm kind of tired tonight," she had said when he'd asked her. "Plus, my ma and I did some washing earlier and I should go see if it's dry yet." She had then absently walked away from him.

Then there was last night. Rachelle had spent the whole evening with some clown named Charles Chuckwood, he'd heard her call him, with curly brown hair, a striped shirt, and trousers. Apparently it was Charles Chuckwood's turn to be Rachelle's infatuation *du jour*. She spent two hours with him, holding hands and dancing with him. Tyler hadn't seen Chuckwood kissing Rachelle, but he might have at some point.

So obsessed was Rachelle with Charles that not even Van Buren Colledge could get at her, though Tyler saw him looking at her often with clear longing in his eyes.

Adding to Tyler's misery was the increasing dustiness of the trail along the North Platte. Those at the back of the wagon train suffered most, but all ate their share of dust. When Tyler blew his nose with his handkerchief, the handkerchief was black with dirt.

The dryer air also started talking its toll on man, beast, and wagon as Chimney Rock came into view. Thirst became more common, more pervasive. However, water had to be boiled before it could be safely drunk. A day's supply of water had to be carefully husbanded.

Thinner air as the wagon train ascended above 3,000 feet forced oxen, horses and the occasional mule team to work harder to pull the wagons. Nor did it help that upgrades along the trail became more common.

Tyler knew that Drake and Dru were a strong team and would keep up the good pace. He worried, though, about the MacNaughton oxen team. Renford MacNaughton's decision at the start to buy a smaller pair of lead oxen looked like it was starting to catch up with him. Save money in Independence, pay more later at Fort Laramie to buy a fresh pair of oxen.

That is, if the MacNaughtons even made it all the way to Fort Laramie, 150 miles distant. Their team of oxen did a fair share of bawling and complaining, and sometimes came to a dead halt struggling to pull the MacNaughton wagon up a rise.

Wagon wheels had started drying out, creating small gaps between the wooden wheels and the iron rims. Many a wagon wheel would have to be replaced by the time Fort Laramie was reached. This problem would grow even worse on the other side beyond Fort Laramie.

Tyler took a look at his own wagon wheels and ran his fingers along the rim of one. They looked okay for now. He, Pa, and Penny had taken turns keeping the axles well greased, and so the axles looked okay.

"You're fine," Alain said, coming up beside Penny. "I know what you're thinking. Your wagon wheels are okay. The ones that are starting to break apart are on the wagons that were too heavily loaded down at the start. Those folks are going to start bitching at their luck before too much farther."

CHAPTER TEN

It seemed to take forever and a day to reach Chimney Rock, the pinnacle stretching several hundred feet toward the sky and one of the key markers along the Oregon Trail. Chimney Rock was visible for several days before the wagon train reached it, and was visible behind the wagon train for several days following.

As he walked along the light brown dusty trail, Tyler turned to look back one last time at Chimney Rock. His attention was arrested, however, by the sight of a broken-down wagon about fifty feet back, with a front wheel that had fallen off. An angry man, his wife and three children gathered around the broken axle. The wife buried her face in her hands to weep. Tyler recalled the names of the two parents, Zach and Ella Bennett.

Stonehouse's wagon rolled right past them without stopping.

"Somebody help us," the suspendered man beseeched. "You're not going to just leave us here! There's wild Indians around here, and outlaws. You can't just leave us here."

"Why not?" Stonehouse called out as he walked by, driving his team with his whip. "You took your chances, Bennett, just like we all did when we started out on this journey. You took an even bigger chance than most, by not taking along a spare axle. Now why should any of the rest of us inconvenience ourselves just because you didn't think ahead?"

Ella Bennett spread her arms. "But you can't just leave us!" she shrieked. "We'll die out here by ourselves, with no wagon and no way to get back East again."

"A hundred fifty miles back is Fort Kearny," Stonehouse bellowed. "If you walk fast, you can maybe get there in five or six days."

Zach Bennett slapped his hat against his thigh. "With no food or water? And two kids to carry, plus our son Blaise?"

"Not my problem," Stonehouse declared.

Tyler noted that not only Stonehouse, but a couple of other wagons passed the stranded Bennetts. Tyler was about to say something to Pa when he saw Jonas Smith hurry over to the Bennetts.

"I've got an extra axle," Smith said. "You can pay me for it and I'll buy another one at Fort Laramie."

"You'll be eating dust at the back of the train, Smith, by stopping to help Bennett," Stonehouse muttered.

"And why are you concerned about me eating dust when you weren't the least bit aggrieved about Zach and his family being marooned out in the middle of nowhere?" Smith demanded.

Tyler looked away again. Zach Bennett and his family would truly have been in the butt end of nowhere if they had been left behind. Sand hills, in some cases a couple of hundred feet high, dominated the landscape. Trees had almost entirely given out. Even the prairie grass was growing thinner and shorter.

"There 'tis! There 'tis!" a man named Credence Armagast shouted, pointing toward the northwest. "Scott's Bluff—we're almost to it. Getting to Scott's Bluff means we must be halfway to Oregon now."

Yeah, right, Tyler thought to himself. They would be halfway to Oregon, maybe, in another five hundred miles. All Scott's Bluff represented was a gigantic geological promontory that signaled that whoever reached it had successfully completed their Oregon Trail apprenticeship. Well, that *was* something. After all, the pikers and the pretenders hadn't made it this far. Ten wagons had turned tail and headed back to Missouri. Seventy-six were left in the train.

Directly ahead Milon Crabbage's wagon had stopped. The back axle had stuck. Pa had to stop his wagon while Crabbage leaped down cursing and swearing at his back axle. He kicked the wheel and kicked it again.

"Damn shit wagon!" Crabbage bellowed. "I don't have time for this."

Pa half-rose in his wagon seat. "You haven't greased your axles well enough," Pa declared. "Fact is, it doesn't look like you've greased 'em at all in quite a while."

Crabbage boiled over. "Well who in the damn hell asked you for your opinion, Linders?" he barked.

Pa sat back down. "I was just trying to point out—"

"Well, I don't need your bitching at me, so just shut the hell up."

"Hey!" Tyler jumped in front of the angry, thin-faced Crabbage. "You don't tell my Pa to shut up."

Crabbage swung at Tyler and he ducked. Alain ran forward to grab Crabbage but the brute was too big. He hurled Alain to the ground. Tyler took a swing at Crabbage that barely grazed him. Crabbage leveled a fist at Tyler that felt like a sledgehammer hitting his upper lips. Blood spurted out of his lips and nose.

A rifle shot rang out above Crabbage's head. Tyler wheeled. It was Van Buren Colledge leveling a Spencer squarely at Crabbage.

"Sounds like Magnus Linders just gave you some really high-quality advice, Crabbage, that you're too much of a professional ass to take," Van Buren declared. "You're holding up a lot of people behind you. So shut up, grease your axles, and get moving again."

Crabbage backed up and held up his hands. "I didn't mean nothing."

"That's exactly right, Crabbage," Van Buren declared. "You didn't mean nothing. You meant *something*. You meant that you've always got a chip on your shoulder and you're always daring someone to knock it off. A lot of good people on this wagon train are getting fed up with your attitude, Crabbage."

Crabbage clenched his expression, looking like he wanted to grumble some more, but he evidently thought better of it.

"Just grease your axle and everything's fine," Pa muttered.

While Crabbage moved off to take care of his bum axle, Tyler turned to face Van Buren Colledge, who was working on growing a mustache. He shook Van Buren's hand.

"Thanks," Tyler said. "Obliged to you, Van Buren."

"Not a problem," Van Buren said. "Crabbage is holding up a lot of people. Glad to help."

Tyler looked around. Pa and anyone behind him would not be able to simply go around Crabbage's wagon. There were dense lineups of wagons moving on either side of them.

After several minutes, Crabbage finished greasing his back axle. He climbed back up into his wagon box and got his wagon moving again.

Pa snapped the reins. "Ho!" he shouted, and Drake and Dru started moving once more.

Tyler stepped back close to Pa. "Let's not get behind Crabbage ever again," Tyler suggested.

Pa nodded. "I don't think anyone's gonna want to be near Crabbage. He's making himself into a regular pariah on this train."

Tyler walked on. One thing he was learning on this trip was that on the treeless Great Plains, distances could be deceiving. The wagon train traveled for four more hours after the first sighting of Scott's Bluff, but the promontory seemed no closer at the end of the day than it had been after the nooning.

There was no dance that evening. The wind picked up and blew dust around mightily. Pa tried to fix a potato and beef jerky soup for supper, but the dust got into the broth and it was no use. Tyler had to eat his beef jerky straight as he sat on the ground. Pa boiled three unpeeled potatoes for himself, Tyler, and Penny. Alain brought some lentil soup that his mother had fixed while huddled down underneath their wagon.

Pa had made sure to park the wagon away from Crabbage and close to the Allertons and the Ellises.

"I still don't like the idea of having to pay someone a million dollars for ferry service," Ephraim told his wife Abigail, as Tyler overheard while biting off a piece of jerky. "I think I showed that ferryman a thing or two by crossing the wagon box without having to pay for a ferry. Yep, I showed him good, I feel."

"It wasn't a million dollars," Abigail retorted. "It would have been four dollars at the Platte Crossing. Well worth it if you ask me to avoid that quicksand I heard about in the Platte, and spare me the worry I felt when we crossed without the ferry. Someday, Ephraim, I swear you're bull-headedness is going to get you in some real trouble at one of these river crossings. Just you wait."

"I'm telling you, Abby, I'm getting tired of these high-way-robbing ferrymen who think we got no alternative but to pay 'em," Ephraim insisted. "Why I got me half a mind to go first across the next river we come to, and show everybody behind us that they don't need no ferry."

"That's right, you got half a mind, Ephraim Allerton, if you think you're gonna risk driving our team and our wagon across when we come to a really deep river," Abigail declared, hands on her hips. "Some of the rivers up ahead are a lot deeper than the Platte. We could lose everything we got if the current breaks our wagon apart. And how you know you won't drown? And where would that leave me if you did?"

"I don't plan on . . ."

Tyler turned his attention back to Pa.

"We got plenty of money for ferries," Pa murmured. "It's not a problem for us. I think we're going to hit it lucky with Drake and Dru anyway. They're holding up well, unlike some other folks' teams. I don't think we'll need to buy new oxen at Fort Laramie. That'll save us a ton of money."

Tyler drove the team the next day while Pa walked. Penny read one of her books in the wagon. Scott's Bluff looked close enough to reach in an hour. Instead it took all day. As the day ended, the wagon train reached Scott's Bluff.

Buckman called a halt for a day. He rode up and down the line of wagons shouting, "Well done! We've made it to Scott's Bluff and we're on schedule to be at Independence Rock by the Fourth of July. You've all earned a day of rest and relaxation."

With the wagon train circled up beneath the red-gray-brown Scotts Bluff promontory, an air of celebration took over. Bruce Mallory hauled out his fiddle and the party was on, except for Tyler. Pa wanted him to watch Drake and Dru and the other oxen as they grazed on better grass farther away from the much-used Scotts Bluff wagon campsite.

His insides seethed as he saw in the distance Rachelle dancing with Van Buren Colledge and then Brent McGuigan. At the very least, Tyler felt, he should ask Rachelle to dance. Even if she said no for whatever reason, at least she would know that he was still interested in her. As it was, Tyler worried, with every young guy in the whole wagon train lining up to dance with Rachelle, except for him, she would probably think he'd forgotten all about her, if she thought about him at all.

Tyler could not bring himself to dislike Van Buren Colledge. After all, Van Buren had helped him out with Crabbage. Still, Tyler saw Van Buren Colledge as one of his arch-rivals for Rachelle, along with Brent McGuigan. Colledge had practically stolen Rachelle away that other night. After awhile, Tyler noted Brent dancing with Rachelle once more. Well, at least she hadn't completely settled yet on either Van Buren or Brent, apparently.

Tyler looked around for Penny. Maybe she wouldn't mind watching Drake and Dru for a few minutes just long enough for him to ask Rachelle to do one dance with him. He screened his eyes from the sun setting over impressive Scott's Bluff rising at an angle out of the surrounding plain and he looked around for Penny. He saw her sitting on the ground next to Alain, reading stories from her books to a rapt collection of fifteen or more children. A few of the mothers stood in back, looking gratefully at Penny, her long dark hair wrapped in a pony tail. The children seemed enthralled with Penny, and he did not feel it would be right to interfere with Penny's growing collection of admirers.

Sighing, Tyler looked at Drake and Dru and Pa's other two teams of oxen, placidly munching on the buffalo grass near the reeds along the North Platte. He watched the oxen for the next hour, trying to avoid looking at the dance. It was too painful to watch Rachelle with other young men as the sun slipped beneath the golden western horizon.

"I'll watch Drake and Dru and the other oxen." Pa finally approached, rifle in hand. "You go have yourself some fun."

"Thanks, Pa!"

Tyler hurried toward the dance. Rachelle was still there, but she looked to be leaving, wrapping a white lace shawl around her shoulders and heading back to her family's wagon. Tyler hurried up to her.

"Rachelle, you want to dance?" Tyler asked breathlessly.

"Tyler Linders, where you been hiding?" Rachelle demanded. She playfully punched him in the shoulder. "I was looking for you earlier, but I guess you felt you had better things to do, huh?"

"My Pa made me watch over our oxen while they were grazing," Tyler responded, his thin face reddening. "I couldn't get away till just now."

Rachelle's face fell. "Well, after dancing for over two hours, I'm kinda tired, Tyler."

Tyler made no effort to hide the disappointment on his face.

"But hey, a bunch of us, Billie Kay, Brent, Van Buren, Tim, Justin Maybrie, that Hapsburg girl, and one or two others, we're going try to climb to the top of Scott's Bluff tomorrow. You want to join us?" Rachelle placed a hand on Tyler's shoulder. "You got to join us tomorrow. It'll be great fun."

Tyler was ready to melt with joy. "Why—why sure, Rachelle," he declared through his broad toothy grin. "Wouldn't miss it. Count me in. Definitely."

"Bring something to eat and share," Rachelle instructed. "Doesn't have to be much, some bread, a bit of dried fruit, whatever. We're going to have a picnic on the top of Scott's Bluff, or as close to it as we can get. I heard you can see a hundred miles in any direction from there."

"I wouldn't doubt it," Tyler agreed. "I'll be looking forward to it."

Rachelle waved him a goodbye. "You better be there, Tyler." She winked at him and added in a low, coy tone. "It won't be as much fun if you're not there. See you tomorrow."

With a wide smile that sparkled her blue eyes and fair skin, Rachelle took her leave of him.

Tyler needed nothing more to happen to him that whole evening. He couldn't have planned it any better. Whatever might have happened with Rachelle if he'd danced with her, the result could not have been better than what had just happened. Rachelle thought he was special, apparently very special.

Walking on the edge of the dance, Tyler scarcely noticed the music or the dancers, his insides were so giddy.

"I heard you talking vis Rachelle about going to Scott's Bluff vis us tomorrow. It vill be a lot of fun, *ja?*"

"Huh?"

Tyler's reverie was interrupted. He turned around. There was buckskin-clad Angelique Hapsburg looking at him, her long brown hair flowing down the front of her deerskin outfit. Her brown eyes looked quiet, interested.

"Oh, *ja*, I mean, yeah," Tyler said absently, turning away.

"It vill be much fun, I think. I vill be excited to see the view all around."

"Yeah, that'll be fun, I guess," Tyler again said absently.

He drifted off, but he felt Angelique continuing to watch him. Tyler thought he would see what Penny was up to again. Pa had asked him to sort of drift in and out of the picture when she was with Alain.

Tyler found Alain still with Penny, reading stories to small children.

"'N' is the 15th letter of the alphabet," Penny told the children. "The letter can stand for Nancy, for nurse, for napkin or for nose."

"What are you doing, Penny?" Tyler asked. "Are you school marming now?"

"The kids like my stories and all," Penny said defensively, pushing her hexagonal-shaped glasses up.

"Yeah, we do," little Jenny Clevenger said.

"And the mothers appreciate having a place to send their kids to keep 'em busy," Alain declared.

"Reckon they do," Tyler said. He looked at Alain and pointed a thumb in the direction of Scott's Bluff. "You and Penny going on that picnic tomorrow?"

"What picnic?" Penny asked.

"A number of us are going, me, Rachelle, Brent, Billie Kay, and about a half-dozen others," Tyler said. "We're going to climb to the top of Scott's Bluff and have a picnic up there."

Alain leaned forward, rubbing his clear chin. "I heard something about that. You sure it's safe up there? On those warm rocks closer to the sun, that's perfect rattlesnake habitat."

"Then bring your gun and shoot a few of 'em," Tyler replied. "It'll be a good time."

"Let's go tomorrow, Alain," Penny beseeched, her hands clasped under her chin.

"Might be fun at that," Alain agreed. "If I do shoot a rattlesnake, I hear they taste like chicken."

"If you kill a rattlesnake, I'm going to keep it and shove it down either Milon Crabbage or Brinton Stonehouse's throat," Tyler declared. "I think before this journey is over, they're probably going to force us to deal with them."

* * *

It was a hard climb. The elevation combined with the upward slope made it real exercise getting to the top of the Scott's Bluff incline. Tyler worked up a sweat doing it. All of the others made it, however much they huffed and puffed in the thin air.

Rachelle, Angelique, Billie Kay Ellis, Van Buren Colledge, Justin Maybrie, Quimby Freding, Brent McGuigan, and Alain and Penny, all made it to the edge of Scott's Bluff.

Kelly Jay had to stay behind, a bit of altitude sickness, Billie Kay had said.

"You can see a hundred miles from here—two hundred miles!" Rachelle exclaimed, shielding her eyes from the sun. Her yellow bonnet hung down around her neck.

Tyler thought Rachelle looked spectacular in a pair of brown culottes and a lace-fronted white blouse. She had a light blue ribbon in her hair. He intended to play it cool, though. He would be friendly with Rachelle, as he would be friendly with them all. But he would not try to monopolize her. Brent and Van Buren would never let that happen anyway, and a too-obvious competition for Rachelle's attentions might make her feel uncomfortable.

Tyler settled down to enjoying a smoked ham sandwich from a circular basket he had brought. He tried to sit fairly close to Rachelle, as did Brent and Van Buren. Billie Kay sat with Justin Maybrie, a thin-bearded and muscular, tanned young fellow. Billie Kay laughed and joked with Justin, apparently having found her man. Off to one side, each alone, sat Quimby Freding and Angelique Hapsburg, quietly eating dried fruit.

Alain and Penny sat together overlooking the bluff, facing west with their backs to the others. Alain had an arm around Penny's shoulders.

Tyler looked at the scenic view. Indeed, the view extended for hundreds of square miles in any direction. He could not quite see all the way to Fort Laramie, but the panorama was spectacular. Red-brown hills and far-distant outcroppings toward the south and west beckoned, as if showing a glimpse of the promise ever westward. Again, Tyler felt a sense of the promise of the West Coast, a land of abundant rain, greenery everywhere, tall trees, and fertile soil. The very landscape led them onward in thought.

"You're Irish, aren't you?"

Tyler's thoughts were interrupted by Van Buren's question to Brent McGuigan as they sat cross-legged on the hard ground.

"Well, my parents are Irish," Brent replied. "They came over, actually, well before the famine of the 1840s. I guess they saw it coming twenty years ago. I was born in this country. I am an American from the start. That's why I don't have much accent."

"Really? You raise a very good question, Brent," Van Buren said, biting into an apple. "Do immigrants' children *become* American over time, or *are* they American?"

"Now what's that supposed to mean?" Brent demanded, putting down a plate of dried cherries. "I wasn't trying to raise a question."

"Oh nothing, nothing," Van Buren hastened to say, shaking a hand. "I'm sorry. Forget I said anything."

Tyler noted that Van Buren looked furtively at Rachelle, making a split-second of eye contact with her. Van Buren had been trying to make a subtle point about his rival Brent McGuigan for Rachelle to consider. Rachelle was smart and intelligent. She would grasp the point Van Buren had been trying to make without him having to be blunt about it. Was Irish-American Brent McGuigan really someone that Rachelle's Anglo-Saxon Protestant parents would ever want her to actually marry?

Brent leaned back on his hands, his suspenders stretched taut over his muscular frame and thin-striped shirt. "You know, Van Buren, I do wish I had your money. I'll bet back East you had every young woman in the state of Tennessee wanting to marry you. I'll bet it'll be the same in Oregon. You'll have your pick of dozens of young, beautiful women. You'll have dozens of young women fighting over you."

Tyler saw Brent make eye contact with Rachelle. Brent had been trying to make a point about Van Buren for Rachelle to consider, a point she would grasp. Van Buren Colledge had plenty of money, yes, but that would make him desirable above all other young men, and the competition for him could be stiff and merciless. Rachelle would now presumably wonder if she really wanted to deal with a fray like that.

All this helped his cause with Rachelle, Tyler reflected. Let Brent and Van Buren tear each other down in Rachelle's mind. Tyler figured he would be the ultimate beneficiary with Rachelle.

Brent's point did not escape Van Buren. "Well, yeah," Van Buren muttered. "I'd rather have money than not have it."

"My folks have always had enough," Brent declared, leaning forward and scowling.

"Yeah, but do *you?*" Van Buren demanded.

"Shut up, you two!" Angelique shouted. "Vee have bigger problems now than your gamesmanship. Look!"

Tyler turned to glance behind him in the direction Angelique pointed. What he saw startled and numbed him. There, blocking the only path down from Scott's Bluff, a dozen Sioux men sat on horses, watching the picnic gathering. Tyler jumped to his feet, as did Rachelle, Alain, Penny, and the others.

The Sioux, with bows and arrows, sat their horses with stark, unmoving, tight-lipped, expression-less faces. Tyler assumed they were Sioux, for their clothing was different from the Pawnees, with more bangles and thin chains about their necks. The Sioux appeared to be assessing him and his friends, gauging them, trying to determine what the white young people were up to, and what their next move should be as they faced the white young people.

Tyler licked his dry lips nervously and breathed heavily. What a time to be without either his Sharps rifle or his Colt revolver. He saw Rachelle gulp. Billie Kay held a hand to her mouth as Justin put an arm around her shoulders protectively. This time, it was just them and the Indians. This time, there was no Buckman in sight. This time, there was no convenient white missionary to act as an intermediary. This time, Tyler realized, it was just him and his companions facing potentially hostile Indians directly, with nothing and nobody in between.

CHAPTER ELEVEN

"Try to relax," Angelique told them all, taking a deep breath. "They don't have war paint on. They were probably just out hunting buffalo and antelope. I think that's all they were doing, I think."

One Sioux in the middle moved his horse a couple of steps forward. "*Ota wasicula ekta kaipsilyalake wana!*" he shouted, his face bitter. He pointed a stiff finger all around him. He lowered his arm and looked with a pouty lip at the young people, as if expecting some sort of response, and it had better be a good one.

Brent gulped. "I think h-he was saying h-hello."

"That's not what he was saying," Justin declared quietly.

"I-I hope he wasn't saying he wants our scalps," Van Buren said.

Tyler had no idea what exactly the Sioux hunter-warrior had said, but he guessed it was something along the lines of, "This is our land, not yours. What are you trespassers doing here?"

Angelique took a step forward, with her right hand extended across her chest, palm downward. She would make a great white Indian squaw, or else her long brown hair would make a trophy scalp, but Tyler figured she probably knew that.

Two of the Sioux gave the same gesture, somewhat disgustedly, saying nothing. The other Sioux watched stoically, including the one who had spoken.

"I think they'll be satisfied just to do some trading," Angelique murmured.

"We're not traders," Justin complained. "We don't have any trade goods."

"We got food," Angelique declared, looking around. "I'm pretty sure that's what they're wanting."

"Let's hope you're right," Brent said quietly.

Quimby Freding grabbed his wooden lunch bucket and started moving toward the Sioux hunter on his far right.

Rachelle caught her breath. "Quimby, be careful," she begged.

"O-oh, you-you think I'm not gonna be?" Quimby responded.

Gingerly, Quimby made his way forward with half-steps. He opened one lid of his lunch bucket in invitation to the nearest Sioux. Quimby tried to half-smile, likely to keep his nerves in check.

The nearest Sioux suddenly got down off his horse and stepped forward. He grabbed Quimby's lunch bucket and looked inside. The Sioux peered at the lunch bucket contents for a couple of seconds, then pulled out a smoked ham sandwich on wheat bread. The Sioux hunter threw the bucket down and threw away the bread, preferring instead to bite deeply into the two smoked ham slices and cheese.

In three swallows, the Sioux had the ham and cheese down as Quimby watched and gulped.

Quimby started to back away. The Sioux hunter pulled a blanket off his horse that had thunderbird and underwater panther designs on it. He put it around Quimby's shoulders and shoved Quimby away.

Tyler had stood next to Quimby and he surmised that everyone would expect it was his turn next. He grabbed his lunch basket. Three apples were left from his lunch, that he had intended sharing with Rachelle. Instead, he would give all three apples to the Sioux.

He stepped forward cautiously, as Quimby had done. No fast moves here. The Sioux were armed and unpredictable. They could decide to do anything in an instant. Tyler approached the mounted Sioux hunter next to the one with whom Quimby had exchanged goods.

The Sioux hunter dismounted and took the lunch basket from Tyler. The Sioux hunter looked inside and took out an apple to look at it. The Sioux inspected the apple, muttered a word or two to his companions, and half-smiled.

Tyler gathered that he liked apples, thank God.

The Sioux put the apple back in the basket and suddenly from his belt sash he took out a knife. Tyler leaped backward to avoid being stabbed. All of the Sioux roared with laughter.

The Sioux who had taken the apple fingered the blade of the knife as if admiring its sharpness. The Sioux then turned the knife around, and, handle first, presented it to Tyler.

"He wants to trade you his knife for your food, Tyler," Angelique said. "Smile and say yes, Tyler. Say yes."

Tyler forced a nervous grin and took the knife very carefully from the Sioux Indian. The Sioux smiled and took the three apples, leaving the basket behind. Tyler grabbed his empty lunch basket, and put his new Indian knife inside one of his suspenders. He tried to walk away as casually as he could, without giving an impression of being scared.

"Like Angelique said, they just want to trade," Tyler remarked with as much nonchalance as he could muster.

"Let's not stretch our luck too soon," Angelique warned. "Keep doing what we've been doing and keep hoping."

"Saying a prayer might not be a bad idea, either," Billie Kay murmured.

"I'll go next," Justin said as Tyler returned. Justin grabbed a few dried orange slices from his bucket. "Wish I had more than this left."

"Here, here, take a couple of sandwiches," Billie Kay said breathlessly. She put the sandwiches into Justin's bucket.

"Take my stuff as well," Rachelle said. She thrust a wheat bread sandwich and several slices of cheese at Justin.

Justin carried his lunch bucket down toward the Sioux. He walked more quickly, Tyler observed, possibly with greater confidence now. Three of the Sioux dismounted and helped themselves to the contents of Justin's bucket. For his trouble, Justin received a buffalo blanket.

"Let's go next," Brent said to Van Buren.

"I'm all out of food," Van Buren said, gulping.

"Then give 'em your shirt bands, something," Brent urged. "Just try giving 'em nothing and take your chances on what happens to you."

Brent approached with two pears and some jerked beef. Van Buren took off his purple shirt garters to present to the next pair of Indians. The two Sioux dismounted and approached Brent and Van Buren.

One of the Sioux grabbed Van Buren's garters and put them on as Van Buren fell backwards, trying to get away quickly. The Sioux hunter put one purple garter on each arm.

"Eeee-yewwwayy!" the gartered Sioux shouted in exultation, turning to his fellow hunters to show off his new arm decorations.

The other Sioux hunter took Brent's jerky and pears. He gave Brent a knife in return. Van Buren received nothing.

Tyler observed that only Angelique, Alain and Penny were left.

"I've got plenty of food," Alain said. "I didn't eat much because I wasn't really hungry."

Penny ran her tongue over her lower lip nervously. Nevertheless, when Alain and Angelique started forward, Penny went right with them.

Tyler watched with held breath what happened next. The last Indian dismounted and stood beside the other two dismounted Sioux. Angelique exchanged more sign language with the Sioux as the three Indian hunters helped themselves to the contents of Alain and Angelique's baskets. Angelique gestured toward Penny.

The Indians nodded, looked at Penny, and turned to wave at someone behind them. Tyler looked past the Indian hunters and saw that they were not alone by themselves. About a dozen other Sioux on ponies and with attached travois had watched the scene from well behind the first group of Indians.

An old Indian woman pulled a pony forward dragging a travois with a large bundle on it. When the old Indian woman neared the hunters she stopped and opened the bundle carefully.

Tyler walked over to the scene just to be near Penny and Alain.

"Wow!" Penny exclaimed.

The wrinkled Indian woman pulled items out of the bundle. She pulled four multi-colored Indian shirts out of the bundle. Two of the shirts were buffalo-skin, with thunderbird, underwater panther, and solar, star, and moon designs on them. The other two shirts were silk, no doubt gotten in trade, one red with geometric designs on it, and the other green with multi-colored stripes.

"Wow!" Penny said again. "They're beautiful!"

The elderly Sioux woman smiled at Penny and pointed to her while holding the shirts. "They yours all now," the elderly Sioux woman said.

"Thank you," Penny exclaimed. "Thank you very, very much. May I try one on?"

"They yours all now," the Sioux woman repeated.

Penny took the red silk shirt and put it on over her calico dress.

"They are gorgeous," Alain agreed. He took the other three shirts to hold for Penny.

The Indian woman took a couple more buffalo hide shirts out of the bundle. "They yours all now," she told Penny. Then, the woman pulled two pairs of children's moccasins out of the bundle and a pair of Indian leggings to give to Penny.

"Thank you again," Penny said excitedly. She gave them to Alain to hold onto.

The Sioux woman smiled again and pointed a finger upward for Penny to wait some more. She reached back into her bundle and pulled out several chains of beads—red, blue, green chains and beads. The Indian woman put them all around Penny's neck.

"They yours all now," the Sioux woman reiterated.

Penny looked at the sparkling Indian jewelry draped around her neck and over her shimmering silk shirt. Penny's radiant smile indicated how fully she understood the honors that were being bestowed upon her and how deeply she appreciated it.

Tyler heard the sound of horses rounding the bend of Scott's Bluff. It was Buckman riding with his rifle out. A dozen armed men rode with him. Pa was among them, as were Dennis Palmerston and Ephraim Allerton.

A bunch of men ready to shoot was the last thing the situation needed. "It's all right!" Tyler yelled at Buckman and

Pa. "We're just doing some trading and I daresay we're getting the better end of the deal here."

Buckman pulled up on his horse and raised his rifle to signal the men behind him to halt. "Just the same, I'll keep my rifle ready till this is over," Buckman hollered.

The Sioux woman took six long silver and turquoise chains out of the bundle.

Angelique's eyes went wide. "In the Indian economy, these items are priceless," she declared. "They must have been obtained in trade with the Navajos further south."

The Sioux woman smiled anew at Penny. "They yours all now," she said, grinning at Penny and placing the silver and turquoise chains around Penny's neck.

"What the . . ." Pa exclaimed.

Next, the Sioux woman took five solid gold chains with beaten solid gold panther pendants out of the bundle and put them around Penny's neck.

George Ellis's eyes nearly popped out of his head at sight of the gold jewelry. "The Sioux got gold?" Ellis declared. "Let's ask 'em where they found it. They can't have gotten it all the way from California. Let's ask 'em where that gold is from."

"Let's not," Buckman sternly responded. "Even if any of 'em spoke English, and they could tell us where they got that gold, do you honestly think they would tell us?"

The Sioux woman took two solid gold baubles out of the bundle. She clasped one of the baubles to Penny's long brown hair. The Sioux woman took her blue cloth headband and put it on Penny's head. She attached the other gold bauble to the headband.

The Sioux woman stepped back, smiling, to admire Penny and her shimmering collection of jewelry. "Very beauty," she said.

Penny fingered the silver, turquoise and gold chains to admire them. "Wow," she whispered in awe. "I can't believe this." She looked at the kindly Sioux woman. "Thank you, thank you a thousand times."

Tyler saw Pa on horseback gaping at Penny. Pa leaned toward Buckman and said, "I can't believe what I'm seeing. How much—how much is all that jewelry Penny is loaded down with worth?"

Buckman stretched forward in his saddle to inspect Penny's collection of Indian jewelry more closely. "Out here, in the middle of nowhere, it's debatable. But if we were in New York City or back East somewheres, that jewelry Penny is wearing, I'd say, would fetch every nickel of ten thousand dollars easily, maybe even fifteen thousand. Why you asking? You thinking about selling it?"

"Ain't mine to sell," Pa replied in breathless wonderment. "That stuff belongs to Penny. It's hers to sell if she wants to. Somehow, though, I don't think that's real terrible likely."

Tyler walked around the Sioux to get closer to Buckman. "What's this all about?" Tyler asked. "We gave them a bit of food, some meat, a few pieces of fruit, not a whole lot more. Why are they giving us all this valuable stuff in exchange?"

"I'll explain in a minute or two," Buckman said. "Let's let the Sioux leave first."

The old woman took her empty bundle and walked away. The Sioux hunters remounted their horses. All of them turned around to leave. As they left, the Sioux exchanged stony glances with Buckman, Pa, Dennis Palmerston, Ephraim, and the others with them. Both sides silently looked each other up and down, scowling, indicating no love lost between any of them.

One of the Sioux pointed a finger at himself. "La-ko-ta," the Sioux hunter declared.

When all of the Sioux were out of earshot Buckman said, "Yeah, right, whatever you say, fella." He looked at Tyler, then at Penny and Alain, at Angelique, and then at Rachelle,

Quimby and the others behind them. "Let me explain what I think—I think—just happened here. The Sioux or Lakota or whatever they call themselves were buying our cooperation. We're a very large wagon train and they don't want us hunting their buffalo that they need for survival. By accepting their gifts, you've indicated agreement to their terms."

"We weren't—"

"It's all right, Tyler," Buckman said, stroking his now bushy beard. "We've got plenty of food. No one is starving. We don't need to kill any more buffalo after all the hunting Press, Silas and some of the other men have been doing lately. We can agree to what the Sioux want in exchange for them not harassing us or stealing our livestock. The Sioux will spread the word to leave us alone. It's a fair exchange. We won't have any trouble with the Sioux on this trip. That's a good thing you've all accomplished. We'll have plenty of other things to worry about as we head into the desert, but thanks to all of you, we won't have to worry about the Sioux."

Tyler turned to grin at his companions. "Well, thanks to Quimby for implementing a smart idea," Tyler said, wanting to show up both Brent and Van Buren.

"Thanks to Angelique for suggesting it," Quimby said.

"Yes," Billie Kay agreed. "Thank you, Angelique, for knowing what to do and keeping your cool about you. Your knowledge of the Indians saved us from acting scared and running and who knows what the Indians would have done in that case."

Angelique smiled self-consciously.

"I think we'd all better get back to the wagons," Buckman declared. "We don't need to be out here stretching our luck."

* * *

Tyler sensed the dance that evening wasn't quite as much fun for everyone as it should have been after a day of relaxation. Some of the emigrants were indeed celebrating and rejoicing that peace had been guaranteed with the Sioux. Tyler and the other young people who had been at the picnic on Scott's Bluff received thanks aplenty from others in the wagon train for ensuring that the Sioux would not harm any of them. But others, friends and family of the other young people who had had the nerve-wracking encounter with the Sioux, and the men who had come riding to rescue them if necessary, spent a lot of time talking about what might have been but for quick thinking on the part of Angelique and Quimby. People had fun, but it was as though some of them were forcing themselves to have fun.

The unnerving encounter with the Sioux had cast a pall over the proceedings.

Searching for Rachelle, Tyler observed Billie Kay Ellis and Justin Maybrie holding hands but not dancing with their glum expressions. The encounter with the Sioux had been discomfiting, but, still, they should have been happier to be back safe and sound. Tyler didn't know Justin very well, but he still considered Billie Kay a friend.

"What's the matter, you two?" Tyler asked. "You look like you've both seen ghosts. Was it really that bad meeting the Sioux?"

"I haven't seen a ghost but I think my father has," Billie Kay somberly said. "When he saw that gold the Sioux had, the fever gripped him again."

"The fever?" Tyler asked.

"Gold fever," Billie Kay clarified disgustedly, running her fingers through her long dark hair. She sighed and looked at Justin. "He's been wanting to go to California, not Oregon. He figures now, though, there's gold somewhere right around here. If there is, he won't take another step toward Oregon.

If there isn't gold around here, then I'm sure my father will want to split off from the wagon train and head to California. That's why he wasn't all broken up when Ma died. Ma didn't want to go on this trip at all. She only agreed to go if Pa agreed that we'd head to Oregon, not California where all those wild mining camps are. Now, though, with Ma dead, there's nothing stopping him from heading to California."

Sighing, Tyler pulled on his suspenders. He had no answer for Billie Kay. He could only nod, purse his thin lips and move on, aware that if Justin's parents were determined to stay the course for Oregon, Billie Kay could face the heart being ripped out of her in another five hundred miles or so when the two trails split off.

He observed Penny briefly, with Alain, and with the awe-struck children admiring Penny in her Indian jewelry and clothing even as she tried to read to them sitting cross-legged on the ground. In her Indian moccasins, headband, clothing, and bangles, and with her tanned skin, Penny looked more Sioux than white except for her hexagonal glasses.

"Settle down, kids," Penny requested, smiling.

"Ain't easy," one little girl said, "what with you all shiny and everything."

Penny laughed. "I'm not the sun."

Finally, Tyler espied Rachelle, right by her wagon. She sat alone on the ground, slumped with her head pressed against her knees. Tyler started walking toward her to ask her to dance, but as he neared Rachelle he heard her sobbing.

Here was a chance, if he played it right, to really move several steps forward with her. Rachelle looked up at him, seemingly with her tear-drenched eyes inviting him to join her.

Tyler did not have to be asked twice. He sat down on the ground next to Rachelle and, cautiously, put his hand on her shoulder. She looked at him but did not shrink away. Tyler felt emboldened.

"What's the matter, Rachelle?" he murmured.

Rachelle leaned back, wiping the tears off her face and trying to compose herself. "I can't—can't help thinking what might have happened today," she said. "I've heard stories about women who were kidnapped by Indians. I've heard stories, Tyler, about—about—rape. Or worse. Sometimes Indians like to burn their captives alive. That could have happened to us."

"Hey, it didn't happen," Tyler said as gently as he could. He kept his hand on her shoulder and gave her a couple of comforting pats, looking into her moist blue eyes. "Lots of bad things could have happened to us before now, but didn't. We could have been among those who died of the cholera, but we weren't." He bowed his head, then looked up at her again. "Remember that, Rachelle, and think on it."

"I will," she promised, nodding. "But thank God they didn't kill Quimby when he approached them, or you, or any of us. There was no way to tell ahead of time what those Indians were gonna do."

"I know, I know," Tyler agreed, patting her shoulder again. "But what could have happened, and what did happen, are two different things."

"Well, yeah," Van Buren declared.

Tyler saw Brent and Van Buren approaching, belatedly, to be with Rachelle. He had no interest in competing with them. If Brent and Van Buren were coming, he was leaving. Tyler rose, wanting to send a subtle message to Rachelle, that he was above competing and would not involve himself in a triangle or quadrangle situation. He was above it all. Let Brent and Van Buren beat each other up verbally. If Rachelle wanted more of him, then she needed to distance herself from Brent and Van Buren.

"Take care, Rachelle," he murmured.

"Take care, Tyler," Rachelle said quietly, "and thank you—for being there for me."

Tyler nodded, half-smiling. He walked past Brent and Van Buren. "Fellas," he acknowledged them casually.

The party broke up early. Tyler again volunteered for the first night watch. It would continue to separate him from Van Buren and Brent, and from anyone else who had designs on Rachelle. As darkness fell and Tyler walked with his Sharps rifle on the outskirts of the circled wagons he saw Angelique again, also on the first watch. Interesting that she seemed to enjoy the night watch so much and that he saw her so often when he was on night watch duty. She crossed paths with him.

"How is it that you know so much about Indians any-way?" Tyler demanded of Angelique, his brow tensing. "It's like you know more about wild Indians than all the rest of us put together. How can that be? You're from Germany or somewhere, right?"

"Austria. I'm from Austria," Angelique said with an excited smile. "I haf books, many, many books I haf, Tyler. Vestern America is a fascinating place. I couldn't stop reading about it in Austria, and I knew I haf to see it for myself. It is a fascinating subject and I haf many books vith me. I'd be happy to share them vith you, Tyler. You'd probably learn a lot and it vould help you."

"Yeah, well, maybe."

"Vould you like to borrow some of my books, Tyler? They are in English, mos' of them. I'd be happy to lend them to you!"

"Well, maybe sometime, maybe." Tyler turned to walk onward, then half-turned back toward Angelique. "Let me give you some advice—learn to speak proper English all the time. You sometimes slide back into a weird accent. It's 'would,' not 'vould,' and 'with,' not 'vith'."

"See you, Tyler," Angelique said, waving a hand. "I vill—vill—will—let you borrow any of my books you want, anytime. Feel free to ask. Just let me know."

Tyler walked on, but he had a sense again that Angelique's quiet eyes were watching his every move.

"Just let me know, Tyler," she said hopefully.

Tyler saw Pa observing him from a distance with a scowl. "Don't be out too late tonight, Tyler," Pa demanded. "I'll need you tomorrow morning early when we get started again."

"I'll be there when you need me, Pa."

Tyler continued on his rounds, past more of the seventy-six wagons remaining. Men in cotton shirts and suspenders, and women in bonnets, talked in low tones around their campfires, about Indians, about the approaching desert, about how the worst of the journey lay ahead. Children scurried around, playing hide-and-go-seek, marbles, or settling down to sleep.

The Clevenger kids caught Tyler's attention. Agnes Clevenger, all of ten years old, looked to have fixed a pot of beans for her and her siblings to eat quietly. Agnes scooped out a plateful of beans and salt pork for little Jenny.

"I miss mommy and Pa," Jenny said tremulously.

"I know you do, muffin," Agnes murmured comfortingly, giving Jenny a precious hug. "We all do. But we have each other still . . ."

Tyler moved on, past wagons which were dark and quiet, their occupants apparently already having retired for the night in their tents. He neared the Colledge wagon, with its oversized water barrel. All was quiet, the elder Colledges either retired for the night or else still visiting with the Zurich family, as Tyler had seen earlier

He heard a low muffled voice talking on the other side of the Colledge wagon. Tyler would not have thought anything of it except he noted that as he approached the Colledge wagon, the voice suddenly stopped, as if not wanting to be heard.

"Hmm." Tyler raised his rifle carefully. Something was going on in the darkness. He wondered if he should investigate. Was it an Indian sneaking into camp and trying to maybe steal one or more of the Colledges' eight horses? Indians often tried to steal horses and stock in the deep dark of night. Tyler asked himself if he should stay safe and move on, pretending he'd heard nothing.

No. Ignoring trouble was not what night watchmen were supposed to do. Tyler knew he was duty-bound to see what sort of trouble was brewing near the Colledge wagon. He resolved to investigate and take action. Also, the Colledges had money. Everybody knew it. Maybe, someone was trying to see if the Colledges' strongbox could be broken into.

CHAPTER TWELVE

If there was real trouble afoot, he would fire a warning rifle shot to alert Buckman and then grab his waist pistol. Tyler walked about twenty feet past the Colledge wagon and then doubled back between a pair of other wagons to look back at the Colledge wagon and see who was there and what mischief they were up to.

A shadowy form had grasped one horse's bridle and was carefully and quietly leading it out from behind the wagon into the open.

"Van Buren?" Tyler asked.

The shadowy form froze, as did Tyler's raw nerves.

"Mista—Mista Tyla?"

It was Tuck, the Colledges' slave.

Tyler relaxed and lowered his rifle. "Tuck, what're you doing?" he asked.

Tuck put a quick finger to his lips. "Shh—not so loud. I is leavin'."

"Leaving? To go where?"

"I's leavin' for good," Tuck declared in a low tone. He nodded toward the horse he was leading. "I was jist tryin' to calm Ol' Gray here down a bit. I was jist goin' to borrow him for 'while."

"Yeah? And when were you thinking about returning him?"

Tuck breathed heavily. "Please, Mista Tyla, don' give me away. I'm a free man now, on free territory. I's gonna find them Injuns and join up with 'em. I'm a free man now, not belongin' to anybody. I done served Mista Colledge and his fam'ly for over twenty years now, with not one nickel of pay as a slave. I paid my dues. I'm owed a horse at least, ain't I? Well, ain't I?"

Tyler didn't know what to say. He lowered his rifle still further. If Tuck was leaving, well, yeah, he would need a horse. Setting out alone on foot in this wild country would be suicidal.

Apparently surmising that Tyler wasn't going to give him away, Tuck led the horse forward and between the Colledge wagon and the wagon behind it in the circle.

Ahead, maybe fifteen wagons in the fire-lit distance, Tyler saw Van Buren heading this direction, walking with Rachelle. Tyler looked at Tuck. "Get outa here quickly, will you? I'll try and hold Van Buren off as long as I can."

Tuck saw the danger. "Just distract him for a couple of minutes. That's all I's needin' to get clean outa here. Nobody'll know that you helped me."

Tyler hoped that Tuck could lead his horse far enough into the darkness to take off without anyone seeing him clearly and being able to follow. Tyler headed as fast as he could walk for Van Buren and Rachelle. They weren't holding hands. That was good. They were still just friends, although Van Buren surely wanted more.

"Hey, Van Buren, Rachelle."

Rachelle smiled. "Hey, Tyler."

"Tyler," Van Buren said with somewhat less enthusiasm.

"Out for a walk?" Tyler asked.

"As you can see," Van Buren said.

"Van Buren and I were just debating what's the hardest challenge we've all faced so far," Rachelle said spritely. "What do you think, Tyler—was it O'Fallon's Bluff, that two-mile-long California Hill, or Windlass Hill?"

Tyler wished he knew what Rachelle's opinion had been so that he could agree with her. "Well, um, O'Fallon's Bluff was quite a trudge uphill, but not for that long," he said, taking care to gauge Rachelle's reaction. "California Hill a hundred miles back, um, wasn't that high, just too long a trail to the top. I think Windlass Hill was the toughest challenge we've all faced to this point."

"That's what I said!" Rachelle declared, beaming. She looked at Van Buren with a proud smirk of triumph, causing Van Buren to look at Tyler with a pout.

Tyler did not want to cut Van Buren down too far, remembering his previous help with Crabbage. "Well, the reason I say that is because Windlass Hill forced all of us to work together," Tyler declared, thinking fast. "Remember how all of the men and even a lot of the women worked as teams to hold onto the axle ropes for all of the wagons, even wagons that belonged to total strangers, to keep them from going down the other side too fast."

"That's what I thought as well," Rachelle agreed. "People started seeing one another as being in this all together as one united group, really for the first time. Van Buren was also just telling me that we're going to have to start conserving our water more carefully. Desert up ahead. People are going to need each other."

"No rivers there, and it never rains," Van Buren said disgustedly.

"There's rain all right," Tyler declared. "The problem then becomes the Trail turning to thick mud—yellow gumbo, I think I heard it was called—and wagons getting stuck in it."

Rachelle seemed worried. "You think though, that if some people do run out of water, that others with water will share some of it?"

Not a chance in hell. "I'm sure they will," Tyler said cheerfully. No sense upsetting Rachelle.

"They will if you come at them with a gun," Van Buren muttered. "Mark my words, once supplies and water start giving out past Fort Laramie, you just watch how quickly any teamwork disappears and people start turning against each other Your good friend today may be the guy who shoots you tomorrow if you got water and he's dying of thirst." Van Buren folded his arms. "You know, Tyler, aren't you supposed to be making rounds or something?"

"Right." Out of the corner of an eye, Tyler saw only darkness. Tuck was probably safely vanished into the night by now. He could let Van Buren continue on with Rachelle. The missing horse would likely not be discovered until morning.

"Yeah, I better be moving on," Tyler declared.

"See you, Tyler," Rachelle said, smiling at him. "Always good talking with you."

"Thanks. Rachelle, Van Buren, see you both later."

Tyler moved along, content that Tuck had merely done what he was entitled to do. Once they had left Missouri, the wagon train was no longer on slave territory. What's more, Tyler smiled with the thought, he'd scored a couple of points with Rachelle without even having planned on it that day.

Early next morning, Tyler was awakened in his tent before the pre-dawn horn when he heard Jonathan Colledge cussing out his son five wagons back. "It was your job to watch the horses, Van Buren!" Jonathan stormed. "If you'd a-spent more time keeping an eye on the horses and less of an eye on that Palmerston girl, we'd still have eight horses this morning, plus we'd still have Tuck."

Also, as the day wore on, Tyler learned that Pa knew what he was talking about. Tyler felt tired but thirsty as well. The land turned brown and more sere, except in the narrow ribbons of land within a few hundred feet of either side of the North Platte. The river was running high with snow melt out of the Laramie Range 150 miles ahead. Already on the horizon, the hazy purple of the front range of the Rockies loomed.

Tyler walked beside the wagon as Pa drove, with Penny reading her books inside. He watched carefully, and nervously, as some of the wheels of the wagons around him looked ready to fall off. Indeed, the wheels were starting to come off some of the wagons.

The wagon driven by Credence Armagast lost a wheel when the wood under the wheel pulled away from the iron rim. Armagast hardly felt inconvenienced.

"I was expecting this," Credence said as he pulled a replacement wheel out of the back of his wagon. "The dry air does that to wheels."

Others weren't so fortunate, and had not had an element of foresight. Tyler heard a lot of cursing and swearing about a hundred feet behind him. He turned and there was a bespectacled, gray-haired man kicking a wooden wheel that had fallen partially off its rim. Tyler did not know anything about the man except his name, Nels Sogstad, and the name of his wife, Essence, and that they had six children. Thus it was no surprise that their wagon was among the first to break down. However, Sogstad had evidently not anticipated this, as he shook his fist at the broken wheel and kicked it again.

Tyler glanced ahead to his right and to the third column of wagons. The Anderson wagon had a back left wheel that wobbled precariously.

Silas Maple rode back to look at Nels Sogstad cutting loose with a blue streak of swearing. "We'll have to stop an hour early," Silas said. "Several wagons need fixing and we can't leave anyone behind in this desert."

Three wagons back on his column, Tyler heard Milon Crabbage bitterly shouting at Silas. "These people should have known what to expect. They should have brought extra supplies but they didn't. If we wait for them, they'll hold us all up and we'll all get stuck in the first snows."

"Who or what is that coming?" Nathan Zurich asked from his wagon board, pointing toward the plains to the west.

Tyler looked in the direction Zurich was pointing toward. "I ain't never seen nothing quite like that before," Tyler said.

"You can say that again," Tim MacNaughton agreed, shading his eyes while walking next to his oxen. "Strange-looking, and it's coming straight toward us."

"Whatever it be, it's heading our way," Press Doolittle said from horseback. "I'd best go take a look-see before it gets any closer."

When Doolittle rode off, Billie Kay stepped out from behind her father's wagon to look westward. "Knuckleheads, haven't any of you ever seen a Catholic priest before?" she demanded.

Billie Kay hurried forward to meet and greet the priest riding on horseback. Buckman rode forward on his horse as well to meet the visitor.

Tyler walked slowly forward to see this phenomenon. The priest was dressed in black from head to foot, with a Roman collar and dark pants. Out of nowhere, in the desert west of Scott's Bluff and east of Fort Laramie, a Catholic priest had appeared.

Curiosity got the better of Tyler. The priest rode to the head of the wagon train, which slowed and stopped for this one man. Tyler got close enough to hear the conversation between Buckman and the priest.

"Who are you and what are you doing out here, all by yourself, in the middle of nowhere?" Buckman demanded.

The priest doffed his broad-brimmed black hat, smiling. "Reverend Father Seamus Coogan at your service, sir."

"Fine. You've told us your name," Buckman said. "I'll ask it again, who are you and what are you doing out here in the butt-end of nowhere all by yourself? The Indians will kill you as likely as listen to any preaching of yours."

"Huh, and what of that?" Fr. Coogan said with a slight brogue. "If such befalls me, then my fate will be no worse than many another purveyor of the Gospel."

Buckman cocked his head to one side. "I reckon not."

"A missionary priest I be, yes, from Ireland originally, come to preach a Word or two to the heathens, both Indian and white. I travel among the tribes, aye, and also between the forts, and from wagon train to wagon train go I, being of service where I may. The commandant of Fort Laramie, Major John Sanderson, asked me to check on the status of the emigrants coming in. You've another thirty miles to the fort. The commandant wishes to know if any assistance from his troops need be rendered."

Buckman looked behind him, lifting the brim of his plainsman's hat. "Well, the wheels are starting to come off, to coin a phrase, on some of the wagons."

Coogan let out a sigh from his round, ruddy face. His light eyes darted about in their glance at the wagons. "You've not been keeping your wagon wheels watered, have you?"

"Hmm, well, no." Buckman looked around at the wagons, then turned to the priest again. "Water is going to start becoming precious. We'll need it to drink."

"You don't just need drinking water, my dear fellow," Coogan said. "Any water out of the North Platte will do to keep the wheels moist in the dry air. It won't eliminate the problem, but it will greatly reduce it."

Buckman rubbed his bushy chin. "Well, yeah, I knew that. You've got a point there. I'll tell everybody. It's worth trying."

"Father Coogan," Billie Kay said, clasping her hands next to Buckman, "will you be able to spend some time with us—even a day or so—saying Mass, hearing confessions and such?"

"Can you do a Protestant service?" Buckman asked. "We had a minister with us but the cholera took him. There's folks that might enjoy some good preaching from any quarter. I ain't one of 'em, mind you, but there's others that would, I'm sure."

The priest looked first at Billie Kay. "Why of course I'm here, my dear, for that as well. I shall be happy to say Mass and administer the sacraments to them that be Catholic among you." Coogan turned to Buckman. "I can do Protestant as well, when the need requires it."

That evening, the Reverend Father Coogan said Mass in the center of the wagon circle using a small table from the Hanclicek wagon as an altar. Among those in attendance at the Mass, Tyler observed, was Billie Kay Ellis, whom he wasn't aware had any religion at all. Obviously that was not the case, as Billie Kay entered into the Mass with all fervent-ness, veiled with a lace cloth.

Kelly Jay watched her sister's devotions from a distance, by their father's wagon. Pout-faced Kelly Jay stood with arms folded over her green sweater, as she observed Billie Kay.

Tyler walked over to Kelly Jay. "You're not joining your twin sister?" he asked, curious.

Kelly Jay let out a disgusted sigh and put her hands on her hips. "Billie Kay is Catholic, as you can see, but I am not, as you can see," Kelly Jay declared. "I am as Presbyterian as they come, and proud of it. Let Billie Kay follow the Pope. I'm not a part of that at all."

Interesting. Billie Kay and Kelly Jay, two identical twins, Tyler reflected, who seemed not to mind it and in fact to revel in it and their ability to fool people. They had the same color of brown hair and eyes, same thin noses and facial features, of course, and even close to the same length of hair. Billie Kay and Kelly Jay often wore the same kind of pinafore dresses, just to have some fun confusing people. Yet one was Catholic, and the other was Presbyterian Protestant. Tyler was curious how that one strange divergence had come about, but he felt it was none of his business, and so did not ask.

"What about your Pa?" Tyler inquired, though. "Is your Pa much of a church-goer?"

"Our Pa? Church?" Kelly Jay laughed without mirth, folding her arms again. "It's been a long, long, very long time, Tyler, since I've heard the words 'Pa' and 'church' used in the same sentence. Our Pa's religion is gold. That's what he worships. Our Pa hasn't been inside a church, any church, in, I bet, forty years or more. He plans to ask at Fort Laramie where the Sioux got that gold. If the soldiers at Fort Laramie won't tell him, then he plans to go to California, not Oregon. A cousin of our Pa's went to California in '49 and after only three days of panning he found several big chunks of gold worth $20,000. Pa figures the same'll happen to him."

"That was three years ago," Tyler said. "Most of the easy-found gold is gone now in California."

"You try telling that to our Pa. Me and Billie Kay have certainly tried," Kelly Jay said ruefully. "He won't listen."

Enough said. What George Ellis decided to do was of no concern to Tyler. He looked again at the Mass just to see who else was there. Angelique Hapsburg was at the Mass along with her father and the four Austrian soldiers—no surprise there—as were the Hancliceks, all six of them including Marta and her four brothers, and the McGuigans, of course, including Brent.

Interesting, though, that the four Clevenger children were at the Mass—Brit, Agnes, Luke and even little Jenny.

After losing both of their parents to cholera, Tyler would have thought the Clevenger kids would be pretty mad at God.

Then, sitting on the grass a bit further back, Tyler saw the Laurent family, Alain, his parents and two younger brothers. Penny sat with Alain. Penny, the $10,000 Penny, Pa now called her, or the Golden Penny, with all of her Indian jewelry about her neck. Penny attending a Catholic Mass would be a sight to horrify Pa. Fortunately, Tyler observed, she did not participate in the Communion part, and her presence seemed to be more with Alain than anything else. Good thing, though, that Pa was out watching Drake and Dru as they grazed, and so did not see Penny at the Mass.

The Protestant service which Father Coogan conducted was well attended. Alain and Penny stayed for it. Tyler observed the service from a distance. The Allertons, Ephraim and Abigail, the MacNaughtons, including Tim, the Elston Tanner family, Quimby Freding, Bruce Mallory, the Colledges including Van Buren, the Clayton Finlayson family, and the Palmerstons including Rachelle, all were there along with about three dozen others. Apparently there was a pent-up spiritual hunger among many in the wagon train after all they had been through thus far.

Repairs to wheels were made that evening so that all were ready to move on time the next morning. The wagons rolled close to the North Platte with its cool water from the mountains that quenched many a thirst after boiling as the dry desert air took over. Tyler grabbed an occasional bucket of water from the river to pour over the wagon wheels to keep them moist and attached to the iron rims.

Ten miles east of Fort Laramie, the wagon train passed a group of eight wagons headed eastward.

"Seen the elephant, they have," Pa declared, cracking his whip over the oxen heads. "Some folks just ain't fit for heading West."

Four wagons from the Buckman train decided to join the East-bound travelers. That left seventy-two wagons in the Buckman train of the original eighty-seven. Tyler felt that was actually pretty good. He would have expected more than that to have dropped out prior to Fort Laramie.

That evening at Pa's request Tyler watched Drake and Dru graze on the short buffalo grass. He missed out on the dancing, but he didn't mind. A drizzle fell throughout much of the evening—good for wagon wheels, but bad for dancing. Tyler soon heard the fiddle music from Bruce Mallory die out. Brent and Van Buren would have been vying with each other for Rachelle's attention anyway.

Staying away from that competition played into Tyler's developing strategy with Rachelle. Let Brent and Van Buren continue tearing each other down before Rachelle. He would stay aloof, giving Rachelle attention when those two weren't around. He knew that less was more. Quality time with Rachelle was better than quantity time. Let the times with her be times that she would savor and remember as being special, not routine. Let Rachelle want more of him, Tyler figured, and let him not become mundane to her, as Brent and Van Buren surely would with time.

A short haul the next day brought the wagon train to within sight of the white-washed buildings of unstockaded Fort Laramie, a welcome piece of civilization amidst the sere plains. The adobe remains of the original fort stood close by.

Renford MacNaughton hurled his hat in the air. "Yessssuhhh!" he exclaimed, and others like Elston Tanner and Dennis Palmerston joined the shouting acclaim.

From his position beside his wagon, though, Pa looked somberly at Tyler and Penny walking near him. "Like the expression I've heard," Pa said, "Fort Laramie isn't the half-way point, and wishing doesn't make it so."

"You got that right," Press Doolittle said, riding alongside Pa's wagon. "All getting to Fort Laramie means is that we've arrived at the mountains. The longest and hardest part of the journey is ahead of us."

Tyler held his breath at what lay just ahead and he shook the bangs out of his eyes. Beyond the spread-out buildings of Fort Laramie, the Laramie Mountains loomed purple-blue and capped with snow. Mt. Laramie, over 10,000 feet high, lay ominously to the northwest, the direction in which the wagon train was heading.

"We're not gonna try and cut straight through the very teeth of that mess up ahead," Press declared, seeing Tyler's concerned expression. "We'll follow the North Platte around the Front Range of the Rockies and then down to the Sweetwater and South Pass."

That evening, the wagon train made camp by the Laramie River, near a bridge leading to the fort. Indian tepees of the Sioux, Arapahoe, and Cheyenne tribes practically surrounded the fort. A Fort Laramie sentry explained to Tyler and Pa that the Indians hereabouts were friendly, wanting to engage in trade, and were not to be feared as long as they were treated with decency.

"No chasing after Indian girls, please," the blue-uniformed, white-sashed sentry said at his box. "Some of the Indian braves might not take kindly to competition from white men for the attention of their women."

Tyler spent much of the evening watching Drake and Dru and the other two pairs of Pa's oxen. Amused, he enjoyed seeing Van Buren and Brent sullenly watch Rachelle occupy her time entirely with enchanted soldiers from Fort Laramie. The soldiers no doubt enjoyed the sight of any woman at all, let alone one as eye-popping beautiful as blonde, blue-eyed Rachelle. For her part, Rachelle appeared to glory in the attention which the soldiers lavished upon her at the fiddle-music dance. This confirmed for Tyler that his strategy with Rachelle was the correct one. She was tiring of Brent and Van Buren all the time. When someone different came along, such as the Fort Laramie soldiers, Rachelle welcomed the attention and fresh admiration. The time for decisive action with Rachelle was drawing nearer.

CHAPTER THIRTEEN

Tyler poured more water from the Laramie River on the wagon wheels, happy to lay over for a day or two at the fort, with Buckman saying they had all earned another rest prior to the next leg of the Trail journey.

Around him Tyler saw people fixing loose wagon wheels, greasing their axles, turning their oxen out for grazing. Others built campfires and fixed fresh bacon, eggs, beans, corn on the cob, even boiled potatoes, amenities which the fort afforded and which the emigrants hadn't seen in bulk since leaving Fort Kearny, and in some cases, since leaving Independence, Missouri.

Others were busy trading their trail-weary oxen for fresh ones at the fort, sometimes for a price. Pa sat eating a plateful of beans beside the wagon while watching Drake and Dru. Tyler finished his beans and turned his attention to the MacNaughton oxen as other emigrants nearby haggled over oxen prices with the blue-uniformed soldiers.

"You think they'll make it, Pa?" Tyler asked.

"What's that?"

"The MacNaughtons' oxen," Tyler said. "They were a small pair to begin with and they've come pretty far."

"Renford told me he isn't buying any more oxen," Pa said uncertainly, rising to feel one of his large rear wagon wheels. "He said if he can exchange 'em, then fine. But he isn't buying any more. If I was him, I'd spend the money and get me a good pair of oxen. If he doesn't, I expect the MacNaughtons'll be in trouble before too much further."

Tyler looked around to see what else was going on. Becoming more of a rare sight, trees lined the Laramie River. Brit and Luke Clevenger had a couple of long-branch fishing poles in the water of the narrow river. He saw the Fort Laramie commandant, Major John Sanderson, his expression angry, stalking straight for George Ellis, busy greasing his axles fifty feet away.

"You the one asking about gold?" Sanderson demanded, epaulets shaking.

"Yeah, I'm the one," Ellis replied. "The Sioux we saw back at Scott's Bluff had gold from somewhere around here, I'm sure."

"Well, hear me and hear me good," Sanderson bellowed. "Gold is of no value to the Sioux, but they know that white people value it highly and so they find it and use it to trade with. So yeah, there's gold out where the Sioux live. I'm not going to tell you exactly where, because, mister, if the Sioux find any whites off the beaten trail, the Sioux will torture and kill them ten or eleven times over. I'm not risking my men to chase after you and rescue you. So there!"

"Well then, I'm heading for Californ-y," Ellis said.

Tyler turned to Pa. "I guess that settles it for the Ellises. They'll be peeling off for California in a few hundred miles."

"Reckon it does, and reckon they will."

"How are our oxen?"

"Drake and Dru and the others are fine," Pa declared. "I paid a little extra for 'em in Missouri but it's proving to be worth it."

Loud shouting from the east side of the wagon circle away from the river drew Tyler's attention. "Looks like there's a fight going on." Tyler leapt up to head for the excitement. "I got to see what this is."

Running toward the action, Tyler saw Brinton Stonehouse and Elston Tanner pummeling each other as the crowd whooped it up, with most of them on Elston's side.

"Get 'im, Elston! Teach him a lesson!" Credence Armagast shouted, shaking a fist.

"That's it, Elston, hammer his stomach!" someone else yelled.

Stonehouse leveled a fist to Elston's jaw that sent him reeling backwards.

"Get in there, Elston. You're bigger than he is. You can take 'im!" another man shouted.

Others yelled excitedly and whooped and hollered for the combatants to charge one another and they did. Even several soldiers enjoyed the action. Elston grabbed Stonehouse by the thigh and tripped him to the ground and kicked him in the ribs. Stonehouse was on his feet in a second but Tanner dodged his fist and leveled a right to Stonehouse's jaw which stunned him backwards.

Stonehouse wiped a trickle of blood from his lower lip, eyeing Elston Tanner warily, apparently sensing that Tanner would prevail in a prolonged fistfight. Breathing heavily, eyes fixed and blazing at Elston, Stonehouse drew a small knife out of his pants pocket.

Elston backed away as the crowd grew somber and silent.

"There's no call for that, Brinton," Credence said worriedly. "It ain't worth a killing."

Stonehouse had an evil sparkle in his eyes. "I'll show you that I'm fair," he murmured, leaning forward. "I'll let you get a knife from your wagon, Tanner, so it'll be an even fight. Then we'll settle this. The winner gets to live, and gets to pronounce that word any way he wants."

"It—it ain't something worth killing or being killed over," Tanner said, shaking his hands. "I got a wife and kids. It ain't worth it."

"Coward!" Stonehouse bellowed. "I'll come after you with my knife and you unarmed then. You won't save your skin by turning chicken."

A gunshot over the heads of the crowd sent people ducking.

"All right, that'll be enough."

As Tyler looked up from the ground, he saw a young captain from the fort approaching with a new cylinder revolver pointed squarely at Stonehouse.

"Put that knife away, now," the captain snapped.

Stonehouse straightened up, smirked, and obeyed, putting the knife back in its sheath and back in his pants pocket.

"What started all this?" the ruddy-faced captain demanded, keeping his revolver leveled.

"Me an' him was talking," Elston said. "We was talking about how much further it is to Oregon, the Willamette Valley, I mean. I was just trying to tell him the proper way to pronounce Oregon. It's OR-e-gon, not Ore-GON. And he got all huffy and upset."

The captain looked first at Stonehouse, then at everyone else, taking them all in. "I've heard it pronounced both ways. If you folks are ready to kill one another now over a trivial thing like that, then what's going to happen in another two or three hundred miles, when you're fighting over water and food?"

Stonehouse glared at the captain's pistol, then at Elston. "Huh," he snorted at Elston. "See you later." Stonehouse walked sullenly away.

"Anybody that commits murder is going to face a hanging," the captain declared.

Tyler got the clear impression that this episode had a "to be continued" feel about it.

The wagon train got moving again the next morning by five a.m. Another river crossing of the Laramie River to keep following the North Platte, meant another four dollars to the Army for every wagon using the ferry.

All did. Ephraim Allerton complained about having to pay again.

"Look, will you just pay the man and let's get across," Abigail Allerton demanded at the riverside.

"Oh, all right," Ephraim declared. "But I'm getting tired of this. We got across the South Platte just fine without any ferry."

"I hear the Laramie and the North Platte River are deeper than their cousin," Abigail declared.

Buckman pushed the wagon train hard across land that was littered with badlands—sod tables, needles, and pinnacles amidst stretches of green grass turning brown. "It's a week to the Fourth of July. I want to be at Independence Rock by the Fourth," Buckman told everyone several times. "That will mean we're on schedule and in less danger of being caught in the early snows. If we're not at Independence Rock by the Fourth, we could get caught in an early blizzard before we hit the Willamette."

Tyler didn't mind. During the first few days of the journey leg to Independence Rock, the Palmerston wagon rode directly next to the Linders wagon. Tyler liked to think that Rachelle wanted it that way. The long stretch with the McGuigan and Colledge wagons far to the other side of the train and in back gave Tyler ample time to walk, alone, with Rachelle. She was more beautiful than ever with her tanned, light brown skin, sun-bleached waist-length blonde hair and blue eyes.

They talked of mundane things, their lives back in the Midwest and East, the journey so far, and, most interestingly, their plans for Oregon. Rachelle talked of being a farmer's wife in the fertile Willamette Valley, with the nearby cool coastal pine forests of Douglas Fir stretching 250 feet into the sky.

This type of talk, on the third day of the leg, stirred Tyler to his depths. His plan was working faster and unbelievably perfect. Rachelle spent time dancing with him, as much or more than with Brent and Van Buren put together, or so it seemed to Tyler.

A bold plan came to Tyler's mind. Strike while the iron was hot. He had planned to ask Rachelle to marry him when they got to Oregon. But why wait that long? No, he wouldn't wait, and risk Rachelle drifting back to Van Buren or Brent, or someone else like Charles Chuckwood. He would ask Rachelle to marry him when the wagon train got to Independence Rock, and he and Rachelle would face the rigors of the second half of the journey as husband and wife. They were getting toward Mormon country, and surely there would be some kind of preacher man around who could get them hitched. Worst-case scenario, there would surely be a preacher at Fort Hall. He and Rachelle would start their lives in Oregon together—married.

Sitting on a small stool eating a supper of dried bacon and beans with Pa and Penny, Tyler discussed his plan with Pa as Penny listened, weighed down by her gold, silver, and turquoise jewelry. "I feel like this was meant to be," Tyler declared. "It's not just me, Pa. It's Rachelle—I'm sure she's feeling it too. She's the one who's been talking about settling down and setting up a farm. I haven't had to lead her on one bit. She's leading *me* on now."

Pa grinned as he shoved baked beans into his mouth. "I'm happy for you, Tyler," he said, swallowing. He put his plate down. "Rachelle is one beautiful catch, a wife to make other men envy you. And I think you're right. It sure sounds like Rachelle is taking a serious shine to you." He turned to grab something behind his stool. "Oh, by the way, Angelique Hapsburg stopped by earlier with this book that's kind of heavy."

Tyler took the book to look at it, with the imposing title, *North American Indians—an anthropological exposition and discourse* by Prof. George Bainbridge.

There was a note within the book:

Hi, Tyler. Hope this book helps you. Keep it as long as you need it. All the best.

Angelique

"I'm not much of a reader." Tyler tossed the book aside. "Maybe Penny will get some use out of it, even if it is a little thick. Anyway, when we get to Independence Rock, just before the Fourth, I'm going to ask Rachelle to marry me. The other guys, Van Buren, Brent, Charles and all of them, they'll be envious of me something wicked. But I think now's the time with Rachelle. Our relationship is on a fast rise. I'm not going to give it a chance to plateau out and start slipping backwards. I've got to move Brent and Van Buren out of the picture for good."

"Well," Pa said. He took a guzzle of coffee. "I wish you luck, Tyler. It sounds like a winning strategy, just like I had with your Ma when she was Rachelle's age."

"I'm really, really going to ask Rachelle Palmerston to marry me," Tyler breathed, half to himself.

Pa's smile grew excited. "I wish you the best of luck. Maybe we'll be having an engagement party real soon."

With Pa's robust encouragement, Tyler became a mental whirlwind. That evening he spent time doing four dances with Rachelle. After he finished dancing with her, he watched her every move. Glory be—she didn't dance at all with Brent or Van Buren. Clearly, Tyler told himself, he was now way ahead of those two. Indeed, Brent and Van Buren themselves barely noticed Rachelle. Maybe they knew that Rachelle had made her choice, and it wasn't either of them. Rachelle did do a few dances with other young men, but with no one more than once, and with apparently little enthusiasm. She danced with Tim once, Quimby Freding once, a couple of others once, and Justin Maybrie once. Justin was handsome and the only other young man that Tyler felt could give him real competition.

But just as soon as Justin had finished one dance with Rachelle, he quickly returned to Billie Kay Ellis, with whom he had spent most of the evening and with whom he spent the remainder of the evening and upon whom he was clearly fixated.

When Bruce Mallory put his fiddle away, Tyler approached Rachelle. "May I walk you back to your wagon?" he asked her.

"Of course," Rachelle replied, smiling mildly as she pulled a white lace mantilla over her shoulders. "Did you have a good time tonight, Tyler?"

"Yeah, I sure did," Tyler replied earnestly. "I enjoy our time together, Rachelle."

"Yeah, so do I," she responded casually. Rachelle talked about how there seemed to be fewer dancers lately, proba-bly because so many people were just plain tired after having walked fifteen or more miles a day, for most of the 800 miles since leaving Independence, Missouri.

As Rachelle talked casually about the journey so far, Tyler barely heard her as he tried to work up the courage he needed. He felt his body going numb, especially his knees. His fingers began to tingle. He wished right now that he had a more handsome face, maybe a smaller nose. Breathing hard, he slipped a hand into Rachelle's as he had done before, and she quietly half-smiled at him, but she noticed his sudden anxiety.

"What's the matter, Tyler?" she asked.

Nothing ventured, nothing gained. Tyler just knew he had to do it. "Rachelle, there's a question I've just got to ask you."

She stopped. "What is it, Tyler?" she asked, looking concerned. She apparently had no idea what he was getting at.

Tyler took both of Rachelle's hands in his. He looked into her worried-appearing blue eyes. There was nought to do but say it. "Rachelle Palmerston, will you marry me?"

Tyler's heart stood still. Rachelle's breathing suddenly shortened. Her jaw dropped. She looked stunned, utterly stunned, and worried and concerned still, unsmiling and not looking the least bit excited or happy.

Not exactly the response that Tyler had hoped to see.

"Uh-h . . ." Rachelle let out a deep breath and glanced away, letting her hands fall out of his grasp. She cocked her head to one side, then she looked at him again. "Are you serious?"

Not exactly the response that Tyler had hoped to hear.

Tyler put his arms akimbo. Now it was his turn to cock his head to one side and look at Rachelle askance. His tone became slightly annoyed. "Do you think I would ask a question like that as a joke?"

"Oh, no—no, not at all," Rachelle hastened to assure him, waving her hands. "Not at all, Tyler. It's just that, uh-h, um," she finally broke into a smile, but it was a remorseful smile, a consolation smile.

She clutched his hands. "Tyler, that was sweet, it truly was," Rachelle said. "I'm flattered, truly flattered."

There was that dangerous word, "flattered." Tyler had heard it many times before, from other girls and young women. It never, ever presaged a positive answer. It was a consolation word.

Rachelle bowed her head momentarily, as if composing her next words. She looked up at him. "Tyler, you're one of the nicest friends I've ever had."

There was that dangerous word, "friends." He had been after much, so much more, than mere friendship, with Rachelle.

"I—I know that's not what you were hoping I'd say," Rachelle continued. "I truly have valued you as a dear and cherished friend on this trip, someone I can count on whenever there's danger around, much more so than most of the other young men in this wagon train. But, uh, Tyler, I have to be honest with you, as I've been honest with Brent and Van Buren, who both asked me the same question. Brent proposed a week ago, and I had to tell him what I'm about to tell you. I had to ask Brent to tell Van Buren also, since I could tell that Van Buren was starting to talk about marriage as well." Her gaze was steady, heartfelt. "I'm engaged already, to a wonderful man back in Pennsylvania. His name is Everett Lueckens, and he's studying at Harvard University. He's going to be a doctor. We met in Pennsylvania when he was home from school a year ago. He's going to make the journey to Oregon as soon as he's finished with his studies next year. He asked me to marry him before my parents and I left to head West, and, Tyler, I said yes. I said yes to him. Everett is a wonderful young man, handsome and smart. You'd like him. He's going to do some farming in Oregon while he gets his practice as a doctor established.

"I'm sorry, Tyler," Rachelle murmured. "I'm sorry I can't give you the answer you were wanting so badly, the answer that I know you really, really wanted to hear." She clutched his arm. "I owe you a sincere apology. I sincerely and truly apologize, Tyler. I deeply apologize if I raised your expectations by giving you the impression that I was after anything more with you than simply friendship. Forgive me?"

Tyler had had enough of this. He yanked his arm loose from Rachelle and started walking away, pouting. "I think it's best that I not finish walking you back to your wagon," Tyler muttered. "People might get the wrong impression about us, and I'm sure you wouldn't want that. Nor would Everett Lueckens. God forbid."

"I—I'm sorry, Tyler," Rachelle said earnestly and sincerely. "We're still friends, right? Right?"

Tyler raised his hands in bitter frustration, half-turning. "Rachelle, please just leave me alone from now on. I feel like I've made an absolute fool of myself with you. Now I know why Brent and Van Buren have been avoiding you." He continued walking away, not looking back at her. Why didn't she wear a ring or something to tell other men that she was not available? Well, because she enjoyed flirting too much with other men, even as she was already taken.

"See you, Tyler," Rachelle said quietly.

He stomped away from her. Friendship—bah! Friendship was useless. This was not the first time that he had mistaken platonic friendship for something greater, that he had been led to believe that a young woman was interested in a romantic relationship that went way beyond mere friendship. Why did women do that? All his hopes, crushed. Tyler felt numb and utterly stupid.

As he walked back to his wagon Tyler saw Pa leaning against the sideboard with arms folded, one foot propped up against a wheel. Penny and Alain were there, conversing with Billie Kay Ellis and Justin Maybrie.

Pa leaned forward. "I saw you talking with Rachelle. Any news?"

Tyler could not respond right away. He felt that probably his sad, embarrassed expression with his head hanging down would tell them everything they really needed to know. He let out a bitter sigh and shook his head. "Not so much."

Pa let out his own sigh and gave Tyler a pair of comforting claps on the shoulder. "I'm sorry, son," Pa murmured. "You're a fine young man, Tyler, a fine young man. You'd have made a good husband for her."

"You deserve better than Rachelle anyway," Penny declared. "I always thought she was just about leading men on and just enjoying all the attention she was getting."

Alain half-smiled, brushed his sandy blonde hair back, and put his arms around Penny's waist. "While Rachelle's been soaking up all the interest and attention from the single men," he said, "there's been plenty of other young women in this wagon train that nobody's noticing."

Billie Kay took Tyler by the wrist. "Come with me, Tyler, I want to talk with you for a moment," she said.

Tyler let Billie Kay gently take him aside thirty feet where they could talk in semi-private. Tyler wished, now, that he would have paid more attention to Billie Kay early on. She was as beautiful as Rachelle but in a different way, with her long dark brown hair, brown eyes, thin nose that was slightly larger at the end, and clear features, and the light blue bow in her hair. Too late now. Billie Kay and Justin Maybrie were a definite pair.

"Look at me, Tyler," Billie Kay implored, holding his hands.

Tyler looked into Billie Kay's quiet, sympathetic brown eyes.

"Rachelle missed out on a wonderful opportunity just now to have a tremendous husband who would have loved her and cherished her and her children for the rest of her life," Billie Kay said with compassionate sincerity. She raised her eyebrows. "It's her loss, Tyler. She was the loser here."

"I've heard people use that expression before," Tyler muttered, hardly consoled. "If Rachelle ends up marrying this doctor man from back East that she told me about and they end up living happily ever after, how does that make Rachelle a loser? Or, at best, how in the blazes would Rachelle even know that she's a loser?"

Billie Kay smiled mildly, unperturbed by Tyler's anger and seeming to understand his need to vent. She put a hand on his arm. "Tyler, there's somebody here for you. You're going to find someone. Or, maybe someone is going to find you, just like I found my Justin. Tyler, I believe that with all of my heart within me."

"Yeah, right. I'm just—"

"Tyler, I promise you from my heart, I'm personally going to find someone for you," Billie Kay continued mildly. "I'm going to help you. I've gotten to know a lot of the young women on this trip. I'll be your matchmaker. Don't you even worry about it. I'll find someone for you."

Tyler tried to force a smile. Despite his mood, he appreciated Billie Kay's attempts to comfort him and help him in his anguish. "When people talk about friendship, too many of them don't even know what the word means," he said. "Billie Kay, you are a true friend."

She smiled and chuckled lightly. "I try to be."

"I don't suppose Kelly Jay is available?"

"No, unfortunately not." Billie Kay clutched Tyler's arm a little more tightly. "She's going to be heading to California with our Pa to watch over him. Justin's parents said I'm welcome to keep traveling with them to Oregon. But Kelly Jay's hoping that our Pa can find enough gold in California so that they can afford to travel back to Pennsylvania. Kelly Jay's not liking the West—the altitude, the desert, the lack of trees and civilization, worrying about water and Indians and such. She wants to return East. But Tyler, there's plenty of other young single women around that aren't spoken for. What Alain said was right. Rachelle's got too many of the single men on this trip centered on capturing her. The other single women are there for the taking, if anybody'd notice them."

Tyler smiled more firmly. "Thanks, Billie Kay. I guess I needed to be reminded of that."

"I'm going to keep my eyes and ears open for you, Tyler," Billie Kay reiterated. Her sympathetic quiet eyes tenderly looked at him, and Tyler knew she truly felt bad for him. "I promise you I will. I'll talk you up good, Tyler."

Tyler couldn't help chuckling despite his mood. "I'm sure you will, Billie Kay. You'll tell the other young women that I'm Davy Crockett and Daniel Boone all rolled into one."

Billie Kay laughed and gave him a playful punch in the shoulder. "Just you wait. I'm going to find somebody for you, Tyler Linders. That's going to be my special project. I'm going to get you hitched to somebody if it's the last thing I ever do—and I'm sure it won't take that long."

CHAPTER FOURTEEN

"There's Independence Rock!" someone shouted. "I can see it on the horizon."

Tyler turned his attention from his nooning meal of corn biscuits and coffee to the horizon. There, a grayish blur almost due West seemed to gain height toward its northern face.

"That's it," Pa declared. "Independence Rock all right, maybe another fifteen or twenty miles. It's July 2nd. We'll be there by the Fourth."

"That mean we'll get to Oregon on time?" Penny asked, leaning back on her hands.

"That's what it means," Pa confirmed. "We'll be in the Willamette Valley probably by mid-September. We won't have to worry about getting stuck in the early mountain snows."

"All right, let's get rolling again," Buckman said, riding by and dodging sagebrush and greasewood. "We've had our noon grub. I'd like to get another four or five miles in today so that we're at Independence Rock by no later than tomorrow afternoon."

Pa got up in the wagon box just to get the oxen moving. Tyler knew he'd be walking again. No matter. His mood remained somber. That morning, he'd asked Pa to get in line behind the Ellis wagon, as they had previously done on the journey, and not behind the Palmerston wagon again. He had not seen Rachelle since last night, nor did he care to.

The Ellis wagon ahead of them got rolling, and Pa snapped the reins to follow. Toward the southwest, dark clouds were coming over the horizon. Bad weather suited Tyler's mood just now. Still, he felt mildly pleased when he saw the dark clouds and accompanying distant flashes of lightning heading away from the direction of the wagon train.

The dance that evening had a festive air amidst the blue-green sagebrush and greasewood shrubs. Everyone sensed that the journey was approaching its halfway point. They'd made it this far. That was something to celebrate.

Tyler was in no mood to celebrate anything. Van Buren Colledge walked past him at one point, grinning. "Heard you asked Rachelle to marry you and she turned you down flat," Van Buren said with a thin-faced smirk. "Welcome to the club."

"Just leave me alone," Tyler demanded.

"Hey, relax. Just get on with your life and forget about her like Brent, Charles, and I are doing," Van Buren advised out of his thin face. "I saw Rachelle holding hands a couple of hours ago with some new sucker named Blaise Bennett, I think his name was. I just know the same thing will happen to him. She'll lead him on; he'll fall for her; he'll ask her to marry him in a couple of weeks; and she'll tell him all about this damn doctor back East. It never changes."

Tyler nodded a thanks, shaking bangs out of his eyes. Van Buren Colledge was really not a bad person. Tyler wondered if Rachelle had told others that he'd asked her to marry him and she'd said no. How else could anyone have known? A true friend would never reveal a confidence like that.

He wandered idly along the line of wagons, his mind numb until Billie Kay caught up with him.

"You've got to get back into circulation, Tyler," Billie Kay said, clutching his arm. "Marta Hanclicek's been standing there for a long time, waiting for someone to ask her to dance."

Tyler turned and smiled at Billie Kay. "Look, I appreciate what you're trying to do, but give me a day to recover. I'll be in a better mood tomorrow."

Billie Kay nodded and put a hand on his shoulder. "I understand. That's fine. But tomorrow, Mr. Tyler Linders, you'll be dancing if I have to drag you over there." She gave him a warm smile and a gentle, friendly smack on his arm.

So Billie Kay had appointed herself his guardian angel. Well, fine. He would rejoin the wagon train's social circle tomorrow to keep her happy. Tyler did watch from a distance. Rachelle did a couple of dances with Quimby Freding. The only reason that Tyler could figure for Rachelle dancing with Quimby Freding was that she would have felt embarrassed to be standing, alone, with no one paying any attention to her or dancing with her. Sure enough, as soon as a tall, thin, blonde young man came along—presumably Blaise Bennett— Rachelle drifted straight over to him and poor Quimby, ever hopeful, was quickly left behind and abandoned.

Tyler had a notion to tell both Quimby and Blaise that they were wasting their time and hopes on Rachelle, but he barely knew them and so did not.

Another group of people, largely men, had congregated toward the east end of the large circle of wagons, near someone's Dutch oven. There was plenty of yelling and hollering. Tyler moved closer. Credence Armagast was walking away from Brinton Stonehouse, or trying to.

"I asked you what you meant by that," Stonehouse moodily demanded. "I want an answer, damn you."

"I told you, one of your oxen nearly stomped over one of my kids because you weren't keeping a close enough eye on your livestock. That's what I meant," Credence declared. "Shouldn't be hard to understand."

"Or maybe you should keep better watch over your little brats," Stonehouse retorted. "I can't tell my oxen to avoid every little bastard that gets in their way."

"You calling my kids bastards?" Credence erupted, fists balling.

Stonehouse swung at Credence's jaw and missed but the fight was on.

"Get 'im, Credence!" Elston Tanner hollered.

Credence swung and missed while Stonehouse leveled him. Credence got up instantly and charged Stonehouse, pushing him backwards.

"Kick his ass good, Creed!" someone else shouted.

Men exclaimed and shook fists, all screaming their support for Credence Armagast. Stonehouse had thoroughly alienated everyone in the wagon train.

Credence got the better of Stonehouse, leveling rights and lefts to Stonehouse's bloodied jaw and cheeks with his longer reach.

Stonehouse tried to grab Credence but the latter was too quick and dodged to the right giving Stonehouse a hard kick straight in the left ass. Stonehouse fell to the ground but quickly got up. When he did so, he pulled out his small pocket knife.

The laughter and shouting died instantly.

"Ain't no call for that, Stonehouse," Elston declared.

Stonehouse fixed his tight eyes on Credence Armagast. Slowly through his bloodied teeth and whiskers, he breathed, "What the hell good does it do to own a knife if I never get to use it on anyone?"

He charged at Credence who turned to run. A shot rang out and a bullet ripped into Stonehouse's upper right chest.

Stonehouse's eyes bulged as much with shock as with pain. He clutched his chest where the bullet had penetrated. Blood curled around his fingers.

Buckman walked forward with his drawn revolver. Other men nervously made way for him as he approached Stonehouse.

Stonehouse fell to his knees, then fell to one side on the ground. He was not dead.

Buckman aimed his revolver directly at Stonehouse's head. Tyler thought for a second or two that Buckman was going to help Stonehouse. But Buckman kept his pistol pointed straight at Stonehouse's forehead as horrified onlookers watched, surmising what was about to happen. Buckman fired one shot straight into Stonehouse's head right between the eyes, drawing a spurt of blood that rose a foot in the air.

Two women screamed at the sight. Men backed off in terror. Buckman raised the barrel of his pistol, taking them all in. "This man needed killing. He was nothing but a cancer on this wagon train."

No one argued with him, whether because they agreed or because they worried about how many bullets Buckman had left in his late-model revolver.

"Get this and get it good, all of you," Buckman snapped, looking around. "We're about to head into the most dangerous and deadly part of this whole journey. We're entering a stretch of a hundred miles where there's hardly any water. Any water you find is probably loaded with alkali. What's more, there's no organized law or government. People have been driven crazy mad by thirst. If Stonehouse was a problem before, just picture him driven out of his mind by thirst and heat."

"We could have taken"—

"We could have taken care of him?" Buckman cut off Eliza MacNaughton. "Anyone who would have taken responsibility for nursing Stonehouse back to health—if he even could have been—would be so slowed down that within a day or two they'd be left behind and completely on their own right in the middle of Indian country in a waterless desert. Tantamount to a death sentence for any family that would do that. And I wouldn't ask anyone to do that for a hateful bast—son-of-a-gun like Stonehouse. Better to kill him and be done with him."

With that, Buckman walked away. "Bury him," he said casually.

As Buckman walked away, Tyler drew in a deep breath. Several others, including Eliza MacNaughton, Prudence Smith, and Tomas Hanclicek, did likewise, looking at one another with puzzled, worried expressions. Ella Bennett shook her head and walked away in silence.

Buckman was a different man now. He had been tough but reasonably business-like before; now he was someone who had killed, and who could and would kill again if he felt there was need. Buckman had imposed a sort of martial law on the wagon train as they headed into lawless territory, where the only rule was by the gun.

Tyler did his best to make excuses for Buckman in his mind. Perhaps Buckman was worried that Stonehouse would seek out either Credence Armagast or Elston Tanner or both of them in their sleep and kill them, and proactive action had to be taken to prevent that, There was no jail out here in the middle of unorganized territory that Stonehouse could have been sent to. Rule of the gun, therefore. Buckman was not someone to be trifled with now, if he ever had been.

As Renford MacNaughton and Dennis Palmerston took up the task of putting Stonehouse in a grave with a cross of twigs over it, the dancing wound down. It just didn't seem appropriate.

The next day, Tyler saw clearly what Buckman was talking about. The North Platte River, the old friend of every wagon train, arced away to the south, away from the Oregon Trail. In its place, for a while anyway, was the undependable Sweetwater River. Independence Rock was upon them, a chance to celebrate the halfway point of the journey. Beyond Independence Rock, however, as far as the eye could see, was naught but rock, bare, treeless, promontories in various shades of brown and gray, a hundred miles of brown rock with a million sagebrush plants for variety. And there was no Moses around to strike the bare rock and produce water, precious, cool, wet water. Every drop of treasured water from this point onward must be carefully husbanded. Tyler read in the guidebook that the Sweetwater could often dry up completely in the summer desert heat. Every barrel of water could be drunk dry within a matter of hours after leaving Independence Rock, but each barrel must last a week or more until the next reliable water at the Little Sandy River was reached on the other side of the Continental Divide.

Tyler saw the land growing much more brown and sere. There were patches of grass here and there, which the oxen and other livestock grazed upon as best they could during the nooning. When the journey resumed in the afternoon, the hot sun not only beat down upon one and all, but reflected back from the sere ground just for good measure.

About forty feet away, Tyler as he walked saw Prudence Smith fall down to the ground and stay there. She tried to get up but could only half lift herself in the oven-like heat. Jonas Smith hurried over to his wife with a cupful of water, which seemed to revive her.

"Does anyone have a little extra water that we could have?" Jonas cried out as he helped his wife to sit up. "Prudence could use a little extra water."

Tyler observed several wagons roll right past the Smiths without offering to help. Maybe Van Buren Colledge had been right in his prediction. Tyler looked at Pa, almost shame-faced as he tried to pretend not to see the Smiths. Tyler turned to look again at Prudence Smith. Lucas Pfister was hurrying up to her with a canteen. Praise be somebody, at least, was still capable of thinking of others.

Glancing at Pa walking next to Drake and Dru, Tyler asked, "Would we have helped them if nobody else came?"

Pa did not face him when he answered, after a long, drawn-out moment of hard contemplation. Tyler thought he heard Pa mumble, ". . . thinking of you and Penny, and Drake and Dru, before we can think of . . ."

Maybe Pa was changing on this trip. Maybe it was making him harder. Tyler wondered if the Pa that he had known in Missouri would still be the same Pa at the end of the journey to Oregon.

"What if it had been us needing water, Pa?" Tyler asked. He brushed his long bangs out of his eyes. "Maybe it will be us next time."

"And if it is, people will ignore us as they must, just like a lot of them ignored the Smiths," Pa declared, turning and scowling. "That's why I'm hoarding water for the three of us and our oxen. Don't argue with me, Tyler."

The heat and thirst were getting to Pa. Or, Tyler hoped that was the reason for the change in Pa's personality, and that it would not be a permanent change. There was nothing to be gained by making Pa angry.

The wagon train made camp for the night at the foot of Independence Rock, arching 130 feet away from the wagons. Stonehouse had been put out of everyone's mind. People wanted a chance to celebrate. Bruce Mallory's fiddle cranked out a Reel, and away the dancers went.

Tyler watched with pleased amusement as Blaise Bennett, apparently Rachelle's new boyfriend *du jour*, vied for her undivided attention as other young men formed an entourage around her. Rachelle seemed to need that. It was just a matter of time before Blaise, and many other young men, would hear the same speech from Rachelle as he had been given.

Tyler walked away from the dance but there was Billie Kay Ellis right there Johnny-on-the-spot to thrust her hands out to stop him.

"You're not going anywhere, Tyler Linders," Billie Kay declared. "Beverly Tanner is all alone watching the dancing. I spoke to her a couple of minutes ago and she said she'd love to dance with you. She's waiting."

Billie Kay was eminently sincere in her efforts to help him. Tyler wanted to show respect and appreciation to her.

"Thank you," he said. "Yeah, maybe I could do a couple dances with her. I don't know her that well, but, what the heck?"

Tyler headed over toward short, auburn-haired Beverly Tanner. She saw him coming. Her arms were folded.

"Hmm," Tyler said to himself. To Beverly he asked, "I was wondering if you would like to dance?"

"Well, okay. I guess that would be fine."

Beverly's unenthusiastic response bespoke that Billie Kay's sincere efforts to help him might sometimes cause her to overestimate how effective her attempts to intervene actually were.

Nevertheless, he did a couple of emotionless Reels with Beverly, thanked her, and moved on.

Tyler walked away from the dance. He had no interest in watching Penny and Alain having fun together. But maybe, if Billie Kay was determined to watch out for him, maybe he could adopt someone himself to sort of keep an eye on.

As Tyler walked past several wagons and his feet crunched on the dry, brittle grass, his attention was drawn to the orphaned Clevenger kids. Brit, Agnes, Luke, and Jenny sat around a pot of beans and bacon.

"How you kids doing?" Tyler asked.

Thirteen-year-old Brit Clevenger looked up from his haunches. "We're doing okay," he replied somewhat defensively.

"How you fixed for water?" Tyler asked. "It's a long ways to the Little Sandy."

"We're fixed pretty well so far," Brit said more casually. He rose to his feet and put his hands in his butt pockets. "Why, you need some?"

"Naw, we're fine, but thanks for the offer," Tyler replied. He started to move on.

"Is it true there's no water for a thousand miles?" ten-year-old Agnes asked, peeking out from her light blue bonnet.

Tyler turned. "More like about ninety miles," he said, "till we get to the Little Sandy River. At least I think that's how far it is, maybe farther."

"'Sides, it'll rain eventually," Luke said.

"It has to," little Jenny chimed in.

"It ain't rained in this desert for a hunnert years," Brit declared. "But we'll be okay. We got water."

Tyler looked away for a moment, turning pensive as he again brushed brown bangs off his slightly sunburned forehead. "I've been wondering," he began, facing the Clevengers once more, "what do you plan on doing when you get to Oregon?"

"We still got our Pa and Ma's money," Brit declared. "We'll buy a piece of land and we'll put in some crops and be just fine."

The problem was, Brit Clevenger, at thirteen years old, was too young to buy land. The Clevenger kids would be sent to an orphanage, if there was one, when they reached Oregon, or worse, forced apart and split up among different adoptive families possibly quite far apart. Tyler thought about saying something further, but decided against it for the moment. This was a problem that needed careful thinking-over.

"Well, if you need anything, just let me know," Tyler said by way of leaving.

"Thanks," Brit said uncertainly. "Obliged to you."

The next day Tyler became aware of how seriously the concern over water had not been misplaced. He drove the wagon, with Penny watching the scenery while sitting beside him. Pa kept the whip, snapping it occasionally over the heads of the oxen while walking beside them. The inside of Tyler's mouth felt so dry and scratchy with thirst that his tongue swelled up along with the inside of his cheeks. Every breath in and out sent parched air over his swollen tongue and inner cheeks which screamed for moisture with every breath. Tyler tried his best to shorten his breathing.

He looked at Penny next to him. The blazing, bone-dry, mercilessly beating summer sun was turning Penny brown as an Indian, to go with her Indian outfit and collection of gold, silver, and turquoise-obsidian jewelry.

"How are you doing, Penny?" Tyler murmured.

"I want water," Penny replied plaintively. She pushed her yellow bonnet back.

"What you do that for?" Tyler asked. "Now the sun'll be right in your eyes."

"Wearing a hat makes my head feel too warm," Penny declared.

"Well, I'm keeping my hat on," Tyler said, pulling the brim of his plainsman's hat down lower.

"I want water," Penny repeated plaintively.

"I know you do, Penny, I know you do. But you heard what Pa said. Only one small drink every two hours. We have to make our water last another four days till we get to South Pass at least."

Penny looked around. Tyler knew what she was thinking. They had passed Hell's Gate between two high promontories. Now the wagon train had entered a long stretch of sere, dry badlands, sod tables, pinnacles, and needles. Nowhere was there a drop of water to be found. Not even a mud puddle. The very sereness of the landscape, the brown, parched, bare landscape, emphasized to people and animals that this was the "thirst stretch" of the journey. Oregon, with its wet, moist, dense, tall-tree rainforests, seemed to mock man and beast alike now.

"You can have my drink next time. You look like you need it," Tyler told Penny.

"No, that's okay," Penny said huskily. "I don't want to take your water, Tyler. You're working. All I'm doing is sitting here."

Drake let out a plaintive bawl, which got Dru to doing the same. The other oxen echoed the complaint, as did the oxen pulling other wagons. Tyler knew the animals were thirsty too, and tired on top of it, having hauled their wagons faithfully for close to a thousand miles at an ever increasing elevation. How long before the animals simply started giving out?

Tyler looked to his left. The MacNaughtons' wagon, which had kept pace with theirs all the way from Independence, Missouri, had started falling behind. The smaller-sized MacNaughton oxen bawled piteously with thirst and the strain which was catching up to them.

"Shit! Shit!"

Tyler looked to his right. The Tanner wagon had lost its left hind wheel and had a cracked axle as well. Elston and his brother Bayliss both threw their hats down on the ground in disgust and anger. There was precious little water now for keeping wheels moist. The problem with wheels drying out and breaking apart would resume with a vengeance.

Beverly Tanner and her mother and two small brothers came around to worriedly examine the broken wheel.

"The right front wheel's about to come off too, Pa," Beverly said apprehensively. "What're we gonna do?"

Bayliss Tanner kicked the damaged wheel. For good measure, he slammed a fist into the "Oregon or bust" sign on the side of his wagon.

Yeah, that'll help, Tyler thought.

"We'll walk to Oregon if we have to," Elston bellowed. He also kicked the wagon wheel good and hard.

"As if that'll do us any good," snorted Mrs. Tanner, about to cry. "You brought us all out here to the middle of nowhere with a broke-down wagon. Now what'll we do?"

"We'll shut up and walk. That's what we'll do," Elston shouted with his fists balling.

"Walk—another thousand miles?" Mrs. Tanner charged her husband with her fists, trying to pummel him.

Elston swatted his wife hard on the cheek, sending her reeling backward against the wagon box.

Beverly jumped between them and extended her arms. "Father! Mother! Just stop it," she cried. "You've never once had a fight with each other before in twenty years. Please, don't start now. You're scaring Tommy and Louie. You're scaring me as well. Plus Ma's expecting. She'll miscarry."

Tyler looked far ahead to his left. Press Doolittle sat his mount, watching the wagons moving. Tyler put his fingers to his teeth and whistled at Press as loudly as he could.

"What's the matter?" Pa asked.

Doolittle rode toward Tyler. The scout's growing beard snapped in the breeze.

"Problem with the Tanner wagon," Tyler called out to Doolittle as he neared. "Can't we stop for the night so they can fix it?"

"It's only three-thirty in the afternoon," Doolittle muttered. "Some of these wagons are getting beyond fixing, anyway. We're gonna have to start doubling some families up. The Eisenbarger and Teagarten wagons have also broken down." He swung his horse around. "I'll see to the Tanners."

Tyler drove on as the wind started picking up steadily. Dust and sand swirled around him and Penny. Drake and Dru bawled anew in protest.

Tyler turned to look at the MacNaughtons again. Renford lashed his whip and cursed his oxen mercilessly to keep them moving. Eliza gamely walked rather than rode. The MacNaughton oxen could not last much longer.

Trying to focus again on the Ellis wagon just ahead, Tyler felt his thirst once more. The sand particles hitting his sunburned left cheek and nose didn't help As quickly as it had started, though, the wind died down. Surely, however, it was an ominous portent of what was to come with dust storms.

CHAPTER FIFTEEN

That evening after another two hours of travel, several young people made a brave effort to hold a square dance. Tyler sat disinterestedly against a wagon wheel, but here came Billie Kay.

"I just spoke with Charity Tewksberry, the cute girl with the long strawberry blonde hair," Billie Kay announced, holding her brown calico skirt. "She said she'd love to dance with you and get to know you."

"Hmmm," Tyler said, turning away. "How does someone get a name like Charity Tewksberry?"

"Probably by having a couple of parents named Tewksberry who named their daughter Charity, smarty-guy," Billie Kay huffed. "Now will you never mind that?" Billie Kay helped Tyler to his feet. "Just go dance with her. I'm trying my darndest to help you, Tyler. Work with me here."

"I know, I know. Don't get me wrong. I appreciate you helping me, Billie Kay." Tyler glanced toward the evening dance. There was Charity Tewksberry, long braided hair and all, in a nice pink pinafore over a yellow calico dress, watching him. She smiled when they made eye contact.

Pa looked up from where he had been giving Drake and Dru a sip of precious water. "Go dance with her," he said.

"Maybe she's thinking that 'Charity Linders' would have a nicer ring to it than 'Charity Tewksberry.'"

It was good to see Pa returning to normal. Tyler nodded. "Well, okay, maybe I should."

Tyler walked over to Charity. He had to admit, she was pretty with her long hair, sea-blue eyes, and American-freckled face. She clasped her hands together as he neared.

"Hi, Tyler," Charity exclaimed. "Billie Kay said you'd be coming."

He smiled gamely at her. "How's it going, Charity? Care to dance?"

"Sure!" She led him out to the dance area, where Bruce Mallory was trying to play his fiddle and call the square dance at the same time. It didn't work too well, but no matter. The young people had a chance to be together for the evening and have some fun, and that was what really mattered.

Charity seemed to know what she was doing, which made things easier for Tyler. Charity did have a feel-comfortable, easy-going way about her. Tyler liked her. Maybe there was life after Rachelle Palmerston after all.

Tyler did two dances with Charity before she asked, "Can we take a break and talk for a moment?"

"Certainly," Tyler agreed. He did not want to do too much dancing anyway. He was mindful of his thirstiness.

Hand-in-hand with Charity, Tyler led her off to the side. "I'm glad it's not too hot this time of day," he said to make conversation. "That makes this desert easier to endure, if not easy."

"Um, Tyler, can I ask you something?"

He noted how she looked slightly worried. "What is it, Charity? Is—is something wrong?"

"Oh, no, no, nothing's wrong." Charity waved a dismissive hand. "I wanted to ask you, though, um, uh, well—"

"What is it, Charity?" Tyler asked, concerned. "Does your family have enough water? Do you need some more?"

"No, no, nothing like that." Charity looked him in the eyes. "I have to ask you, um, how well do you know Tim MacNaughton? Is he a close friend of yours?"

"Well, I know him," Tyler replied. "Yeah, I guess you could say that he's a good friend of mine, I guess."

"Why doesn't Tim MacNaughton come to these dances more often?" Charity asked.

So that was it. Charity Tewksberry saw him as nothing more than a bridge to get through to Tim.

Sighing and becoming disgusted, Tyler replied, "You'd have to ask him that question yourself. He's probably out herding his family's oxen if they can find any grass around here on this hard clay. Look, I'll tell Tim the next time I see him that you asked about him and that you want to dance with him sometime. I'm sure he'll be thrilled."

"Thanks, Tyler, I'd appreciate it."

He started walking away. There was night guard duty to get ready for.

Between Tyler and his wagon, though, stood Angelique Hapsburg. He started to go around her, being unsure what to say to her and wanting to avoid her.

"Hi, Tyler. Did you have a chance yet to look at the book I loaned you?" she asked.

"A little. Mostly my sister Penny's been reading it."

"It'll help you. I know it will."

Tyler said nothing. He half-smiled politely. She smiled back at him as he moved past her. He only noted in passing out of the corner of an eye how she clasped her hands over her breasts and eyed him somberly as he walked past her.

"Thank you for reminding me to improve my English, Tyler," Angelique said. "It helps me feel more like an American when I don't talk with a big accent."

Tyler saw several people, and livestock, hurrying past him toward the southeast.

"Look, it's water. Water!" a woman shouted.

Zach and Ella Bennett, Nathan and Buela Zurich, Lucas Pfister, and Credence Armagast and three of his children were among those rushing frantically through the sagebrush toward what Tyler now saw was a pool of water surrounded by white dust amidst the clay surface near a dried-up section of the Sweetwater.

"Hurry, it's water!" Buela Zurich screamed.

Two cows that had been grazing far off got there first and started drinking. People were not far behind.

Tyler's first instinct was to join them. He held back when he saw Buckman and Silas Maple on horseback hard-charging toward the mob of frenzied people. Buckman and Silas had their revolvers drawn as they bore down toward the water pool.

"Fools! Don't drink that stuff—it's poison and it'll kill all of you." Buckman raced his horse around sod tables to try to cut off the two dozen emigrants running toward the water pool. Buckman was not going to get there before the Zurichs and Credence Armagast, who were running the fastest.

Buckman leveled his late-model revolver and fired two shots which ricocheted off the hard clay ground a few feet in front of Buela Zurich to stop her in her tracks and those behind her. Firing a gun at a woman, that brought the whole mob to a stunned halt. Nathan almost knocked his wife over as he lurched to a stop. Lucas tripped over Credence's foot and fell down. Everyone fearfully turned their attention to Buckman, whose toothy expression was a combination of terror and fury.

"That water is loaded with alkali," Buckman shouted.

"It'll kill anyone or anything that drinks it," Silas added loudly. "Look on the other side of the pool."

Tyler casually walked halfway toward the water pool. It was about forty feet wide. On the far side of the pool was a cattle skull. Past that, in the distance, were more bleached bones of cattle and sheep that had drank the alkali-laced water.

Silas rode forward in front of the crowd. "Water that salty will kill anyone's kidneys. You can use the salt for preserving meat, but don't drink that water. And don't let your livestock drink it either. Keep your livestock away from it."

Moaning and groaning and bitter disappointment ensued. One older man, Brinks, everyone called him, hurried into the knee-deep water anyway. "If this water is good enough for my two cows, it's good enough for me," Brinks muttered. He cupped his hands and started lapping up the water voraciously.

"I promise we'll find a good place to bury you, Mr. Brinks," Buckman said. "You'll be dead in a few hours if not sooner."

Tyler turned to walk away. Before he reached his wagon, he noted several men with rifles and revolvers gathering. There were about a half-dozen men congregating. Charlie Cullendar and Bronson Chuckwood were among them.

"If they won't give us some of their water, we'll force them to!" Charlie declared, shaking a meaty fist.

"Yeah! Crabbage and them have more water than they need for themselves," another tall and lanky man shouted. "We'll make them share, one way or another."

Bronson Chuckwood, short and barrel-chested, raised a rifle to the air. "Crabbage ain't gonna stop us. We'll do whatever we have to."

Tyler saw Brent on one knee nearby also watching the scene. "Does Buckman know about this?" Tyler asked.

"I'm sure he doesn't," Brent said nervously.

"Then maybe one of us best go fetch him and do it quick."

* * *

Tyler followed at a careful distance. Chuckwood, Cullendar and the four other men with them headed for the far east end of the wagon circle. Milon Crabbage stood and watched them come. Women looked on fearfully at what was coming. Crabbage had a Sharps rifle in his hand and he lowered it. Two other men were with him, also with rifles. Tyler only knew the last names of the other two men, Leitner and Hulworth, and that they were single men with no families, as was Crabbage.

As Charlie Cullendar got to within thirty feet of him Crabbage leveled his rifle right at Charlie's fat belly. "That's close enough," Crabbage bellowed. "I told you it's my water, and I'm holding onto it. I need my water for me. Maybe if you people had shown more appreciation when I kept them cholera-ridden Renwilers away from the rest of us—but not a one of you thanked me for doing that. Now I'm supposed to share my water with you ingrates?"

"I got seven kids that are dying of thirst," one of the men with Chuckwood and Cullendar said. "They need water. They don't have enough. Please!"

"Ain't my fault you had seven kids, Rooker," Crabbage muttered. "Overpopulating the earth, you are."

"Why I oughta—"

Bronson Chuckwood jumped in front of Rooker and faced Crabbage. "We not only got families but animals to water as well."

"Animals? Animals?" Crabbage declared incredulously, his thin face hardening. "No wonder you're nearly out of water if you're sharing your supply with your animals."

"Huh!" Cullendar snorted. "I suppose your idea, Crabbage, is we let the horses and oxen die of thirst and then we walk the rest of the way through this desert to Oregon."

"We're wasting our time talking to these bastards!" another of Chuckwood and Cullendar's group shouted. Tyler couldn't remember the man's name now. "We tried asking Crabbage politely earlier and all he did was tell us to go to hell. Now we're gonna ask in a not-so-polite way and see if that works better."

Buckman rode up, knocking aside someone's folding chair, a Sharps rifle in one hand. "There's not going be any shooting tonight, Lawton, unless I do it."

"Stay out of this, Buckman," Lawton muttered. "This ain't your affair. You heard what I said. We tried asking friendly-like, and that got us nowhere. Now we're just gonna take what we need. Now you listen and listen good, Crabbage."

"I'm warning you, Elrud," Buckman said. "This ain't gonna be settled with a gunfight. I won't stand for it."

"Just like you wouldn't stand for killing Stonehouse?" Lawton grunted. "Stay out of this, Buckman! Our young'uns are thirsty, and as far as Crabbage, Leitner, and Hulworth are concerned, our kids can die of thirst."

Lawton pressed his rifle trigger but caught Buckman's bullet in his right ankle first. Lawton fell to the ground, clutching his bloodied right ankle.

Chuckwood, Cullendar and their group wheeled but Buckman had his new military revolver leveled in his left hand to complement his Sharps rifle. "The next man who moves gets a bullet in the gut where it counts," Buckman promised harshly.

"Damn you and piss all over you, Buckman," Lawton muttered, convulsing with pain. "My ankle's broke for sure. How am I supposed to walk with my oxen and herd 'em while my ankle takes three months to heal?"

"It's a flesh wound," Buckman retorted. "You can dig the bullet out pretty quickly. Your two older boys, Trace and Willie, can handle the oxen for you."

Press Doolittle and Silas Maple rode up with pistols ready. "Everybody just drop your weapons," Press ordered. "I mean everybody."

A crowd hurriedly gathered, anxious women and men, children clinging to their mothers.

Chuckwood, Cullendar, Crabbage and the others carefully put their rifles down on the ground as the barrel of Press' pistol eyed each of them in turn.

"You didn't have to shoot him!" Edna Lawton cried out at sight of her husband and his blood-soaked ankle.

Buckman turned his horse to look over the assembling multitude of emigrants. "Listen to me good, all of you. We're in the most dangerous part of this whole journey, where wagon trains break apart, wagons and animals break down and die, and people die, of thirst or by killing one another. Little grudges that have been building up and festering between people here for the past 1,000 miles have a tendency to boil over in this hot desert. From now on, we're fighting anarchy. There's no government authority anywhere here. So we have to govern ourselves. From this point on, you should all consider the wagon train to be under summary law."

Buckman started riding away. He gestured toward Lawton with his rifle barrel. "See to him."

As Buckman rode away, Tyler walked back toward his wagon. Behind him, he thought he heard Crabbage mutter that children could have some of his water, but not adults.

"You adults should have planned better than . . ." Crabbage muttered as Tyler got out of earshot.

Nearing Pa's wagon, he found Penny again sitting on the ground reading to a dozen children from her McGuffey's books. Tyler watched her. All of the children looked swollen-tongued. Some looked like they had been crying from thirst, including young little Jenny Clevenger.

"What was going on?" Penny asked huskily.

"Water fight," Tyler said. "It's over now."

Penny rose to get her two-hourly cup of water. A strange time to be leaving the kids who admired her so, but maybe she just could not stand her thirst any longer. Tyler's own mouth roof felt like thick, dry cotton.

Penny got a tin cupful of water from their barrel. At this point, water was more precious, and more valuable, than all of the gold, silver, and turquoise jewelry put together that Penny wore. However, she did not drink the water herself. Instead, Penny carried the cup of water back to the children she had been reading to. She sat down next to a little four- or five-year-old girl.

"Here, Susie, have some water," Penny throatily said to the little girl. "Just a sip. We have ten children here that we need to share the water with. Roll it around your mouth. It's cold and wet."

After little Susie had sipped the water, Penny wiped the cup with a cloth and gave it to a small boy next to Susie. The small boy took a sip.

"Swirl the water around your mouth," Penny encouraged.

Jenny Clevenger was next. She took a small drink and gave the cup back to Penny, who embraced Jenny with a big hug.

In this way Penny made sure that all ten children seated around her got some water. Only after the younger children had all had a small drink of the precious cooling water, did Penny drink the little that was left.

Tyler felt a hand on his shoulder. He turned and saw that it was Adelaide Laurent, Alain's mother. "Yes, Mrs. Laurent?" he said uncertainly.

She smiled at him with kindly blue eyes surrounded by crow's feet, and she looked at Penny. "Alain truly chose someone special when he chose your sister for a companion," Adelaide said. "There is something special about Penny, and Alain saw that specialness in her. I thought at first that perhaps the age difference between them might be a problem, but Penny would not take a drink of water or even a small sip until all the children around her had drank first. Truly, Alain must have gotten a hint of that deep caring for others in her, and about her, all the way back in Independence. I asked Francois to fetch a little water. Penny is to drink first. She's earned it with her quiet selflessness. We're proud of our son Alain for connecting with such a wonderful girl like Penny."

Tyler sighed heavily and looked away. "Penny is, as Penny does," he murmured.

"Here, for Penny and the children," said Mr. Laurent, approaching with a wooden cup.

"Thank you, Francois." Adelaide Laurent took the cup from her husband. "You first, Penny."

Penny took a drink, then handed the cup to Jenny Clevenger. In this way, the water cup passed all the way around. Tyler finished the drink. There was actually quite a bit left, as all of the children, following Penny's example, had made sure not to drink too much, so that there was some left for the next child.

"Thank you, Mr. and Mrs. Laurent," Tyler said, handing the cup back to them.

"Yes, thank you for the water," Penny said. "What do we all say to Mr. and Mrs. Laurent now, kids?"

"Thank you, Mr. and Mrs. Laurent," several children's voices rang out.

Tyler had had all he could take of this overly-sugared scene and he walked away. Toward the wagon, Pa had found Drake and Dru and the other oxen a little patch of grass and a lot of sagebrush. The oxen nibbled uncertainly on the sagebrush leaves.

"Will there be any grass at all later on?" Tyler asked.

"Probably not till we get to the Little Sandy," Pa said. "There'll be plenty of this blue sagebrush, though. When the oxen get hungry enough, they'll eat it."

Tyler suspected that Drake and Dru were more thirsty than hungry. Their bawling was for water. Pa knew it too as he put a little water in a bucket and let both Drake and Dru have a cool taste.

The next day the faithful oxen pair bawled and bawled some more for water, precious cold water to refresh their parched, dry throats.

Tyler felt for the straining oxen even as his own mouth and throat were like cotton. He heard the oxen begging for even a little water. The poor beasts could not know how long it would be before the next river was reached. "We're all suffering too," he murmured. It was all he could do. For himself, Tyler preferred to go thirsty during the heat of the desert day and then drink his fill in the evening and satiate himself. At the nooning, Tyler barely touched his cup of water.

"I'm trying to hold out as long as I can, Pa, then drink only when I have to," Tyler said, sitting on the ground in the shade of the wagon box.

"I understand," Pa said uncertainly. "But if you have to take a drink of water, take it. I don't want you getting heat stroke and fainting from thirst. That can happen when it's hot and you don't drink anything."

The relentless sun which bathed the emigrants with oven heat, combined with heartless thirst, produced a collective lethargy. People walked beside their oxen as if in a stupor. Oxen bawled; people walked as if ready to collapse. Tyler surmised it was just a matter of time until someone did.

By mid-afternoon Mrs. Hanclicek walked almost dou-bled-over. She was too tired and thirsty to even carry her rosary beads. That, for sure, meant she was in dire straits. Tomas Hanclicek held the reins in front of her so he probably did not see how badly off she was. Nor did she complain. Finally she fell to the ground.

"Mama!" Tomas reacted to his wife's low moan. "Somebody help us."

Quimby Freding, Beth Renwiler and Eliza MacNaughton hurried over to the Hanclicek wagon. Kelly Jay Ellis ran over to Mrs. Hanclicek with a cup of water, which seemed to revive the poor woman. Looking back, Tyler saw Mrs. Hanclicek getting to her feet to be helped inside her wagon where it was shadier, if not cooler.

A loud bawl to his left drew Tyler's attention, where one of the MacNaughton oxen had fallen down. One other ox, yielding to the power of suggestion, also fell. Renford MacNaughton shot off a muzzle-loader pistol into the air to draw Buckman's attention at the front of the wagon train.

Right behind the MacNaughton wagon, the Kirche wagon had lost a wheel. Harlow Kirche, his wife Betty, and their four young children looked numbly at their broken down wagon.

Buckman and Silas Maple came riding toward the scene. "We're going to have to do some doubling up," Buckman declared.

Renford MacNaughton cursed his oxen soundly and lashed his whip at their heads.

"You bought a team that was too small to begin with, MacNaughton," Buckman hollered. "Unhitch your team and let them walk free until we get to Fort Bridger and I think they'll be fine. You can buy another wagon at Fort Bridger."

"What the hell are we supposed to do until we get to Fort Bridger?" Renford demanded. "Walk for two hundred miles?"

"Exactly," Silas declared. Silas turned toward Tyler but his words were still directed at Renford. "You can double up with somebody till we get to Fort Bridger. Harlow, you'll have to do the same."

Pa turned to look at Tyler. Pa let out a sigh and reluctantly said, "I suppose we could take some of the MacNaughtons' stuff in our wagon, their important stuff, I mean, like their plow and other tools."

"I guess we'll have to," Tyler concurred with little enthusiasm.

Renford, his wife Eliza, and Tim and his younger brother Pete loaded up their plow and seeds into the Linders wagon. Now there wouldn't even be room for Penny to sleep in the wagon. All of them would have to sleep in the tent or else under the stars, with the mosquitoes for company.

Nearby, with the sun beating down, the Kirches unhitched their oxen and had to ask around before finding someone who would agree to take their tools on.

"I don't have room in my wagon for any of you or your stuff," Crabbage shouted at Harlow. For emphasis, Crabbage shook his fist at the unfortunate Kirche family. "You knew you were taking your chances like everybody else was when they started out on this journey. Not everyone who starts out for Oregon makes it all the way."

"Are you suggesting, Crabbage, that my family should be abandoned out here in the middle of the desert?" Harlow angrily demanded, wrapping his bony fists around his suspenders.

"Harlow, it's not worth it," Betty Kirche said, pulling her husband away. "Mr. Crabbage doesn't want to help us and so we'll find someone else."

Observing the scene, Ephraim and Abigail Allerton approached the Kirches. "We've got room in our wagon for your tools and supplies," Ephraim said.

"Your wagon's already loaded down with Stonehouse's belongings, though," Harlow said.

"Doesn't matter," Abigail declared. "If we have to throw some of Stonehouse's stuff away now, we'll have room."

Betty Kirche walked up to Abigail and took her hands. "Thank you. Thank you for your kindness."

"You'd do the same for us, we know," Abigail said.

"We have to take care of one another on this trip," Ephraim declared.

Pa looked at Tyler. "Yes we do," he said. "If our wagon were to break down, hopefully somebody would take pity on us."

Tyler felt grateful that Pa was recovering his old self.

Next, Tyler returned his attention to what was going on in front of him. In the Ellis wagon, Billie Kay was busy swathing Kelly Jay's forehead as their father drove their wagon, walking beside it.

Billie Kay saw Tyler observing them. "She's just had a little too much sun, is all," she said about her twin sister's predicament.

"Will she be okay?" Tyler asked.

"She'll be fine, especially when we get to some water," Billie Kay declared.

CHAPTER SIXTEEN

"**O**h, shee—it."

Tyler turned and saw that the Colledge wagon had lost a wheel and Jonathan Colledge wasn't the least bit happy about it. One of their oxen had also collapsed. The poor beast looked dead, with its tongue hanging out of its mouth. The ox wasn't moving at all. Thirst and strain had killed it.

Buckman rode up to the Colledge wagon on the bare, hard clay ground. "Double up with somebody, and be quick about it," he snapped. "We're not stopping for the night for another two or three hours yet."

"I'm not wasting a good steer," Jonathan Colledge declared as Edith Colledge watched and worried. He looked around. "There's plenty of good meat for whatever family will take us in." He turned to Van Buren. "Grab a knife and start butchering this thing."

"On top of the meat we'd get, how much you willing to pay, Colledge, if we take on the stuff from your wagon?" Tyler heard someone from the wagon adjacent to the Colledges say. "For a couple of hundred dollars, you can put your stuff in our wagon."

"Only a hundred dollars buys our help, Colledge!" someone else shouted.

"Find someone quick, Colledge," Buckman reiterated.

With a foam-flecked horse, Press Doolittle rode up to Buckman and gestured with his thumb behind him. "Speaking of being left behind," Press said, "there's a mother with three children and a broke-down wagon up ahead."

Tyler looked ahead and to his left beyond the nearest sagebrush patch.

"I see something," Pa said.

As Tyler drew closer to the object he saw a mother seated on the back of a wagon with a half-torn canvas cover, desperately clinging to what little shade there was. The woman looked to be crying and half-moaning. Maybe her tears had all dried up. She held one small toddler in her arms who looked to be sleeping, or dead.

Two small children were definitely crying, a boy of about five or six, and a girl maybe a year or two older than her brother.

Adelaide Laurent hurried up to the woman and her three children with some water.

"They just left us here. They just left us here!" the woman wailed. "Wagon train about three days ahead of you. My Charlie died of the cholera. Then our wagon broke down and our oxen gave out. The wagon master, a mean man named Rickley or Brickley—that's what I calls him—he said he couldn't do nothing to help us. Nobody took us in when our wagon broke down. The people in the wagon train I was with was just all too selfish. Brickley said that me an' my kids would have to wait for the next wagon train to come along, or else just plain die out here."

"Oh my God." Adelaide held a hand to her mouth. "You could just as easily have been found by wild Indians as by us, or else died slowly of thirst out here."

"Ain't that the truth, though," the woman said as she held the cups of cool, refreshing water to her toddler's lips. "Ask Brickley if he cares what happens to us, though."

Leeanna Smith, tall older daughter of Jonas and Prudence, approached the woman in the broken-down wagon. "You and your kids are welcome to travel with my Pa and Ma and our family," she said. "You won't be any bother. My Pa said it'd be okay."

"Thank 'ee, ma'am," the woman said. "Forbes is my name. Patricia Forbes. My kids are Dunley, Bernice and little Charlie, Jr."

Tyler turned to look back at the Colledge wagon. Van Buren busily carved out large hunks of meat from the dead ox. Some of the ox blood had gotten onto his face, hands, and vest. Jonathan Colledge and his young daughter Edna stood talking with a barrel-chested bespectacled man that Tyler only knew the last name of Ueston, as he recalled.

Blessedly, there were no more incidents that day. Tyler walked and drove on, keeping a careful watch on his own team of oxen and wagon wheels. When the wagon train formed into a circle for the night, there was no dance afterward. People were too thirsty to enjoy anything. Tyler sat in the shade of the wagon early that evening, as did Pa and Penny. Tyler glanced ahead at the Ellis wagon. Billie Kay and Kelly Jay sat in the shade of their wagon. Evidently Kelly Jay was feeling better.

Ironically, as the sun went down, the heat of the day dissipated. The thin mountain air could not hold the afternoon heat. Tyler looked to the east. Even from over a hundred miles away, 10,272-foot Mt. Laramie loomed as the capstone of the Laramie Range. The chillier air and the snow in the distance made Tyler more anxious to get to Oregon and get settled into a warm, snug cabin before winter.

Strange that he thought of winter right in the middle of a desert summer. The water he drank felt cooler and more effective. Tyler settled into his bedroll inside Pa's tent beside the wagon for the night, feeling comfortable. He put the blanket over his head to keep the flies off him, and he was soon fast asleep.

The next day for Tyler started out hot and dry, no surprise there. Tyler wanted nothing more than to get to the Little Sandy River. Silas Maple had said that another day's journey would bring them to within sight of South Pass, the Continental Divide, and the Pacific Springs-Pacific Creek marker, where they would find westward-flowing water. That is, they would find westward-flowing water if the summer sun hadn't dried up Pacific Springs.

Pa drove the wagon with Penny inside amidst the tools and seed bags. This day, Tyler walked, with Tim right next to him. They walked in near-silence for miles, each too thirsty with a swollen tongue and cottony mouth to talk much. The badlands surrounding them, with promontories and sharp-edged rock formations had long since ceased to be scenic. The barren rock in various shades of brown and gray, showed not even a small puddle of water anywhere, much less a stream. It was all Tyler could do to keep putting one foot in front of the other.

"Charity Tewksberry likes you," Tyler finally said to Tim in a hoarse voice. "I forgot she asked me to tell you that."

"If Charity Tewksberry is someone who has a canteen full of water and she's willing to give some of it to me, I'll marry her five minutes from now," Tim said, equally hoarse with a dried-out mouth and throat.

"Lookey ahead," Pa declared.

Tim glanced up. He'd been looking at the ground so much, half-bent over, that he did not see the dark blue thunderheads moving straight toward the wagon train.

"People say it doesn't rain in the desert, but it do," Pa said. "It rains in the desert no different than anyplace else."

Rain? That would be a godsend. Tyler wondered why Pa sounded like the upcoming thunderstorm was about the last thing he wanted to see.

"Get ready for plenty of lightning and hail, as well as rain," Pa said.

Silas rode by, looking at everyone around him. "Get inside or underneath your wagons. We're all sitting ducks out here in the open," he declared, riding on to spread the warning.

As if to underscore the danger, a jagged streak of lightning erupted from one of the low-lying dark clouds all the way to the sagebrush-littered ground. A sharp thunderclap boomed a couple of seconds later, startling the oxen.

Two sprinkles hit Tyler in the face. Pa opened the water barrel on the side of the wagon to allow it to catch the fresh, pure rainwater when it came down in sheets. Another lightning flash followed, then another, with two bursts of thunder almost directly overhead.

"Get inside!" Pa yelled.

"There's no place to sit," Tyler complained.

"Just get inside where it's safer," Pa demanded.

The rain started coming down. Tyler got inside the wagon and had to stand up between Pa's plow and the MacNaughtons' plow. Penny sat in the only available space on the wagon box itself, toward the front. Pa half-seated himself on several leather bags of seed, keeping his head down below the top of the canvas.

Tim climbed in and squatted between one of the plows and a blacksmith bellows. He worriedly looked around when he did not see his parents anywhere. "Ma! Pa!" he yelled into the rain.

"It's okay, Tim," Renford MacNaughton's voice came from behind. "Your Ma and I are with the Burneys."

The heavens opened and the rain came down in sheets.

"I got a water cup," Tim said. He held the tin cup outside the back of the wagon and let it half-fill with rainwater. Tim took a drink and handed the cup to Tyler.

Tyler drank and smacked his lips, then gave the cup to Pa, who did not drink until Penny had tasted the refreshing rainwater.

Outside the wagon, dense rain driven by sharp wind soaked sagebrush and trail alike. Looking toward Drake and Dru, Tyler saw the oxen eagerly lapping up rainwater with their parched tongues. They would be drenched, but probably were not minding.

A scream sounded. "That came from the Ellises' wagon," Pa said.

Tim got out, followed quickly by Tyler. Pa also jumped out.

The white canvas top of the Ellis wagon was half ripped off by the wind. George, Billie Kay, and Kelly Jay frantically worked to grab the flapping edges of the canvas as the rain drenched them.

Tyler hurried to grab the nearest section of the canvas that was still attached. He slid his hand up the edge, bringing it under control and enabling George Ellis to grab the left edges of the canvas. Pa did the same on the other side, with Billie Kay and Kelly Jay grabbing the right side of the canvas.

Tim held both edges of the canvas down. With the rain pouring out of the blue-black clouds, George grabbed a hammer and two nails from the back of his wagon. He nailed down the ends of the canvas, then double-nailed it to prevent it flying off again.

A sharp crack and a burst of lightning enveloped the area to the right of the Ellis wagon. Two women's screams followed.

Tyler looked to his left. The upper part of a wagon sixty feet away had burst into flames. A baby's screams pierced the rain from inside the flaming wagon. Tyler raced over to the wagon. Reaching around the burning canvas, Abigail and Ephraim pulled two bodies, a man's and a woman's, out of the flaming wagon which had evidently been struck by lightning in a direct hit. On the other side, Patience Burney pulled a small, crying baby out of the back of the wagon as Renford MacNaughton ripped canvas away from the wagon box. Patience's dress hem had caught fire. She screamed as she put the baby down on the ground and then fell rolling to the ground herself. Will Burney swatted the flames on his wife's dress with his outer shirt. Tyler joined him, swatting the flames with his light coat. The heavy rain and wet ground plus Will and Tyler's efforts put out the fire on Patience Burney's dress before it grew. Patience clutched her blouse, her mouth wide open.

"Two dead," Ephraim declared on the other side of the wagon.

"And one live baby," Patience said, breathing heavily as she rose.

"You okay, dear?" Will asked as he clutched his wife's shoulder.

Patience looked down at her burnt hem. "I'm all right." She glanced at her husband and then at Tyler and she nervously smiled. "Thank God for the rain and for the two of you. I might have burned to death."

"It was the rain that caused the lightning in the first place," Will muttered.

Tyler looked at the clothes of the young-looking dead man and woman. "Who were they?"

"All I know about them is their name was Cortland, or Corheart, or something like that," Ephraim replied.

Pa asked, "Who's going to take care of the baby?"

"It looks like we will," Patience said mildly, smiling through the rain. She took the baby in her arms again.

Tyler felt a ping of hail against his face, a quarter-inch in diameter. He turned his shirt lapel up to give himself some minimal protection. Two dead people from a lightning strike and an orphaned baby. Now hail.

The hailstones bounced off the top and sides of the white canvas-covered Linders wagon. Pa had bought good material to go with the wagon box. Others were not so lucky. Tyler saw five or six different wagons, including the Lawton and Rooker wagons get ripped nearly wide open by hail, some of it a half-inch in diameter.

Small wonder that Pa did not look forward to heavy rain.

Mercifully, the rainstorm did not last long and was over within a few more minutes. Desert rainstorms were typically intense, but brief. It had lasted long enough, though. While some rejoiced at replenished water barrels and wet mouths, others, including the Allertons and the Kirches, moved to bury the two dead Cortlands, or whatever their names were, or had been.

For one of the few times during the day since Independence, Tyler saw Buckman not mounted, but walking. "Hurry up and bury them," he ordered Ephraim Allerton. "We need to get this wagon train moving again. The rain held us up."

With that, Buckman stomped away. There would be no prayer or service by him this time. Death was becoming simply too common on the trail by now to make much of a fuss over it. Buckman apparently felt the Cortland bodies were just so much waste to be disposed of. The Allertons, Kirches, and a dozen others buried the Cortlands even as the other wagons got rolling again.

As Pa got the oxen moving once more with his whip, Tyler wondered as he walked if, out of respect, he should join the brief graveside ceremony. He decided against it. Tyler next wondered if perhaps he, too, was becoming inured and callous toward death. Death had not struck the Linders family. He asked himself if he was getting to the point where other peoples' misfortunes really mattered to him anymore. A death here, another death there, Tyler felt he just didn't have enough emotion left within him to handle it properly.

The wagon train got rolling again but only for an hour. The trail began turning muddy and Buckman must have seen it. The rain returned, not a downpour, but a gentle wetting. Buckman ordered the wagons to form their circle for the night.

Once the wagon circle had formed, Pa let Drake and Dru graze in the rain on the blue sagebrush. Tyler helped him despite the fact that even in his coat he was soaking wet. It was a cold, clammy feeling. Sometimes there was just too much of a good thing. One day in this desert, a person could be dying of thirst and heat, the next, a person could be worrying about flash flooding, or about the possibility of freezing to death at night in wet clothes as the temperature plunged.

Elrud Lawton approached, walking with a crutch and breathing heavily through his beard and growing mustache. Tyler's guard instantly went up. Pa saw him coming too, and his expression became worried. This was not going to be anything pleasant.

"I've been going around talking to people," Lawton started.

Not smart, Tyler thought. *You should be resting that foot, not putting weight on it.*

"Some of us have decided it's time to replace Buckman as our wagon master," Lawton said through the rain. "He always has been high and mighty, but lately, he's become downright dangerous and arrogant."

Pa exchanged glances with Tyler.

"He shot Stonehouse dead like it was nothing. Then he tried to kill me," Lawton continued.

Pa looked uncertain. He rubbed his dark whiskers thoroughly.

He didn't try to kill you, Tyler thought to himself. *He easily could have shot you dead-center in the chest if he'd really wanted to.*

"Well, who you got in mind to replace him with?" Pa asked.

"Maybe Josh Rooker, or Mase Edwell said he'd be willing to take over."

Pa leaned on one of the back wagon wheels. "Don't know either one of 'em. Either one of those guys got experience traveling through the mountains?"

"Well, no, but they read all the guidebooks before starting out, and they ain't the type to shoot somebody who disagrees with 'em. We'll be safer with one of them in charge."

"Safer?" Pa declared. "Too many of those guidebooks were written by people living in the East who think they know something because they heard a thing or two second-hand. People that know the West real well, people like Buckman, ain't got the education to write a book. Do Rooker and Edwell have any direct experience dealing with the Indian tribes up ahead, the Snakes and such? The Snakes aren't going to know or care about our agreement with the Sioux. And do Rooker and Edwell know anything about mountain passes or the best shortcuts?"

"Suit yourself, Linders, if you don't want to join up with us tomorrow," Lawton snarled. "At least some of us aren't afraid to stand up to Buckman."

As Lawton stalked away on his crutch, Pa turned to Tyler. "I rather suspect there's going to be one ugly turn of events tomorrow morning," Pa said. "Lawton's a hothead and I want no part of any scheme that he's hatching."

* * *

"Buckman, we need to talk!"

Even from a hundred feet away Tyler could hear Lawton's booming voice. Groggily, Tyler rose to one elbow on his bedroll to see what was going on. Walking with a cane, Lawton had gathered a following behind him. There was Josh Rooker, Mase Edwell, and about a half-dozen other men around them. An equal number of worried women and older children with them stood watching behind them. Trace and Willie Lawton stood close to their father.

Buckman calmly rode up to the group challenging him in the early dawn light. He dismounted to face them directly. "I heard tell about some of you folks not liking my leadership. There's nothing preventing you or anyone who's unhappy from striking out on their own."

"There's safety in numbers," young, pudgy Willie Lawton muttered. "We just need the right leader."

"And the right leader is somebody who's never been west of Missouri till now?" Buckman muttered "Like I said, strike out on your own. I'm not stopping you."

Elrud Lawton drew a muzzle-loader pistol from his pants, pointing it straight at Buckman. Clearly, Lawton was spoiling for a confrontation with Buckman and would not be satisfied until he'd had one.

"No need for that," Buckman declared. "Just go, if that's what you want."

"Oh we're going all right," Lawton snapped. "We're going all the way to Oregon, without you."

Pa grabbed his rifle, as did Dennis Palmerston, Elston Tanner and Lucas Pfister nearby. Tyler clambered to his feet and grabbed his rifle to follow after Pa. He assumed that Pa was going to the scene to help avoid a bloody confrontation.

Lawton raised his pistol to shoot. Buckman pulled his revolver out of nowhere.

"Drop it, Lawton!" Tyler screamed.

Pa leveled his rifle along with Dennis, Elston, and Lucas. Lawton wheeled to fire at Tyler. Buckman fired and Lawton was hurled sideways and down, a bullet in his left side. Willie fingered his rifle trigger to kill Buckman.

"Don't do it or I'll shoot!" Elston hollered.

A bang and Trace Lawton's rifle shot caught Elston in the chest right above his heart.

"Rifles down everybody!" Press Doolittle bellowed, riding up with a drawn revolver. "Everybody, guns down on the ground!"

"That's twice now I could have belly-shot you if I'd have wanted to, Lawton," Buckman snapped.

"I'm hit—hit," Elston moaned, clutching his chest. Blood rolled out in gushes from Elston's chest. "Fetch my wife, and my kids. Fetch 'em now. I ain't got long here."

Silas Maple rode at a gallop with his revolver leveled at the Lawtons. "Hands up, Trace, Willie, Mase, and the rest of you with Lawton," Silas bellowed. "I'll shoot the next one of you that moves, and I'll shoot you right between the eyes. No flesh wounds."

Rifles down, Lucas, Tyler, and Dennis hurried over to kneel next to Elston.

"There's nothing you can do for me," Elston moaned as blood gushed out of his mouth now. He coughed more blood out. "I'm a goner. Somebody fetch my wife and kids so I can see them one last time. P-please, fetch them."

"I'll get them," Pa said quickly.

Pa hurried away but he didn't have far to run. Brenda Tanner, with Beverly, Tommie and Louis were all of them already rushing to the gunfight scene.

"Father!" Beverly screamed, hands clutching her cheeks.

"Elston!" Brenda shrieked

A very pregnant Brenda Tanner and her three children threw themselves down beside Elston. Brenda lifted Elston in her arms. He caressed her face with a bloodied hand as he half-smiled at her, then at all three of his children individually.

"Elston . . . Elston . . ." Brenda wailed as the tears streamed.

He coughed more blood, then gave his family one last smile. "Love . . . I love all . . . of . . ." Then Elston's head gently fell to the side, and he was dead.

The shrieks of Brenda and Beverly Tanner were so loud that a flock of sage grouse nearby rose up and hurried into the sky, seeming to accompany Elston Tanner's soul heavenward. Tommie and young Louie burst into tears in spite of themselves.

"Pa! Pa!" Louie shouted.

Brenda Tanner gently lay her dead husband's head down on the ground, and numbly she rose to her feet, facing Trace Lawton. She pointed a stiff, long finger at Trace. "This kid shot my Elston down dead. I saw it," she wailed. "I say we hang him."

"Yeah, hang him!" Tommie echoed.

Trace jerked his gaze around, from the Tanners to Buckman and back to the Tanners. Breathing hard through his thin-lipped mouth, he looked scared and going numb.

"I say hang him," Brenda Tanner shrieked again. "I want some justice!"

"Ain't no trees anywhere to hang him from," Louie said, observant of the rocky desert.

"Then shoot him," Brenda demanded.

"Don't kill my boy," Elrud Lawton begged from the ground. "He's only sixteen years old. Don't hang him. I started this. I did. If you want blood vengeance, kill me instead, but please dear God leave my boy be. This ain't his doing."

Trace looked again at Buckman, his wide-open eyes beseeching for help.

"You want vengeance, I'll give you some, if you just leave my boy Trace alone," Lawton begged anew. He lifted his pistol. Buckman backed up in reaction. But Lawton did not aim at Buckman. Instead, he put his pistol to his own head and fingered the trigger.

"No!" Beverly screamed with arms raised. "There's been enough bloodshed." She raced over to Lawton and grabbed the pistol out of his hand.

Beverly held the pistol, looking at Lawton and breathing hard through tight teeth. She glanced away from him, though, and turned to look at Trace. She raised the pistol and pointed it squarely at Trace Lawton's chest.

Buckman backed away, signaling that he was not going to interfere. Press and Silas sat their mounts in silence, indicating they had no intention of stopping what was about to happen. Beverly took a deep breath. Trace did the same. He did not run, probably knowing it was useless. Tyler watched, unable to think what to do.

Beverly pulled the trigger hard, and the bullet sailed away, over Trace's left shoulder and harmlessly out into the desert. Beverly dropped the pistol to the ground and burst into tears anew. Brenda hugged her daughter tightly.

With a haggard thin face Buckman glared at Elrud Lawton. He put his pistol away between his pants and shirt. "I want you and your wife and Trace and Willie, Mase Edwell and anyone else with you to hitch up your wagons and head south, away from the direction we're heading. If I ever see you again, Lawton, or Trace, I'll kill the both of you on sight. I mean it! I'm giving you and your gang a half-hour to hitch up your wagons and head out on your own away from the rest of us. If you're still in camp a half-hour from now, I'll kill you and Trace and leave both your bodies out in the open for the wolves to feed on."

CHAPTER SEVENTEEN

Buckman walked over to Brenda Tanner. The whole family was hugging one another and weeping together next to Elston's dead body. A father and a husband was gone. "Elston was a good man," Buckman murmured. "I don't say that lightly. He was always willing to do more than his share to help the rest of us. We won't start for the day until he's been given a proper burial."

With that, Buckman headed back to remount his horse, the discussion over as far as he was concerned. His eyes locked with Tyler's. Tyler wasn't sure what, if anything, to say.

"You can thank me by taking the second watch tonight, Tyler," Buckman said.

"Yes sir, I'd be happy to." Tyler was numb. Lawton had meant to kill him.

Tyler turned to walk away and Pa hurried to catch up with him.

"If the Tanners need anything, anything, we'll help them," Pa declared. "That family is going to need time to grieve. Maybe we can spare them some buffalo jerky."

Tyler nodded, brushing brown bangs out of his eyes. "I agree. I feel like we should do something, Pa. Maybe if we'd have talked to Lawton more last night, this could have been avoided."

"Now don't go starting that," Pa snapped. "Lawton and Lawton alone is responsible for what happened. He wanted a showdown with Buckman, and by damn, he got one. Let's not go blaming ourselves for Lawton not being able to control himself.

"Buckman's got us safely this far," Pa continued. "I trust him to get us the rest of the way to the Willamette Valley. He hasn't shot anybody that wasn't asking good and loud to be shot."

"I reckon not," Tyler agreed. Still, it was unnerving, what had just happened. Elston Tanner had not exactly been a friend, just a sort of acquaintance. Still, Tyler felt deeply for the Tanner family. It was a reminder that they were literally in the middle of nowhere. There was no organized government or law or judicial system, where they were at. Force of habit in obedience to social norms, backed up by guns and the willingness to use them, was the only source of law in these parts. Another 100 miles would bring the wagon train to within the remote purview of Utah Territory and its laws. But even then, Tyler figured there would be no organized law or constitution outside the immediate vicinity of Salt Lake, a place the wagon train would skirt around by several hundred miles.

It was Pa's turn to briefly sit in the wagon box and drive the team, after Elston Tanner's burial. Tyler walked, still trying to absorb the impact of Tanner's death. He watched the Tanner wagon about a hundred feet to the right. Clayton Finlayson drove the Tanner wagon as the grieving family walked together beside it

The rain returned again, creating a distraction, but thankfully not with thunder and lightning and hail, just a steady all-day shower, just enough to soak clothes all over again. Blue sagebrush drooped. Wet rocks and promontories turned a darker shade of brown.

"What sort of self-respecting desert lets it rain all the time?" Pa demanded.

Tyler wondered that himself over the next few days of travel, with more rain and general discomfort.

* * *

"There it is! Up ahead, I see it—South Pass," Dennis Palmerston shouted. "Once we're over the hump of the mountains, it'll be downhill all the way from there."

"Well, not quite," Tyler mumbled to himself. Some of the most rugged terrain lay ahead. Still, South Pass was a major milestone. The journey was indeed more than half over now. People could start to truly believe that they would make it all the way to Oregon, not partway, but all the way to the Willamette Valley.

Pa looked at Tyler walking beside the oxen. "Don't get too excited yet. It's another ten or fifteen miles to get there."

There was reason not to get excited. After two days of pouring rain, in the desert, the trail was turning to mud, actually a special kind of mud "gumbo," Tyler remembered it was called, that was downright sticky.

Whatever it was called, it was pure misery. Heavy wagons, many loaded with the possessions of families that had doubled up, became bogged down in the thick, gooey, yellow mud. Tyler spent much of the day helping Pa push their wagon out of one foot-deep quagmire after another, as Penny and Tim MacNaughton drove the team, and then helping others with their stuck wagons. After the rain stopped, the residual high humidity—unexpected in the desert—made Tyler and others around him sweat buckets.

Ahead, the Ellis wagon's left front wheel sank eight inches deep in a mud hole. Tyler gritted his teeth. George Ellis plus his two daughters would need help. Along with Pa, Tyler labored to help push the back end of the Ellis wagon with Billie Kay and Kelly Jay. George Ellis stood beside the wagon box, cracking a whip over his team's heads.

No sooner had the Ellis wagon been freed than the Palmerston wagon, both front wheels, became bogged down in several inches of thick yellowish muck. Tyler had no use for Rachelle Palmerston anymore, but he liked her father Dennis and her mother Helena, and so he helped them. In the case of the two front wheels, it was necessary to attach ropes to the front wagon axle and help the straining, complaining oxen pull the darn thing loose from the mud.

Once this fun chore was done, the ropes had to be detached from the axle, and Tyler, Pa and Dennis had to get in back of the wagon and push the back wheels through the muck.

This agreeable task completed, Tyler started walking away, loaded with sweat and breathing hard as the desert heat beat down once more.

"Thank you, Tyler, we appreciate it," Rachelle said.

Yeah, whatever, Tyler thought. *Your fiancé doctor isn't here to help you, but I am, not that it does me any long-term good.*

Much of that day, as he drove Drake and Dru, Tyler saw the same scene playing out. People would lighten their wagons by removing prized, if heavy, possessions—a heavy bureau, a clock with a tooled ornate case, a cabinet, chairs, a small table, a crib, a clothing box—in order to make it easier to push or pull the wagons out of the gumbo. Once their wagons were free of the mud, families would pile their possessions back in their wagons, only to have to unload them again after another hundred yards.

Heartbreaking decisions again had to be made by some families about what possessions to keep. Was it really necessary to keep grandma's favorite dresser, mother's favorite high-backed chair, or a favorite heavy quilt handed down from colonial ancestors? It was either leave some of these things behind, and make it to Oregon, or else have oxen and wagons not be able to move another foot.

At the end of the day, though, South Pass was reached.

The Pass itself was hardly anything glamorous. Tyler felt a little disappointed. South Pass was just a gentle rise over the Continental Divide, with the Wind River Mountains, so named by mountain men twenty years earlier, in the distance to the right. Interesting, though, there were patches of snow scattered around. The elevation, over 7,700 feet above sea level, was responsible, or so Silas Maple said. There was no cause for alarm. The wagon train was not behind schedule or in any danger yet of being caught in early snowstorms.

To the left were the Oregon Buttes, and Pacific Springs and Pacific Creek. Westward-flowing water that meandered toward the Pacific, not the Gulf of Mexico and the Atlantic. Plus a few more snow patches at the mile-and-a-half elevation above sea level.

"Hip, hip, hooray for Pacific-bound water!" Dennis Palmerston raised his hat and repeated his exclamation. "Hip, hip, hooray! I can almost see the Pacific Ocean now."

Many tired men and even women repeated the shout. Strain his eyes though he did, Tyler saw nothing that looked like the Pacific, and he was sure Dennis couldn't, either. He knew what Dennis meant, though. They were on the other side of the Continental Divide.

West Coast, here we come!

The Oregon Trail could throw up all sorts of obstacles in their way that it wanted, they were overcoming them.

That evening with the wagons circled near Pacific Creek, the dance seemed like more than the usual celebration at the end of a hard day of travel. It was a celebration of near-triumph. To be sure, there would be more blood, sweat, and tears and maybe even more deaths up ahead. But they had made it this far. Men and their families felt their confidence growing that if they could make it this far, there were no obstacles ahead which they could not overcome, as they had overcome everything in their way to this point.

Tyler watched the dancing from a distance, near his wagon, leaning on his rifle. He'd labored hard that day and was tired. Maybe he could dance again some other night.

Here came Billie Kay, though, smiling at him. She was back at it again. "I've been talking with Marta Hanclicek all about you, Tyler," Billie Kay said. "She told me that you're someone that she'd like to get to know better. She's got nobody to dance with right now."

"My legs are pretty well shot for today," Tyler begged off.

"Okay, so don't dance with her. Just go talk with her. I spent a lot of time chatting with her to work up her interest in you."

Tyler put his rifle down as Billie Kay pushed him in the direction of the dance and Marta Hanclicek, but Tyler hesitated.

"I don't know about Marta," Tyler said. "She's too . . . too . . ."

"East European? Slavic?" Billie Kay finished Tyler's thought for him. "Tyler Linders, I'm ashamed of you. Now do I have to drag you over to Marta? Don't make me do that, Tyler."

"Well, I'm not sure that—"

"Don't make me do that, Tyler." Billie Kay grabbed his left arm hard. She meant business.

"All right, I'm going," Tyler said. "I'll try anything once."

"Give someone besides Rachelle a chance," Billie Kay encouraged.

"I haven't even thought about Rachelle for over a week now," Tyler said.

He headed toward the music and dance. Marta Hanclicek was beautiful—dark-hair in a bun, dark eyes, and a thin, clear, squarish face. Tyler approached her and she smiled at him as she stood next to Brent McGuigan.

"Hey, Tyler, how are you?" Marta said excitedly.

"Very good," Tyler replied. "Billie Kay told me you'd like to dance."

"Yes, yes, I would," Marta declared. "I'm just catching my breath for a moment. I'm doing one dance with Brent and then I would like to dance with you."

"Fair enough," Tyler said, happy to rest for a moment. "That'll be fine."

After another minute, Marta went back into the square dance with Brent. Tyler waited patiently. The dance ended, and Marta did another dance with Brent.

Then another. And another. And another. Marta appeared to have developed eyes this evening only for Brent. Tyler did not even see her make any eye contact again with him. Marta seemed to have completely forgotten about him.

Tyler walked away.

He headed back toward his wagon, next to the Ellises. Billie Kay stood holding hands with Justin Maybrie. She looked distressed.

"You saw what happened, right?" Tyler asked.

Billie Kay nodded reluctantly. "I saw." She took his hands in hers. "Tyler, I feel so sorry for you. When your heart breaks, mine does too, for you."

Tyler assumed an air of smugness. "Is that so?"

"Yes, that is so," Billie Kay said mildly. "Tyler, I know that it's going to happen for you. I'm not giving up. My heart tells me it's going to happen for you."

Tyler saw the earnestness in Billie Kay's softening brown eyes and her expression. Truly, she suffered for him. He could not deny it. She wished so dearly for him to have the desire of his heart, and to see him failing truly hurt her.

She gripped his arm anew. "Tyler, listen to me," Billie Kay declared mildly. "I feel for you. I am not giving up. So surely as I have belief and a heart within me, I know that I am going to succeed in fitting you with a wife. I promise you, Tyler, that before we reach Oregon, I am going to find you a young woman who has eyes only for you, and who can gladly and joyfully and confidently decide that she can spend the rest of her life with you." She placed a comforting hand on his shoulder.

"Hmm." Tyler bowed his head and looked at the ground. Maybe it was his fate to be unlucky in love. He looked up again. Billie Kay still looked at him. She was half-smiling now, her eyes happy for him. Her hand still rested upon his shoulder.

Billie Kay gave him a couple of cheerful, affectionate pats. "I'm going right now to check out one or two other options that I've had in mind for you."

As Billie Kay turned to leave, Justin looked at Tyler. "And when Billie Kay says she's going to do something, I believe her." Justin pointed a friendly finger at Tyler, and grinned. He walked on to follow Billie Kay in her matchmaking efforts.

Pa sauntered over. "By this time tomorrow, we'll be well past the Little Sandy and beyond the Wind River Mountains."

"And then on to the Seeds-kee-dee," Tyler said, putting melancholy thoughts aside for the moment.

"They're calling it the Green River now," Pa said. "Easier to say."

Tyler took the first night watch. Tim MacNaughton helped him. As he observed the stars coming out, Tyler dawdled near the Ellis wagon. On the other side he heard arguing.

". . . not want to go to California!" The voice sounded like Kelly Jay's.

"We've been over this a hundred times," George Ellis bellowed. "I'm heading southwest to California at Fort Hall. There's no gold in Oregon."

Tyler moved on with Tim.

"I heard there's five or six other families that'll be heading to California," Tim said. "Truth is, I been thinking about doing that myself."

"You can't be serious," Tyler declared. "I'm sticking with Oregon. I'm not going to chase after fool's gold."

"And that ain't the half of it," Dennis Palmerston said, overhearing as he threw coffee on his evening campfire. "In California, I hear that a loaf of bread costs two dollars. Two whole dollars for a loaf of bread! Can you believe it? A bag of coffee beans is four dollars. You got to be a gosh-darn millionaire to afford to buy food at those prices. I'm sticking to Oregon too."

The next day Tyler had to walk while Pa drove alongside him. The sun felt surprisingly hot. High humidity added to the misery. The nooning was a welcome respite although the sweat underneath Tyler's armpits made him feel clammy.

As Tyler drank coffee with Pa, he watched George Ellis arguing anew with Kelly Jay outside their wagon. Billie Kay did not participate in the discussion as she was off a ways talking with Angelique Hapsburg. From what he could hear, Billie Kay's conversation with Angelique centered on Indians and the likelihood of seeing more of them near Fort Bridger.

George Ellis's arguing made it hard to hear anything else. "If I find gold, I won't have to work another day in my life," he bellowed anew.

"If, if, if you find gold," Kelly Jay declared. "What if you don't find gold, or not enough to amount to anything? What then? We'll never get back to Pennsylvania. We'll be stuck in California forever."

"I'm not discussing this any further! I've made my decision and that's final."

Tyler saw Kelly Jay run off in tears.

The journey resumed with more high mountains in the distance. Tyler felt a discouraging numbness in the pit of his stomach. The roughest part of the journey lay ahead in about another eighty to ninety miles. The Little Sandy River, a narrow, shallow, gentle stream came up. The wagons crossed it without incident. It was a welcome chance to fill up water barrels minus the drenching rain of recent days.

Evening camp was made midway between the Little Sandy River and the Green River. As per usual, Pa pulled the wagon up behind the Ellis wagon, with the Allertons close behind.

Tyler sat on a three-legged stool and ate his typical evening meal of beans and smoked bacon, with Pa and Penny. After awhile Penny left to go talk with Billie Kay. Tyler watched carefully. As Billie Kay and Penny conversed, Tyler saw them cast furtive glances at him and then chuckle together.

"I'm telling you, I can do it."

Tyler turned. Ephraim Allerton talked to Abigail loud and strong as he led his oxen out to munch on the short grass.

"I'm telling you, Abby, I can get our wagon across the Seeds-kee-dee without having to pay one nickel to a ferryman," Ephraim said.

"And I still say you're a fool to try." Abigail put her hands on her hips. "I hear the Green River is twenty feet deep in places. It isn't worth the risk to save a few dollars."

"A few dollars will buy a good acre or more of wheat seed once we get to Oregon," Ephraim insisted.

"We got plenty of seed but we could lose it all if we lose our wagon tomorrow," Abigail retorted.

Tyler turned back to watch Billie Kay and Penny. They had vanished, nowhere in sight. They were up to something, but Tyler doubted that either Billie Kay or Penny would ever tell him what, until the plot was hatched and in the open.

The next day's journey carried the wagon train to the Green River, a hundred feet wide, swift and looking deep at the center. Cottonwoods and aspens lined the banks. As the first set of wagons neared the Mormon-run ferry, Buckman rode past.

"We're making good time," he said. "We can avoid a waterless cutoff and head southwest toward Fort Bridger and take on supplies and new oxen if there's need."

"Fine with me," Pa declared. "If there's a new pair of oxen we can get at Fort Bridger, maybe that's a good idea. Drake and Dru have given us fine service on this trip and they don't owe us a thing. They've earned a rest."

"Why, Pa?" Penny asked plaintively. "Drake and Dru have been good friends. I'll miss them."

Walking beside the oxen, Pa turned and gently smiled at Penny. "I know you'll miss 'em, Penny-golden. So will I. But we got to think of what's fair for Drake and Dru. If they could talk and tell us what they wanted, what do you think they'd say at this point? Would they tell us they want to keep pulling the wagon for another eight hundred miles? They're both a lot thinner than when we first started out. They need rest and recuperation, and then they can be of service to some other family on the next wagon train once they've filled out again. That other family will love them the same as we have."

First, though, there was the matter of crossing the Green. Pa paid four dollars to the Mormon ferryman without a second thought, as did everyone else in front of them. A few grumbled, but all paid.

All with the exception of Ephraim Allerton. Ephraim tried to negotiate. "I'll pay you fifty cents," he told the thick-bearded ferryman. "That's a fair price and high at that."

The ferryman shook his head vigorously, having none of it. "The price is four dollars, take it or leave it, and I don't much care which you choose, mister. If I cut the price for you to fifty cents, then everybody behind you will want to pay only fifty cents. Plus, I'll have to give money back to them's that's crossed ahead of you. Four dollars, take it or leave it."

"I'm leaving it," Ephraim muttered, kicking a riverside bush for emphasis. "I'll get my wagon across the river without any help from any highway robbing ferryman."

"Ephraim, I'm crossing ahead of you with the Palmerstons," Abigail said. "Stubborn old fool, you cross whatever way you want."

"You need a couple of bucks?" Clayton Finlayson asked Ephraim. "Wouldn't be no trouble for me to help you if you can't af—"

"Thanks for the charity but no thanks just the same," Ephraim replied. "I got money. That ain't the problem. It's the principle of the thing. I not gonna stand for being nickeled and dimed at every fort and river crossing for things I shouldn't be having to pay for."

Tyler listened to the arguing from the other side of the river. Once it was clear that Ephraim had made up his mind, Abigail crossed the river with the Palmerston wagon on the ferry, which the ferryman and his assistant pulled along with ropes strung across the river.

Watching carefully from the opposite bank, Tyler saw Ephraim snap his team's reins and head his oxen and wagon straight into the Green River. He didn't even bother removing the wheels this time.

The six oxen drove forward pulling the wagon. To steady the oxen Ephraim walked beside them through the water, walking on the sandy river bottom. All looked fine.

As the water deepened, however, the first pair of oxen panicked. Bawling with fright the oxen flailed their legs, churning the water. Ephraim was pushed away from the oxen and the current caught him. He flailed his arms, bobbed up and down in the water, slamming the river surface with his hands.

"Help—help me! Help!"

"Ephraim! My God—Ephraim! Ephraim!" Abigail shrieked. She stumbled into the water splashing and swirling with her sight limited to one eye. "He can't swim. Neither can I!"

Tyler dove into the water, clothes and all, swimming with all his strength toward Ephraim Allerton. On the opposite bank someone else dove into the river. It was Angelique Hapsburg.

"Help me—somebody!" Ephraim beseeched for his very life, his head bobbing above and beneath the surface as he fought to keep from dropping into the eighteen-foot-deep water.

Tyler swam toward him along with Angelique. She grabbed a tree branch as she swam furiously.

"Use this!" Angelique shouted to Tyler, pushing the tree branch ahead of her. "Don't get too close to him. He's panicking and he'll just pull you down with him."

Angelique threw the tree branch ahead of her toward Tyler with his stronger arms. Tyler grabbed the tree branch and thrust one end forward toward Ephraim. Clutching the end of the tree branch, Ephraim pulled his head back above water. Tyler began pulling him toward the opposite bank. Angelique got behind Tyler and clutched him about the chest. With one arm she swam, pulling Tyler pulling Ephraim toward the river bank as Ephraim clutched the tree branch.

"I can't swim!" Ephraim screamed and flailed his legs. "I can't stay above water. I'm going to drown!"

"Shut up!" Angelique ordered. "Just shut up and let us help you. Let your legs and body relax. You'll float more easily that way. We're pulling you toward the shore. It's not that far."

Tyler used one arm to help move his body toward the river bank. Buckman and Silas Maple also dove into the water. As Angelique and Tyler pulled Ephraim along they finally hit shallow water where Ephraim's feet could touch bottom again. Coughing and spluttering, Ephraim fought through the water toward shore. Buckman and Silas reached Ephraim.

"We got him," Silas declared. He and Buckman got on either side of Ephraim and helped him steady himself.

Abigail helped Ephraim the last ten feet to the riverbank. She pounded his shoulder with her fists. "Stupid, stupid fool! What did you think you were doing?"

Press Doolittle guided the oxen to solid ground pulling the Allerton wagon behind them. Miraculously, the current hadn't carried the wagon away. Ephraim Allerton had gotten his wagon across the Green River without paying anything to the ferryman, but at nearly the cost of his life and goods.

Buckman got on top of a large boulder on the riverbank to look hard and furious at those still on the other side waiting to cross. "Anybody else that tries a stunt like that, far as I'm concerned, you can go ahead and drown," Buckman hollered angrily. "One man nearly died trying to save himself four dollars." Buckman gestured at Tyler and Angelique coming out of the water sopping wet. "These other two people had to risk their lives to save him. Use the ferry and I don't mean maybe from now on."

CHAPTER EIGHTEEN

The wagon train made camp for the night about five miles southwest of the Green River. Tyler sat with Pa in the shade of the wagon, watching the oxen graze on the blue sagebrush. The dry desert air and warm breeze had evaporated the water in his wet clothes within half an hour. There must have been billions of these sagebrush plants around. Still, Drake and Dru looked markedly thinner lately. They would never make it all the way to Oregon. Pa was right. They would have to get a new pair of lead oxen at Fort Bridger.

Uh oh, here's trouble. Tyler saw Billie Kay and Penny looking at him and chuckling together. Billie Kay said something to Penny and the two of them burst out laughing together. They took a few more steps toward him and stopped. Penny said something to Billie Kay and the two of them burst out laughing anew.

Enough of this. Tyler jumped to his feet. "I wasn't aware that I was doing something funny just by sitting here," Tyler muttered. "If you're talking about me, I want to know what you're saying."

Billie Kay looked at him with a bright, grinning face framed by her long dark hair. "Don't look so clueless, Tyler," she said playfully.

Penny burst out laughing again. She covered her mouth, trying unsuccessfully to hide her mirth at Tyler's expense.

"You two are up to something. Out with it."

"Uh, Tyler," Penny began, "Mr. and Mrs. Allerton are requesting you to share supper with them tonight. I think they'd like to thank you, proper-like, for helping to save Mr. Allerton's life."

"Yeah? Well, what's so funny about that?" Tyler demanded.

"Come with us, please," Billie Kay said.

Billie Kay and Penny led the way and Tyler followed, walking around the sagebrush, more curious than anything. Ahead was the Allerton wagon, near where their oxen grazed placidly. Angelique Hapsburg was there also, sitting on a wooden folding chair.

Abigail Allerton smiled graciously as Tyler approached. His beard looking a little grayer after the experience earlier, Ephraim rose to his feet from a wooden crate he'd been sitting on. He extended his hand to shake Tyler's hand vigorously.

"Welcome, Tyler," Ephraim said. "Abigail and I felt we should do something a little extra special to show our appreciation for your help earlier today. I wouldn't be standing here if it weren't for you and Angelique and what the two of you did."

"Glad to have helped," Tyler said, slightly self-conscious. "You've been a good friend on this trip, Mr. Allerton."

Tyler sat down on the crate.

"No, no, over here," Abigail said. She unfolded another chair and placed it right next to Angelique. "Please, Tyler, sit here."

Angelique looked away and hid a surreptitious smile as Tyler sat down next to her. Tyler looked at Billie Kay and

Penny, who took seats on a pair of crates. They were gently laughing together again, apparently enjoying the moment. No doubt, this event had been at least partly their idea. Sitting with Angelique on the folding chairs while the others sat on crates, Tyler could see that he and Angelique appeared to be, literally, head and shoulders above everyone else, apparently by design of the Allertons, Billie Kay, and Penny.

"Ephraim and I wanted to share our supper with all of you tonight," Abigail said. "We don't have much. Ephraim and I can't afford to eat fancy. But you're all welcome to eat as much as you want."

Angelique helped herself to a plateful of baked beans and salt pork. Tyler did the same. Billie Kay, Penny, Ephraim, and finally Abigail helped themselves to beans and pork from the kettle over a Dutch oven.

An uncomfortable silence followed. Abigail broke it up by saying, "I'm curious, Angelique, how did you happen to develop such an interest in the American West?"

Angelique wiped her lips with a cloth napkin and put her plate down. Her long brown hair ruffled slightly in a sudden breeze. Her brown eyes sparkled. "There's a museum in Vienna that I liked to visit," she began. "They have some revolving displays. When I was eleven or twelve years old there was a temporary display called 'The American Frontier.' There were actually some Indians there who showed some of their crafts. They were eastern Indians, Iroquois, I think they were. Anyway, they showed arrowhead making, pottery making, open fire cooking. I was fascinated. The museum had another American frontier display a year later, with more Indians, and someone who was dressed like a mountain man.

"I was hooked," Angelique continued excitedly. "I knew I had to see the American West for myself. I read every book I could about the United States frontier. I learned English. I begged my father to let me go to the U.S. and see real live

Indians and mountain men. He said no way was I going alone. Finally, when I turned eighteen my father got tired of me begging him and he agreed to go with me on the journey. My father's heading back to Austria by ship after we get to Oregon, but I'm staying. My father said I could if it meant that much to me."

Tyler noted Angelique's features, how her nose was so well-formed, long and slightly larger at the end.

"That's quite a story," Ephraim said. "I've heard of Europeans who come here to get a taste of the Wild American West. Is it what you expected?"

"It's more than what I expected," Angelique declared. "I'm glad I came and got to see Indians and buffalo and mountain men like Henry Buckman and Silas Maple and Press Doolittle with my own eyes." She looked at Tyler. "But enough about me. What about you, Tyler? What made you decide to come West?"

Tyler chuckled uncomfortably. "There's not much to tell. The short answer is, my Pa decided to go to the Far West. The longer answer is I encouraged my Pa to do it after Ma died. Pa always had a westward hankering, I guess from his own parents. He was born in New Hampshire, raised in Ohio, and plowed his first farm in Illinois, then in Missouri. This time, he says he's not stopping till he sees the Pacific. I reckon we're not that far from the ocean now, though."

"Another 800 miles and we'll be there," Ephraim said, half-facetiously.

The conversation continued with everyone sharing stories of their lives back in the Midwest, the East, or in Europe, prior to starting out on the Western adventure. Billie Kay told of life in Pennsylvania and of her parents' decision to head West, partly to get Kelly Jay away from a suitor who liked to drink too much. The real reason for heading West, though, Billie Kay said, was so that her father could try his luck in the California goldfields. "He'd only said we were going to Oregon to get my mother to reluctantly agree to journey West," she declared.

Once she'd had her fill of beans and pork, with black coffee, Angelique looked furtively at Tyler and said, "I think I'll head over to the dancing now. Thank you very much, Mr. and Mrs. Allerton, for a wonderful meal and a wonderful time."

"It was our pleasure, dear," Abigail said. She and Ephraim looked at Tyler.

"I'll be along soon," Tyler said uncertainly as Angelique headed toward the evening dance.

Billie Kay locked eyes with Tyler. "She's admired you from afar for a very long time, Tyler," Billie Kay said solemnly. "All joking aside, she has a huge crush on you. Face it, Tyler, you've shown on this trip that you have a sense of adventure that's equal to hers. That didn't escape her attention, and that means a lot to her. She wants you, Tyler, and she means business about it. Angelique hasn't shown it much because she knew for a long time that you had eyes only for Rachelle. Every time Angelique, the poor thing, tried to get your attention, all you did was act like you just wanted her to go away and not bother you. But when Rachelle didn't work out for you, Angelique was hoping you'd pay some attention to her. She's still waiting. And she's made it clear that she's not going back to Austria." Billie Kay nodded toward the dancing. "You want a wife—there she is. Now you get your fat butt over there and dance with her, Tyler Linders."

Tyler couldn't help smiling. "You plotted this evening, didn't you, Billie Kay?"

"Well, me and Penny together. And the Allertons, Ephraim and Abigail. Angelique came to me for help with you, and I told her I would. I told her to stay close to you, be friendly but not overly aggressive, and she'd eventually find an opportunity to have her chance with you."

Tyler felt all eyes on him—Billie Kay, Penny, Ephraim, Abigail—waiting for him to make a move. "Reckon I'll head over there," Tyler said, not wanting to disappoint anyone.

Billie Kay got up and put a hand on his shoulder. She looked at him with earnest eyes. "You're making the right decision, Tyler."

Tyler nodded and headed toward the dancing. Angelique had joined the group of young women waiting for someone to ask them to dance. Tyler walked toward Angelique, and she smiled broadly and expectantly as he approached, inviting him closer. Her bright eyes were on him, and him alone. Tyler could see that for Angelique, there was no one else around but him, nobody who mattered but him.

"Angelique, would you care to dance?"

Angelique's eyes lit up with a precious sparkle as she looked at him.

"Why, I . . . I . . . yes, yes, Tyler!" Angelique exclaimed excitedly. "Why, I thought you'd never . . ." She grabbed his arm and, beaming, she took him out to the dance. Angelique did a Reel with him, her face glowing at him with every musical note from Bruce Mallory's fiddle. Why hadn't he noticed Angelique sooner? Tyler could tell that this was a magical moment for her, and it gave him proud pleasure that he had made Angelique so happy. After the Reel, Bruce Mallory took a breather. As Angelique walked with Tyler back to the edge of the crowd, Brent McGuigan walked up to her.

"Would you care to dance the next one, Angelique?" Brent asked.

Angelique smiled politely and took Tyler's hand in hers. "Thanks, Brent. I appreciate the thought, but I'm with Tyler," she said mildly, but nonetheless firmly.

Tyler spent the rest of the evening dancing with Angelique Hapsburg. He truly noticed her for the first time. She had light brown eyes that sparkled with laughter and joy.

She had beautiful wavy waist length brown hair, a clear face, piquant nose that was minutely larger at the end. She was beautiful, not someone that every man would feel he had to have, but beautiful in her own way. There were thousands of different kinds of flowers in the world, each variety colorful and beautiful in its own unique way. That was the kind of beauty that Angelique had. She was beautiful in her own special way, with the life joy within her showing through to the outside of her, making her skin, her eyes, her even teeth, her personality, all of it shine and glow. Angelique was the kind of young woman who had a radiant sun-like glow about her, and she could spread her glow to those everywhere around her.

With clear pride in their eyes, Ephraim, Abigail, and Pa watched Tyler and Angelique together. During a break in the dancing, Ephraim and Abigail approached Tyler and Angelique.

"Ephraim and I, like we said," Abigail began, her voice catching for an instant as she beheld Tyler and Angelique hand-in-hand, "we don't have a lot of money. We can't give you anything material as our way of thanking you both for . . . for saving Ephraim's life. But Ephraim and I, well, Tyler, well, Angelique, we thought that maybe we could pay you both back in a very, very special and heartfelt way with a very special gift, the gift of each other."

Ephraim took Abigail in his arms. Tyler looked at Angelique and traded smiles with her. Tyler took Angelique in his arms, looked into her tender eyes, responding to her invitation, and he kissed her tenderly. She leaned into his arms, sharing the kiss. Nor did Tyler care who was watching. Nor likely did Angelique appear to care, either.

*　*　*

"How many stars are there in the sky, do you think?" Angelique asked, standing and looking upward. With her arm around Tyler's shoulders, she joined him in looking up at the moonless night sky.

Tyler sighed happily. "Thousands, I'm sure." He exchanged another kiss with Angelique. This was for real. There was no turning back. Angelique had claimed him, and Tyler was the gladder for it. He gently stroked Angelique's long brown hair and she snuggled right into it, leaning her head against Tyler's shoulder.

"Angelique," Tyler gently said, looking into her gentle eyes, "I carry you in my heart, and you are all things beautiful, all things wonderful, all things delightful, all things peaceful, and all things graceful." He exchanged another soft kiss with her as her eyes sparkled at his words, and she quietly smiled at him. "My precious and treasured Angelique, can you ever forgive me for taking such a long time to notice you? I feel like a total heel."

Angelique's response was a quiet chuckle. "I appreciate you saying that, Tyler, but please be assured it's all right," she murmured. "I am grateful that you finally did notice that I was noticing you, and we are together now."

It was a beautiful night, slightly cool. The Milky Way shone light in color but luminous. The multitude of stars, strangely, made Tyler think of the multitude of Indians that he had expected to see but which had not been in evidence west of Fort Laramie.

"You know so much about Indians," Tyler began, "how is it we haven't seen any for awhile?"

"Huh!" Angelique looked at him quizzically. "Have you been paying attention to the landscape? Badlands, no trees, no shelter, a lot fewer buffalo. This region is no more attractive to Indians than it is to us. But we'll see more Indians soon enough. There'll be Shoshones and Utes near Fort Bridger."

Angelique leaned forward. "I'm a little nervous about heading all the way south toward Fort Bridger like Buckman intends to do. It's a little off the main trail that goes toward Fort Hall, and it's right in a border area between the Shoshones and the Utes. Those two tribes love to make war against each other. We'll need to use plenty of caution around Fort Bridger."

"How far you reckon it is to Fort Bridger?" Tyler asked languidly.

"Hmm, another two or three days, I'd guess," Angelique replied. "Depends on the weather. If we get more heavy rain, it's going to slow us down."

The next day there was no rain, but there was heat, with little humidity. Tyler felt no relief. The dry heat felt like an oven as he drove the team with the whip. He tried to go easy on Drake and Dru. The two oxen had performed yeoman service and Tyler felt Drake and Dru owed them nothing at this point, well over 1,000 miles into the journey.

The evening dance was refreshing joy for Tyler. He spent the whole evening dancing with Angelique. Nor did she dance with anyone else, or have eyes for anyone else. Her beautiful long brown hair flew in the wind. Billie Kay and Justin looked happy for them. Penny and Alain looked happy for them.

As he walked around hand-in-hand with Angelique, Tyler noted that Penny had seated herself among her usual coterie of admiring young students. She shared her books and her knowledge with the children around her. Alain sat next to Penny, his arm around her waist, proudly admiring her intelligence and her selfless sharing of her knowledge.

"Penny has the makings of a good teacher," Angelique said. "Her first thoughts are always of others."

"Penny is, as Penny does," Tyler said, recalling how he had said that before.

The next day Tyler drove the team as Pa walked. He carefully watched Drake and Dru. Drake gamely soldiered on though he was thin. Dru looked like he could hardly move. The only reason the wagon didn't fall behind was that many other oxen in the wagon train were in the same shopworn condition.

As they passed Silas on his horse, Pa asked him, "How much longer before we get to somewhere with fresh oxen to sell?"

"We're getting closer to Fort Bridger. There's a few settlers hereabouts that have fresh stock from other wagon outfits ahead of us. Let's get to Fort Bridger first."

During the nooning, Tyler checked on the Clevenger kids just to see how they were doing. Cross-legged and eating some jerky, Brit Clevenger glanced up at Tyler and asked, "How far are we from Fort Bridger?"

"We'll arrive there tomorrow," Tyler said, "probably by mid-afternoon."

"Will Jim Bridger be there?" Brit asked excitedly.

"Well, I hear that Jim Bridger travels a lot, but during the summer he'll probably be there."

Brit looked at his siblings Luke, Agnes, and curly-haired little Jenny. "Just think of it, Jim Bridger hisself," Brit exulted. "I read about him in a couple of dime novels. The most famous mountain man in the history of the universe, and we're gonna meet him, Jim Bridger hisself!"

Penny walked up to Tyler. She looked at Brit. "Jim Bridger himself, Jim Bridger *him*self, not 'hisself,'" Penny said mildly.

"What-ever."

Yep, Penny was going to be a teacher someday. As Tyler walked away past other wagons with Penny, he said to her, "I hope Mr. Bridger is at Fort Bridger, for Brit's sake. Sounds like he'll be real disappointed if he doesn't meet him."

"Pa says he's going to find one of the settlers around Fort Bridger to sell him a new pair of lead oxen," Penny said, changing the subject. "He says he'll need you to help him, so don't go spending all your time with Angelique."

"You mean like you're spending all your time with Alain?"

Penny smiled. "Alain," she said dreamily. "Alain, Alain, Alain." She adjusted her hexagonal glasses and played with the gold, silver, and turquoise jewelry around her neck. "I can't imagine what life would ever be like without him."

* * *

Tyler saw his prediction come true. The following afternoon, with Angelique at his side, Tyler caught sight of the unpretentious log palisade of Fort Bridger. The brains of the operation, trader Louis Vasquez, presumably, stood at the front beyond the gate, watching the wagon train, what was left of it, form into a circle. Fifty-eight wagons remained of the original eight-seven. The area around Fort Bridger was a luscious oasis after the desert—pine, birch, aspen, and cottonwood trees, several cold streams, and green grass for the livestock.

No sooner than all the wagons were settled for the evening, but Tyler saw Brit Clevenger heading into the fort.

"This should be good," Tyler murmured to Angelique. He decided with Angelique to follow Brit, along with the rest of the Clevenger kids.

Inside the fort, if such it could truly be called, Tyler noted a tall, thin-faced, thin-nosed man, stubble-faced, wearing a wide-brimmed plainsman's hat. He sat on a log-hewn bench, whittling outside a log blacksmith shop.

Brit stopped short as the man in the plainsman's hat looked up. His eyes appeared dark-colored, deep-set, and focused squarely upon his young visitors.

"Are . . . are you Jim Bridger?" Brit asked.

The man looked to his left, then to his right, then he turned to Brit again. "Don't see none other around, so yeah, I reckon that makes me Jim Bridger."

"Wo-ow!" Brit exclaimed. "The real Jim Bridger." He took a graphite pencil out of his shirt pocket along with a small piece of paper. "M-Mr. Bridger, sir, c-c-could you please give me your autograph—sir?"

Bridger grinned. "Why certainly, son. I'd be happy to oblige." Bridger took the pencil and piece of paper from Brit and made a large "X" on the piece of paper. Bridger handed the pencil and piece of paper back to Brit. "There's my autograph, son. I'm not one to be pretentious."

Brit looked at the "X" with a puzzled expression.

Tad McGuigan, Brent's fifteen-year-old younger brother, approached with folded arms and a pouty look. "I heard he can speak six languages but is so illiterate that he can't even write his own name," Tad muttered to Brit.

"Still, I'm never going to throw this piece of paper away," Brit said. "I heard, Mr. Bridger, sir, that you once wrestled an eight hundred pound grizzly bear and won."

"That was Daniel Boone," Tad snorted.

Bridger gestured for his admiring young visitors to approach him closer. "C'mon over here, kids. Let me tell you a story about *my* encounter with a grizzly bear. Daniel Boone had to actually wrestle a bear. I fought off an angry bear without ever having to even touch him."

"Really? Wow," little Jenny Clevenger said. "How?"

"Well, gather around kids, and I'll tell you."

Five-year-old Jenny and a dozen other small children took seats on the ground in a semi-circle around Bridger.

"I was fishing for trout a couple of months ago," Bridger began. He gestured toward the outside of the fort. "You probably seen all the little creeks we got around here, offshoots of the Blacks Fork River. Anyway, there's good fishing hereabouts. But when I was fishing around here, maybe a half-mile from the fort a couple months back, I seen this grizzly bear maybe a couple hundred feet away, watching me with a real mean expression on his grizzly bear face.

"I tried to ignore him, but finally this bear says to me, 'You there, you're fishing on my territory and catching my trout. Now you get your fat butt outa my stretch of this creek or else I'm gonna eat *you*.'

"Well, I says to that bear, 'Bear, do you realize who you're talking to here?'

"'No, I don't,' the bear replies. 'Should I care?'

"'Bear,' I said, 'my name is Jim Bridger, and that's *Mister* Jim Bridger to you, bear.' And you know what that bear says next?"

"How can you believe anything this old coot says?" Tad demanded, gesturing with frustration. "Everybody knows bears can't talk."

Bridger fingered his knife, using the point to punch a piece of food out from between two of his yellowed front teeth. He looked down and started whittling again, slowly, emphasizing the movements of his knife.

"You wouldn't be, maybe, possibly, trying to call me a liar there, now would you, son?" Bridger asked.

"N-no." Tad shook his hands for emphasis.

Jenny pulled on Bridger's pants leg. "What did the bear say?" she asked.

Bridger returned his attention to his listeners, ignoring Tad. "Well, that bear apologized to me real quick-like and real sincere-like. 'I-I didn't know it was you, Mister Bridger,' the bear says. 'I-I-I didn't mean no disrespect, Mister Bridger, sir. P-please, feel free to fish here anytime, anytime you want."

Tyler turned to look at Pa, who was apparently arguing with Louis Vasquez near the entrance to the trader's store.

With Pa's back to him, all Tyler could hear was Pa muttering "too expensive" and "anyplace else to go."

"Well then, go there instead if that's what makes you happy," Vasquez retorted at length. "Deal with the Overfields if you can, but I'm warning you they're a couple of ne'er do-wells that got kicked out of the Mormon settlement at Salt Lake. Take your gun with you and . . ."

Tyler had to turn away at the sound of Bridger's hard laughter.

"Me and that bear's best of friends now," Bridger declared.

CHAPTER NINETEEN

"Tyler, you need to help Pa," Penny said, tugging at his sleeve.

Tyler turned away from Jim Bridger's tall tale yarns.

"Pa's over at the trader's store," Penny said. "He's waiting for you."

"All right, I'm going," Tyler said, irritated. Bridger could certainly be entertaining.

"I'll catch up with you later, Tyler," Angelique said.

He kissed her goodbye for now and squeezed her hand.

The trader's store, or what passed for it in this remote location, was another rough log structure, with a low log roof. Two crude stone fireplaces bookended the structure. Bridger and Vasquez's sleeping quarters were at the far end.

Inside Tyler entered and saw Pa with three other men, including Ephraim Allerton looking at merchandise. Pa was examining the smell of different varieties of tobacco in brown leather pouches.

"How do you come by all this stuff out here in the middle of nowhere?" asked Pa.

"We got connections in St. Louis," the fat, bearded trader replied.

The trader noted Ephraim fingering a greasy print shirt on one of the wooden tables. "That shirt is a genuine Jim Bridger shirt," the trader said, "worn by Jim Bridger himself on several occasions. Over there," the trader pointed down the table, "are several Jim Bridger knives, used by Jim Bridger himself on several occasions."

"I'll wait for you outside, Pa," Tyler said disgustedly. All of these Jim Bridger souvenirs would probably mean a lot to someone Brit Clevenger's age, but to Tyler they meant diddly. Tyler counted himself beyond the stage of hero worship.

Pa emerged from the store. "There's a ranch about a half-mile north of here," Pa said. "It's right along Black's Fork. That trader told me they got fresh oxen there for less cost than they charge here at the fort. Guy named Overfield owns the ranch."

Tyler rode north along Black's Fork with Pa, Penny, and Alain on horses borrowed from the herd kept by Buckman, in order to get a good look at the country away from the trail. It was green, wet, and cool for a change. Penny rode with her full regalia of jewelry; she felt she didn't dare leave any of it behind in the unguarded wagon. After a ride across a refreshing evergreen tree-sprinkled meadow they neared a rough adobe hut—it could hardly be called a house—outside of which sure enough a herd of about a dozen oxen grazed placidly. A short, bearded, barrel-chested man sat on a rough wooden bench in front, watching them come. A younger clean-shaven man, taller than the first, and leaner, presumably the fat, barrel-chested man's son, also watched them approach.

As Tyler neared, the fat, barrel-chested man rose from his bench, looking at Pa.

Pa declared, "You got oxen for sale, I hear."

"You heard correctly," the fat man said, working a chew of tobacco.

"You're Overfield?" Pa said.

"You heard correctly," Overfield replied. He head-gestured toward his son. "My boy Clubb."

Tyler, Pa, Penny, and Alain all dismounted.

"How much for a pair?" Pa asked.

"Eighty dollars," the fat man replied, "for a pair."

"Eighty dollars!" Pa exclaimed. "I heard at the fort that I could get a pair of good lead oxen out here for no more 'n fifty dollars."

"You heard incorrectly," Overfield said. He spit out his tobacco.

Pa took in a deep breath and exhaled. "What good does having a lot of money out here a thousand miles from anywhere do you anyway?"

"Well now, that's my affair, I reckon," Overfield retorted. "Costs me money when I have to buy supplies at Salt Lake that I can't get at Bridger."

The man's tall, lean son, with hands on his hips, moved closer to his father.

"Isn't there some way we can negotiate a bit?" Pa asked hopefully. "Our lead oxen are plumb wore out. Eighty dollars is a lot of money out here for two oxen."

Overfield spit out more tobacco. His glance drifted from Pa to Penny, and his eyes raked Penny from head to foot, and all points in between. Tyler saw Penny shift nervously on her feet and take a deep gulp, fear transforming her expression as she took shortened breaths. Tyler thought that maybe Overfield was going to demand some of Penny's gold, silver, and turquoise jewelry. Poor Penny, however, gulped again fearfully, holding her breath and looking like she suspected that Overfield had something far more sinister in mind as he rubbed his beard and assessed her. She moved closer to Alain.

Alain gave Penny a quick kiss on her right cheek and he put his arms around her protectively in front of him.

"You know what, mister," Overfield said, cocking his head to one side as his smile turned cruel, "it gets lonely out here, with just me and Clubb. Now, you got a mighty fine-looking daughter there, yessiree, mister, that's one mighty fine-looking daughter you got th—"

Pa belted the man's left chin with his right fist, reeling him backwards despite his weight. Pa knew exactly what Overfield had been hinting at.

Tyler leaped at Clubb Overfield shoving him backwards but the lean son was pure muscle. He reeled Tyler around and drilled a fist to Tyler's jaw, staggering Tyler. Overfield raced at Pa as Alain charged. Overfield slammed Pa's jaw but Alain grabbed Overfield and hammered a full blow to Overfield's fat belly.

"Get behind me, Penny," Alain declared. "I'll defend you and I won't let them hurt you."

"Ah, the white knight comes to defend the damsel in distress," Clubb Overfield mocked.

Tyler charged the younger Overfield again to keep him from helping his father against Pa and Alain. Rage fueled Tyler and this time he drilled the younger Overfield's stomach, doubling him over. Tyler staggered the younger Overfield to the ground with a hard right to his temple. Tyler wheeled to help Pa just as Overfield drew a knife.

"Penny, get back!" Alain shouted. "We'll take care of these guys."

Alain turned a split-second toward Penny. Overfield slashed Alain across the midsection, creating a gash in his shirt and a large red cut across his lower chest. Blood gushed from Alain's wound.

"Alain!" Penny screamed, hands to her cheeks. She rushed to embrace Alain as he fell to his knees and then to the ground.

"Hah!" the younger Overfield mocked again. "Looks like your white knight ain't much protection for you, is he? He cain't even defend you."

Penny cradled Alain in her arms and she looked at the Overfields and wailed, "Just leave us alone! Enough. We don't need your oxen. Just leave us be!"

Pa whipped his pepperbox pistol out of his pants pocket and shot the older Overfield in the lower ribs.

"There's no need to kill anyone, mister. We was just funnin'!" Clubb Overfield shouted, rising. "We weren't gonna really do nothing to her, just have a little fun with her for a few minutes, that's all."

"Fun my left ass!" Pa shrieked. "You were both fixing to rape a twelve-year-old girl. I gave your lecher of a father a flesh wound that ain't even half as bad as what you done to Alain here. If there was any law around here, I'd have both of you sons of bitches hauled off to prison."

The younger Overfield helped his father to his feet, blood reddening the latter's lower shirt.

"Now move back, both of you, or next time I shoot it'll be to kill ya both," Pa bellowed.

Penny embraced Alain as he tried hard to get to his knees. She began to cry for her hero who had tried so valiantly to protect her. Alain tried to hug Penny but the pain was too great and he slumped back to the ground. Penny wept uncontrollably.

"Not much of a champion for you, is he, girl?" Clubb Overfield smirked. "Tries to stand up for you and all he does is get hisself all cut up."

"Shut up and leave us alone!" Penny begged, weeping.

"We'll have to get him to Fort Bridger—fast," Pa declared. "They'll know what to do. As for these bastards," Pa gestured with his pistol toward the Overfields, "they're not getting a nickel of my money. We'll buy our oxen at the fort."

Pa glanced toward a small open wagon on the side of the adobe hut. "We'll borrow this wagon to haul Alain in, and when I say borrow, I mean take it. He'll never make it alive back to the fort any other way."

* * *

"I've stitched him up as best I can," Bridger said. "That knife cut into him pretty bad and I ain't no doc. You've got to keep him level and as immobile as you possibly can. If he starts to bleed internally . . ."

Penny put a gentle hand on Alain's, who was fully conscious after the painful procedure. She looked at Bridger. "Is he going to live?"

The mountain man let out a hefty sigh. "I don't know; I can't say. I ain't the kind to give people false hope," Bridger muttered. "He might make it. That's the best I can say. I will say this—he was powerful lucky that knife didn't slice into his inner organs like his liver. It tore up mostly muscle. But there could still be internal bleeding and dangerous festering." Bridger threw the bloody rag down disgustedly on the dirt floor. "His survival depends entirely on your boyfriend's internal constitution. It'll help if the wound—it's a pretty big one—doesn't fester. And if it does fester, it'll depend on whether or not his body is strong enough, or not, to fight off the fever he's gonna be dealing with."

Bridger lowered his tone. His voice became more sympathetic. "Little lady, I wish I could say that your Alain made a narrow escape and he's gonna be okay. But I wouldn't want you to get your hopes all up, and then . . ."

Penny let out another little cry and she wiped the heavy tears away from underneath her glasses.

Alain took her hand in his and he looked at her with all tenderness. "My little Golden Penny," he murmured. "You are crying, and I hurt to see you cry so hard."

"Keep still, son," Bridger ordered. "Talking too much uses up your energy."

Tyler saw Pa coming, with Francois and Adelaide Laurent. Francois and Adelaide entered the back room of the trader's store. Adelaide gasped but did not scream at the sight of her son Alain lying bloodied and stitched on three slabs of cut timber across a pair of sawhorses.

"I've had better days," Alain weakly told his parents as he tried to smile.

"I'm so sorry," Penny wailed, fresh tears streaming down her face.

"Oh Penny-dearest, Penny-precious." Adelaide hugged Penny close and took out a handkerchief to wipe Penny's tears away. "It wasn't your fault, Penny. Don't even think that."

"Not at all, little Penny," Francois declared in his French-Canadian accent. "Zat man zat tried to buy your body, he and he alone is responsible for zis tragedy."

Penny took Adelaide's handkerchief and wiped her eyes, then her glasses. Penny's breaths came short, halting, sniffling.

Adelaide clutched Penny's arms and looked tenderly at her. "Penny, you're the best thing, the best thing, that's ever happened to Alain since he was born," Adelaide declared. "Alain was trying to protect your honor against a man who wanted to harm you. We're proud of Alain for doing that. He did that because he cares deeply about you, treasures you and loves you, just as Francois and I do. We would not expect our Alain to do anything less than what he did do in defending you from harm."

Penny looked at both Adelaide and Francois. "I promise you I will look after him with every tenderness," she said.

"We know you will, sweetheart," Adelaide said. "We all will."

Penny gave Adelaide a big hug. Adelaide wrapped her arms around Penny. Francois gave Penny several good pats on the back.

Alain tried and failed to lift himself up on his elbows. "Don't forget about me," he said quietly.

Penny and Alain exchanged a hug and Alain kissed Penny on the lips. He took her hands in his and kissed them.

"I am going to watch you every minute of every day," Penny said to Alain. "I'm going to will you to live, Alain."

He stroked her brown hair. "Precious Golden Penny, my little guardian angel."

"I hate to break up this majestic scene," Pa began, "but we have to get Alain back to his wagon. He'll need rest before we start on the trail again, whenever that is, if he even feels up to it."

"Keep him flat and immobile," Bridger declared. "No rough spots when you're traveling, no going over deep chuckholes. You need to get him to a real doctor who can stitch him up and care for him proper."

"How far to a real doctor?" Pa asked.

Bridger's partner, well-dressed Louis Vasquez, entered. "Two hundred miles to Fort Hall, and it's not an easy two hundred miles. You'll have to cross the Wyoming Range to get to Fort Hall. The trail goes through some nearly vertical ups and downs getting through the Wyoming Range."

Adelaide looked tearfully at Vasquez. "What about Salt Lake? Isn't that closer?"

"It is," Vasquez said, rubbing his short, dark, clipped beard. "But you'll never make it through the desert to Oregon by going to Salt Lake. You'd all perish once you got past Salt Lake. You have to stay on the main trail."

Angelique entered with Buckman. "He needs iodine," Angelique said, thrusting her long hair back. "We couldn't find a drop of it anywhere in the whole wagon train. Nobody's ever even heard of it, but that's what Alain needs, iodine, and lots of it. Iodine can make wounds that might have been fatal years ago become more simple to treat."

"I know we don't have any of that stuff here," Vasquez said. "I've never heard of it, either. What is it?"

"Some new-fangled European medicine," Angelique said. "I don't know exactly how iodine works, but it has properties that seem to help prevent wounds from festering. It's not widely known in the United States yet, but Fort Hall is an old Hudson's Bay post and they might have some."

"Well," Vasquez began, "they may have some of it at Fort Hall, if you can keep him alive for another 200 very difficult miles. There's not only mountains ahead of you, but unfriendly Indians as well."

"Two hundred miles is a ten- or fifteen-day journey," Tyler said.

"If you can get through the mountains okay," Vasquez reminded them. "It will be more than ten days if you can't."

Tyler looked at Buckman. "Is there is any way we can maybe move ahead of the rest of the wagon train and get to Fort Hall faster?"

"Not if you're planning on just two wagons," Buckman said. "It's too dangerous. We're in crossover territory between the Shoshones to the north and the Utes to the south. The Shoshones and the Utes are mortal enemies which creates danger enough right there. Now the Shoshones have been fairly friendly to the whites. I think they see the future and, like it or not, they can see that they will have to learn to coexist with the white man.

"The Utes, however, have come to no such conclusion," Buckman continued, his deep-set eyes narrowing. "The Utes have attacked and will attack whites when they have the chance. They won't attack a large wagon train, but two wagons all alone by themselves, yeah, the Utes could attack and kill everyone. I'd say you should have no less, no less, I'm saying, than fifteen wagons in a train to discourage attack, and even then, that's still chancy. But yes, you could cut the time to Fort Hall to ten days, maybe eight days, maybe just seven, by tracking faster in a smaller group, eliminating the evening camaraderie and traveling till dusk. Forget the dancing and just concentrate on reaching Fort Hall."

CHAPTER TWENTY

In all, thirteen families agreed to plunge ahead with the Linders and Laurent families. George Ellis was the first to agree, if only because the sooner he got to Fort Hall, the sooner he could turn south toward the Humboldt River and the California goldfields beyond. The Maybries at Justin's urging agreed. Tyler felt strangely surprised but not especially joyful when the Palmerstons decided to join the group—probably Dennis's decision. Dennis, after all, had been friendly at times.

Quimby Freding told Tyler that he would be glad to help out by coming along. "Buckman is right," Quimby declared. "You'll need people traveling along with you for protection deep in Indian country."

Tyler put his hand on Quimby's shoulder. "You're a true friend, Quimby, and a brave one, and we're happy, and lucky, to have you," Tyler said.

The McGuigans and the Colledges agreed to come with the ahead-plungers, largely, Tyler guessed, because Brent and Van Buren had still not entirely given up pursuit of Rachelle, despite their protestations to the contrary. The Colledges with their money had purchased a small new wagon at Fort Bridger.

Ephraim and Abigail Allerton quickly agreed to come, as did the Hapsburgs.

The Clevenger kids agreed to go. The MacNaughtons, with a new wagon and oxen purchased at Fort Bridger, said they would come. The Hancliceks, Bruce Mallory, the Bennetts, and Tewksberrys agreed to come. A few, like the Allertons, did so because of friendship. Others, like the Bennetts and the Tewksberrys, hoped to catch up with one of the wagon trains further ahead at Fort Hall and get to the West Coast and the land offices there more quickly. The fun of traveling had worn thin after 1,200 miles.

Silas Maple agreed to go with the intrepid adventurers hurrying on ahead.

The next day the group of fifteen wagons headed the group of fifty-eight. However, when Buckman called a halt for the day, Silas Maple kept his group of fifteen wagons moving on another five miles, until darkness fell.

There was no dance. Bruce Mallory was too tired, as was Tyler. When Tyler checked on Penny and Alain, he found Penny as she had been all day, near the Laurent wagon with Alain, talking softly to him, trying to keep his spirits up. Penny had watched over him, making sure that his body remained steady and did not bounce around. It was crucial to Alain's survival that he not begin bleeding again, especially internally.

The wagons were back on the road again early the next morning. To the south, the snow-capped Uintah Range loomed. To the north, even more ominous since they were directly ahead, the Wyoming Range and the Salt River Range loomed snow-capped and purple-green. At least, though, the Salt River gave comfort since its waters via the Snake River emptied into the Columbia, and the Columbia meant—Oregon.

There were more immediate concerns, however. As the wagons rolled along, Tyler walked with Angelique surveying the surroundings. They saw two Indians, then five Indians, then a group of fifty Indians sitting on horseback. Tyler smacked his lips nervously while holding hands with Angelique. This was unneeded trouble right now. Nothing must interfere with getting Alain to Fort Hall rapidly.

"They're wearing war paint," Angelique said, observing the Indians.

Tyler looked ahead to Silas on horseback. "What's this mean, Silas?" he asked. "They're wearing war paint but they're not attacking, well, yet."

Silas turned his horse around to draw close to Tyler and Angelique. "They're Shoshones," Silas said. "They're not after us; they're looking for Utes. Still, there's plenty enough danger if we're right in the middle of an Indian battle zone."

Tyler warily watched the Shoshones watching him and the wagons moving past. Grim-faced, unsmiling, the Shoshones watched the lumbering wagons. This was no place for a wheel to fall off, or for an axle to break. The Indians sat on their still horses, their lances with butt ends to the ground, some with bows and quivers of arrows slung over their shoulders.

Penny got out of the Laurent wagon and jumped down. She eyed the war-painted Shoshones nervously.

"How's Alain doing?" Tyler asked.

"He's doing fine," Penny said with an anxious tone. "For now, anyway, he's doing fine."

The wagons were almost past the fifty Shoshones. Their silent but hostile demeanor, the uncertainty which the thick, tense atmosphere created, seemed almost as threatening as if they had let out war whoops and gotten their attack over with.

Two of the Shoshones peeled away from the group and rode toward Silas, sitting his horse about forty feet away. Tyler immediately thought of Tim.

Turning toward Tim he said, "Don't forget the lesson you learned about 600 miles back."

"Don't worry," Tim said. "I'm not going to shoot. I learned that lesson with the Pawnees."

"Good. Let's just let 'em talk to Silas and head back to their group."

Tyler watched the Shoshones trying to communicate with Silas, partly in sign language since Silas hardly spoke a word of Shoshone. Tyler could not hear what was being said, if anything was being said verbally. One of the Shoshones pointed toward the northwest and the mountains, the direction in which the fifteen wagons were headed. Although Tyler could not hear what was being said, the Indian looked angry. He gestured with his arm, in a dark silk shirt that he had no doubt gotten in trade. He wore brass armbands on his arms, a red headband kept his long hair in place. The Indian's hair extended halfway down his back.

The two Indians turned their horses around to head back to their compatriots.

Pa put the reins down and looked at Silas. "What did they say?" he demanded.

Silas rode toward the Linders wagon as Tim, Renford, Ephraim, Abigail, Dennis, and Paddy McGuigan gathered around to hear the news.

"They said, if I understood them correctly, that they've been trailing a party of Ute hunters for several days now and they've almost caught up to them." Silas looked toward the northwest. "The Utes are roughly two hours away, and the Shoshones said the route we're headed in will take us straight to them. When the Shoshones catch up with the Utes, basically they said there's gonna one hellacious battle, and we'd be right smack in the middle of it."

"That's about the last thing we need," Renford declared.

Pa looked at the assembled men. "We have to get Alain to Fort Hall as quickly as we can," he said. "We can't just sit here waiting for the Indians to get out of our way." He turned to Silas. "Is there any other route we can take?"

"Huh!" Silas leaned forward in his saddle, extending a buckskinned arm toward the snow-capped peaks ahead. "Another route? There ain't no other route that would keep us on halfway level ground. But hey, if you know some way to get a two or three thousand pound wagon up a twelve thousand foot high mountain and then down the other side, then hey, yeah, we can try another route like you said, sure."

Francois stepped forward. "Alain is hanging on," he said, "but a trail that is too rough would be dangerous for him. The bouncing and bumps would loosen his stitches holding his body together."

"Oh-h." Silas let out a grunt. He looked at the assembled men and women, making eye contact with each of them as he pondered what to do. "All right, here's how we'll handle it. We have to think of Alain but we also need to think of our own survival. We'll keep moving, as far and as fast as we can, until we see signs of an Indian battle up ahead. Then we'll have no choice but to stop. With a little bit of luck, though, we'll avoid whatever is going on up ahead of us, or maybe the Indians'll be done with their battle before we get there."

Penny headed back over to the Laurent wagon. Tyler glanced at Angelique and together they followed Penny. Adelaide stood by the wagon, her expression worried as she held a hand to her cheek.

"What was that all about?" Adelaide asked.

"Indians fighting other Indians up ahead," Tyler replied. "We're moving on just the same."

Francois approached and took Adelaide in his arms to explain what the situation was in detail.

Penny stood and the back of the Laurent wagon and looked in on Alain. He was sitting up in the crowded wagon bed.

"How are you doing?" Penny asked.

"As well as could be expected," Alain replied.

"We're heading into some danger, Alain," Penny tried to say. She stopped as she started to cry.

"The Shoshones and the Utes are at war with one another," Tyler said. "We just passed a bunch of Shoshones. The Utes are up ahead somewhere close. The Utes don't care for whites and they don't care for Shoshones. We could find ourselves in the middle of a big Indian battle."

Alain looked at Penny. "Just so my beautiful Golden Penny is safe," Alain said weakly. He brushed a loving hand against her cheek. "That is above all other considerations."

Penny pressed his hand between her hands, looking at Alain with a gentle smile and admiring soft eyes. Tyler couldn't help but think that the love between Alain and Penny was something dear and sweet.

Alain tried to lean forward a little bit with his arms outstretched. Penny climbed into the Laurent wagon, and she and Alain hugged each other. Penny cried relentlessly as Alain hugged her with all tenderness and kissed her tear-filled cheek.

"Let's leave them be," Angelique suggested.

Tyler nodded. He and Angelique moved away from the Laurent wagon. Pa had already gotten his wagon started. The new team of lead oxen whom Pa had named Elijah and Elisha, lurched forward.

Angelique returned to her father's wagon and Tyler took up his position beside Elijah and Elisha with his whip in hand.

Mountains, snow-capped and dark underneath, loomed on all sides now. Tyler wondered how the trail could possibly wind its way around or through these barriers. Indeed, Silas's remark about driving oxen and wagons straight up the side of a high mountain, and perhaps more than one, did not seem so facetious now, but rather an ominous reality up ahead, if they could get past the Indians first.

The trail grew rougher and narrower. Fewer wagons had made it this far, 1,250 miles from Independence, Missouri, to keep the trail in good shape. Whenever a particular pothole or declivity loomed ahead, Tyler glanced worriedly at the Laurent wagon, which Penny marched beside.

The wagons had to cross a particularly rocky stretch strewn with stones. Tyler called out to Penny, "How's Alain doing?"

"Mrs. Laurent is in the wagon with him, holding his body steady over the bouncing," Penny replied.

"Look up ahead," Pa shouted.

Tyler saw it—a gathering of what looked like a couple of hundred Indians, rampaging at each other from horseback with lances and club-like weapons. Yips and angry shouts of the warriors carried across the rocky terrain.

"Everybody halt right here." Silas held up his hand as a signal to stop.

Tyler recalled that he had read in Angelique's book that Indian warfare was more a matter of counting coup than anything else—touching an enemy in battle. But what he saw happening up ahead looked deadly. Rifle shots rang out. The white man's idea of a battle and how to fight had influenced the Indians.

Clouds of dust obscured some of the scene, but Tyler could see Indians on horseback circling around one another, shooting at one another with rifles or with bows and arrows. Other Indians jabbed at one another with feathered lances or clubbed one another with stone or iron clubs on handles.

"The Utes look like the ones in the middle," Silas called out.

Peering through the dust, Tyler saw more clearly that a few dozen Indians on horseback fought in the center. Other Indians, presumably the Shoshones, circled them on their horses, picking them off with rifle or arrow shots or engaging them in single combat with their knobbed clubs. The angry shouts and yips of excitement continued as the Shoshones and the Utes lit into one another.

Outnumbered by their Shoshone enemies, the Utes looked to be getting the worst of it. Two Indians fell off their horses to the ground, rolling and tumbling over one another as they raised their own cloud of dust and cried and shouted defiance at one another.

Finally, one Indian got on top of the other and dashed his antagonist's brains out with a knobbed club. Two more such engagements ended similarly with one Indian finally clubbing the other to death. Tyler had never thought of Indians fighting other Indians in such a bloody, fanatical manner.

The Shoshones whom the wagon train had passed now came hard-charging on their horses crying out their excitement to join the battle.

Already outnumbered, the Utes still on their horses broke away from the battle and sought escape.

Pa rose in his seat. "They're coming straight at us."

"Take cover!" Silas shouted. "Get ready. They're gonna be mighty ornery after losing that fight with the Shoshones."

Tyler dove underneath the wagon along with Pa and took cover behind the wheels. They saw others doing the same or else jumping to their wagon boxes. Tyler's legs went numb and he held his breath. His heart skipped a beat and then thudded hard.

Young Ute warriors raced past on their horses. As they spotted the Trail emigrants about a dozen of the Utes slowed down. Two of them fired rifle shots at Tyler. He dove hard left to avoid being hit.

Three other Utes went after a pair of horses belonging to Jonathan Colledge. One of the Utes used a knife to slash the ropes holding the horses to the back of the Colledge wagon. Other Utes, yelling and shouting, herded the two horses away to steal them.

"Hey!" Jonathan angrily rushed out from beneath his wagon with a Sharps rifle in hand. "Bring those back."

"Hey yourself," Tim exclaimed. "What the hell do you think you're doing?" Tim ran to grab Colledge's rifle barrel and his shot went harmlessly into the desert air.

"They're my horses they're stealing, not yours," Jonathan bellowed. "Let me shoot."

"They can bury us all," Tim exclaimed. "You'll be dead. We'll all be dead and your horses will be stolen anyway."

The rifle shot had nevertheless drawn the Utes' attention. Instead of simply riding on with the stolen horses, now they reassembled in a group of about two dozen grim-faced, war-painted warriors. They faced the wagon train, perhaps debating what to do. The Shoshones looked to be moving on and not giving chase. The Utes were free to attack the wagon train if they so chose and the Shoshones were not interested in doing anything to stop them. The Shoshones probably wanted some of the Utes to escape in order to spread the word about how fierce an enemy the Shoshones were and that it would be best in the future not to intrude on Shoshone territory.

"What do you think they're up to?" Pa asked.

"Wish I knew, wish I knew," Tyler replied, shaking one way and then another.

Attacks by Indians on wagon trains were the stuff of dime novels, Tyler reminded himself. He told himself that again, then again. He could not convince himself. These were real Indians, and they looked like they were deadly in earnest about attacking.

Tyler looked in the direction of Silas Maple, standing behind Elijah. "What do we do, Silas?"

"What do you think we're going to do?" Silas snapped. "If it comes to a fight, then by God, we'll fight. What do you think we got rifles for?"

"If that's what it comes to, then so be it," Tyler muttered.

"Yeah, right," Pa said sarcastically. "Half of us will be dead before the Indians are driven off. Alain would never forgive himself, ever, for causing people to die in an Indian attack."

Tyler turned to look back at the Utes. "What the—"

Angelique and her father were leading two horses over to the Utes. They presented them to the nearest Ute warrior, who took the reins and grunted.

"What do you suppose they're doing?" Tyler wondered.

"I'm pretty sure I know," Pa murmured. "Our lives are worth a few horses."

Dennis Palmerston climbed out of his wagon and cut one of his two horses loose to take to the Utes. Clarence Tewksberry did the same.

The Ute who had taken two of Colledge's horses brought one of them back toward Jonathan and returned the reins to him. The Utes kept the other one, and the four other horses they had been given.

With a shout from one of the Utes, they turned and galloped off with the emigrant horses, leaving the wagon train in peace.

Tyler got out from underneath his wagon. He went straight toward Angelique and the two of them fell into one another's arms. Tyler stroked Angelique's long brown hair and looked into her quiet brown eyes, seemingly full of concern for him.

"That was a very brave thing you did," Tyler said.

"They seemed to want horses more than anything else," Angelique responded. "The Utes knew we had rifles and plenty of ammunition. They knew if they attacked they'd pay a high price for any of us they killed, after the Shoshones had already given them a beating. But while most Indians are intelligent enough not to attack an armed wagon train, they will try to snatch livestock, especially horses, if they can. By saving them the trouble, we got rid of them without any bloodshed, and not only that, now they're less likely to come skulking around at night looking to steal livestock. We can always buy more horses at Fort Hall."

The excitement over for the time being, the wagons rolled on. Still, Tyler walked with his rifle at his side and not in the wagon. There were no more Indians around, but there were plenty of high mountains. The trail took a sharp turn to the north. Silas said it was to avoid having to go straight through the Wyoming Range.

Again, the wagon train made good time. Silas estimated they had made an incredible twenty-two miles that day. There was no dance as the travelers were just too tired as darkness fell. Despite that, Tyler took his turn on night guard duty. Around here, night guard duty actually meant something.

Tyler listened to the sounds of the star-filled night, the crickets, the antelope and the elk herds settling down. But also there were sounds that he did not recognize. There was shuffling amidst the dark sagebrush. Tyler readied his rifle. The shuffling continued. Had the Utes returned? Were they trying to sneak up on the wagon train? Would the emigrants be able to organize themselves into a defense if the Utes staged a surprise attack while most in the wagon train slept? Tyler's breathing became heavy, pointing his rifle at the shadows.

Suddenly out of the bushes, came a group of a half-dozen sage grouse. Tyler relaxed and lowered his rifle.

"Hey there."

Tyler wheeled and leveled his rifle. It was Angelique.

"Well, you're certainly jumpy tonight," she greeted him.

Tyler relaxed again, putting his rifle down. He took Angelique into his arms and kissed her. His actions, he felt, were too mechanical.

Angelique sensed it. "What's the matter, Tyler?" she asked.

Tyler put his hands on Angelique's shoulders and looked into her quiet dark nighttime eyes. The moonlight silvered them. "Angelique, you are so much smarter than I am that I feel inferior to you," Tyler admitted. "You always seem to know what to do and how to do it, better than me or anyone else."

Angelique gently put a hand on his arm. She looked at him with her eyes softening, full of sympathy and love for him.

"I'm never going to let you sell yourself short, Tyler," she murmured. "I won't let you. I won't let you do that. Hear me, Tyler. What I do, I do to protect us all as you do. You were ready to fight to protect not only yourself but everyone around you. That's more than what I was ready to do. I got lucky. What if I had guessed wrong with the Utes? I would have needed you, Tyler, to fight for me, and I know you would have. You are my brave hero, Tyler."

Angelique gently kissed him. Tyler looked into her admiring eyes. He put a finger underneath her chin and drew her lips to his.

When he drew back from her, Tyler again saw the admiring pride in her eyes for him.

But beyond her, Tyler saw Penny looking at him and Angelique from a distance. Penny's arms were folded. The star light caught her jewelry and sparkled with reflection.

"We weren't doing anything," Tyler declared, "and we weren't going to do anything. So you needn't chaperone us."

"Just making sure," Penny admonished.

Angelique chuckled quietly as Penny disappeared.

Tyler was actually grateful for the change of subject. "I worry about Penny," he said.

"Why?" Angelique cocked her head to one side.

Tyler leaned back against his wagon. He sighed and gestured in frustration. "Well, I worry about how Penny will take it if Alain dies, to be blunt. She's been partnered with Alain ever since this journey started. I worry about how she's going to react when—I mean if—Alain dies. She's just twelve years old. It would be the first major crisis in her young life. When our Ma died, Penny was younger and not understanding much about it."

"Penny is a strong young girl." Angelique clutched Tyler's arm. "She has a powerful will. She's courageous and she's very brave. A journey like this can break, and has broken, far greater people. But not Penny. Whatever happens, Penny will deal with it."

Tyler nodded, but still with a degree of uncertainty. "I'm sure you're right."

Angelique kissed him again and moved on as Silas approached to make sure they were attending to their rounds.

The next day Tyler struggled with some of the roughest terrain of the whole Oregon Trail. There was plenty of up-and-down.

"I'm glad we got new, fresh lead oxen," Pa declared, walking beside the team. "Drake and Dru, bless them, could not have handled these rises."

"Rises" was a polite term, Tyler felt. At about 7,000 feet above sea level, a 50-foot rise felt like climbing 200 feet at a lower elevation. Legs ached and became sore to the point of numbness. Lungs burned. Tyler couldn't imagine what it must be like for the oxen trying to lug the heavy wagon uphill.

Out of a sense of guilt, Tyler helped push the wagon up one hill after another. He wasn't sure how much help he was giving the oxen, but it felt a lot better than walking beside the poor beasts cracking a whip.

The scenery was breathtaking as Tyler pushed. Snow-capped, dark, pine-mantled mountains surrounded them. It seemed they were up in the sky. Light clouds floated below them near the valleys, not above them.

Making it to the tops of the latest rise, Pa allowed the oxen to rest and catch their breath. Tyler caught up with his breath, with his hands on his hips.

"We need to attach ropes to the axles for the down slope so the wagon doesn't overrun the oxen," Pa said. "We don't have time to unhitch the oxen; that will take too long and I'm afraid the oxen could run."

With Pa's help, Tyler attached ropes to the back axle. Penny drove the team on the down slope while Tyler and Pa held ropes helping the wagon to descend down the 100-foot slope at a gentle pace, not at runaway speed. Dennis Palmerston and Ephraim Allerton helped them with the ropes.

When their wagon reached the bottom of the slope, Tyler and Pa helped Ephraim with his wagon to get down the slope safely. Then it was the turn of the new MacNaughton wagon, then the Palmerston wagon.

After helping Dennis get his wagon safely downhill, with Rachelle watching and thanking him, Tyler trudged back up to the top of the rise. It was time for the Laurent wagon to make the descent. Alain stood beside his family's wagon, half-smiling.

Tyler felt uneasy watching him. "Why aren't you lying down?" he asked.

"I'd add extra weight to the wagon," Alain said, "so I decided to get out."

Tyler wondered if Alain's real, unspoken concern was more what would happen to him if the ropes broke, or if the men couldn't hold the wagon ropes, and the wagon went careening downhill with him in it. If the wagon rolled over and over and smashed, Alain would surely be killed.

Down below, Penny watched nervously, with her hands clasped together over her young little heart.

Francois attached ropes to the back of his wagon. Alain grabbed one of the ropes.

"What do you think you're doing?" Francois demanded.

"I'm going to help you with the ropes as the wagon goes downhill."

"Oh no, you're not," Francois declared. "Are you insane?"

"Please don't, Alain," Penny begged. "You're not well enough yet."

Alain stepped aside as Francois, Adelaide, Jonathan Colledge, Ephraim, and Tyler grabbed the ropes. The bawling oxen started down the slope. Tyler and his companions held on tight. The wagon wanted to take off. The slope looked to have about a hundred-foot descent at about a ten or fifteen degree angle. The yoke pushed against the oxen team's necks. The creatures bawled and complained.

Tyler felt the heavy rope partially slipping through his fingers. His hands burned. He could not let go. The wagon weighed almost three thousand pounds even without Alain in it. If it slipped out of their fingers, the yoke could snap and the wagon would overrun the oxen, cripple them, and then probably tip sideways and crash.

Francois struggled with his rope. He was a smallish man, maybe 5'8", and thin as a rail. His arms looked like pure skin over bone, no muscle.

The rope slipped partway through Francois's fingers.

"Just make it to the bottom," Tyler said to his companions. "Another thirty feet and we're there."

Suddenly Francois slipped and let the rope go.

"Father!" Alain cried out. He rushed over to grab the rope and hold the wagon steady.

"Let go, Alain, we got it," Ephraim shouted.

Alain did not let go but instead strained to hold onto the rope.

Just as the wagon reached the bottom of the incline Alain fell to his knees and clutched his lower midsection. His light brown shirt was bloodied. His stitches were coming loose.

"Alain!" Penny screamed, hands to her face.

"Somebody help me," Alain begged.

CHAPTER TWENTY ONE

Penny held Alain in her arms as Silas rushed up the incline to the scene.

"Crazy fool. Now you've started bleeding again," Silas snapped.

Alain said nothing. The pained look on his face said plenty as he clutched his midsection.

"Lie down," Silas ordered.

Penny laid Alain's back on the grassy ground and she moved out of the way.

Silas pulled Alain's shirt up to look at his wound. Tyler drew closer. One end of the stitches had come loose and was bloodied and getting bloodier.

Pa rushed up as did Francois and Adelaide. Pa asked, "Can you close the wound?"

"I ain't no doctor," Silas bellowed.

Francois clutched Silas's shoulder. "You must have done this before," he declared.

"Please help him," Adelaide begged. "It's not important what you are or aren't. Can you fix him?"

"Fix him?" Silas rose to his feet, hands on his hips. "If you got a needle and thread I can try to stitch up his skin. He could still be dead if the wound isn't completely closed and he bleeds to death. And even if it is closed, there's a possibility the wound could fester now and the fever could easily kill him."

"He needs a real doctor," Francois declared quickly. He looked past the snow-capped ridge and pine trees ahead. "There's one at Fort Hall, right?"

"Yeah, probably," Silas muttered, "if he makes it that far. And there's no guarantee that any doctor can keep him alive if he's too far gone."

"How far is it to Fort Hall?" Adelaide asked.

"It's still a good hundred miles to Fort Hall," Silas said. "If we bust our butts and the oxens' butts as well. We can be there in, maybe, four and half days."

Alain looked at Silas. "Am I going to live four or five days till we can get to a doctor?"

Silas folded his arms. "I'll be honest—I don't know, son. I'm no doctor, and I certainly ain't God."

Pa stepped forward. "Maybe we can send a couple of riders ahead to Fort Hall and fetch the post surgeon back here."

"If he isn't tied up taking care of men at the fort," Silas said. He rubbed his grizzled whiskers and his narrow eyes looked down fearfully at Alain. "But yeah, a rider could make it to Fort Hall in two days if he busted his tail, and his horse's as well. We'd be heading toward Fort Hall as fast as we could; we'd probably meet up with the doc heading toward us in three days, maybe two and a half even. That might be the difference between life and death for Alain, if we send a rider or two or three for safety's sake, on ahead to Fort Hall to fetch a doctor back here."

Tyler rubbed his hands. "Any Indians between here and Fort Hall?" he asked.

"What do you think?" Silas snapped. "Yeah, there could be a few wide-ranging Utes between here and Fort Hall. Maybe some Shoshones. But mostly around here you got Bannocks."

"How they feel about whites?" Pa asked.

"I don't know," Silas replied, looking askance. "I ain't that familiar with the Bannocks. I know the Pawnees, the Sioux, the Shoshones and the Utes, but the Bannocks are a tribe that lives further west than I've ever been but once or twice."

"The Bannocks are friendly, though, right?" Ephraim asked.

"I just said I don't know!" Silas snapped. He thrust his broad-brimmed hat back. "You know what, Ephraim, why don't you ride to the nearest Bannock village and ask 'em."

Pa raised his arms. "All right, all right. This isn't what Alain needs right now."

"Well, who's going to ride to Fort Hall through Indian country and fetch the doc?" Silas asked. "I can't go because I have responsibilities here to all of these other people."

"I'll go," Tyler declared.

Pa jerked his head around.

Tyler faced Pa. "Alain means everything in the world to Penny. If you don't believe me, just ask her."

Pa scratched the back of his head, looked down, and sighed. "I believe you, Tyler," he murmured. "But if you're going, then I'm going with you."

"If you go, who will drive our wagon?" Tyler asked.

"Don't worry about it," Silas said, "I'll help. I can also have Dennis Palmerston, Ephraim Allerton, and Van Buren Colledge take turns driving the wagon."

"I'll go as well," Francois declared stepping forward. "Alain is my son, and I need to do this for him."

"I will come with you as well."

Tyler turned. It was Angelique who had spoken.

"It's too dangerous, Angelique," Tyler said. "We'll be riding through—"

Pa clutched Tyler's shoulder. "She knows Indian sign language," Pa said quietly. He let out another low sigh. "We may—

hopefully not—but we may need her help on this trip. I'll talk to her father about how important Angelique's Indian knowledge is."

"With four of you," Silas said, "it'll be better than one person traveling alone. If one or two of you don't—" Silas stopped in mid-sentence, perhaps thinking twice about what he was on the verge of saying. "Stay away from riding right next to the Snake River if you can. That's where you'll find Indian villages, most likely. I'll give you our fastest horses that we got left."

"We don't have any time to waste," Pa said. "We'd best get moving."

* * *

The first day's hard ride took Tyler and his companions to within sight of Soda Springs, a wealth of cool, refreshing water. However, Pa felt it would be too dangerous to make camp overnight right at the springs themselves. Probably, Indians visited the springs regularly.

At Pa's suggestion, no fire was made. Supper consisted of a plateful of jerked beef.

Next morning, with no Indians around, Tyler and his companions filled their canteens with cool water from the luscious spring. Then it was time for another hard ride. Tyler kept his horse's legs pumping, sometimes until the poor beast was foaming at the mouth. Then Tyler would slack off for awhile, as would Pa, Francois, and Angelique in her riding culottes.

"It's not going to do us any good if our horses pass out," Angelique said at one point. "If they do, then where are we?"

A good question, Tyler thought. Distant a couple of miles as they rode was the Snake River. They rode along a rough trail through the blue-green sagebrush, sometimes having to lead their horses up and down rises. Evidently others before them had had the same fear of contact with the Bannocks.

Occasionally far-distant smoke let Tyler know that the Indians were present, but fortunately, not close by. The end of the second day came and Fort Hall was nowhere in sight. Silas's prediction that Fort Hall could be reached by fast travel within two days had proven false and overly optimistic.

"Well, it's not quite two days yet since we set out," Pa said at suppertime—more beef jerky. "We started out about a day and a half ago. Probably we'll be there by early tomorrow afternoon."

"At least we know the land is getting flatter and lower hereabouts," Tyler said. "The wagons will have easy traveling through this area."

"Easier maybe, but not easy," Francois declared. "There are narrow passages in some places."

"I think we're on a volcanic plain," Angelique said. "The rocks and boulders are darker and there's a lot fewer trees. The wagons will be okay traveling if the Indians leave them alone."

The journey resumed early the next morning, just as soon as there was enough dawn light to see the trail ahead and avoid badger holes and sharp black stones littering the ground. Low-lying mesas topped by rows of volcanic black rock loomed everywhere around.

About an hour after setting off, however, Tyler saw that their luck had run out. "Pa, Indians up ahead," Tyler shouted.

"I see 'em," Pa declared.

Tyler pulled up on the reins of his appaloosa. Pa, Angelique, and Francois also pulled up short on their reins. Tyler strained to see how many Indians there were. It looked from a distance like there were not a lot, maybe fifteen or sixteen. Bannocks, he assumed, sitting their horses and not moving.

"They're not wearing war paint," Angelique said.

"That mean anything?" Pa asked.

"Well, uh, um, not really," Angelique said.

The Bannocks did nothing, nothing except sit on their still horses, their expressions as nearly as Tyler could tell, looking grim, purse-lipped, and generally unhappy. The Indians gave no indication of what their purpose or intention might be. They merely watched Tyler and his companions, the Indians making themselves more ominous simply by their unmoving and ambiguous presence.

Angelique leaned forward. "If we turn tail and run, they'll be after us like a pack of wolves chasing down prey," she murmured. "Our best bet, probably our only bet, is to act unafraid of them, and find out what they want."

Francois looked ashen-faced. "I have every confidence in the world, that they know we are afraid of them."

"I didn't say *be* unafraid; I said *act* unafraid," Angelique declared.

Pa snapped his reins. "All right. I guess we don't have a choice," he muttered. "Let's see what they're wanting from us."

Slowly Pa moved forward on his horse. Tyler followed closely, along with Angelique and Francois. The Bannocks remained ominously impassive. When Pa got to within thirty feet of the Indians, he halted. Tyler, Angelique, and Francois did likewise.

For several tense seconds, the two groups simply faced one another, with no one speaking. The Bannocks looked dark, sinister, but unmoving, sitting their horses almost like bronze statues. Only the occasional swish of a horse's tail provided evidence that the Bannocks were not grim-faced statues. Tyler felt the very air hardening around him.

Finally, one of the Indians in the center of the group extended his hand, palm downward.

"The peace sign," Angelique murmured, sounding cautious. She returned it slowly, extending her hand outward with the palm down.

"That peace sign from them mean anything?" Pa asked.

"Your guess is as good as mine," Angelique said. "Hopefully they are sincere and aren't trying to pull something."

The Bannock who had made the peace sign looked behind him and gestured for someone to come forward. Tyler watched as another Bannock rode to the front, hauling the reins of another horse behind him. The horse's rider caught Tyler's attention and shocked him. He could scarcely believe his eyes. The little rider had long blonde hair and a round white face. She wore Indian clothes, a deerskin shirt with geometric designs, deerskin leggings, and moccasins.

She looked nervous, indeed, terrified with her short breaths and half-open mouth.

Tyler, Pa, Angelique, and Francois exchanged puzzled glances among themselves.

Pa turned to face the young white girl, who looked to be maybe nine or ten years old. "What's your name, girl?" he asked.

The little girl only pursed her lips and gulped, her eyes wide and fearful as she looked at Pa. Tyler felt for her.

The Bannock leader knocked the little girl on the side of her head. "Ho!" the Indian declared, and he pointed toward Pa.

"My name is Sarah," the little girl said, terrified and breathing heavily.

"Sarah what?" Pa asked. "Sarah Smith? Sarah Jones? Sarah Ivanovitch? What?"

The little girl pursed her lips again and caught her breath. "Sarah Van Oerton," she half-whimpered, and exhaled.

Tyler leaned forward, interested. "Where are you from, Sarah?" he asked.

"From New York," she said weakly. "From the Hudson Valley."

Pa looked at Tyler. "Figures, with a last name like she's got." Pa turned to the little girl again. "What are you doing out here? How did you get here?"

"Indians attacked our wagon last year near a river. My Pa called it the North Flat. They killed my Pa and Ma. My two older brothers and my sister escaped with my uncle. But they captured me and then sold me to these people."

The Indian leader gestured at the little girl and made more signs. Tyler looked at Angelique for an explanation of what the Indians meant.

"They want to sell this little girl to us," Angelique said.

"What?" Pa was incredulous.

"They're not going to just give her to us," Angelique said. "They want something in return. It doesn't have to be much, but it has to be something of value."

"I have a little bit of tobacco," Francois said.

"I'm not giving them my knife or rifle," Pa declared.

"You got any money?" Angelique asked.

"Money?" Pa asked in disbelief. "Do these savages even know what money is?"

"Yes, they do," Angelique declared in a low tone, looking askance at Pa. "Or let me say, they probably do. They no doubt go trading at Fort Hall every so often and they can use money to buy things. Even though it's still Hudson's Bay-owned for the moment, Fort Hall is on American territory now and so they would accept American money."

"I have ten dollars in silver coins that I can give," Pa said. He pulled his parfleche forward.

Tyler, Pa, Francois, and Angelique exchanged glances.

"Well, who's going to give the Indians our stuff?" Pa asked.

"I will," Francois said. "Alain is my son. It is my responsibility."

Francois took the ten silver coins from Pa and held them, his tobacco, and his reins as he slowly moved forward on his horse. Sarah bit her lip nervously.

Tyler half-expected the Indian leader to move forward slightly on his horse as well, but this did not happen. The Bannocks glumly watched as Francois approached. He had to approach all of them together, not just the leader. Tyler tried to read some measure of reaction in the faces of the Bannocks. However, the Bannocks remained scowling, or otherwise impassive.

Francois approached the Indian leader next to Sarah and held out the tobacco and the silver coins. The Indians stared at the proffered gift for a long, thick several seconds. Without warning, the nearest Indian in a lighting move grabbed the tobacco and then the coins. He sniffed the tobacco to see that it was genuine, then he whipped his paint horse around and took off. The other Indians did the same, with their legs guiding their horses as much as their reins.

Little Sarah was left behind with Francois.

With the Indians gone, Francois and Sarah stared at each other. Suddenly Sarah began to cry.

Tyler looked at Pa, both of them unsure if Sarah was crying out of sorrow for the loss of her parents, or out of relief, or fear.

Pa made a sighing, head-shaking expression. "We don't have time for this," he murmured. "Alain's waiting for us and that doctor."

"Come." Francois gestured for Sarah to ride forward and join him.

Instead, Sarah stood still on her horse.

Seeing she wasn't sure what to do, Francois grabbed the horse's reins and pulled Sarah's horse to follow him.

"Let's move," Pa said.

"We were on our way to Fort Hall to get help for one of our company who is wounded and dying," Tyler explained urgently. "We need to get riding again quickly."

Tyler, Pa, and Angelique started again for Fort Hall. However, Francois hauling Sarah along slowed progress down to a crawl. Tyler knew they had to get to Fort Hall pronto.

Sarah, of course, had no knowledge of the nature of their mission or of the critical importance of speed here. She lagged behind Francois, who lagged behind Tyler, Pa, and Angelique. There was no time, now, to explain in detail who and what they were, or to learn more about Sarah's story.

"I have an idea," Angelique said. "Follow my lead." She snapped her reins and her appaloosa took off at a fast gallop. Pa's horse took off and so did Tyler's. Francois's horse took off as well.

Tyler looked back. Sarah's horse instinctively galloped after them, with Sarah holding onto the reins confidently.

"She's got a trained Indian horse," Angelique said. "It's reacting like I thought. And after living with the Indians for a year, Sarah knows how to ride."

Tyler looked back at Sarah. "We have to get to Fort Hall quickly," Tyler told her. "We need to get a doctor for an injured man at our wagon train."

Sarah snapped her reins and launched her horse fast and hard, with seeming determination and dawning realization of her rescuers' situation and of the need to get far and fast away from her erstwhile captors.

Tyler alternately rested his horse with a slow canter when his companions rested theirs. Then, they were off at a fast pace again. Within a couple of hours Fort Hall came into view, unpretentious white adobe, but civilization.

As they rode into the fort, wild shouts greeted them. What that told Tyler was that this was an intensely isolated post over the winter and their arrival as one of the first wagon trains through was probably a welcome treat. The fort interior looked like frontier basic—a long log house, presumably the living quarters for trappers and traders staying at the fort, and then three ramshackle adobe huts. One of the huts looked to be a blacksmith shop, with a wooden roof that was partly caved in.

"We've got a little girl with us," Pa said. "She's been a captive of the Indians for the past year."

Several Hudson's Bay trappers gathered around them. One older trapper-dressed man approached them. "I'm Horace Buggert, sort of in charge of this fort. And who might you be?"

"People who need help, that's who we be," Pa replied.

"My son on a wagon train fifty miles back needs a doctor," Francois said. "He was attacked with a knife."

"Providing a medical guy, that we can do," Buggert said. "But who is this little girl dressed in Indian clothes?"

"All we know about her," Pa said, "is that her name is Sarah Van Oerton, and that she's from the Hudson Valley of New York. Her parents were killed by Indians on the Oregon Trail a year ago. The Bannocks sold her to us about ten miles back."

Another older clean-shaven trapper in buckskins and a raccoon hat, though looking younger than the first, came forward from one of the ramshackle adobe huts. "I'm factor Ben Lockwood of the Hudson's Bay Company. Did you say this girl's name was Van Oerton?"

"Sarah Van Oerton to be precise," Pa declared.

Lockwood's face turned into an excited half-smile and his breaths came quick. "Can it be?" he declared. "Glory, can it be? Can it actually be? Can it actually be that you found the Van Oerton girl, alive and unharmed?"

Pa exchanged puzzled glances with Tyler, who shrugged his shoulders. Tyler exchanged glances with Angelique, smiling and seeming to grasp the significance and the joy of the moment that others around them were feeling.

Lockwood turned to a pair of other men near him. "Fetch Dirk Van Oerton," he shouted. "Fetch him quick!"

The men hurried into the long log bunkhouse. Tyler was not sure what to think. Something momentous was going on here, though.

In an instant a buckskin-clad man with a feathered wide-brimmed hat emerged, and at sight of Sarah, his eyes practically bulged. "Am I seeing right?" he declared. "Are my eyes really seeing what they're seeing?"

Sarah nodded and smiled, her blue eyes shining. "Yes, Uncle Dirk, you are," she said mildly. "It is I, Sarah Van Oerton, your niece. I am returned to you."

"Sarah, praise be. It's Sarah!" Dirk Van Oerton ran toward his long lost-and-found niece with outstretched arms. Sarah dismounted and fell into his embrace.

"Sarah. It's Sarah!" a teenage boy exclaimed. He raced toward her to embrace her.

"Sarah!" A teenage girl hurried out of the log hut followed by an adolescent boy.

All of them hugged Sarah close, and Sarah hugged them all to her young heart as she wept for joy. Tyler could only surmise that these were Sarah's siblings that she had spoken of. It was a fine scene but one that was slowing them down from finding help for Alain.

"We waited for you, Sarah," the teenage girl exclaimed, wiping away tears. "We couldn't leave you behind."

"We've been living at the fort for the past several months," Dirk Van Oerton declared. "We never went all the way to Oregon after we heard rumors here at the fort that a lone white girl might be living as a captive with the Bannocks. We hoped and prayed it was you and that you weren't dead.

Like Hannah said, we couldn't leave you behind. We'd never forget you, ever."

"Thank you," Sarah said. She turned to Angelique, Tyler, Pa, and Francois. "And thank you to these brave people who rescued me. For ten dollars and some tobacco, they rescued me from the Indians. You thought me dead, I am sure, but praise be, I am alive and returned to you."

Pa dismounted, followed by Francois. Pa looked to one of the trappers and handed him the reins of his horse. "Can our horses get some water? I'm sorry, but we are in a bit of a rush."

"Of course," the trapper replied, taking the reins.

Tyler and Angelique also dismounted as trappers stationed at the fort came to take their horses away. The horses could only rest a short while, as the post surgeon was fetched. Then they would have to be off again.

The Van Oertons, all of them, were not about to let Tyler, Pa, Francois, and Angelique get away. Dirk hurried over to Pa and practically shook his arm off in thanks. As did Hannah Van Oerton, the two brothers, and Sarah. They shook hands with Francois as well and hugged him, likewise with Angelique and with Tyler.

Tyler felt some discomfort and self-consciousness at this display of tearful affection, but he well understood the Van Oertons' exuberance and rejoicing at finding their lost family member.

"We can't forget why we came here," Francois said.

"No we can't," Pa agreed. He turned to Dirk Van Oerton. "We came here to get a doctor. Francois's son is near death and he needs medical help just as rapidly as possible. We need to get a doctor and quickly."

"And some iodine," Angelique added.

"There's actually a couple of docs here at the fort," Dirk responded. "I'm sure one of them should be able to get away and go with you. As for iodine, if that's some type of medicine, you'd probably have to ask at the post trader's. That's where the pills and potions and stuff like that are sold, if we have any now."

Tyler observed a low-roofed white adobe hut with a "trading post" sign above it in one corner of the fort. "Who's the post trader?" Tyler asked.

"Well, he's—" Dirk stopped abruptly and his face puckered through his white whiskers. He sighed. "Well, I guess you'll have to deal with him if you want medical supplies."

"Well, who is he?" Pa asked. "What's his name?"

"Saurusse," Dirk Van Oerton replied. "His name is Saurusse. Mr. Bulworth Saurusse, or as we sometimes refer to him when he's not around to hear, Mr. Bullhead Sore-ass."

CHAPTER TWENTY TWO

Tyler, Pa, Francois, Angelique, and Dirk all went together to see Saurusse the post trader.

"One person alone can't deal with this guy," Dirk declared, "especially if you don't know him and he doesn't know you."

The post trader's store was little more than an adobe hovel; it could scarcely be called a building. Entering, the atmosphere inside loomed dark and obscure, lit only by light coming in through a pair of narrow windows, one on each side of the door. Tyler felt the gloom pervading the store, filled with cans of food, bolts of cloth, bottles of rum, and rifles, pistols, gunpowder horns, and bullet balls for sale.

A smallish man with thinning hair on top stood behind a counter reading a yellowed newspaper. His lips were pressed together in a tight pout. The man took no note of his visitors. He was short, maybe 5'2" or 5'3", and thin as a rail. But Tyler easily surmised that packed into that bony frame was all the bitterness of an apparently misanthropic personality born of pure cynicism about anyone and anything outside of himself.

The man's bitter pout caused large wrinkles about his mouth that could only have been formed if this was the man's near-perpetual expression. His dark eyes were narrowed, his fingers gnarled as they gripped the newspaper hard.

His nasal breaths sounded like a combination of continual hard sighs and guttural grunts.

"Good afternoon," Pa said casually.

Saurusse did not look up from his newspaper. "Is there something good about it in your opinion that you feel I've failed to notice?" he demanded.

Oh God, Tyler thought to himself, *not one of these continual chip-on-his-shoulder types.*

Tyler leaned over to Angelique and Francois and whispered, "This guy is a piece of work, isn't he?"

"I heard that." Saurusse threw his newspaper down on the counter and glared. "What do you want? I'm a busy man."

Busy reading your newspaper, Tyler thought.

"We need iodine for my son," Francois said. "I'm afraid he'll die without it. I've heard it's some sort of new European medicine. This being a Hudson's Bay post, we thought you might have some."

"He is my daughter's boyfriend," Pa declared. "We need iodine desperately. We must have it."

"Desperately, eh?" Saurusse said. "Must have it, eh? He'll die without it, eh?"

Clearly it had been a mistake to use words like "desperately," "must have" and "he'll die without it" with a man like Bulworth Saurusse, Tyler concluded.

"I have iodine." Saurusse pulled a small bottle, maybe five inches high, off one of the back shelves that was loaded with small pill bottles. The bottle was filled with a dark reddish liquid. "It'll cost you thirty dollars."

"Thirty dollars!" Pa exploded. His fists clenched. "You're trying to take advantage of us."

"Thirty dollars is what I'm charging," Saurusse bellowed. "This is my store, not yours. Business is business."

"What if we need to buy more supplies later?" Francois asked. "A new wagon wheel or more bacon? We'll be short of money. We've traveled a long ways and we've already spent a lot."

"Tell me why that suddenly becomes my problem and not just yours," Saurusse snapped. "Thirty dollars, I said!" Saurusse slammed the bottle down on the counter. "If you really want it as bad as you've said, then the price goes up of course."

Pa drew his pepperbox pistol out of his coat pocket and stuck it squarely in Saurusse's face.

"Magnus—no!" Francois said. "Alain would not want—"

"I'm doing this for Penny as well as Alain," Pa declared. "If Alain dies, it could take Penny years to get over it, if she ever does."

Saurusse gulped, his breathing short and hard. "You—you won't pull that trigger, mister. Justice is quick and swift at this fort. They'd hang you within minutes."

"Oh yeah? Why don't you go ahead and bet what's left of your no doubt worthless and miserable life, Saurusse, that I won't pull this trigger," Pa challenged. "I might regret doing it ten seconds after doing it but that won't bring you back to life, will it?"

Saurusse gulped again, his eyes on the pistol barrel pointed at his nose. His breaths continued short. "Ten dollars. That's my final offer, ten dollars," Saurusse said. "I'll sell it for ten dollars."

"Yeah, Sore-ass?" Pa muttered. "What'd it cost you to buy it? I'll bet no more than the equivalent of two bits."

"I've got ten dollars," Dirk Van Oerton declared, pulling a couple of greenbacks and some coins out of his buckskin shirt pocket. "And I'll buy a pouch of tobacco for this other gentleman." Dirk nodded at Francois. "It's the least I can do after these folks ransomed Sarah."

"That's fine, that's fine," Saurusse hurriedly agreed. "But not until this gun is out of my face."

Pa lowered his pistol, tucking it back into his britches. Tyler doubted that the gun was loaded. Still, 1,500 miles of frontier travel had definitely hardened Pa. Tyler could not imagine Pa doing something like that back in Independence, Missouri.

"That'll be eleven dollars," Saurusse snapped at Van Oerton.

Dirk paid Saurusse his money and Saurusse handed over the bottle of iodine and the tobacco pouch.

"Now get out of my store," Saurusse demanded.

* * *

With hard riding accompanied by Doc Preston, one of the post surgeons, and Dirk Van Oerton, who knew a few words of Bannock should they encounter any more, Tyler, Pa, Francois, and Angelique caught up with the advancing wagon train late the following day. Tyler wondered if Doc Preston was a genuine doctor, or if that was just what he called himself. Whatever, Preston would have to do.

Tyler and his companions headed straight for the Laurent wagon, with Adelaide standing outside, one hand to her upper chest. Penny was inside the wagon, swathing Alain's forehead with a damp cloth. Alain's lower shirt had dried blood on it.

"The bleeding will stop for awhile," Penny whimpered, "then it'll just start up again. We can't seem to stop it once and for all. And now he's developing a fever."

Doc Preston sighed deeply, running his fingers through his gray hair, his wrinkled face tensing. "It's the wagon jolting as it moves along," he said. "He's being jostled back and forth. That's what's causing the periodic bleeding. I'll take a look at him and tighten the stitches. But he's got to be completely immobilized. You've got to tie him with ropes to a flat board that he can't move. He's already lost a lot of blood and the wound has begun to fester. It'll be uncomfortable for him, riding immobilized on a board, but being in a casket and six feet under would be even more uncomfortable for him, I'm thinking. we've got to get him to Fort Hall, where he can be completely stationary."

"Will he live?" Penny asked plaintively.

Not sure what to say, Preston scratched one of his bushy eyebrows. "We can hope, and pray," he declared.

"Penny, come here," Pa said.

She climbed out of the front of the wagon and both Tyler and Pa approached her. Pa gently clutched Penny's shoulders and he knelt to talk to her.

"You're a strong, powerful young girl, Penny," Pa told her. "You have to be strong for Alain. You have to be strong for him. Francois and Adelaide Laurent won't be able to. It would be too much to ask or expect of them. So you have to be strong for all of them. Can you do that, Penny?"

Penny wiped tears out from underneath her glasses. "I can try, Pa."

"I know you can do it, little Golden Penny."

"Penny, when did that fever start?" Tyler asked.

"Yesterday," she replied, "and it's getting worse."

Pa got up and gave Tyler a stern look, as if to declare, *don't say anything more.* "The doc is here," Pa said. "Let's hope for the best."

"I'm hoping the iodine will help curb the festering," Preston said, looking at Pa. "I've heard of it but never used it."

"It's a European medicine," Angelique said. "It may make the difference, I hope."

Penny returned to be with Alain. Francois and Adelaide cut down a large cottonwood tree and constructed a stretcher board to which Alain was strapped.

The wagon journey continued and by early evening of the next day the smoke of the Fort Hall fireplaces came into sight. Silas warned everyone that distances can be deceiving in the West, as they had learned with Chimney Rock. However, the decision among the emigrants was to push on to Fort Hall. It was another ten miles, and close to midnight, before the wagon train approached the fort. The last few miles of the trail had to be traveled by moonlight.

Alain was transferred to a bed in the adobe fort infirmary, such as it was, with its rope beds and dirt floor. Penny sat in a chair by his bedside. Tyler, Pa, Francois, Adelaide, Alain's younger brother Jean-Pierre, and Angelique stood close by. Alain had fallen into a delirium, drifting in and out of consciousness.

"I've done everything I can for him," Preston said. "With the fever so hot now, he is going to literally burn up from the inside out. There is nothing to do now except send for that visiting priest, Father Seamus Coogan, so that Alain can be given his last rites."

Adelaide burst into a sob.

"I'll find him," Francois murmured.

Alain grabbed Penny's hand. "Precious, precocious little golden sugar-Penny, precious little darling of mine," Alain said. His eyes appeared glazed, looking straight up at the ceiling. "I-I don't want to die. I do not fear death, but-but it will mean that I shan't be able to ever marry you and treasure you and love you. I-I want . . ."

He could not go on, and his grasp on Penny's hand loosened. Penny clutched his hand. Tears covered her face.

Shortly, Reverend Coogan arrived, bearing a vial of oil. He looked at them all. "We meet again," he said, "not under the best of circumstances."

"Do you want us to leave?" Pa asked.

"No, it is not necessary," Coogan said. "You may stay, but I must ask you to maintain a respectful silence. I can answer any questions you may have about the rite later, after it is over."

Coogan wore a white lace vestment and a purple stole, rather like a scarf, about his neck. He dipped his thumb in the vial of oil and drew the shape of a cross on Alain's forehead.

"*In nomine patri, et filii, et spiritu sancti*," Coogan began.

The last rites took about fifteen minutes, with Coogan concluding by looking at Francois and Adelaide and telling them quietly, "He's too sick for me to give him Viaticum. But he is ready—ready for his journey, if it comes to that."

Francois clutched Adelaide in his arms closer. "There's nothing to do now except wait," he said.

Pa turned to Tyler. "Let's help out by getting a few more chairs."

Tyler moved quickly to fetch more log-frame chairs from the bunkhouse. This done, he and Pa seated themselves toward the back and settled in for the vigil. Penny held Alain's hand in hers, while Adelaide held Alain's other hand. Alain would either get better, or die.

Alain could not speak. His breathing was labored, his eyes glazed over.

Pa walked over to Penny, placing a comforting hand on her shoulder, saying nothing, but communicating his caring for her and for Alain.

Penny looked up at Pa. "I love him," she said quietly. "I really and truly do love him, with all of my heart."

Pa sighed and gently clutched her shoulder. "Yeah, little sugar-Penny, I think you do," he murmured. "I think you do. I know you do."

Tyler sat in his chair, drowsiness overcoming him. He drifted off to sleep, waking up about an hour later, with the scene unchanged. Penny and Adelaide had their faces fixed on Alain, breathing more gently. Pa had reclaimed his chair. "I'm going outside for awhile," Tyler said quietly.

Pa nodded, half asleep himself.

Tyler went outside and walked around the fort. The parade ground was deserted, and Tyler let the cool air drift over him. He found himself pacing around the parade ground or small central plaza, his hands behind his back.

Pa joined him after a short while. He looked at Tyler, his face in the dark still visibly drawn and worried, and he said, "Let's never forget that Alain is dying because he stood up for Penny, trying to protect her."

A loud scream of exclamation from Penny startled Tyler and Pa. They looked at each other in shock, then together they hurried back toward the adobe infirmary. Inside they saw Penny's face buried in her hands. She was weeping. Quickly, it was apparent that she was weeping for joy.

Alain was half-sitting up in bed and he looked much more lucid. "I feel like I'm starting to get better now," he said weakly, but nonetheless firmly. "I don't feel so feverish now."

He laid a hand on Penny's shoulder to comfort her. "My precious little Penny, precocious little Golden Penny," he murmured. "You are ever and always in my heart, and I would not cause you worry, or do anything to make you cry, for all the riches in Oregon. In a few years, I may get the chance to marry you after all."

Penny wiped the tears from underneath her glasses. She couldn't stop crying for joy and for relief. She managed a smile through her young tears, however.

"I'm not ever letting you forget what you just said," Penny declared.

Alain also managed a smile. He gently laid a hand underneath Penny's chin. "Nor shall I ever forget."

* * *

Alain slowly recovered over a period of days. Preston said that Alain would need time to recover, but that in a week, he should be able to move again.

The remainder of the wagon train arrived at Fort Hall after three days. Buckman was still the wagon master. Tyler became bored stiff with the inactivity. He had become accustomed to the daily grind to the point where he missed it and felt purposeless without it.

Tyler took to walking around and around the exterior of the fort just to kill time. On his third jaunt around the fort, Tyler was surprised to see Rachelle Palmerston sitting against the white adobe wall, her face buried in her hands, crying.

"Tarnation," Tyler exclaimed in a whisper to himself. "Enough with the tears around here lately."

Nevertheless, he approached her. "What's the matter, Rachelle?"

She thrust a letter toward him. Without looking up, Rachelle mumbled, "This letter was waiting for me here at the fort."

She apparently didn't mind if he read it. Tyler took the letter and began to read:

Dear Rachelle,

I would rather have my heart ripped out of me than to have to write you a letter like this. But I must. I have never been anything but honest with you for as long as we have known each other. I will not start being dishonest with you now.

There is nothing to do but out with it: by the time you read this letter, delivered via the isthmus of Panama, and then by courier to Fort Hall, should you get that far, I will be married to a lovely young woman. You may know her—Edna Philpott. After you left, Edna gave me signals that she wanted to be more than just a friend to me. Well, one thing led to another— Edna was pretty persistent—and I ended up proposing marriage to her. There is nothing I could have done to avoid this. Once you left, Edna saw her chance and she took it.

You're a beautiful young woman, Rachelle. I have every reason to believe that you will find someone else, if you haven't already.

Nothing more to say, except—I'm sorry. I will always remember you as my first love.

Sincerely,
Everett Lueckens

Tyler looked up after finishing the letter. Rachelle was trying to dry her tears. "This guy is the epitome of a jerk," Tyler declared. "He knew he was engaged to you. You stayed faithful to him, yet he says he couldn't help himself on his end."

Both of Rachelle's fists clenched. "Eww, that Edna Philpott! I know what she did. She lured my Everett back behind the barn for some sparkin' and spoonin' and then, like Everett said, one thing led to another, and pretty soon Everett married Edna because he *had* to."

Rachelle leaned back and sighed. "But I'm okay. I'll be fine. Quimby Freding invited me on a picnic, just him and me."

"Ah—Quimby." Tyler would never have guessed. "Quimby is a good man. I'm glad to hear he invited you to a picnic. You'll have fun."

Rachelle took the letter back. "Quimby is a little shy, but that's okay."

"I'm sure all he needs is a little encouragement. You'll have fun, I'm sure of it."

Tyler walked on. Rachelle Palmerston and Quimby Freding. Rachell had undergone a remarkable maturation process on this journey to have shown interest in a young man like Quimby Freding. Rachelle Palmerston, maybe Mrs. Rachelle Freding someday—who would have thought that such a thing was possible back in Independence?

It occurred to Tyler that maybe if he had still hung around Rachelle as a friend even after she had told him that she was already engaged, then this might have been his big chance with her. Or would Quimby have still beaten him to her?

No matter. Angelique Hapsburg meant everything to him. "Hmm," he said, smiling. He was glad that Rachelle had rejected him hundreds of miles back. It was Angelique's beautiful face that he saw in his mind's eye, her gentle brown eyes, clear skin, straight nose, slightly rounded at the end, and a flow of brown hair that went nearly to her waist.

"Hey, you."

Tyler turned. Billie Kay looked at him, with a smile on her quiet face. "I am very, very, very proud of you, Tyler," she said, and meant it.

"Why is that?"

"You stayed loyal to Angelique," Billie Kay said.

Tyler couldn't help returning her smile.

"Angelique is the right one for you," Billie Kay said. "I am proud of the way you stuck with her."

"Indeed she is the right one for me," Tyler agreed. "Not only is she beautiful, but she has a frontiersman's head upon her shoulders."

Billie Kay cocked her head to one side. "You're coming to the wedding, aren't you?"

"Wedding?"

"Mine—and Justin's," Billie Kay replied. "The priest is here now. It's time."

"When?"

"Day after tomorrow, at noon."

* * *

The wedding was like a celebration. Many had harbored unspoken doubts that most of them would get this far. But here they were, 1,500 miles from Independence, Missouri, and 500 miles from their goal, the Willamette Valley.

Tyler knew there were still obstacles to overcome—more deserts, more Indians, more rivers to cross, more mountains to get around, or over. But there was nothing ahead that represented anything new or different from the many threats which the emigrants had already faced down.

Billie Kay and Justin said their "I do's" in front of the Reverend Father Seamus Coogan. Billie Kay Ellis became Billie Kay Maybrie.

Bruce Mallory chipped in with his fiddle at the reception. No one seemed to mind that they had heard Bruce's entire repertoire many times before.

The day after the wedding, Billie Kay had a sad duty to perform. Kelly Jay had tried heroically many times to convince their father to give up his quixotic dream of heading to California to pan for gold.

"Our father is stubborn as a mule," Kelly Jay muttered as she hugged Billie Kay outside the fort wall, and Tyler and many others watched.

"You don't have to go with him, you know," Billie Kay said, wiping away tears.

Kelly Jay bowed her head. "I know, she murmured. "But our father needs someone to watch out for him in California. I'm just afraid that if I don't go with him, he'll get roped into a poker game somewhere and lose anything he does find to some sharper." She looked up. "But-but maybe if our Pa can keep all of the gold he finds, if he finds any, he will decide to head to Oregon in another year or two."

"Well, yeah," Billie Kay acknowledged, sighing. "At least you won't be alone crossing the Sierras."

Ten other families had decided to veer southwest from Fort Hall and head for California. Not all of them were interested in the gold diggings.

"The San Joaquin Valley has the best farmland in all of North America," Ben Renwiler declared, heading his oxen toward the Humboldt. "You can get in three crops a year there."

Justin kept his arm tenderly around Billie Kay as she watched her twin sister and her father leave her behind. She and Justin would continue on to Oregon without them. It was the first time she'd ever been apart from them.

Even so, Billie Kay still smiled gently as quiet tears fell down her cheeks, watching her father's wagon growing ever smaller, heading toward the southwest horizon.

Tyler wanted to cheer her up, as she had tried to do for him when Rachelle had rejected him several hundred miles back. Tyler knew there was nothing he could really say that would cheer her.

Instead, he quietly asked her," Billie Kay, you and your twin sister Kelly Jay were—are—identical twins in every way—looks, clothing, and mannerisms. But I am curious about this one thing."

Billie Kay wiped a tear off her cheek and smiled. "What's that?"

"Well, um, uh, Kelly Jay is Presbyterian and you are Catholic," Tyler said. "Why aren't you both one or the other? For the sake of consistency, I mean, since you try so hard to be identical in all ways."

Billie Kay gently chuckled from her heart, and clasped her hands together. "Our grandfather on our father's side was a Presbyterian minister for forty-five years," she began. "I wish more of our grandfather's preaching would have rubbed off on our father, but I guess not enough did. Our mother was Catholic. Both Kelly Jay and I made our choices. Kelly Jay chose our grandfather's religion. I chose our mother's religion. Kelly Jay prefers her religion simple and basic. 'Jesus, period,' she calls it. I prefer my religion to have a little more richness. Kelly Jay prefers a simple, quiet meetinghouse, plain and unadorned. I like stained glass windows, thought-provoking statues, and cool, dark aisles. Why can't both have their place? Like the Bible says, there are different charisms but the same Spirit."

CHAPTER TWENTY THREE

The dust blew so hard that it was like a blizzard of sand, with visibility down to maybe thirty feet, and the sky filled with brown. Tyler kept the oxen going hard to stay close to the Maybrie wagon in front and the Clevenger wagon to the right. To the left, the MacNaughtons' new white canvas wagon seemed like it floated above the ground, so poor was the visibility. All of the wagons tried to stay within sight of their neighbors. To have lost sight of one's neighbors in this sandy mess would be to enter grave danger of becoming completely lost and alone once the sandstorm let up.

Tyler had asked Pa to stay close to the Clevenger wagon so that he could keep an eye on the four Clevenger kids and see that they were all right. Billie Kay Maybrie, perhaps out of force of habit, had asked that her wagon stay close to that of the Linders'.

The Clevenger kids bravely soldiered on through the sandstorm which the heavy wind forcefully blew, stinging faces and forcing handkerchiefs and bandanas over eyes.

Through a white handkerchief Tyler saw the four Clevengers, with the oldest, thirteen-year-old Brit, gamely controlling their oxen. All of them took turns carrying little Jenny, who cried and cried as the sand blew.

Tyler looked ahead to Pa, walking in front of him. "How far to Fort Boise?" Tyler asked Pa through the wind.

Pa looked back with his wide brim down over his eyes. "We're three days past Fort Hall," he declared, "so it's probably another nine or ten days to Fort Boise. It depends on the Snake River, how easy the Trail is near the river."

Tyler looked again at the Clevengers. Ten-year-old Agnes, who'd said she was almost eleven now, bravely carried little Jenny. Tyler had also seen Brit and even seven-year-old Luke carrying Jenny at times. The Clevenger wagon was on the other side of the Linders oxen, so Tyler could not talk to the four Clevenger kids, but on they went. Little Jenny was scared, but her three siblings did their best to comfort her.

Penny was traveling with Alain and the Laurents, on the other side of the Clevenger wagon, and Tyler felt certain that the Laurents and Penny were watching the Clevenger kids as well.

"Magnus! Tyler!"

Through the sandy wind Tyler saw Press Doolittle approaching on foot, shielding most of his face with his right arm. The sandstorm was too severe for riding on horses.

"Buckman says we're gonna form our circle early today," Press declared. "It's too dangerous to travel any farther today. We'll have to wait out this storm."

"Sounds good to me," Pa responded.

The wagons formed themselves into their familiar circle as the wind let up slightly and mercifully. Oxen were unhitched and kept inside the circle with the rest of the livestock. They could not be allowed to wander off into the sandstorm. By the time that the emigrants were ready for supper, the wind had died down enough to permit cooking. Salt pork and beans, the usual fare, could be cooked out-doors. Tyler, Pa, Penny, Angelique, and Justin and Billie Kay Maybrie sat eating their tin platefuls together.

Tyler sat on the ground next to Angelique, but his attention continued to be drawn to the Clevenger kids, eating their soup by themselves.

"What is it, Tyler?" Angelique asked, noticing his restless distraction.

Tyler looked at Angelique, then at Pa. "What's going to happen to them, Pa? The Clevengers, I mean, when they get to Oregon? Brit isn't old enough to buy land, not for several years yet."

Seated on a three-legged stool, Pa took a swig of coffee from a tin cup, looking intently with narrowed eyes at the Clevenger kids about fifty feet away.

Angelique also looked at the four Clevengers. "My heart goes out to them," she murmured. "They've lost both parents, but they have been so brave about continuing on."

"But when they get to Oregon, will they be able to stay together, all four of them?" Tyler asked. "Or will they be split up among different families, or sent to an orphanage, maybe in California?"

Pa hurled the last of his coffee against one of the front wagon wheels. "Too much sand," he muttered. Pa looked at Tyler, then at Penny, Angelique, and Justin and Billie Kay. He bowed his head, sighing and shaking his head. Looking up, he slowly murmured, "Asking one family to adopt four kids, that's asking an awful lot. You might get someone to agree to adopt the two younger ones, or the two older ones, or the two boys by themselves, or the two girls by themselves, or maybe one of them here or there. But some family adopting all four kids, and keeping them all united together? Golly, Tyler, I'm sorry, I just don't see that happening. I sure couldn't take in all four of 'em, and I'm afraid that anyone else you talk to would like as not feel the same. I'm just afraid that, yeah, them four Clevenger kids may get split up among different families, or one or two of 'em sent to an orphanage somewhere, and like as not, they'll never see each other again."

Sighing through growing whiskers, Justin leaned back on his arms propped against the ground. "Same story here," he said reluctantly. "I could take in possibly one of 'em, but taking in all four of the Clevenger kids together, gosh, I wish I had that kind of money but I don't."

Billie Kay, Angelique, Tyler, and Penny exchanged somber glances.

Penny spoke first. "Pa, they have to stay together, they have to."

Angelique put a gentle hand on Billie Kay's shoulder. "I see another project in your eyes, Billie Kay," Angelique softly declared. "I know what you are thinking."

"I am certain that you do," Billie Kay murmured in reply. "I have another project in front of me to see through to completion. And complete it, I shall. But this time, I will need help. If I am to find a family to take in four children all together, I shall need help."

Angelique and Billie Kay exchanged an embrace; both of them with moist eyes, and the two young women were one in heart. "We shall help you, Billie Kay," Angelique again gently declared. "This shall be our project, all of us, together."

Tyler nodded. "We should probably let the Clevenger kids in on what we're doing."

"Ask them to come over here," Pa said. "Wait—on second thought, just ask Brit to come over here."

"I'll get him," Justin said, rising.

Within a few minutes Justin returned with Brit Clevenger, looking concerned, indeed, looking worried.

Brit seated himself cross-legged on the ground, next to Tyler.

"What's this all about?" Brit demanded, brushing long sandy-blonde bangs out of his eyes.

Pa didn't look directly at Brit. He folded his hands together across his knees, looked downward, and asked, "Son, what are your plans for when you reach Oregon? Tyler's told me that you plan to buy land. Son, you're thirteen years old, too young to buy land."

"I know that," Brit muttered. "Mr. Buckman's already told me that, two weeks ago when he asked me the same question that you're asking me now."

Billie Kay leaned forward, clasping her hands together. "Did Mr. Buckman make any suggestions about what you should do?" she asked mildly.

"He told me that we—me, my brother Luke and my two sisters—we should try to get ourselves adopted by one of the other wagon families, or at least find someone who'd be willing to be a legal guardian for us, someone who could buy land on our behalf and hold it in trust until I turn eighteen. I been too scared to talk to anyone until the past day or two. We want to stay together, Luke, Agnes, Jenny, and me, and not be split up among different families in different places far apart. I asked Mr. Sogstad if he'd be willing to think about adopting us into his family. We've gotten to know him a bit because he's traveled close to our wagon sometimes. He got kind of mad, though, and said he already had a big family and that he couldn't take us in and he kind of asked us to leave him alone."

"I'm sorry to hear that," Angelique said. "I thought Mr. Sogstad was nicer than that."

Billie Kay looked at Brit with soft, heartfelt eyes. "Brit, would you mind the next time you try to talk to one of the other wagon families about adopting you and your siblings, if maybe some of us tagged along behind you and listened to what you're saying?"

Brit pursed his lips for a couple of seconds, and then shrugged his shoulders. "I guess that'd be all right," he said uncertainly. "We'd like to do this mainly ourselves, though."

"Of course," Billie Kay agreed readily. "We might be able to make some suggestions, though, about how to approach people with a question like that."

"Trust me, Billie Kay is good at making suggestions," Justin said, chuckling.

Chuckling herself, Billie Kay gave her new husband a playful punch in the shoulder.

"Who were you thinking of asking next?" Tyler wondered.

"Um, well, uh, we thought of maybe Lucas Pfister," Brit said. "He's not married, so maybe he'd appreciate having a family of his own. And because he's been single and alone, he'd probably have enough money saved up to support four kids."

"Lucas Pfister is a good man," Tyler said. "He was willing to help when we needed men to visit the Pawnees and straighten things out after Tim shot at them. Lucas would be a good place to start."

"And hopefully finish," Angelique said.

* * *

Agnes carried little Jenny in her arms. Jenny squirmed and looked this way and that at the wagons encircled around them. Brit and Luke Clevenger walked together, their expressions grim and uncertain.

Tyler walked with Angelique and Billie Kay, trailing the Clevengers by about twenty feet. They wanted to hear what approach the Clevenger kids were using to try to get someone to adopt all four of them together. Walking around a wagon tongue to the outside of the circle, they saw Lucas Pfister sitting in a folding chair, simply gazing out at the black rock volcanic plain of the Snake River. The snow-capped Sawtooth Mountains loomed purple and white in the far distance.

"Mr. Pfister," Brit began.

Lucas looked up from his reverie. "Y-yes?" he said uncertainly.

Tyler thought Lucas was interesting in that he was one of the few individuals who had started this journey 1,500 miles ago and who still looked as plump in face and middle as he had in Independence.

"Mr. Pfister, can we talk with you about something?" Brit asked.

Lucas's face turned into a mild pout. "Out with it, kid, what do you want?"

"We were hoping that maybe, uh, er, maybe, um, well, maybe that you would think about adopting us, or being our legal guardian once we get to Oregon?" Brit asked, his tone rising at the end.

Lucas's mouth went wide open and he jerked forward before slumping backward in his chair hard. "Run that by me again?" he said incredulously.

"Our parents are dead," Agnes said. "We need someone to adopt us so we can stay together and not have to go to an orphanage or be split up among a bunch of different families. We wouldn't be no trouble. We're good kids."

"We can't buy land on our own," Luke said. "We need an adult to buy land for us—using our parents' money—and then to be our legal guardian until Brit turns eighteen."

Lucas Pfister's half-open mouth in his moon-like face was a sure indication that the idea had hit him like a mallet blow to his head. Lucas looked at Brit, then at Luke, then at Agnes, still holding little Jenny looking at him with her bright, nervous brown eyes. Jenny had her thumb between her lips.

"How old are you kids?" Lucas asked breathlessly, Tyler thought, because he likely had no clue how to react to this bombshell of a question.

"I'm thirteen," Brit said. "I'll be fourteen early next year. Luke is seven. Agnes is ten."

"I'll be eleven in a couple of weeks," Agnes said, running her fingers through her blonde-streaked brown hair. She set Jenny down with her free hand. "Jenny is five."

Jenny smiled at Lucas. "Shix next year," she said gaily. "I be a big girl when I be shix. Will you be our new papa, Mishuh? We need a new papa."

Lucas looked at little Jenny's eyes, hopeful and trusting. His heavy breathing and the terror on his face grew, however. He looked past the Clevenger kids to Billie Kay. "What's this all about?" he demanded, still in shock.

"Exactly what you heard," Billie Kay said.

"Is this something you could at least think about?" Angelique asked, clasping her hands together.

"You weren't afraid when we went to visit the Pawnees," Tyler said. "Why are you acting scared now?"

"No, I wasn't afraid when we visited the Pawnees," Lucas said, "but right now I'm scared as the bejeebers."

"You don't wanna be our new papa?" Jenny asked plaintively from her precious heart.

"We wouldn't be no trouble," Agnes repeated. "We wouldn't be any trouble, I mean. We'd obey everything you tell us to do. You don't have a family, Mr. Pfister. We could be your family."

Gripping his chair handles with his hands turning red from the effort, Lucas appeared to shove himself as far back into the recesses of his chair as he possibly could. "It's not—I swear it's not that I don't want to be your new papa, kids," he said in a frightened tone. "It's just that, well . . ." he looked past the four little Clevengers and at Billie Kay again. "Me and that Hanclicek gal, Marta, well, I asked her to marry me. She's thinking about it. She sounds real positive, though. I'm sure she'll decide to say yes sooner or later. But if I tell her that she'd have to accept an instant family, not one, not two, not three, but four kids right from the get-go, well, that might, that kinda might cause her to change her mind quite a bit, you know."

The four faces of the Clevenger kids fell. Little Jenny started to cry. "He don't like us. He don't want us," she wailed. "We need a new papa."

Trying hard to control her own emotions, Agnes took Jenny back in her arms in a hug and gave her a quick peck on the cheek and stroked her hair comfortingly. "It'll be okay, muffin, we'll keep trying," Agnes soothed, looking like was trying to avoid breaking down and crying herself.

"It isn't that I don't want to, kids," Lucas went on defensively. "But, you know, a man's got to look to what's best for himself, you know. Marta's gonna want some kids of her own, you know. How do I tell her she'd have four kids on her hands right from the very start? How do I tell her that we'd be raising—"

"Don't worry about it." Brit waved a hand dismissively. "It's all right. We'll find somebody else. Don't trouble yourself."

"Let's try someone else," Luke said disgustedly. "This guy doesn't want us."

Angelique tried to force a smile. "Maybe we'll have better luck elsewhere," she said.

They looked around. The far snow-capped mountains caught Tyler's attention, then Jonas Smith at the second wagon beyond Lucas. Jonas had been listening to the conversation with Lucas.

"Jenny, get your thumb out of your mouth," Agnes demanded. "Your thumb is dirty. 'Sides, it's not a good habit. Here—play with Dolly. Dolly needs you to hold her."

Agnes held out a plain, eyeless cornhusk doll to Jenny, which the little girl took and held onto dearly.

"Mr. Smith," Brit called out. "Can we talk to you for a minute?"

Brit headed toward Jonas Smith, followed closely by Luke, then Agnes holding Jenny's little hand and pulling her along. Unfortunately, Tyler saw the same look of fear come over Jonas's face as he had seen with Lucas.

"What do you kids want?" Jonas asked uncertainly. He'd shaved off his beard, and now his face looked triangular and rigid, with narrow, sharp features.

"Maybe you heard us talking with Mr. Pfister," Brit began hopefully. "We-we need someone to adopt us so we can stay together when we get to Oregon. It's not something you'd have to say yes to real quick—we know that's not real likely. But with our parents dead, we need a new home—me, Luke, Agnes, and Jenny."

"And Dolly," Jenny said, smiling and excited again. She thrust Dolly forward in her small hand toward Jonas. "Dolly needs new fam'ly."

"We could help you on your farm in Oregon," Luke said. "We can sow crops, harvest 'em for you, help you out in a lot of ways."

"Me and Dolly help too," Jenny said eagerly and happily.

Jonas put his hands up defensively. "Look, kids, I'm sorry about what happened to your folks. Everyone is." His tone was worried, nervous. "But—but I heard what you said to Lucas. Look, me and Prudence, we already have three kids of our own to feed, three kids of our own to help with the chores. And Prudence's still young, she'll probably have two or three more kids before she's done. We just can't try—"

"S-so you don't want us, either," Agnes said, heartbroken.

"Dolly and me, you don't want Dolly and me?" Jenny asked with disappointment. She drew her simple little corn-husk doll close to her heart as her eyes teared up again.

Jonas shook his head this way and that, struggling for words. He gestured toward his torn canvas wagon behind him. "Look, me an' Prudence, we got next to nothing. We can't afford four kids all at once. We may not even go into farming when we get to Oregon. I been thinking about maybe building a mill. I wouldn't need a lot of help if I started a mill. I could pretty much do the work by my—"

"Aw, forget it," Brit muttered, thrusting his hands down disgustedly. "We'll keep looking."

Billie Kay stepped forward. "Help us out in one way, though, Mr. Smith," she asked, her hands clasped together. "Spread the word. Let people know that the Clevenger kids are looking for help, looking for someone to adopt them together."

"Well, yeah, I guess I could do that," Jonas said.

"C'mon kids, we'll try again tomorrow," Billie Kay suggested.

Jenny put her head against Agnes's hip and, holding little Dolly, she began to softly cry.

"It'll be okay, muffin," Agnes soothed her, giving Jenny a much-needed hug. Agnes was in tears herself. "We'll find someone to adopt us, I promise."

"It's early still," Tyler said. "We could maybe try a couple more families."

Billie Kay gestured for the Clevenger kids to follow her out of earshot of Jonas Smith. Tyler and Angelique also followed her.

"I have a plan in mind," Billie Kay said. "If we just go up to a bunch of families this evening and ask them, 'would you like to adopt four kids?' we're going to keep getting the same kind of answers that we've been getting. But if we give the word time to spread among all the families in the wagon train about the Clevenger kids . . ."

"Ahh," Tyler murmured, "maybe they'll have a chance to think about the idea first, and maybe it won't be such a surprise when we ask 'em, and maybe they'll have thought of some ideas of how adopting four kids could be worked out."

"That's one part of it," Billie Kay murmured. "Even better, though, is the possibility that maybe—"

"I know what you're thinking," Angelique said. "Maybe, possibly, someone will come forward on their own and offer to adopt the four Clevenger kids."

"Precisely," Billie Kay said. "My hope is—my prayer is—that someone or some family will come to us of their own accord, or come to the Clevengers, and make an adoption offer."

"You hear that, kids?" Tyler asked. "We're going to shake the bush for you around here."

Brit sounded hopeful, unfolding his arms. "You think that idea will work?"

Billie Kay put her hands on Brit's arms and looked at him squarely in the eyes. "I can't promise it will," she said, "but I think that strategy gives us our best chance of finding some family or someone that will take in all four of you kids. I'm going to believe for you, Brit, and for Luke, Agnes, and Jenny." She let go of Brit and looked at all of the Clevenger kids, winking at them. "If we hope and we pray and we believe hard enough, maybe, possibly, we're about to see a miracle happen."

The next day the only miracle that Tyler saw was a clear blue sky—no sand, no dust. Possibly a second miracle occurred when he saw Alain walking for brief periods next to his wagon, with Penny, Adelaide, and Francois watching his every step carefully. Alain was slowly getting better. Penny encouraged him to take it easy, not to stretch his luck, and this time, he appeared to have listened to her and to his parents.

Tyler observed the hilly, grassy landscape. The Snake River, named after an Indian tribe, could just as easily have been named for snakes, the way it twisted and curled. The trail was narrow in places next to the river, but fortunately, no more Indians. The oxen seemed to be doing all right, though, a fact Tyler pointed out to Pa.

"The elevation is lower here than what we've been having to deal with most of the past several hundred miles," Pa said. "The animals aren't so starved for air."

There was no miracle at the nooning, however. Tyler walked hand-in-hand with Angelique among the wagon families, spreading the word about the four Clevengers. Several people politely had to decline.

"I'm sixty-two years old, and Abigail is fifty-eight," Ephraim said resignedly, sitting on one of his folding chairs in the shade of his wagon. "At our ages, we're just a little old to be taking on a new family, much as we'd like to."

Angelique looked at them mildly. "I know," she said quietly. "I wasn't really thinking that you could. But maybe you could talk to some of the other families, see if anyone's interested, see if you can convince someone to think about it."

"We'll certainly do that, we'll absolutely do that," Ephraim assured Angelique and Tyler.

A few others were less friendly about saying no.

"You're cracked if you think someone is going to adopt all four of those kids," Jonathan Colledge said. "I could see maybe adopting one of them, and other families maybe taking in one or two of the others, but all four of them together? You've got to be kidding, or smoking opium to think of a plan like that."

Angelique's face turned pouty. "Smoking drugs, are we?" she demanded. "If this is what we have to put up with in order to help four orphans who want to stay together as a family, then I'm willing to put up with it until we—"

"We'll try somebody else." Tyler pulled her away.

Nor could Angelique's father consider the idea. Duke Hapsburg was still planning to return to Austria after getting to Oregon. In any case, Franz Hapsburg said, he was not an American citizen, and thus his ability to adopt four American kids would be debatable.

The journey resumed in the early afternoon. The trail continued along the Snake River now, heading toward Fort Boise. At times the trail between the river and the surrounding low plateau was so narrow that the wagons had to go single file. Luckily there was no rain, or the journey might have come to a dead halt, or worse, flash flooding could have occurred, demolishing wagons and drowning animals, and people.

Angelique walked with Tyler, observing the meandering, twisting Snake River, about a hundred fifty feet wide. Looking closely, they could see occasional trout swimming near the riverbank and its sharp drop-off.

"How I'd love to put a line and some bait in the water," Tyler said.

"We're getting close to Nez Perce country, past Fort Boise," Angelique said. "The Nez Perce may have some smoked trout or salmon they'd be willing to trade."

That evening, the wagons formed into their usual circle to keep in the livestock after finding an open meadow. Bruce Mallory took out his fiddle and sat on a tree stump overlooking the Snake River to play some favorite tunes for the hundredth time. There was no dance. People were too footsore by this stage, but still they enjoyed listening to Bruce's energetic fiddle.

Tyler and Angelique ate their usual supper of beans and salt pork with Pa. Justin and Billie Kay joined them after awhile, bringing some jerked buffalo meat to add to the bean pot. Penny ate with the Laurents on this evening.

As they finished their meal, they saw the four Clevenger siblings approaching. "We gonna talk to some more people tonight?" Brit asked while still at a distance.

Billie Kay, Justin, Tyler, and Angelique exchanged glances. Billie Kay quickly looked at the four Clevengers, though. "Of course we are," she said, smiling. "Let's take a look around and see who we find to talk to."

The four young adults and the four Clevenger siblings began their walk, talking to people wagon by wagon. Philo and Mary Jean Eisenbarger politely said they couldn't afford four new kids, but they wished them all the luck in the world with their quest to find an adoptive family.

Mabel Armagast saw the Clevenger kids coming and she quickly half-ducked inside the back of her wagon. She pulled a broom out of the back of her wagon and she wore a pouty expression.

"Not exactly the sort of response we need," Justin commented.

Little Jenny Clevenger nevertheless smiled broadly at Mrs. Armagast, and Agnes, Brit, and Luke tried to do the same as they approached her.

"Hello, Mishash Armagasht," Jenny said spritely. "Maybe you help us."

"I know what you're here for," Mabel Armagast muttered harshly. "The story's goin' around. You're lookin' for someone to adopt you. Well, keep lookin'! Credence and I ain't got money enough to take in four little runts."

"We're good kids," Agnes said in a tremulous, halting voice. "We wouldn't be any trouble to you. Maybe in time you could learn to love us even if you don't right off. We understand."

"Just give us a chance," Brit beseeched. "That's all we ask, just a chance."

"Get out of here before I wallop all four of you!" Mabel Armagast shrieked at the Clevenger kids. She hammered Agnes's behind with the broom. "Git! Git, I said! I raised five kids already and they were all nothin' but grief and trouble and mischief and jail bail. That's all you'd be, you little hellions! Nobody's gonna want to buy the kind of trouble you little delinquents would bring. Now git!"

Mabel Armagast raised her broom at little Jenny and Luke. Brit and Agnes pulled them away before Armagast could hit them with the broom. The Clevenger kids hurried away from Mabel Armagast, followed quickly by Billie Kay, Tyler, Angelique, and Justin.

Jenny hugged her Dolly and fell into Agnes's arms, crying her precious five-year-old heart out. Agnes could no longer hold back her own tears and crying as she hugged Jenny close.

Tyler glanced at Billie Kay and Angelique. Both of them had moist eyes of their own. Angelique laid a sympathetic hand on Luke's shoulder, then on Brit's. Billie Kay hugged both Agnes and Jenny.

"I promise you kids," Billie Kay began, her own voice nearly breaking, "I promise you kids, I promise all four of you, we're going to find someone in this wagon train who has a heart." After a moment of collecting herself, Billie Kay encouraged, "Let's keep walking."

"I saw it first!"

"No, I saw it first!"

Tyler turned to his left to observe the commotion. Milon Crabbage was at it again. Crabbage shook his fist while using his other hand to lead one of his cows toward a patch of long green grass about twenty feet wide. Credence Armagast was also leading a cow toward the same patch of grass.

"There's only enough grass here for one animal, not two," Crabbage muttered. "I saw it first. So go find yourself someplace else to graze your homely old hag of a cow."

"What!" Armagast bellowed. "The only fair thing to do is for us to share the patch of grass."

"What did I just say?" Crabbage snarled, his narrow face twisting. "Two animals trying to eat this grass is one too many. I tell you, I saw it first. It's mine!"

Buckman had also heard the commotion. He came riding up on his mount with his eyes narrowed and his face rigid with anger. "I'm getting damn sick and fed up with your belly-aching, Crabbage," Buckman roared. "All you've ever done on this whole journey is belly-ache about one thing after another, right from Missouri onward. You're never happy unless you're arguing with somebody and bitching about something or whatever."

Brit stepped forward, about twenty feet from Crabbage. "I think I did see Mr. Crabbage leading his cow toward the grass first, Mr. Buckman," Brit said. "And what I know of cows, there probably isn't enough grass there for more than one."

Buckman looked stunned. Tyler could only surmise that Brit had taken Crabbage's part in the argument because of the way Armagast's wife had acted toward him and his siblings a few minutes earlier.

Looking first at Credence Armagast and then at Crabbage, Buckman muttered, "All right, Milon, you win this round. But you like arguing so much that when you actually do have a valid point, nobody wants to admit it." Buckman looked at Armagast. "C'mon, Credence, I'll help you find another place for your cow to feed."

As Buckman and Armagast headed away, Crabbage was left with the four Clevengers and the four young adults near him. He glared with deep-set rigid eyes at Billie Kay and Justin, and then at Tyler and Angelique.

"Well, what are you staring at?" Crabbage asked the four young adults. "I know what you think of me. I know what all of you think of me. I'm the one everybody loves to hate. Yeah, I know it and don't you deny it. You all hate me! I'm the ogre and the villain of this whole wagon train. Yeah, don't deny it; you know that's what you've all thought of me, every one of you that's been in this wagon train.

"Yeah, I got mad at the Renwilers when they showed up with their cholera," Crabbage went on ranting, shaking a bony fist. "I told 'em to stay clear away from the rest of us with their disease. Maybe if they had, these Clevenger young'uns would still have their Ma and Pa. The Renwilers showing up with their cholera killed these young 'uns' parents, I say!"

"Mr. Crabbage, there is no way to ever know that for sure," Angelique said.

"But I might be right. Don't deny it," Crabbage bellowed. "But when I tried to tell the Renwilers to keep their distance from the rest of us, well, instantly everybody sees me as the mean bad guy for doing it. Yeah, I'm the big, bad villain here! Everybody hates me. Everybody thinks I'm nothing but anger and hate and spit. Everybody thinks that about me. Everybody thinks I'm nothing but mean old Mr. Crabbage who hates everybody else. Well, let me tell you something— you grow up with a name like 'Crabbage' and have to live all your life with a name like that, people *expect* you to be nothing but a mean old cuss. People that I hardly even know want to believe I'm a mean old cuss. So there!"

Billie Kay took a deep breath, and she took a step forward. "Then prove them wrong, Mr. Crabbage," she declared. "Prove how wrong we've all been about you. Prove that people are wrong about you, Mr. Crabbage. Show all of them how wrong they've been about you and how badly people have misjudged you."

Crabbage's expression assumed a puzzled look and he scratched his head underneath his plainsman's hat.

Billie Kay looked at the four Clevenger kids one by one, and then at Crabbage again. "There's four children here that need someone to adopt them," she said. "You're without a family, Mr. Crabbage. Brit, Agnes, Luke, and Jenny could be your family. Please just think about—"

"I knew you were going to get around to asking me that," Crabbage huffed. "Don't bother explaining—I know you've been going around asking people. Gotten nothing but rejections, haven't you?"

Before Billie Kay could respond, Crabbage went on, "Well, that doesn't surprise me, what with all these so-called good people in this here wagon train. Yeah, they're wonderful folks, ain't they?—right up to the point where you ask 'em to actually do something to help somebody else, then it's every man for himself."

Tyler knew that wasn't true, but he forced his argue instinct to reign itself in.

"Taking in four Clevenger kids?" Crabbage muttered. "I'll have to think about it."

Angelique half-smiled. "Mr. Crabbage, that's all we can ask of—"

"I said I'd think about it!" Crabbage muttered. "That doesn't mean yes, that doesn't mean no, it means I'll think about it."

Billie Kay couldn't help a grateful grin. "Mr. Crabbage, that's more than anyone else in this whole wagon train so far has said they'd do." She gestured for the Clevenger kids to follow her. "Come, children, let's be fair to Mr. Crabbage and give him a chance to think about it like he said."

As they walked away, Jenny smiled and waved a hand at Crabbage, with Dolly in her other hand. "Bye, Mishuh Cwabbage, thank 'ee you," she said.

Tyler turned around to see Crabbage's reaction. Strangely, Crabbage slowly lifted a hand to give a stiff, unmoving wave back at Jenny. The expression on Crabbage's face, however, looked almost haunted, as if he had seen a ghost, so frightened did he look with wide eyes and a half-open mouth at the Clevengers, little Jenny and her Dolly cornhusk doll in particular. Not a good omen.

When the four young Clevengers had gone off to bed, the four young adults had a chance to talk among themselves about what they'd just witnessed with Crabbage, as they faced each other around a small cottonwood branch campfire.

"I'm thinking," Tyler began, "that early tomorrow morning, before we head out for the day, that maybe we should talk with Crabbage just by ourselves. I don't think that Crabbage getting all upset and telling those poor Clevenger kids to quit bothering him is something they need to hear right now."

"I think you're right," Justin reluctantly agreed.

Billie Kay and Angelique slowly nodded, apparently with reluctance as well. But Tyler could tell that they sensed the same as he and Justin.

"It's agreed then," Justin said. "Let's all meet together just before sunup and we'll talk to Crabbage."

Angelique looked at Tyler. "My heart goes out to those four kids," she murmured. "Maybe they could be adopted by different families living close together."

"Maybe," Billie Kay said without conviction. "But once we get to the Willamette Valley, all of the families in this wagon train are going to scatter apart over 300 miles of territory. I want in my heart for all four of those Clevenger kids to stay in one place together."

* * *

Early August had come, and with the wagon train making good time, Buckman was allowing people to sleep in, all the way to 6 a.m. if they wanted. Tyler was up before sunrise, as were Angelique, Billie Kay, and Justin. Tyler's attention was instantly drawn to the Clevenger wagon about a hundred feet away, just to be sure the young Clevengers were still asleep. He did not want them joining the discussion with Crabbage.

But his eyes nearly bulged with shock at the sight before him. Angelique, Billie Kay, and Justin also went open-mouthed with shock and surprise at the sight they saw. The four young Clevengers were up, and were sitting cross-legged on the ground, listening to a man seated on a stump bench. Tyler strained his eyes in the morning light. He could scarcely believe it—yes, indeed, it was truly Milon Crabbage, smiling and talking with all four young Clevengers.

Tyler looked at Angelique and Billie Kay. Astounded, he murmured, "What in the blazes is going on over there?"

Billie Kay's astonishment gave way to a soft, broad smile. "A miracle," she quietly said.

"Hmm." Tyler looked at Angelique and Justin, then at Billie Kay. "You'll forgive me if I say that there's probably a more rational explanation."

Billie Kay nodded gently, but she responded, "Miracles often come about in seemingly rational ways, Tyler."

"Let us go and see what it is that has happened," Angelique suggested.

Together, as others brewed their morning coffee and ate their hard biscuits, Tyler, Angelique, Billie Kay, and Justin approached Milon Crabbage and the Clevenger kids, who sat apparently enraptured by what he was saying.

Crabbage kept his focus upon the Clevenger kids. "I have to tell you the rest of the story," he was saying. "My wife Elena and I had our two children, Michael, a fine young lad of about eleven years, about your age, Agnes, and our precious little girl—Aranis, we named her. She was right about your age, Jenny, and she looked a lot like you. Little Aranis had a doll just like Dolly, she did." Crabbage looked at a simple corn-husk doll he held in one hand. "Aranis named her doll Lissa, and Aranis loved her doll Lissa, and I truly believe, Lissa loved Aranis every bit as much. Aranis played with Lissa every single day, and Lissa kept Aranis good company. We had a satisfying, happy life in Illinois, all of us together on our farm."

Crabbage smiled mildly, extending his arms as he spoke. The simple, eyeless cornhusk doll he held in one hand was similar to and only slightly smaller than the one which Jenny held.

"Then came the cholera," Crabbage continued, still smiling mildly as Tyler listened. "I woke up one morning about two years ago a happy man, with my wife, and our Michael and our little Aranis. By late afternoon, I was a childless widower." Crabbage paused and looked briefly at Agnes. "Is she understanding any of this?" he asked Agnes as he gestured at Jenny.

"She will someday," Agnes quietly assured him.

With what must have been great effort, Crabbage smiled mildly again. "Cholera strikes without warning and very quickly, you know. You start feeling a little feverish, and within just a few hours, you either get better, or you're dead. The cholera took my Michael, then my Elena, and then, last of all, my dear little Aranis. She died peacefully, she did, with a soft smile on her face, cradling her little doll Lissa in her arms to the very last. I truly believe little doll Lissa cried for the loss of her dear friend Aranis."

Crabbage paused for a moment, running a finger under his nose as he looked down in thought. He composed himself, however.

"Maybe, maybe it was just the moisture in the attic where I had to store Lissa away," Crabbage went on quietly. "But I truly believe that I saw that little doll Lissa shedding real tears as she lay alone now, in a box, in an attic, after the loss of her little playmate Aranis, who loved her, hugged her, played with her always, and cherished her as her dearest friend."

Crabbage's expression brightened, though, as he focused upon Jenny, and his voice became happy-mild. "But now, thanks to you, Jenny, little doll Lissa once again has a little girl to love her, to play with her, to hold her, to hug her, and to cherish her forever." He held the small doll out to Jenny. "See? For the first time in over two years, I think Lissa is smiling again!"

Jenny eagerly took the simple, eyeless, faceless cornhusk doll and gave it a big hug. She held her Dolly in one hand and Lissa in the other. She brought the two dolls together, with their arms permanently extended, face-to-face in a doll hug.

"Dolly likes her new little sister Lissa!" Jenny exclaimed. "Dolly and Lissa and me will all be good friends, won't we, Dolly?"

Jenny held Dolly to one ear. Jenny's eyes sparkled. "Dolly says yes, we will be! Dolly likes her new little sister Lissa."

Crabbage extended his arms. "And now, thanks to all of you, Brit, Luke, Agnes, and Jenny, I have a family again, to take the place of the family that I lost." Crabbage took all four Clevenger children in his arms and hugged them, and they hugged him back, all smiles.

"Ah, Mr. Crabbage."

Tyler saw Patricia Forbes approaching the scene, with her own children, Dunley, Bernice, and Charlie, Jr. who sat in her arms.

"I was going to offer to adopt these four wonderful Clevenger kids, but I see you beat me to them," Patricia said gaily. Her tone became coy, though. "I don't suppose, however, that there's some way we could someday share them?"

"Well, I don't see why not," Crabbage said. "I'm sure that . . ." Then the full import of Patricia Forbes' words suddenly hit him. Half-seriously, half-jokingly he added, "Whoa there. Give me a chance to get set up on a farm in the Willamette Valley before I go to courting anyone now."

Patricia grinned and put her free hands on her hips playfully. "You're not the grumpy old grouch you pretend to be, Milon Crabbage," she said with a laugh

"I will have you know, madam, that I can grump and I can grouch with the very best of them," Crabbage said in the same tone. "Ebenezer Scrooge has got nothing on me."

"Yes," Patricia agreed, "and from what I know of you, Milon Crabbage, I can certainly vouch for that. But as I recall the story's ending, even Ebenezer Scrooge turned out to have a heart of gold finally."

Crabbage rubbed his chin thoughtfully, looking up at the sky. "Aye, so he did, so he did."

"Maybe we should leave them be to continue their bonding," Angelique suggested.

"Probably a good idea," Billie Kay concurred.

As they started walking away, Tyler said, "I wonder why Crabbage never told anyone before now about losing his whole family to cholera. I'm sure people would have understood him better if they'd have known he was in mourning."

Justin gave him a quick glance. "My guess is, Crabbage was trying to suppress his grief."

"I think you're right about that, Justin," Billie Kay said. "Grief has to be let out in some fashion or other. And whether he realized it or not, or wanted to admit it to himself or not, Mr. Crabbage was still grieving the loss of his family to cholera. Because he tried to suppress his sorrowing, it came out in unhealthy ways like anger, bitterness, and hate."

Angelique took a quick look back at the happy scene, with Patricia Forbes and her family joining Milon Crabbage and the four Clevenger kids. "I think Mr. Crabbage will always fondly remember his family back in Illinois, and he should fondly remember them," Angelique said. "Now, though, he has a new family that, with time, he will learn to love and cherish just as much as he did his deceased loved ones."

Tyler looked at Angelique and took her hand in his. He glanced not only at her, but also at Billie Kay and Justin. "Even if we all live to be a hundred," Tyler began, "we will never, ever, any of us, be able to thank Milon Crabbage enough for what he has done this day."

Angelique smiled mildly at Tyler. "Amen."

CHAPTER TWENTY FOUR

The remainder of the journey to Oregon was a joyous, happy victory celebration for Tyler. He knew now that they were going to make it. The wagon train followed the Snake River. Dirk Van Oerton acted as a guide. Forty-eight wagons of the original eighty-seven that had started out in Independence were still on the road to Oregon. In addition, five new families had been picked up at Fort Hall, including the Van Oertons, who now sought to finish the journey they had started a year earlier.

Fort Boise consisted of little more than a small white adobe enclosure. The fort, if it could properly be called that, was another Hudson's Bay outpost which reminded Tyler of one of the major reasons why the United States Government was encouraging Americans to move to the Oregon Territory—by right of number of bodies living there, the United States could lay permanent claim to Oregon once and for all, and help the British to see that their claim to partial ownership of the Pacific Northwest was a lost cause.

At Fort Boise, the emigrants stayed long enough for Mrs. Tanner to have her baby, a boy which she promptly named Elston, Jr.

For Tyler, the main event was a joint birthday celebration for Agnes Clevenger and for Penny. Their birthdays had been on the same day, August 12, two years apart. Agnes was eleven now, and Penny was turning thirteen. The two girls decided to celebrate their birthdays together, with plenty of sugary biscuits and honey.

Agnes suggested that they have the party outside the fort on the shady side of the fort wall, an idea with which Milon Crabbage readily agreed.

As Jenny hopped and skipped and jumped around inside the fort playing with her two dolls, Tyler overheard Crabbage bark, "We better grab the shady side quick, before some other group decides to camp out there. I don't want to have to kick somebody else out of our spot. I will if I have to, but if we grab it quick I won't have to do that."

Well, Tyler reminded himself, it probably wasn't realistic to expect Milon Crabbage to turn into a saint overnight. Clearly, though, a process had begun within Crabbage.

As Penny ate her birthday biscuits, and sat cross-legged and as bejeweled as ever, Alain approached her with a bouquet of blue pasque flowers.

"Alain, Alain, Alain," Penny said joyfully and dreamily as she took the flowers.

"It's not much of a birthday present, but it shows how I will always feel about you, Penny-Golden," Alain declared.

Penny got up and she hugged and kissed her dear Alain. "Having you well again, precious Alain, is the only birthday present I shall ever need," she said loud enough for all to hear.

At thirteen now, Penny was beginning to blossom into the beautiful young woman that she would someday be. Tyler again felt a pang of jealousy at the amount of attention that Penny always seemed to garner. Interesting that Tad McGuigan had decided to attend the party. Tad, along with other young teenage boys, had started hanging around Penny a bit more lately, trying to get to know her. However, Tyler was certain beyond a doubt that Penny would always and evermore be one with Alain Laurent.

Tyler folded his arms and glared at the scene of Alain and Penny holding hands and smiling at each other. "Penny is, as Penny does," Tyler muttered to himself

"What was that, Tyler?" Angelique asked, standing close to him.

Tyler unfolded his arms and chuckled at being overheard. "Oh, nothing, nothing."

Tyler spent his free time during evenings and noonings, and other times as well, with Angelique, and with her father, the duke. Eating a plateful of beans with Angelique one evening in the final desert stretch beyond Fort Boise, Tyler listened to Duke Franz Hapsburg talk about his future.

"I've decided that I'm not going to return to Austria," Hapsburg declared, sitting on the ground with an arm propped over his upraised knee. "I'm going to stay in Oregon. This is a raw frontier land where a man is what he makes of himself, not how he was born. Europe is all about inherited rank and privilege. This frontier land, this United States, is where you are what you have made yourself become. I'm staying, and I will send for Angelique's mother to get on a ship and sail to join us. And I'm changing my last name from Hapsburg to Hobbs. I think 'Hobbs' sounds a little more American, and a lot less pretentious."

"I think so, father," Angelique quietly declared. She laid a hand on his arm, even as she looked at Tyler. "And you know I'm staying."

This one last desert stood between the emigrants and the Willamette Valley. This time, however, the emigrants knew how to preserve their wagon wheels, and how to conserve water. Tyler felt thirsty at times, but he was used to feeling thirsty by now, and he knew it was only a temporary discomfort. One hundred miles from the Columbia River, a gentle rain replenished water supplies and relieved parched throats.

Then, after another five days of wagon travel, there it was—the broad, pristine blue waters of the Columbia River. A cool breeze from the Pacific Ocean ruffled the water into waves.

Buckman decided the easiest way to travel the last couple of hundred miles was by rafting. Tyler gladly agreed with him. After 1,800 miles of wagon travel, rafting would be a fun change of pace.

Tyler and the other men got busy with their axes, building rafts out of the thick cottonwood groves along the Columbia's bank. There were two wagons to a raft. All was well until one raft tipped over. Bruce Mallory saw his wagon spill into the Columbia, along with the Tewksberry wagon, and himself and the Tewksberrys.

"We're okay," Bruce called out. "We can swim."

Bruce, Charity Tewksberry, her older brothers and their parents swam a dozen feet over to the raft with the Palmerston and Teagarten wagons. They had lost everything—tools, seed, clothing, and fiddle.

But by this point in the journey, people were close enough to one another, Tyler reckoned, that Bruce and the Tewksberrys would have no trouble getting replacement tools and seed from their fellow emigrants. Bruce could buy another fiddle in Oregon, although he would surely miss his old fiddle, which would have been a cherished souvenir from the 2,000-mile journey on the Oregon Trail.

Even as he climbed onto the Palmerston-Teagarten raft, Bruce dove back into the water and swam about twenty feet.

"I've got my fiddle and bow," Bruce proudly announced, holding them aloft. "They were floating in the water."

After holing up in an inlet for the night, the emigrants resumed their journey early the next morning. By mid-morning a stiff wind blowing straight in from the Pacific ruffled the water and then kicked up waves, close to two feet high. The men struggled with their poles to keep the rafts level. The wagons had been nailed and bolted to the rafts, which both kept the wagons steady and also kept them in danger of going to the bottom of the river if the raft should capsize or break apart.

As so often had been the case on this long journey, Angelique knew what to do. "Rope several rafts together and then pole toward shallower water," she declared, looking at the dark clouds ahead. "That will make it harder for the waves to capsize one raft by itself."

Tyler knew that Angelique was smart and savvy, but she had no monopoly on intelligent thinking. Other men and women on rafts well behind and in front of them were getting the same idea at the same time. Heading for another inlet of the Columbia River, the emigrants waited a couple of hours for the wind to die down before resuming their journey.

That evening, Tyler looked at Angelique on the expanded raft with him and grinned. "I think that was our last crisis, earlier today," he mused.

Tyler took both of Angelique's hands in hers as he looked at the golden sunset ahead of them, with its mauve, red, orange, and yellow clouds framing the gateway to the Promised Land ahead. Billie Kay, Justin, Penny, Alain, Rachelle, Quimby, and Pa joined them near the front of the raft. Ahead, just past the glowing sunset, lay the Promised Land of the Willamette Valley of Oregon Territory. All of them stood in awe, in silence and inspired wonderment, at the scene before them. No one spoke. The grandeur of the magnificence of the sheer overwhelming splendor of the West Coast made words seem feeble and unnecessary.

Finally, it was Tyler who quietly murmured, "This is what west of the sunset looks like, and privileged are we to see it."

The emigrants passed the Columbia River Gorge, and after several more days of rafting, they approached the big bend of the Columbia—tall Douglas Firs, moss-covered, greeted them. Lush, Pacific Northwest rainforest vegetation replaced the sere sagebrush of the dryer land behind them. They had traveled 2,000 miles from Independence, Missouri. Straight ahead was the Willamette Valley, and home, in Oregon.

As Tyler helped Angelique off the raft, he looked in her eyes, and quietly murmured, "What we have done—all of us in this wagon train—may not be apparent to us now, but after deserts, Indians, sandstorms, thunder, lightning, thirst, and mountains, and everything else nature threw at us, I believe that with the passage of time, history will magnify our accomplishment ever higher, and maybe forty or fifty years from now, we will be able to proudly say that we were part of one of the greatest movements not only in American history, but in all of history."

EPILOGUE

Tyler smelled the fresh, piney spring breeze coming in off the Pacific. Rows of wheat had begun to push up from the fertile dark Oregon soil. With steady rain in this far part of the country, Tyler had every expectation of another bumper crop this year of wheat, rye, and vegetables.

He turned. Angelique stood in the cabin door, gently holding little Bethany in her arms.

"Hey you," Angelique said. "We're going to be late for the big wedding."

"Now we can't have that, can we?" Tyler agreed.

He prepared the buckboard and then helped Angelique with Bethany into it. The little baby slept quietly, oblivious to the momentous events surrounding her.

The horse trotted contentedly a couple of miles toward another cabin, low-roofed and cozy-looking with a curl of smoke coming out of the chimney and twisting about the 250-foot tall Douglas firs in back.

Billie Kay, Kelly Jay, Quimby and Rachelle Freding, and Tim and Charity MacNaughton greeted them. In the background, Tyler saw Milon and Patricia Crabbage, and the growing Clevenger kids, including Agnes with her beau,

Tad McGuigan, and Brit with his love interest, Patty Zurich. Luke was busy playing soldier with the other young boys, while Jenny talked and laughed with the other young girls. Dunley Forbes was busily engaged in conversation with Sarah Van Oerton.

"Penny is getting ready inside," Rachelle said. "Alain is off with Van Buren and with Brent, trying to do a bit of morning rabbit hunting to calm himself down."

Pa emerged from the cabin. "Alain's not the only one around here who's nervous," he said. "Penny's as nervous and excited as I've seen her since we headed out on the Trail from Independence, Missouri to Oregon three years ago."

Angelique looked at Tyler. "Getting married is not something you do every day," she murmured.

"I'll hold her for awhile." Tyler took Bethany away from Angelique to allow her arms a rest.

Another buckboard arrived, bearing their old friend from the Oregon Trail days, Rev. Seamus Coogan, still traveling the back roads of the American West. Coogan would officiate.

Tyler looked to his left, where a long table laden with ham, bacon, corn, vegetables, pies, beer, and wine stood ready to feed the revelers afterward.

Angelique pulled on his sleeve. "Tyler, look. She's coming out."

She pointed toward the cabin. Penny was emerging, dressed in a beautiful white-lace wedding gown and veil. Over her wedding dress, she wore all of her gold, silver and turquoise jewelry from the Oregon Trail journey, an odyssey which had such cherished memories for all of them. It was the first time Tyler had seen Penny wearing her Indian jewelry in at least a couple of years. But today was appropriate. The jewelry, the gown, gave emphasis to the beautiful young woman that Penny was fast becoming after sixteen years.

Penny pushed her glasses back up on her nose. Alain came out of the forest with Van Buren and Brent. Alain had bagged a couple of rabbits which he handed off to Brent along with his Spencer rifle.

Alain hurried over to Penny and they embraced and kissed. Coogan said the words. Both Penny and Alain said their "I do's" with fullness of heart. Coogan then gave the sermon.

"Stamina, courage, perseverance, fortitude, commitment, is what these two demonstrated on that long journey to Oregon," Coogan said at one point. "They brought those virtues, all of them, to their relationship with each another. Alain and Penny have already shown how committed and dedicated they are to each another, even in the most difficult of circumstances. Truly, they are worthy of each other, the equal of each other, and deserving of each other, till death do they part."

Holding hands, wreaths of flowers on both of their heads, with the wreaths joined together by a blue silk garland, Alain and Penny looked into each other's eyes and smiled, maybe a little self-consciously, but with joined hearts. They did not need an invitation from Reverend Father Coogan to kiss.

After the service, Alain and Penny seated themselves at the center of the head table. Tyler sat with Angelique on the other side of Alain. Pa held Bethany on the other side of Penny.

Tyler looked across the table at Justin and Billie Kay Maybrie, with Billie Kay holding their little James in her lap. Kelly Jay Ellis sat directly across from him. Tyler was about to ask the question that was on everyone's mind, but Penny beat him to it.

"So tell me, Kelly Jay," Penny began, "exactly how much gold did your father find in California?"

"About enough to buy me a ticket on a steamship for Oregon," Kelly Jay replied, resigned but smiling. "Now there's more rumors of gold and silver just east of the Sierras, and further east still, near Pike's Peak in Colorado. I 'spect one or both of those places is where our father is headed next."

Alain looked at Penny. "I've got all the gold treasure I need right here," he said, grinning at Penny and placing a hand on her back, "and I don't mean the jewelry around your neck." He looked into her eyes. "I will never forget the way you cared for me when I was dying."

Penny smiled shyly. "Well, if Pa and Tyler and me would've stayed away from that oxen-selling pervert, you wouldn't have been hurt."

"Penny, my love, you were worth fighting for and pro-tecting, even dying for."

Alain shared another kiss with Penny.

Tyler looked at Angelique. "Oregon is nice, but it wouldn't have been worth dying for," he murmured. "I'm glad that you, at least, did your homework before we headed out three years ago. You saved us in many difficult situations that could have brought our trip to a tragic conclusion."

Angelique chuckled lightly with embarrassment. "It's not important what didn't happen," she said. "What did hap-pen was, we made it. We got here. We're here."

"And we have nothing but the future in front of us," Tyler said with a grin.

ABOUT THE AUTHOR

Paul F. Murray grew up in Tawas City and Essexville, Michigan, and attended Michigan State University where he received his B.S. from the James Madison College division of MSU. The author studies ethnic, racial and religious intergroup relations. The author also earned a Master's of Business Administration degree from Grand Valley State University in Grand Rapids, Michigan. After having worked as an energy cost consultant for business and industrial clients for many years, the author went back into journalism, living in Minnesota, Montana and finally Wyoming, where he currently covers local and state government news and local sports.

www.ingramcontent.com/pod-product-compliance
Lightning Source LLC
Chambersburg PA
CBHW052025220726

48293CB00015B/274